*Steamy praise for the novels of*
Jasmine H...

"Deliciously erotic and completely...
—*New York Ti...*

"An erotic, emotional adventure of discovery you don't want to miss." —*New York Times* bestselling author Lora Leigh

"So incredibly hot that I'm trying to find the right words to describe it without having to be edited for content . . . extremely stimulating from the first page to the last! Of course, that means that I loved it! . . . One of the hottest, sexiest erotic books I have read so far."
—*Romance Reader at Heart*

"Delightfully torrid." —*Midwest Book Review*

"More than a fast-paced erotic romance, this is a story of family, filled with memorable characters who will keep you engaged in the plot and the great sex. A good read to warm a winter's night."
—*Romantic Times*

"Bursting with sensuality and eroticism." —*In the Library Reviews*

"The passion is intense, hot, and purely erotic . . . recommended for any reader who likes their stories realistic, hot, captivating, and very, very well written." —*Road to Romance*

"Not your typical romance. This one's going to remain one of my favorites." —*The Romance Studio*

"Jasmine Haynes keeps the plot moving and the love scenes very hot." —*Just Erotic Romance Reviews*

"A wonderful novel . . . Try this one—you won't be sorry."
—*The Best Reviews*

"With sizzling love scenes that will stir both the loins and the heart."
—*CK²S Kwips and Kritiques*

# YOURS FOR THE NIGHT

## Jasmine Haynes

HEAT
*New York*

**THE BERKLEY PUBLISHING GROUP**
**Published by the Penguin Group**
**Penguin Group (USA) Inc.**
**375 Hudson Street, New York, New York 10014, USA**
Penguin Group (Canada), 90 Eglinton Avenue East, Suite 700, Toronto, Ontario M4P 2Y3, Canada
(a division of Pearson Penguin Canada Inc.)
Penguin Books Ltd., 80 Strand, London WC2R 0RL, England
Penguin Group Ireland, 25 St. Stephen's Green, Dublin 2, Ireland (a division of Penguin Books Ltd.)
Penguin Group (Australia), 250 Camberwell Road, Camberwell, Victoria 3124, Australia
(a division of Pearson Australia Group Pty. Ltd.)
Penguin Books India Pvt. Ltd., 11 Community Centre, Panchsheel Park, New Delhi—110 017, India
Penguin Group (NZ), 67 Apollo Drive, Rosedale, North Shore 0632, New Zealand
(a division of Pearson New Zealand Ltd.)
Penguin Books (South Africa) (Pty.) Ltd., 24 Sturdee Avenue, Rosebank, Johannesburg 2196,
South Africa

Penguin Books Ltd., Registered Offices: 80 Strand, London WC2R 0RL, England

This book is an original publication of The Berkley Publishing Group.

This is a work of fiction. Names, characters, places, and incidents either are the product of the author's imagination or are used fictitiously, and any resemblance to actual persons, living or dead, business establishments, events, or locales is entirely coincidental. The publisher does not have any control over and does not assume any responsibility for author or third-party websites or their content.

PRINTING HISTORY
Heat trade paperback edition / November 2009

Library of Congress Cataloging-in-Publication Data

Haynes, Jasmine.
    Yours for the night / Jasmine Haynes.—Heat trade pbk. ed.
        p. cm.
    ISBN 978-0-425-22999-6
I. Title.
PS3608.A936Y68    2009
813'.6—dc22                                        2009019532

PRINTED IN THE UNITED STATES OF AMERICA

10  9  8  7  6  5  4  3  2  1

*To Linda Simi, for all the brainstorming over the years*

# ACKNOWLEDGMENTS

Thanks to Jenn Cummings, Terri Schaefer, Kathy Coatney, and Rita Hogan, for always being there to keep me flying straight. To Renee Bernard, for telling me about the wonders of port, and Janice Beach, for letting me borrow her gambler's chain. To Bella Andre, Shelley Bates, and Pam Fryer, for the writing days and the unending support. To my agent, Lucienne Diver, and my editor, Wendy McCurdy.

# CONTENTS

# THE
# GIRLFRIEND
# EXPERIENCE

# 1

"I AM NOT BAILING YOU OUT AGAIN."

"I'm not asking for a bailout, Dad. I'm asking for a small loan." Marianna had paid back every loan he'd ever given her. With interest, both monetary and emotional.

Asa Whitney rocked heel to toe in front of the picture window overlooking San Francisco Bay, hands clasped behind him like Captain Ahab searching for a whale to harpoon. She was pretty sure he wasn't admiring the water sparkling in the bright sunshine. January in the Bay Area could be short-sleeve weather, a respite before the rains of February.

Marianna wasn't in a position to enjoy either the view or the weather.

"You're thirty-five, Marianna. At some point, you have to start taking care of yourself."

As usual, he'd made her feel like she was fifteen. "I take care of myself. I just had some extraordinary expenses this month—"

Her father cut her off with a slash of his hand. "Enough." He turned toward her, gray eyes glittering, hard and cold as the bay. Tall, with a full head of steel-colored hair, at sixty-two he was imposing, autocratic, and omnipotent, with the ability to slice her to ribbons. "That's where the old cliché about saving money for a rainy day comes from."

She bit down on a curse. It wouldn't help. "The Bay Area is a very expensive place to live, Dad, and you and Mom didn't want me to move to Nevada last year when I had that job offer." Marianna knew that was a cheap shot, but she didn't take it back. She would have despised Las Vegas. She hated hot places.

"Your mother didn't tell you to buy those choo-choo shoes." He pointed at her blue suede Jimmy Choos, which, by the way, were more than a year old. She'd gotten them at Nordstrom's half-yearly sale for a steal at 75 percent off.

"I'm in *sales*, Dad, I have to dress for success." How did he even *know* they were Jimmy Choos? Oh yeah, Mom loved her Choos as much as Marianna did.

"Dressing for success obviously hasn't helped you."

He always managed to push the right button, making her feel worthless. A failure. A total fuckup. In the world according to Asa Whitney, she should be married, driving the kids to soccer practice in a Porsche SUV, and living in Atherton. Or better yet, in Pacific Heights, in the same building as her parents.

"Why can't you be more like your sister?"

She *knew* he was going to say that. Everything was about money and the lifestyle one could afford. Marianna, however, had graduated from college with a degree in library science, and she'd gotten a job right away. She loved books; she loved reading them, touching them, talking about them. She especially loved the kids' reading groups, where she'd gotten the little ones to fall in love with books. She'd adored her job. Except that in the Bay Area, you couldn't live on a librarian's salary. In San Francisco, you couldn't even afford a studio, let alone a room in someone else's house. Unless you liked bed lice in the Tenderloin district.

So she'd run into a money problem. Her dad helped her out. On the condition that she find a career with a better pay scale.

Five career changes later, she was still looking for the magic combination that would please her while making her father proud of her at the same time. One of San Francisco's elite, a pillar of the business and social communities, her father knew everyone who was anyone, and *she* was his embarrassing disappointment.

"Dad, I honestly can't help it that the economy is in trouble and the real estate market has taken a nosedive."

"I told you that you were getting into it three years too late. If you hadn't taken so long to get your real estate license . . ." He let the sentence dangle.

If, if, if. If she'd remained a librarian and moved to Kansas, where she could afford a house. If she'd gotten away from her father so he didn't micromanage every decision she made. If her Beemer hadn't taken a rock to the windshield. If the tiny chip hadn't become a fissure that snaked across the driver's side. If this weekend she hadn't gotten a fix-it ticket for it. She survived the cracked radiator by filling it up with water all the time. Not to mention the bald tires she shouldn't be driving on. But if she told her dad about all the issues with the car, he would go into the whole lecture about how he'd told her to lease instead of buy in the first place.

"I promise this is the last time I'll ask."

"You'll have to find another way." He smiled. It wasn't a nice smile. "You could sell some of the shoes in your closet."

She tried not to take a deep breath, because he'd accuse her of sighing to try to make him feel guilty. But she knew Asa Whitney was not going to feel guilt. He'd made up his mind. She'd have to figure out another way to pay for the repairs.

Was it too late to move to Kansas?

\* \* \*

THAT VERY SAME EVENING, JEWEL BISHOP STARED INTO MARIANNA'S crammed closet. "You're not going to get a damn thing for these," she said. "Every pair is at least a year outdated."

Most were several years out of fashion, not that it bothered Marianna. She bought on sale at the end of the season, she didn't toss a pair until she wore them out, and most were more than two years old. She loved shoes as much as she loved books, and her closet was as full as her bookshelves. "So it was a stupid idea." Besides, selling her shoes on consignment wasn't going to get her the money fast enough. Nickie, her car guy, wouldn't buy the new windshield without cash up front.

"I can loan you some money."

"No." It came out a little too harshly, but she was not bumming off her friends. It was bad enough bumming off her dad. She was still reeling from this afternoon's confrontation. "I mean, thanks, but I've got to solve my own problem this time."

"You can pay me back," Jewel continued. "With interest, if it makes you feel better."

They'd gone to college together, and even though they were poles apart in everything, they'd become good friends. Jewel had dark hair, brown eyes, and was a petite five foot two, while Marianna was blond and hazel-eyed, and a full four inches taller. Looks weren't the only thing differentiating them. Jewel had started her own accounting firm five years ago, and bought a house in San Mateo last year. *That* was the last sale Marianna had made. Jewel had helped her out that way, and Marianna couldn't accept any more charity.

"Thanks, but no. I'll figure something out." Maybe her sister could help. God, what was she thinking? Her sister was the *worst* person to ask. Besides, Marianna knew she'd be in the same boat next month. She needed big cash. She needed to make a damn sale.

"You could always declare bankruptcy."

Marianna snorted. "Right. My father would disown me."

"Who gives a fuck what your father thinks?" That was Jewel, telling it like it is.

"I'm thirty-five years old. At some point I've got to grow up and start taking care of myself." She parroted her father, a familiar lump in her throat. "I'm a loser," she whispered.

Jewel grabbed her arm, squeezed. "You listen to me. You're just in a slump."

"I've been in a slump for thirteen years. I should have made better decisions, gone into something high-paying like accounting, the way you did."

"It's not everything you think it is."

"You've got a house, your own accounting firm, all those galas up in the city that anyone who's somebody goes to."

Jewel was quiet a long moment, tension flitting across her face. "The business isn't doing as well as I tell everyone."

Marianna's heart dropped to her toes. Jewel was her shining beacon, the example she tried to live up to. "But you could afford the house."

"I needed some supplemental income to swing that."

"You mean like a second job?"

"Sort of." Jewel tipped her head, pushing her long, glossy black hair over her shoulder. "Do you really want a way to make some fast money and pay off your bills?"

"I'm desperate." Tension rode her spine, floated up to her eyeballs, pounded in her head. She had to prove she wasn't a failure, and for her father, money was the only yardstick.

"This requires a champagne cocktail while I explain." Jewel tugged Marianna to the kitchen. Which didn't take much tugging, since Marianna's apartment was the size of a postage stamp.

"I've got the cheap stuff." With a cocktail, you didn't dare use good champagne. You simply added bitters and sugar. It had become one of her favorite drinks because it tasted decadent without being hell on her budget.

Only minutes later, ensconced on the couch—two steps from the kitchenette—champagne in hand, Marianna clinked Jewel's glass. "Now spill."

She was giddy with the thought of a way out.

"All those parties and galas you talked about? Well, I get paid to go."

"Paid?"

"Yes, I receive money to attend."

Marianna tapped her finger to her chin. "You mean the organizers want to make sure they have enough women?" She had to admit she didn't understand.

Jewel shook her head slowly. "No. The men I attend with pay me. They like a pretty woman on their arm." Jewel was gorgeous, with flawless cheekbones, full red lips, and all the right curves.

"Uh-huh." Marianna nodded even though she still wasn't sure exactly what Jewel was saying. "And you make enough money to pay for a house?"

"I make a lot of money for an evening." Jewel set her champagne on the table and linked her pinkie finger with Marianna's. It was a childish thing they used to do right before a big test or a speech in college. A show of solidarity. "And after the party I have sex with them."

A flush rode through Marianna's body. Her face burned. The champagne bubbles made her head spin. "They *pay* you to have sex with them?"

Jewel held her gaze steady. "They pay me a *lot*."

"That's like being a . . ." Marianna couldn't say the word.

"It's being a *courtesan*," Jewel finished for her. "I please men. They tip me well."

Marianna's heart beat wildly in her ears. "How much?"

"I attended a five-hundred-dollar-a-plate charity dinner last week and the man I went with gave me four thousand dollars."

Marianna's jaw dropped.

"You're catching flies, Marianna."

She didn't know what to think or how to feel. "Was he gross?"

"No. He was quite decent-looking."

"Was he ancient?"

Jewel shrugged. "About fifty."

Fifty wasn't bad at all. "Did he hurt you?"

"I don't allow anyone to hurt me."

"Did you have to do awful, disgusting things?"

"Define awful and disgusting."

Marianna didn't want to even imagine.

"It was standard sex," Jewel supplied. "The basics. His wife doesn't like giving oral. I love it. And quite frankly, with how good he is at giving *that* in return, he could be as old as Harrison Ford or look like Quasimodo."

Marianna suppressed a shiver at the "oral" comment. She wasn't a prude. She enjoyed sex. And Harrison Ford was still pretty darn hot even at his age. The shudder she experienced was purely sexual. "So he's married."

"Most of them are. Being with a courtesan is a safer route than having an affair. They're not worried their mistress is going to start making demands on them, and they like the power of paying for what they want."

A courtesan. What Jewel was talking about was more like a whore. A hooker. A call girl. A prostitute. But *four thousand dol-*

*lars?* This was no street-corner shindig. It would pay for Marianna's windshield, the radiator, the new tires, with money left over.

"I can't even *think* about doing that," she said aloud.

"It's not so bad, Marianna. I like sex. I like men. And I love the money."

"But what if you get stuck with someone totally disgusting?"

"You never have sex unless you want to. You never do anything you don't want to do. And you always use protection."

"But—" She stopped. She couldn't use that word with Jewel. Not *whore*.

"You think I'm a terrible person, don't you?"

"No, I just . . ." Honestly, Marianna didn't know what to think. Four thousand dollars in one night. It was mind-boggling. But what about the morals of it? "Don't you feel sort of . . ." She couldn't define it. She loved Jewel, counted her as one of her best friends.

"Go ahead and say it." Jewel sipped her champagne cocktail, her fingers tight on the glass stem.

Okay. "Doesn't it make you feel sleazy and dirty?" Marianna was dying to know.

The smile was slow to grow on Jewel's lips, but when it came, it was sexy, sultry, secretive. "Getting paid for it is the hottest thing I've ever done, and so damn sexy. This is better than a one-night stand, and you don't have to worry about how to get rid of him in the morning. Oh my God"—Jewel rolled her eyes—"if a one-nighter is looking for a *relationship* . . ." She punctuated with finger quotes. "If I decide I don't like a guy, I tell my consultant not to put his calls through."

"You have a consultant?"

"That's what we call them, the person who answers the calls for me and sets up the dates." She laughed, her voice musically sweet. "Maybe we should call them matchmakers."

Marianna couldn't judge, especially when the thought of all that money set her pulse racing. "I'm still in shock."

"I get paid for having sex with no complications." Jewel touched Marianna's knee, lowering her voice to a whisper. "What more could a girl ask for?

# 2

A GIRL COULD ASK FOR A LOT MORE THAN SEX WITHOUT COMPLI-cations. Marianna, however, was having no sex and a whole bunch of complications.

And Jewel? She'd wanted her own business, to be her own boss, to have her career totally in her control, but with the Sarbanes-Oxley rules instituted after the Enron debacle a few years ago, the personal liability an accountant had to bear on audits made it harder for small single-person firms to stay in business. Marianna hadn't realized it affected Jewel to the point that she had chosen to become a call girl on the side. Jeez, what was the economy coming to?

"I never dreamed of happily ever after, Marianna. Sex is just biological. If I couldn't get it on my own terms, I'd probably pay for it, too."

Marianna had started to believe happily ever after would never come her way either. "You don't have to explain. I don't think badly of you."

"It's something I want you to consider. You could be out of your money problems like that"—Jewel snapped her fingers—"as long as you don't feel guilty about it later."

"I don't think it's right for me." But . . . she bit her lip. "Is four thousand in one night typical?"

"I've gotten as little as five hundred, and once a man gave me ten thousand for the weekend at his villa in Sedona. He paid for the flight, of course. I never pay for anything." She shrugged. "And sometimes I get jewelry."

Marianna eyed the ruby ring Jewel wore on her middle finger.

"Yes, this was a present from a pleased client. I'd say I average fifteen hundred. That's pretty standard when you're talking dinner, a party, dancing, then back to a hotel room. But I never stay the night. I call a cab by three at the latest." She leaned forward to poke the air. "They pay for that, too."

Marianna laughed, a touch of a scoff in it. "You're really trying to talk me into this, aren't you?"

"I'm just saying you could end your money troubles. Even if you did it a few times, you could get yourself debt-free and start over. Without hitting up your dad."

That was the kicker. Marianna couldn't see a way out of her current situation without going to her mother or her sister now that her father had said no. She laughed again, shaking her head. "So I don't borrow money, I prostitute myself instead. How is that better?" Honestly, she didn't want to make Jewel feel bad about her choice, but she couldn't see herself doing it.

"It's easy if you don't feel immoral about it. And you'd be building your network for your real estate business."

"You're kidding." Marianna's jaw dropped. "I'm going to tell these men my real name and hope they ask me to sell their house? How am I supposed to tell their wives how I met them?"

"They aren't going to reveal how they met you any more than you'll tell on them. I mostly date men from out of town to avoid the problem of running into their wives. But even if I do date someone from the Bay Area, I always get a picture first to make sure it's not a friend's husband or something." Jewel touched Marianna's knee. "These men are movers and shakers, either here in San Francisco or another big city, even internationally. I've gotten a couple of new accounting clients out of it."

"That's one thing I wouldn't do," Marianna said, flapping her hand, "tell them who I really am. What if one of them was a cop? They'd know exactly where to come and arrest you."

"First of all, clients come through referrals only, and second, I never ask for money; it's a gift. It's understood up front that if I choose not to sleep with them for whatever reason, then nothing happens."

Setting her empty champagne glass on the coffee table, Marianna wanted another, but she didn't want Jewel to see how badly. "I'm worried. What if something happens to you?"

"Someone knows where I am at all times. I check in, I always have my cell phone with me. I never go anywhere that isn't pre-arranged unless I call in first to let my consultant know. Protection on all fronts is the name of the game."

"What about something you can get from the sex?"

"Protection. Or I don't do it."

Marianna picked at a loose thread on the seam of the leather sofa. Six months ago she'd replaced the ancient flower-print pull-out she'd inherited from her sister. Marianna was always living in hand-me-downs, and she'd finally broken down and bought the brown leather. It had been a floor model.

Jewel sighed. "Maybe I shouldn't have told you about this. I should have just let you sell your shoes."

"I don't know what to think. I'm all messed up."

"Is it going to affect our friendship?" Jewel touched her hand.

Marianna's head popped up. "Of course not. Just because I

don't want to do it, doesn't mean I think you're a horrible person because you do."

Jewel let out a pent-up sigh. "Good, because I wouldn't have told you any of this if I thought you'd hate me."

"You're such a freak." Marianna snorted. "I'm not going to hate you."

Jewel hugged her hard for one second, then bounced off the couch, back to her usual pragmatic attitude. "All right, so let's go pick out what you're going to put on eBay."

Marianna didn't suddenly start hating Jewel, but she did think about Jewel's extracurricular activities long into the night. It couldn't be right to take money from men for sex. But God, she kept seeing dollar signs hovering over her head as if they were angels. She needed money, needed it bad. She was in an untenable position. No matter which way she turned to get the money, she'd be wrong in her father's eyes. No Whitney had *ever* declared bankruptcy. Selling her Jimmy Choos on eBay wasn't going to make her solvent.

But was following in Jewel's footsteps any better?

And then there were the *other* images that ran through Marianna's mind.

She tossed and turned, kicking the blankets aside. She hadn't had sex in far too long. It made her forget she was a woman. Behind her lids, she imagined a handsome stranger picking her up in his limousine. Salt-and-pepper hair. She liked older men. Gerard, her last lover, had been in his late forties, but they'd broken up over two years ago. She hadn't found time for a relationship since. God, she missed sex.

Yes, distinguished gray hair, trim, toned body, a nice smile, sexy voice. She gave herself over to the fantasy. *He helps her into the limo, pours her champagne. Chitchat, light touches, first her hand, her fingers, her arm, then her knee. They're alone, a tinted window between them and the driver. She's chosen a black dress with a high slit, and he slides his hand up her thigh. She's wet, her nipples hard.*

Marianna slipped her hand down between her legs.

*He doesn't kiss her; she's not sure she wants to kiss him anyway. That's more personal. She shifts, spreading her legs for him. She isn't wearing panties, and he strokes along her slit. It's the most amazing feeling, looking into a stranger's eyes as he fingers you. Hiking her skirt higher, she straddles him and rides his hand. Oh, so good.*

Marianna buried her finger inside, then slid out to use all that moisture on her clit. The fantasy had her so wet she didn't need her vibrator.

*Steadying herself on his shoulder, digging her fingers into his suit jacket, she pumps against his hand as if it were his cock. Then she throws her head back and comes. As she climbs off and straightens her dress, he hands her an envelope. Four thousand dollars for the best orgasm of her life.*

Marianna cried out, climaxing to the images in her head. A handsome stranger. And all that money.


THE NEXT MORNING SHE WAS ALMOST OUT THE DOOR WHEN HER cell phone chirped. Rather than worry about trying to get the Bluetooth in so she could drive, Marianna answered without looking, her hand on the doorknob.

"Hi, darling."

Her mother. It could mean only one thing. Her father had talked. "Hi, Mom. I'm off to an appointment." Not. She'd be behind her desk at the brokerage hoping her leads didn't hang up before she got her name out. "I'll call you back when I'm done."

"This'll only take a minute, honey."

Marianna held back a groan. She loved her mom, she loved her dad, but being stuck between Asa and Louise Whitney was akin to Mel Gibson in *Braveheart*. Drawn and quartered. "Okay."

"You know, if you need money, you don't have to go to your father. I've got some spare pocket change."

Her mom would give her the money and not expect to be paid back. But eventually her father would figure it out and accuse her of going behind his back. Then *both* she and her mom would be in trouble. There'd be emotional strings attached, too. "Thanks, Mom, but I'm fine. I've got it worked out. In fact, I'm on my way to a meeting that looks promising."

"All right, baby, but if you need it, we can keep it from your father, I promise."

Marianna didn't want to keep it from her father. She wanted to be in a position where she never had to go to him again. "Really, Mom, everything's cool. But thanks."

"Your sister says she hasn't heard from you in over a week."

*That* was one of the emotional strings. Calling her sister, making sure her sister felt included in her life, listening to her sister tell her how badly Marianna was screwing up. "I've been busy, Mom, but I'll try to give her a call."

"She said she's left you several messages."

Tattletale. Tina, older by two years, had been a tattletale even when they were kids. "I'll call her today."

"Promise?"

"Promise." She hated it when her mother made her promise. "Gotta run, love you, bye."

It took her mother only long enough for Marianna to get to her car and put her Bluetooth in. The cell phone beeped in her ear and announced her sister's name. Mom hadn't wasted a second.

Marianna tapped the answer button. No point in trying to

hide. They'd find her eventually. "Hi, Tina. What's up? Sorry I haven't called you, but work has gone psycho."

"You're such a liar. You've been asking Dad for money again, so work can't be good at all."

That's exactly where Tina learned to be a tattletale, from their mother. "It was a loan," Marianna said tightly.

"You always need a loan. You'll give Dad a heart attack."

Stress would give him the heart attack. Marianna considered herself merely an embarrassment. With her perfect husband, perfect house, and two perfect teenagers, Tina always made her feel small. "I've got a good line on something, so I don't need the loan anymore."

"In one day?" Tina snorted.

"That's how these things happen. Feast or famine," Marianna quipped, then she just couldn't keep her big mouth shut. "I've been going to some events up in the city with Jewel and my contacts list has grown exponentially."

"That's great." Tina didn't sound convinced. "Anyone Dad knows? He could probably put a good word in for you."

"Nope, no one Dad knows," she said quickly. She did not need her father asking who.

"Well," Tina paused, thinking, thinking, "let's do lunch."

Marianna couldn't afford lunch with her sister, neither the cash it would cost for the expensive restaurant Tina chose nor the emotional drain listening to how she, Marianna, needed to get her act in gear. "I'm not sure when I'll have time, but I'll call you as soon as I can. Gotta run, love you, bye."

She disconnected and pulled into a random parking lot, shutting the engine off as she peered through the ginormously cracked windshield. One breath, two. She'd screwed herself now. She couldn't go back and say her "leads" hadn't panned out. Her family would know she'd made up the whole thing. And by God, she needed to stand on her own two feet to show them she wasn't the loser they thought.

She said Jewel's name into the Bluetooth.

She'd only do it a few times. Just long enough to get herself out of debt. Her family never had to know where the money came from.

# 3

CHASE RAMIREZ STOOD BEFORE HIS SAN FRANCISCO HIGH-RISE office window overlooking the Bay Bridge. The afternoon sun was too bright on the water. The reflection burned his eyeballs and made his head pound.

"All I'm saying is you to need to get social again." Behind Chase, Harve drummed his fingers on the arm of his chair as he spoke. "I'm worried about you, bro."

Harve Duesterman wasn't his brother, but they'd known each other for many years, starting as freshmen in college when they'd been on the rowing team and both majored in business. They'd roomed together and, after graduating, had climbed each rung of the corporate ladder in tandem. When Chase finally made CEO, the man he'd wanted for his CFO was Harve. He trusted him.

The last year, though, had been hard. Chase had lost something intrinsic. Waking up in the morning seemed almost pointless. Work didn't interest him. His concentration sucked.

Sometimes it was hard just to breathe.

"I'm not interested in dating."

"It's not a date, it's sex." Harve sighed. They'd had this conversation too many times in the past three or four months. "You need a woman."

In the old days, before Chase married Rosie, he and Harve had done their quota of screwing around. They'd had some nasty times, shared a few women. In college, Harve's nickname had been Deuce, both a play on his name and the fact that he'd preferred doubles, two men and a woman, two women and him, two men with two women. They'd both settled down, gone the marriage-and-kids route, though Harve had gotten divorced about three years ago.

As for Chase, with Rosie gone, the only thing that kept him going was Krista, his daughter. She was a sophomore in college, and he had to put on a good face for her, make her think he was doing fine. She'd lost her mother; he didn't want her to be afraid she'd lose her father, too.

But fuck, pretending anything mattered took its toll.

"Sex isn't always the answer, Harve."

"No. But neither is what you're doing, dude, letting yourself waste away. I'm worried."

It was a wonder the board hadn't fired him, he'd been doing such a shitty job. Maybe he should quit. Yet as hard as it was to get up in the morning, if he didn't have work to occupy him, he'd simply die. And he needed to stick around for Krista.

"I'm fine," he said, but even he heard the apathy as he turned back to his desk and sat in the leather chair.

"One night," Harve insisted, his eyes alight with hanky-panky as they'd been all the freaking time in college. Harve might have lost most of his hair and stand only five-eight, but he was in good shape, and women gravitated to him as if they scented how much he loved sex, how much he liked making a woman come. "I'll find you the perfect lady. It'll break you out of this funk you're in."

This wasn't a funk. Rosie was dead. His fault. He should have done something. Krista had gone off to college, and he'd been working all the time, and one day Rosie was . . . gone. He hadn't even known she'd had the sleeping pills.

God, he was tired. "I'm not into threesomes or any of that crap anymore, Harve. I appreciate your concern, but I'm fine."

"It wasn't your fault."

Chase swallowed hard. "I know." He wasn't a good liar. Some would say working hard, getting ahead, growing the income and taking care of the family was the most a man could do. Rosie had needed more. He hadn't been there to give it to her.

"So get out for once." Harve stared him down.

He didn't want a woman. He didn't want to date. He didn't even care about sex. But Harve wouldn't let up on the questions and the solutions, and maybe it was time to bite the bullet. Maybe he needed a mindless fuck. Besides, if he did it at least once, Harve would get off his back.

"All right. I'll go out with one of your 'courtesans' or whatever the hell you call them." He'd paid for sex before, when he was single. The kinkiness of it had appealed to him then. Now it was simply the anonymity. She wouldn't be expecting him to call her again.

Harve rubbed his hands together lasciviously. "Awesome. When do you want me to set it up?"

"Krista's coming home this weekend, so it'll have to be the following weekend." His daughter was as worried about him as Harve was. But he'd never do anything to himself. Never. When he wasn't feeling guilty, he managed to hate Rosie for what she'd put Krista through. Which was better, anger or guilt? He wasn't sure, but he'd never in a million years do that to Krista.

He held up his hands. "But no tag-teaming like when we were in college, okay? Just a simple date."

"How about dinner? You can talk, get to know the chick a bit, and see where things go." Rising to round the desk, Harve clasped

Chase's shoulder. "And if it's a no-go, that's fine. I'll just feel better if you get out of that apartment."

Okay. One evening out of his life. He could even tell Krista he had a date. She'd be pleased. Maybe she'd think he was getting over it, moving on, healing.

"SO, MARIANNA"—THE WOMAN GLANCED UP FROM HER LEGAL pad—"why are you interested in this area of exploration?"

Marianna wanted to laugh. *Area of exploration?* It was Wednesday, two days after Jewel had first mentioned it, and here Marianna was, hiring on as a high-priced call girl. It wasn't exactly an "area of exploration." It was desperation. But Isabel was completely serious.

Marianna had taken BART into the city, and a cab from the station to Nob Hill. The establishment—or brothel, or whatever you called it—was nestled between two Victorians converted to law offices. Marianna thought it rather amusing. If anyone got arrested, they had lawyers on either side to choose from. The front lobby had been nicely appointed with buffed hardwood floors, dark paneling, a pretty receptionist, and Impressionist prints on the walls. She'd been shown to a small front room, which offered a fabulous view of Alcatraz between the buildings. The coffee was of the highest aromatic quality.

Isabel had arrived just as Marianna seated herself on the expensive yet comfortable chintz sofa.

"Jewel recommended your agency to me." It didn't answer the question, but Marianna needed to think through her reply. She hadn't expected anyone to ask *why*, though Jewel had said they'd interview her to make sure she'd fit the organization.

"We at Courtesans thank Jewel for that. But I'm interested in *your* thoughts." Isabel tipped her head and smiled, like a psychiatrist wanting to put her patient at ease. Or a car salesman trying to unload a lemon.

Somewhere in her forties, she was exceptionally well preserved. Botox, surgery, Restylane? Her blond hair, a thick fall of it over her shoulders, didn't have a trace of gray. Her artfully applied make-up enhanced her eyes and lips, and the wraparound skirt showed off toned calves. The woman obviously took care of herself, exercised, and watched what she ate. Instead of coffee, she sipped a glass of designer water she'd poured from a bottle out of the mini-fridge. Pretty? Attractive was a better word. She'd turn heads even if she was forty-five. Marianna wasn't sure she could hold herself with such poise.

"The money appealed to me." She decided to get her reason out in the open. If Isabel wanted to turn her down, so be it.

"There's nothing wrong with being attracted to money." Isabel wagged an elegantly polished fingernail. "You do realize, however, that we provide companions, and anything that occurs between you and your client is strictly up to the two of you."

The agency charged the client a fee for "matching" them to an appropriate courtesan, which made it sound like one of those on-line dating services.

"If there's an exchange of gifts, that is also within your discretion." The "gifts" could be jewelry or cash. "We don't get involved in any payment nor do we refer to whatever occurs between you as a service."

Isabel was very careful *not* to say Marianna would be paid to have sex, but Jewel had told her how it worked. Payment wasn't required for any act performed, but if the "gifts" were consistently underappreciative of a courtesan's time, the client was simply no longer matched to anyone.

"I'm clear on that," Marianna said because it was expected.

Giving another of those charming smiles, this one a tad friendlier, Isabel arched her brow conspiratorially. "There's nothing wrong with money, or thinking you're worth it." She put a hand to her chest above the cut of her form-fitting sweater. "*I'm* worth it. So are you."

Did Isabel go on dates, too? Interesting. "Jewel said there would be a couple of days of seminars I'd have to attend." Marianna assumed they'd be about protection against disease and the proper blow job technique or some such thing.

"It's a two-day psychological intensive where you'll hone your abilities to read people. Fantasy interpretation. Personality identification. Body language. You're lucky." Isabel smiled. "We have one beginning tomorrow."

Marianna raised one brow. "You teach us psychology?"

"That's what this is about." Isabel crossed her legs and set aside her legal pad. "We pride ourselves on interpreting unexpressed fantasies. A client *says* he wants this"—she leaned forward and lowered her voice—"but he really wants something else entirely, something he can't express, is afraid to voice, or doesn't even know he wants. Your job is to ferret that out."

"I'm not very good at reading people." If she was, maybe she wouldn't pick the wrong jobs or miss opportunities.

"It's easier than you think. You interpret body language, facial expressions. You learn to read between the lines, look for the subtext in what a person says. Sometimes it's as simple as someone saying he *doesn't* want to do something, and you realize you have to help him free himself."

Marianna laughed self-consciously. "I'm not sure I'll be so great at it."

"Don't be modest. Women are very good at reading a man's signals. We'll help you perfect that ability." Isabel picked up her pad once more. "First we have to uncover your fantasies."

"*My* fantasies?" Marianna mentally gulped.

"Yes. That's how we learn to match you. We look at your desires and find a client we think will mesh well."

"But I don't have any fantasies." She thought of the limo scenario she'd played with two nights ago when Jewel first told her how she made extra money.

"Everyone has fantasies. You just might not think of them that way. What do you imagine when you're masturbating?"

Marianna was glad she hadn't been sipping coffee, or she'd have spewed it all over the chintz.

Isabel correctly interpreted her look. "If we're not frank, we can't provide our clients with the ultimate experience. More important, we can't give *you* what you need. This is as much for you as it is for them."

"I thought it was about—"

Isabel put her finger to her lips, cutting Marianna off. "Courtesans was founded over two hundred years ago to give women a freedom they could attain nowhere else. That's still our mission statement today."

They had a mission statement? Marianna experienced an urge to giggle. She held it in.

"We encourage women," Isabel went on, "to realize their full worth. We want to empower women, aid them in exploring their own sexuality, whatever that may be and whether they get paid for what they do or they do the paying. It's all about self-worth."

Marianna didn't have a whole lot of *that*. Nor did she think Courtesans was going to give it to her, but she played along. "That's exactly what I'm looking for."

"Good." Isabel gave her a smile, one that had an almost feral cast to it. "Let's talk about your ultimate fantasy. Have you imagined threesomes, foursomes, watching two men have sex . . ." She spread her hands and raised her brows.

Marianna shuddered at things she'd never even considered. Did Jewel do any of that stuff? "I'd rather stick to me and one man." Then she laughed and added, "How about finding Prince Charming?" It was only after the words were out that she realized it wasn't so much of a joke.

Her biggest and best fantasy was of taking over her sister's life: a handsome husband with a secure job, a huge house, two darling teenagers, and a car without a crack in the windshield. Tina's life was . . . normal. Their father was proud of her for her charity work and her well-mannered children. Like Beaver Cleaver's mom, Marianna would have a made-from-scratch meal ready when her hubby got home, a clean house, perfect kids, such a lady, but ooh, once the bedroom door closed, she'd morph into a whore for him, keeping their sex life spicy. He'd never stray. *That* was her fantasy.

Isabel hadn't said a word. A flush heated Marianna's face. "I was just kidding." She tried to smile it away. Then she dove on the next thing that came into her mind. "How about a little exhibitionism?" She shrugged. "Not so much being totally out there, but the possibility of being caught, doing it in risky places." Like playing naughty out in the deep woods where you *think* you're the only hikers around. Except you're not. Oh yeah, she'd had that fantasy with her imaginary Prince Charming. "Or vice versa, walking in on someone, they don't see me, and I watch." She'd had that fantasy with her dream man, too, sitting out on their hotel balcony and looking straight into someone else's room to catch them. Or an office building. An apartment house. Somewhere they could watch, and get naughty themselves.

Isabel made a few notes on her tablet. "Very interesting. Risky places and voyeurism are universal fantasies. I'm sure we'll easily find several matches."

Marianna shivered. "You mean I'm hired?"

"We don't *hire* you, we don't pay you, we simply match you, with the client taking care of the matching fee. I've got a few more questions, about your personal preferences as to age of your escort, et cetera, but I believe everything will work out. I'll supervise your first few matches personally."

Oh God. She'd just committed herself.

# 4

THREE DAYS LATER, TWO OF WHICH SHE'D SPENT IN "TRAINING" AT Courtesans—she'd found it quite fascinating—Marianna surveyed herself in her vanity mirror.

"You must be crazy," she whispered.

"You'll be great." Jewel popped her head around the bathroom doorjamb from where she'd been primping. "But if you do freak out, I'll be there to talk you down."

"Sure, I'll be just peachy," Marianna muttered. She was scared spitless, but at the same time her panties were damp.

A Saturday night party. In the city. A limousine would pick them up in half an hour. She'd read her date's profile a hundred million times since Isabel sent it to her yesterday. Brock Ransom—the name sounded fake. He was midfifties, 165 pounds, five-eleven, unmarried. Yeah, right.

She gazed at his photo. At least she didn't recognize him. And she had told Isabel she liked older men. "He's not exactly Mr. America." Or Prince Charming.

"You can't judge someone by the package they come in. While looks get a second glance, what's really attractive is up here." Jewel tapped her temple.

Marianna hoped so. While she was given his picture, he did

not get hers. The agency protected their courtesans' anonymity. Isabel had even armed Marianna with a cell phone, paid for by Courtesans, so that her true name, phone number, or location would never appear anywhere for a client to track her down. It was her choice as to whether she used her real name.

"If you're not attracted, don't do anything." Jewel paired her words with a shrug.

To match his height, Marianna had chosen black suede pumps with a two-inch heel. Short and flared, her sparkly black cocktail dress flirted with the lace of her thigh-high stockings as she twirled in front of the mirror.

"You look perfect," Jewel reinforced.

Marianna was sure she couldn't have done this on her own. She'd never even get into the limo. But Jewel wasn't going to let her cry off, she knew. "I like your red velvet."

The dress was strapless, a plunging cowl neckline gracefully draping Jewel's ample breasts. Tight around her waist and butt, the velvet fell in sinuous lines to her matching high-heeled sandals. Jewel's glossy black hair caressed her bared back, setting the dress off to perfection. They were opposites, Jewel's dark hair to Marianna's blond, her olive skin to Marianna's peaches-and-cream, her voluptuous curves to Marianna's slender figure.

Marianna eyed her critically a moment. "Are you wearing panties?" Not a single line marred Jewel's sleek gown.

Jewel merely batted her lashes. "If you're not wearing them, you don't need the time to get them off."

The tips of Marianna's fingers went slightly numb. For a moment, they'd been two friends dressing up for a night on the town. Now they were . . . "I'm wearing mine," she said, "and I don't care what you say."

Jewel tipped her head one way, then the other, her glittering ruby-colored earrings swaying in her hair. "You don't have to sleep with him. You meet him, you decide. If you change your mind, he'll take it like the gentleman he is."

Marianna sat heavily on the end of the bed. "Did you ever do that, tell someone no?"

"I've turned down two men after I met them." Jewel stepped back into the bathroom and raised her voice slightly to carry through the doorway.

"Why?"

"One of them had terrible breath. Call me small-minded, but I wouldn't have sex with a man I couldn't kiss because his breath bowled me over."

Marianna shook her head, allowing herself a smile. Bad hygiene wasn't a *small* thing. Although some people couldn't seem to help it. She flexed her ankles and pointed her toes, a nervous little tic because her skin felt jumpy. "And the other man?"

Jewel gave a snort of disgust. "He was hot as hell, very doable, a little older than us, tall. He really had me going. I was wet and ready. But then he did this really asshole thing."

Marianna rose and leaned into the bureau mirror, checking her makeup once again. "What?"

"We were dining at the Carnelian Room, and the waiter brought him the wrong drink. He made a scene, raised his voice, told the guy he was an idiot and threatened to have him fired. It was unnecessary, not to mention embarrassing."

"What did you do?"

Jewel popped around the doorjamb again, her top lids lined, the lower lids still bare. "I leaned in close, told him I didn't fuck dickheads, then picked up my purse and walked out."

"You're kidding. What did he do?"

"I think he stayed to finish the replacement drink his waiter brought, because he sure didn't follow me outside while I hailed a cab. The next morning"—she waggled her fingers like the Wicked

Witch and smiled—"he called Courtesans and told them to fire me." She stopped dramatically.

Which of course made Marianna demand, "And?"

"Isabel fired *him*, in a manner of speaking. She told me any further requests from him would be politely denied." She spread a hand. "See why this place is so great? They take your word over a man's."

Marianna wished she hadn't gotten ready so quickly. It left her too much time to think, which is why she kept Jewel talking. Nerves. She was so damn jittery about the date, about meeting Brock Ransom, about what he'd expect, measuring up.

She glanced at her watch. "Are you ready? The limo will be downstairs in a couple of minutes."

Stepping out of the bathroom, Jewel caught Marianna's wrist. "Take that off."

"My watch?"

"Clients don't like to know you've got an eye on the clock."

Brock Ransom had hired her for the party. She could do anything she wanted. Or nothing. She could have fun or she could choose to castigate herself. She undid the band, tossed her watch on the bed, and followed Jewel out the door.

Dammit, she was going to enjoy herself at a big gala with delicious food, the best wines, and scintillating conversation. She'd worry about what might happen later in the evening . . . later.


CHASE TOOK KRISTA OUT TO DINNER. HE HADN'T GONE SHOPPING. Besides, he didn't have enough cookware in the apartment. If he'd even known how to cook decently. After Rosie died, he'd sold the house and gotten rid of all the furniture. She was imprinted all over it, and he couldn't live with the reminders. He now had a small, utilitarian apartment—basic two bedrooms, bathroom, kitchen, and one long room that passed for living and dining—with naked walls and cheap, bare-minimum furnishings. Krista had never said a word about it, but he realized it worried her, his lack of interest in anything, not even the creature comforts of a home.

The restaurant he'd chosen was a homey Italian place with cheesy red checkerboard tablecloths, noisy families, and the scent of tomato paste and garlic permeating the air.

"You look tired." Krista leaned in to be heard over the buzz of voices and a burst of laughter from the next booth.

"I'm fine, sweetie." Which was what he'd said to Harve, minus the sweetie. At least Krista had waited until dessert to say something. She had tiramisu, he a coffee, and the waiter had left the check by his elbow.

"You always say you're fine, Dad."

"That's because I am."

Her brow creased. Krista had her mother's curly dark hair and brown eyes, and his square jaw. She wasn't a traditional beauty, but she shone like a star in a dark night. Her college boyfriend Andrew didn't know what a gem he had, and sometimes Chase wanted to knock the kid upside the head. Then again, he wished Krista had more self-esteem than to allow herself to be disrespected. But kids, they didn't listen. Any more than he listened to Krista when she ragged on him about getting out more.

"It's not like I'm saying you should date. But you should do *something* to get out of the house."

"We're out tonight." He smiled.

She wasn't buying it and lowered her voice. "I miss her, too, Daddy." She called him *Daddy* when she was trying to wheedle her allowance out of him early, or when she was worried about him.

"I don't know any women I want to date," he said, still trying to avoid the subject.

"It doesn't need to be a date. You always liked the symphony. You could ask that couple you and Mom used to go with. I'm sure they'd love it."

It was years ago, before Rosie's depression. "I'm pretty sure they're divorced now, and I believe she's moved away." Not that he had the woman's number.

Krista slapped lightly at his hand. "You're not a good liar, Dad. You don't have any idea what she's doing now."

He did know they'd divorced, but only because Dick, the husband, had come to Rosie's funeral. Krista probably didn't remember. Chase remembered everything, especially the way Dick had avoided his eyes, the way *everybody* had avoided him. He felt the long, slow spiral grabbing at him, sucking him down. Not now, not in front of Krista.

He turned the stem of his water goblet on the table. "I wasn't going to mention it, but I have a date next week."

Krista gave an unladylike snort. "No way."

"It's true. Harve set it up for me."

She rolled her eyes. "Oh God, Dad, we're doomed. Harve set you up on a blind date?"

"Harve's got good taste."

"He's a T and A man," she scoffed.

He glanced around to make sure no one had heard. "I can't believe you just said that to your own father."

Her eyes crinkled in a smile, before she turned serious again. "Do you really have a date?"

"Yes, I do." He forced himself to smile. "But Harve bullied me into it." And he sure wasn't telling Krista that it was a date with a hooker. He just wanted to make his little girl happy, to show her he was trying to move on so she didn't worry so much. She was the most important thing in his life. The *only* thing that meant anything.

"Do you know her name?"

Damn. Busted. He smiled wryly. "I admit I've forgotten it."

Actually he'd been hoping Harve would forget the whole thing. Now Chase would have to do it. Krista would ask. And be disappointed if he said he hadn't gone through with the date.


BROCK RANSOM WAS BALD AND WORE GLASSES, BUT HE HAD THE sweetest smile and told the funniest stories.

"So she asked me what that hundred-thousand-dollar payment to the former CEO was for." He wasn't handsome. He was your average Joe, and his nose might have been broken once, yet he held his audience of seven, their attention rapt.

Even Marianna, who'd been an executive assistant for two years—career change number three—was dying for the punch line. Jewel had long since disappeared and Marianna didn't even care that she was on her own with her "date." Jewel was right: it wasn't the looks, it was the man. And Brock's personality more than made up for his lack of Mr. America features.

"I looked her straight in the eye"—Brock gave a dramatic pause—"and said it was a golden shower."

Marianna's lips twitched. Brock squeezed her hand.

"She didn't even crack a smile, just said that must have been some golden shower." He guffawed, a sound straight from his gut that had heads turning in their direction. The man's laughter was infectious rather than obnoxious. "It took almost five seconds for me to realize what I'd said. Then I had to retract and say I meant a golden parachute, not a golden shower."

The man next to Brock snorted out a laugh. "Didn't you ask her how *she* knew what a golden shower was?"

Brock smiled, and really, it was the nicest smile. "I thought it best not to embarrass myself further since it was my first week as

CFO, and she was the new audit manager." He raised Marianna's hand to his lips, kissed her knuckles lightly, and smiled. "If you only knew the number of times I'd stuck my foot in my mouth . . . You just have to learn to laugh at yourself."

Marianna had never been good at laughing at herself and was always mortified if she made a mistake. She figured, though, that with a boss like Brock Ransom, she just might be able to get over it. He made her laugh too much.

"Your drink is empty, dear. Let's get a refill." Pulling her from the crowd they'd become part of, he moved on. He called her "dear" as if she were his daughter, but his gaze assessed and recorded. The man was sharp. He'd guessed she was a little nervous and told her he was proud she'd accepted his invitation. He complimented her and introduced her as if she were someone important. She *became* someone important because of him.

All the while, he touched her, a brush of his fingers at her throat, down her arm, her back. Never out of bounds, just always there. And every time he made her laugh, Marianna got wet.

She didn't know why.

That was a lie. She knew exactly why. It was his fantasy. The one in his profile. This CFO of a Fortune 500 company wanted to skirt the edge of risky, to get naughty at a party of his peers, where anyone could turn a corner and discover him.

Perhaps he wanted to be discovered, to become the talk of the event.

Brock loved a titillating sexual story. Now he wanted to create one of his own. As he grabbed a glass of champagne from the tray of a passing waiter, Marianna slipped closer and nipped his earlobe. Just a little bite. Brock froze.

Had anyone seen?

Marianna hoped so. That's what he wanted. It excited her to give it to him. She wanted to step out of her staid world and get naughty. If she was going to get paid for sex, she sure as hell wanted to enjoy it.

Brock wasn't the handsome man of her dreams, but he made her laugh. Looks only went so far, then there was charisma, and Brock had loads of it. Marianna wanted to give him his fantasy, a little naughty play, the titillation of risky business.

He handed her the champagne. "Tell me more about you."

"I'm a librarian."

He chuckled. "A naughty librarian." His chuckles carried, but his voice was low. "Tell me the naughtiest thing my little librarian has ever done."

Marianna didn't think Brock would mind if she made up a story. Her skin flushed, images racing through her mind.

"We need to be somewhere a little more private for that." She stepped back, pulling on his hand, leading him out to the balcony. The long terrace overlooking Van Ness was relatively unpopulated, but the night being chilly, with fog rolling in off the bay, the management had lit the standing heaters.

Taking him to one end, on the other side of a huge potted ficus, she pushed him back against the wall. Resting one hand at his belt, she tucked her fingers just inside his waistband.

The scent of sex surrounded him, and she knew if she touched him, she'd find him hard inside his pants.

"Tell me," he whispered, his pupils dilating in the dim light.

And she spun him a fantasy.

# 5

"AT MY FIRST JOB OUT OF COLLEGE, MY HEAD LIBRARIAN WAS A VERY commanding man, in his fifties, bald, wire-rimmed glasses." Marianna dropped her voice, just a murmur in Brock's ear. "He made my panties wet whenever he called me into his office."

"I bet he called you into his office a lot." Brock's rising temperature heated the air around them.

"He did." She pouted prettily. "No matter how hard I tried to be good, I always did something wrong."

"Such a bad girl," Brock played along.

He shifted, she shifted, until she was almost flush against him, just a hairsbreadth separating them. He smelled of spicy aftershave, and his hard cock caressed her low on her belly.

"One day, I was in the fourth-floor stacks finishing up after the closing bell, when I heard steps on the metal stairs."

"Were you scared?"

"Yes, I was," she said, wide-eyed. "I knew it was him, and I knew I'd done something wrong. I just didn't know what."

"I'm sure he was about to tell you."

"He said"—she dropped her tone an octave—"'You've been bad.' And I said, 'What can I do to make it up to you, sir?'"

"What did you *want* to do?" Brock's mouth quirked with a knowing smile.

"Oh, I wanted to do a *lot*." She winked.

"Right there in the stacks, you naughty girl."

"Any of the other employees could have come up the stairs." She rubbed his chest, pushed aside his tie and slid a finger into his shirt to touch bare skin. "Anyone," she whispered.

Brock closed the micron of distance between them, and that was definitely an I'm-happy-to-see-you bulge in his trousers.

"So then I said, 'I'll do anything, sir, just don't fire me.'" She enjoyed her story, her nipples tight in her little black dress as she wished she'd had a head librarian of her own.

Brock slid his hand around her waist, his fingers resting on her hip.

"If you take off your glasses, can you still see me?"

He laughed. She glanced to the rest of the terrace to see if anyone heard. No. The few couples braving the chill were busy talking.

"I can see you without them."

"Take them off. We don't want them steaming up at a critical moment."

"Take them off for me."

His arms came fully around her, holding her at the waist, molding her lower body to his erection. She put his glasses in his suit pocket. He had nice gray eyes without them. Then she spread the lapels of his jacket, enclosing herself in them.

"Cold?" he asked.

She shook her head. "Easier access," she whispered.

His pulse trembled at his throat. "So, where were we? Oh yes, you agreed to do anything the head librarian wanted so he wouldn't fire you."

"He told me to turn around and face the shelf. So I braced my hands on the metal. Then I felt his hand on my ass." She shuddered dramatically.

Brock slipped his hands down to cup her butt.

"Then he lifted my short little skirt."

Brock bunched her dress in his hand and raised it.

"I wasn't wearing any panties," she said.

He tested the tops of her thigh-highs with his blunt fingertips, found the edge of her thong. Marianna swallowed. She was warm. She didn't need the heaters, and instead relished the cool air on her backside.

"Then what did he do?" Brock urged, his gray eyes smoking.

"He leaned in close and told me to spread my legs, then he slipped a finger down to test how wet I was."

Brock stroked the crease of her ass along her thong. "How wet were you?"

"Drenched," she whispered, mesmerized by her story, by his touch, by the fact she was letting a virtual stranger stroke her. And she wanted more. "He turned me around."

"And? And?" He sounded like a member of his audience listening to his funny stories and begging for the next line.

"He put my hand on the front of his pants." She eased a fraction from him and, never taking her eyes off his, glided her hand down between them, fitting his erection to her palm. His lids dropped to half-mast. A burst of laughter drifted down the terrace. Neither of them looked. This was what he wanted. Her hand on him when all someone had to do was turn to see.

"He told me to undo his zipper." She slid down the tongue of his, the rasp of metal seemingly loud, attention-getting. "Then he made me put my hand inside and touch him." She wrapped one arm around Brock's shoulders and slipped her hand into his slacks. He'd gone commando, and warm, hard flesh filled her palm.

A part of her stood back and couldn't believe she was doing this. But a bigger part thrilled to the knowledge that she'd made this man so incredibly hard with simply a story and a touch.

"He put his hand over mine and forced me to stroke him." Just as in her story, Brock covered her hand with his and together they caressed his cock, her fingers wrapped around him.

"I heard someone on the stairs, but he wouldn't let me go. He pushed me back against the shelf and rocked in my hand. I felt his come on my palm, and I smeared it all over him, making everything slippery."

Brock swallowed, and his breath puffed. "You naughty, naughty girl." The glint in his eyes said the naughtier, the better. All the while, she stroked him, tightened her grip, loosened it, caressed him until he was steel in her hand.

"The footsteps came closer and closer, and he whispered in my ear, 'Don't stop, don't stop.' As if he were chanting. My panties were so wet even though I was afraid we'd be caught. Then he groaned." She squeezed Brock hard in her hand, droplets of come coasting down her fingers. Leaning in, she pressed herself against him. "Then he made a strangled sound and came all over my hand. And those footsteps, closer, closer, closer."

Brock mumbled incoherently against her throat.

"Then he pulled my hand out of his pants and held my eyes as he said, 'Lick it all clean.' And I did, every last drop."

She gave Brock one last pump, one last squeeze, one last shift of her body against his. His face in her hair, he groaned, and a jet of come filled her palm. He jerked, once, twice, gasped, then held her still against him.

"Je-sus," he murmured on the next breath, shuddering in aftermath. Then he reached in his pants pocket and pulled out a handkerchief. She wiped her hand on it, then he threw it in the potted plant behind which they'd been hiding, and zipped up.

She'd caught him all, without leaving a single stain on his clothing, the only evidence being the handkerchief.

"My dear, you are a very bad girl." He smiled, then, her hand in his, stepped from the shelter of the ficus. People dotted the patio, laughter, voices, talking. Anyone could have seen them. Someone probably had.

Brock put his arm around her shoulder and hauled her close as they passed a group. "George, Roger, so good to see you here." A word to a friend, a smile for an acquaintance. "That," he murmured for her ear alone, "was superlative."

She hadn't truly bought into the whole women's empowerment thing until that moment. But it *was* power. Her blood pumped with it. He'd come fast, he'd come hard, just from the touch of her hand, her voice, and her imagination.

She hadn't even had an orgasm and it was darn near the best sex of her life. Anyone could have seen, but she'd had him in the palm of her hand, figuratively as well as physically.

"Would you like to dance, Brock? I feel like dancing."

He held out his arm. "I'd love to."

Under normal circumstances, she'd have rushed to the ladies' room to wash her hands. But she didn't feel the least bit dirty.

An hour later, her feet pleasantly tired after several dances, she was slightly tipsy from the champagne she'd drunk. She couldn't remember when she'd had such a good time at a party, especially not at one of these affairs, which was much more her parents' speed. Jewel never reappeared, but they'd arranged to make their way home separately anyway. Outside the hotel, Brock handed her into a car he'd called for her. He hadn't asked her to stay with him, hadn't tried anything else. Leaning down to kiss her cheek, he pressed an envelope into her hand. "Thank you for a wonderful evening. We'll have to do this again very soon."

He closed her door, handed the driver some cash, and signaled him to carry her away.

The car was out of the city before Marianna loosened her grip on the cream-colored envelope. It wasn't sealed. Easing it open, she stared at the bills inside. Crisp, green, almost new. Her blood pulsed in her ears, and she didn't know why she'd waited so long to open it. No, dammit, that wasn't right. She knew why. She was afraid she wasn't worth as much as Jewel.

It was lunacy to compare, but Marianna had been comparing herself to others all her life.

Glancing up to make sure the driver wasn't watching in his rearview mirror, she pulled out the bills and fanned them in her lap. Her heart raced. They were all hundreds. She counted like a miser, one, two, three . . .

*Oh my God.* He'd given her three thousand dollars. The thrill that ran through her was almost as potent as an orgasm. Three thousand dollars for a hand job. It had been so fast. The rest of the time, they'd talked, laughed, mingled, danced. If she measured the actual sex time, she'd gotten one hundred dollars a minute.

"DETAILS, DETAILS." JEWEL CALLED MARIANNA A LITTLE AFTER TEN the next morning. "How'd it go? I want to make sure you're fine, okay, not freaking out and all that."

Marianna sipped her second coffee of the day. "It was okay, and I'm not freaking out." She actually felt good. Almost giddy. She could pay for the windshield in cash, buy new tires, and fix the radiator.

"What did you do?"

"We danced."

Jewel huffed over the phone line. "You know what I mean."

She was actually embarrassed to say. She'd never been one to talk about her sex life with friends, at least not in lurid detail. She was even a little uncomfortable when Jewel got explicit. "It was just teenage stuff."

"I haven't been a teenager for so long I don't remember what that is."

Marianna puffed out a sigh. "Hand."

"He did you or you did him?"

She clucked her tongue, feeling her face heat with embarrassment. "It was *my* hand."

"Hmm." Jewel allowed a long pause. "How was it? Not the actual hand *thing*," she said with emphasis, "but the experience?"

"You mean do I want to do it again?"

"I mean was it *worth* it?"

Ah, Jewel was referring to the money. "More than worth it."

"Do you want to do it again?"

Oh yeah. She wanted the money. She wanted the power. And next time she wanted the orgasm.

# 6

"I MADE YOU A DATE." HARVE SHOVED A NOTE ACROSS CHASE'S DESK, then sat in the chair opposite.

Chase didn't pick it up. The thought of entertaining some woman, even if she was paid, carved a hole in the center of his stomach. He could always just *tell* Krista he'd had a great date.

"You don't get the option to change your mind," Harve correctly interpreted. "I've already paid for the woman."

"I didn't need you to pay for it."

"I knew you wouldn't do it if I hadn't paid up front."

Chase closed his eyes. His only option was to tell Harve the truth. He wasn't interested in sex or women. He didn't give a damn about work or making money. Besides Krista, however, there was only one thing he actually had an emotion about, and that was not to appear self-pitying to his friend of twenty-five years.

Rather than do that, Chase reached across the desk and grabbed the note. "Fine. I'll meet her." He didn't ask her name or what she looked like.

"Take the afternoon off. Go home, have a shower, shave, and dress nicely, okay?"

He laughed; it was almost real, and it almost felt good. "Yes, *Dad*."

\* \* \*

A COUPLE HOURS LATER, SHOWERED, SHAVED, WEARING A SUIT, and ready for a late lunch, he pulled up in front of an Italian place in Foster City he'd never been to before and climbed from his SUV.

"You're wearing a suit."

The voice came from behind. Turning, his heart skipped one beat, just one. A picnic basket dangled from her hands, and she'd wedged a plaid blanket under her arm. Tanned legs beneath a flowing white skirt. His gaze traveled up. He'd expected young. When you thought of sex for hire, you thought young, like that New York governor's scandal a couple of years ago. That girl had been in her early twenties. This woman was midthirties and in exceptional shape, her hair a mix of blond and brown streaks, her makeup light, her lips a deep burgundy. And she had a gorgeous pair of breasts beneath a tight long-sleeved red top. He was a breast man; he didn't need them large, but he liked pert. Hers were high, firm, plump above the neckline of her low-cut shirt.

He didn't usually stare at a woman's breasts when he met her. It had been months since he'd paid that much attention. But he was noticing a hell of a lot about *her*. For the first time, he wasn't so put out by Harve's insistence.

Instead, he felt . . . warm. After months of a cold knot in his gut even on the hottest summer day, he almost reveled in the burgeoning core of heat.

"I was told the dress code was high-class," he said, flashing his gaze up and down her entire lithe form, "but now I see that high-class has more than one meaning."

Her nose wrinkled as she smiled. "Is that a compliment?"

"A very high compliment. I can take off my jacket and tie and anything else you'd like me to if that'll make you feel more comfortable." He realized he was flirting, something he thought he'd forgotten how to do.

For a moment, he enjoyed small talk with a beautiful woman.

"You certainly should remove at least some of those clothes." She held up a hand to the sky. "It's a lovely day, and probably one of the last nice ones we'll see before the rain sets in again."

"I do believe it's supposed to rain later this afternoon." From the north, the slow-moving clouds were dark, threatening, but to the south, the sky was a vast expanse of blue.

"Then we'd better hurry or our picnic will be spoiled." She held out a hand.

He liked her smile a little too much. Flirting with her was a little too delightful. He shouldn't enjoy how she made him feel. He even tried to tamp down the sensation, because feeling too good about anything didn't sit right. Yet Chase took her hand in his and the warmth of her touch stoked a fire in the tiny nucleus of heat trying to build inside him.

"I'LL DRIVE," CHASE SAID. "YOU NAVIGATE." HE PULLED HER IN THE opposite direction from her car.

Marianna figured there had to be some sort of symbolism in what he said. "My name is Marianna."

He smiled. He had good teeth, white and straight. But then she wasn't buying a horse. The rest of him was darn nice, too. Beneath the suit jacket, he wore a tailored white shirt over a muscular chest and a flat abdomen. With strands of gray in his black hair and attractive lines on his face, she guessed him to be somewhere in his late forties. Isabel hadn't given her a profile, just an envelope, his fantasy, and his name. Chase Ramirez. He had the swarthy Latin coloring, but his eyes were the shamrock green of a mixed heritage.

"Nice to meet you, Marianna." His voice was deep enough to send a shiver along her spine.

"I guess you weren't expecting a picnic."

He had a nice smile. "Not when you chose a restaurant to meet me at."

"Oh, I didn't pick that. Your friend did." Provided with his physical description, she'd received the instructions to meet him at two o'clock outside a restaurant in Foster City. The more she thought about it, though, the more she started to see that a lunch date at a restaurant was just too . . . ordinary. She wanted to do something special to fulfill his fantasy.

He wanted a girlfriend experience, which, Isabel explained, was simply pretending you were on a date with your girlfriend instead of a courtesan you'd never met before. And what did girlfriends do? They created surprises. They cooked spectacular dishes for their man. They made him feel special. A restaurant, even a fancy one, simply wouldn't cut it.

Especially since his fantasy intrigued her. He wasn't wearing a wedding ring, but if he was married, she'd expect him to have taken it off anyway. Yet no telltale indentation marked his left hand. So why did he want to pretend he had a girlfriend?

Stopping by the front end of a silver SUV parked along the street, he reached in his pocket to beep the remote and unlock the doors. "I'll put those in the backseat."

She handed him the basket and the blanket. If it rained, she would absolutely scream. It wasn't supposed to rain. Or rather, she hadn't looked at the weather channel to see that it might rain until *after* she'd already planned her picnic, and by then she was so in love with the idea she couldn't give it up.

He removed his jacket, yanked off his tie, and undid the top three buttons of his shirt to reveal a dusting of dark hair sprinkled with gray. He tossed the jacket and tie across the backseat, then opened the door for her. "Thank you," she murmured as he ushered her in.

The SUV was clean, no empty coffee cups tossed on the floor. You could tell a lot about a man from how he kept his car.

He climbed in, closed the door, and she smelled him. Aftershave. Something mellow and slightly sweet, expensive yet subtle. It was the kind of scent you'd find all over you once he was gone, a subtle reminder of him you couldn't get out of your head.

"You smell good," she said.

"So do you." He glanced sideways with just the hint of a smile and started the engine.

She didn't usually say things like that, but everything about today was different. She hadn't opened the payment envelope. She'd wanted it to be a surprise when she returned home. Something to look forward to if her date turned out to be dog meat.

Chase Ramirez was the furthest thing from dog meat.

"Where to?" he asked, backing out of the spot.

"Highway 92 to Skyline." She knew a little-known park up there perfect for a picnic. That's what girlfriends did, they found romantic out-of-the-way places.

As he pulled onto the freeway, she shifted to face him and pulled her feet beneath her. "So, how was your day, honey?"

He turned his head slightly, his eyes touching hers briefly.

"Play along," she whispered.

"It was fine."

"You can do better than that."

"We've got a board meeting on Monday, so most of the morning was spent going over everyone's presentation."

"And it was extremely boring," she finished for him. So he was an executive.

He smiled, to himself almost, and nodded. "Very. But I'm always shocked at how ill-prepared people are."

She patted his knee. "Well, I want you to forget about it because I spent all morning making your favorite things."

"The agency told you all that, huh?"

"Of course not, but I'm a woman so I decided for you."

He laughed, then suddenly cut it off as if he'd shocked himself. "Which way did you say?" he asked, completely sober.

They were coming up on the 280 interchange. "Toward Skyline." He concentrated on the winding road as they climbed into the hills. The silence bothered her, yet she had trouble coming up with some decent small talk.

"Take the next left," she directed. The road looked like a driveway and the SUV bumped over it. "To the right."

He pulled in along a small tributary that was even more rugged than the last. She didn't remembered it being this rough, but then she hadn't been up here in . . . good God, two years. She hadn't had a real relationship since then. No one she'd even *want* to spend all morning cooking for.

So why do it for a complete stranger?

"You can park here." Marianna studied him. He had nice hands, capable hands on the wheel. She wondered how they'd feel on her body. He pulled into what had once been a semi-decent parking area but was now so overgrown the macadam had almost disappeared beneath the vegetation.

Beyond the so-called parking lot were waves of long summer grass now long dead. A slight breeze blew the fronds flat in one direction, then picked them up and tossed them the other way, giving glimpses of trees, the reservoir, and the ribbon of freeway in the distance.

\* \* \*

THE CAR WAS SO QUIET, CHASE COULD HEAR HER BREATHE. HE'D crushed her. But he'd heard himself laugh, and he remembered when laughing was an easy reflex. Before Rosie died. When he didn't have a clue how close to the edge she was, and laughter hadn't seemed like a monumental effort or a sacrilege.

Shit, he was a downer. Marianna was trying, even if she was getting paid for it, and he was being an ass.

With effort, he changed gears. "What'd you make me, baby?"

She brightened at the endearment. "It's a surprise."

In the grief counseling he'd attended with Krista, they'd said that if you could pretend for a little while that everything was fine, eventually you started believing it. He hadn't been able to pretend, but maybe he'd never tried hard enough.

Marianna jumped out of the car and grabbed the blanket and picnic basket from the backseat. She was sweet, vivacious, and trying really hard to please him.

"Come on, slowpoke," she called, standing in front of the SUV and waving at him. Her shoulder-length hair blew around her face and neck. Rosie had paid big bucks to get her hair mussed just that way, and she would have been horrified in a stiff wind. Until the last year when she'd stopped taking care of herself. Something he hadn't noticed until it was too late.

Marianna trod across the grass, tamping it down, the wind billowing the hem of her skirt.

Chase yanked the door handle and climbed out.

The blanket blew away from her every time she tried to lay it down, then she lost her grip, and the wind tossed it down the hill. She ran after it and dragged it back, laughing like a child. Her exuberance made him want to laugh with her. Her attitude was infectious.

"I guess it's a little too windy up here," she said, smiling.

"You hold that end," he said, "and I'll put the basket on the other end to keep it down."

She flopped onto her knees, securing her side, as he fumbled to get the basket onto the other.

"Guess this was a dumb idea." But she was laughing still.

And inexplicably the wind died. Her hair settled prettily. He sat next to the basket as she kicked off her sandals and crawled closer on her hands and knees. It was neither seductive nor sultry, but his heart pumped faster as he glimpsed down her shirt to the edge of a pink nipple peeking out from her lacy bra.

He'd been celibate for over a year. Watching Marianna crawl across the blanket was the sexiest damned thing he'd noticed in all those long months. He wanted to feel normal for this one afternoon. Even if they didn't end up rolling around on the blanket. Even if he didn't get his rocks off.

More than anything, he wanted to pretend he was fine.

For today, he'd stop thinking about Rosie. He wouldn't feel the guilt. He would enjoy whatever Marianna brought him.

"Don't you dare open that." She slapped playfully at his hand as he reached for the buckles on the wicker basket. "You'll see all my surprises and ruin everything."

"Yes, ma'am." He stretched out, propping his elbow on the blanket. "I'm all atwitter wondering what's in your magic basket."

She laughed at his word choice, eyes sparkling. "Now, that's more like it."

"I'm starving." For so many things.

"Good." She whisked out a plastic-covered plate. "First we have teriyaki chicken drummies. Then we've got sliced peaches to go with the chicken. The tastes complement each other. And we also have champagne." She pulled the bottle from the basket and handed it to him. "Will you do the honors?"

It was semi-expensive stuff. He twisted off the wire and foil, then held the neck and pushed the cork with his thumbs. With a loud pop, it shot into the air, disappearing in the grass. The scent of champagne misted out, but it didn't foam over.

"How'd you do that?" Sitting back on her haunches, hands on her hips, she surveyed him. "It *always* foams when I do it. And to get it off, I have to stick it between my legs and tug like you wouldn't believe."

He laughed, and it didn't feel bad. He tried it out a second time just to be sure. "It's no wonder it foams all over if you tug on it like that."

She tipped her head. "Why does that sound vaguely sexual?"

Because he'd meant it that way. "Because you have a dirty mind."

She smiled. "You know, I think I do."

And Chase imagined getting down and dirty with her.

# 7

CHASE HAD EXPERIENCED PAID COMPANIONS, BUT NONE HAD BEEN like Marianna. She wasn't practiced. She was real.

From her magic basket, she'd pulled a bowl of sliced peaches and two champagne flutes. She plopped a slice in each glass, then handed him one, which he filled, followed by the other. Tapping her flute to his, she saluted—"Cheers"—and swallowed a quarter of the glass, then closed her eyes, tipping her head back. "Oh God, that's good. I haven't had champagne like that in ages."

He'd have thought she had it all the time.

She opened her eyes. "You haven't tasted."

"I was watching you."

She was still a long moment, regarding him, assessing his words. Then she must have decided she liked what he'd said, because she graced him with another of her smiles and held out the plate of drumsticks.

"One drumstick, then a peach slice. It's to die for."

He chose a piece of chicken, the scent mouthwatering. Like her. "Delicious," he said, licking the stickiness from his fingers.

Instead of giving him the peach bowl, she selected a slice, then fed it to him. After the tang of the teriyaki, the juicy peach was heaven. He savored it along with the flavor of her skin, sweet as the peach. He'd never cheated on his wife. He hadn't had sex with another woman in more than twenty years. Since Rosie died, he couldn't even remember thinking about sex.

But he thought about it with Marianna, enjoying the image as much as he had the peach.

She ate a slice herself, and he took pleasure in the sensual cast of her eyelids, the low, throaty moan of appreciation. Then, going down on her elbow beside him, she pushed the plate of chicken at him. "Eat. I made a lot."

He ate, but he liked it better when she fed him.

"So tell me what you do." She nibbled daintily on a drumstick without getting messy.

"Business." He didn't want to talk about work. That would only lead to bad memories.

She dropped her chin to give him a look through her eyelashes. "That's illuminating."

"Sorry." He stroked a lock of hair from her cheek. Touching her skin, he wanted more. He wanted her to touch him. "I haven't done this in a long time. I'm not good at making conversation, and I'm a little nervous."

"Done *this*?" She flipped her palm out expressively.

He held her gaze. "Gone out with a woman."

"Are you recently divorced?"

A pulse beat at his temple. He thought about lying. "My wife died a year ago."

She gasped. "Oh, I'm so sorry." She laid her hand on the blanket a scant inch from his, their fingers almost touching.

He thought of telling her the truth about why Rosie died. But then maybe he didn't really know the why of it. He only felt the guilt in his gut. Dammit, he was not going there now. He wanted to pretend for a little while longer that he wasn't a basket case.

As if she understood how close to the darkness he was at that moment, she smiled gently. "Got any kids?" she asked.

MARIANNA COULD ONLY HOPE THE QUESTION WOULD SAVE THE situation. Chase's sudden smile dazzled her, the abrupt change amazing. Thank God, because she'd totally blundered that one. Isabel should have told her he was a widower. She wondered why he didn't wear a ring. You took it off for divorce, but not for death. But hell if she'd ask *that*.

"I've got a daughter," he said, a beam of light in his eyes. "Krista. She's a sophomore at Cal Poly in San Luis Obispo."

She gasped. "Oh my God, she's a Poly Dolly."

He chuckled. "I've never heard that one."

She felt the mood lifting. "I graduated years ago. Maybe they don't use it anymore. But it's sure better than being called an Aggie." In the midst of taking a peach slice from the container, she glanced up in case she'd offended him. "Not that I've got anything against Aggies." Cal Poly had been a big agriculture university even when she was attending.

He snagged a piece of chicken. Another good sign. "Don't worry, she's not an Aggie. She's doing graphic design."

"So tell me what she looks like."

He lips creased in a doting-dad smile. "She's beautiful." Everything was different about him when he spoke of his daughter. He came to life. His eyes brightened.

"Duh," she said. "With your DNA, I'm not surprised."

Chase licked teriyaki from his fingers, and she had the most incredible urge do it for him. Suck his fingers clean. Her face heated. So did everything else.

"Is that a compliment?" he asked.

"Yes, you're very handsome." Pretty damn hot, actually.

He blinked, then his mouth curved in a sexy half smile. "Thank you." His lips glistened with a touch of lingering teriyaki. Marianna wanted a taste of that, too.

He was obviously grieving for his wife. He didn't want a *real* girlfriend. He wanted someone to ease the loneliness for a little while. And she'd almost botched everything totally. She'd even had trouble thinking of things to talk about. Which shouldn't have been a problem since she had to make small talk all the time with potential buyers. Chase unnerved her in a way Brock Ransom hadn't. Perhaps because this was more like a date. A blind date one of her friends had set her up on.

And because Chase was much more devastatingly attractive.

She searched for something scintillating to say. "So, Cal Poly is my alma mater, but I'm a real estate agent now." Oh God. She closed her eyes and waited for him to say, *But I thought you were a whore.*

He didn't. Instead, he lifted her chin with the tip of his finger, waiting until she opened her eyes.

"I think we should start over." His eyes were a gorgeous bottle green.

"We should?"

"Yeah. Here I am with a beautiful woman who's prepared a delicious feast for me and I'm making her struggle to come up with conversation."

He had the most amazing eyelashes, thick, dark. "It's not your fault." It was her job to be scintillating. She sucked at being a courtesan. Though the thought of that particular word under these circumstances brought a smile to her lips.

He raised one brow. "Tell me."

Her face always gave her thoughts away. Why not tell him? "I was thinking that I sucked at being a courtesan." Her smile grew, then she laughed.

"An interesting choice of words." His eyes deepened to an earthier shade.

"Then I realized that's what I'm *supposed* to do."

"You are a very naughty woman."

She loved the way he said *naughty*. He stroked a finger down her throat, then slowly pulled away, leaving her skin tingling.

"I haven't done anything naughty"—she fluttered her eyelashes—"yet."

Holding her gaze, he dipped into the bowl of peaches and held one out to her. "Eat this."

Entranced, she took the fruit from his fingers as if he were a hypnotist. A drop of juice slid off her lip. His eyes glued to her, she licked it up.

"Now suck this." His tone was smoking as he stretched out his hand.

She drew his finger into her mouth and sucked off all the leftover nectar. So good, she had to close her eyes to savor his taste mixed with the peach and teriyaki.

"I would say you were a perfect courtesan," he whispered.

He pulled her hand to his crotch, molded her fingers over his hard cock. "Feel what you do to me?"

Her body was suddenly a blaze of sensation, wet at her core, a flush along her skin, her nipples teased to peaks by the touch of her lace bra.

Like Sleeping Beauty, she needed his kiss and she needed it now.

She covered the plate of chicken and snapped the lid on the bowl of peaches, then laid them in the basket. She set the two champagne glasses in the grass, hoping they wouldn't fall over.

Putting her hand on his face, she gave him her lips.

Tentative, sweet, a delicious combination of peaches, teriyaki, and hot male desperation. She swept her tongue across his lips, asking. He parted for her. She'd never felt so in control of a kiss, not the aggressor so much as the director. Touching his tongue with hers, she quickly backed off, teasing. He watched her, his eyes smoky with desire. She leaned in again and gave him her mouth. When she would have pulled away once more, he slid his fingers through her hair, held her to him, and the kiss became his. He used his tongue, his lips, sipped her, tasted her fully, teased, then rolled her under him.

Angling his head, he took her deeply. The crush of his body heated her inside and out. She forgot it was about money. She forgot he was a stranger. She wrapped her arms around him and kissed as if she were the longtime girlfriend he'd fantasized about. He groaned, holding her still. Just when she couldn't bear another moment without his hands on her breasts, her belly, between her legs, he backed off, then laid his forehead to hers, eyes closed.

"Christ," he murmured, his breath fanning her cheek. "You make me feel starved."

"I've got more food."

He chuckled, real laughter, no cutting it off. "Food is not what I'm hungry for." He pressed his hips, imprinting his erection along her thigh, then he slid to the side, laying his hand on her abdomen. "I don't want to rush."

"God, I do." At her words, he laughed again, and she decided she adored his laugh. She could get used to the twinkle in his eyes, the curve of his lips, the square jaw that spoke of strength.

"It's been so long, I'd rather take time to savor it."

She stroked his cheek, his skin freshly shaven, and, to use his word, *savored* the feel of him. She parted her lips to say something sexy and seductive, and a fat raindrop plopped on her cheek. "Oh my God, it's dark up there."

Rain splattered in her hair. The stormy clouds that had been off in the distance were now straight overhead. A drop rolled down Chase's temple. Another, faster, harder. She squealed. "My picnic. It'll be ruined."

Chase grabbed the important things, glasses and champagne, while she slammed the lid of the basket closed. When it was in her arms, he scooped up the blanket, and they ran for the car. Beeping the remote, he got there before she did, and he had the back door already open for her. All she had to do was climb in and crawl across to the far side. Inside the car, she leaned against the opposite door, hooked one leg beneath her, and held the basket in her lap.

As he climbed in and slammed the door behind him, raindrops glistened in his hair. He looked so . . . touchable.

Holding up the champagne, he gestured. "Refill?"

Her glass was still half full, but she nodded. "More, please." The rain pattered on the roof. "I guess this is like tailgating."

He clinked his glass to hers after handing it over. "Better. With tailgating you have a bunch of people around."

She smiled. Oh yeah, being alone was so much better. The champagne had a sweet bite to it. She'd splurged on it for the special occasion. She took two swallows, then licked her lips. Glancing at him, she loved the way his eyes followed the action even as he drank his own champagne. The way a man watched when he wanted, it always set her blood racing, but now, with Chase, it made her burn for more.

Marianna popped the lid of the basket open, gazing at him over the top. "I've still got pasta salad and crackers and Brie and . . ." In the midst of it, with his look eating her up, a flush of heat rose to her cheeks and warmed her through.

She didn't care that this had started with money, that she didn't know him, that tonight might be the only night, that it was all just make-believe. Screw waiting. She wasn't hungry for any of the goodies she'd packed. All she could think of was his touch on her. He'd made his move by putting her hand on his cock. Time for her to let him know how much more she wanted.

Slowly she closed the lid again, then hoisted the basket over the seat and set it in the back of the SUV. She waggled her fingers for the champagne bottle. He handed it to her, and she stood it up next to the basket.

Chase threw the blanket back there himself.

It was time for bold moves. Marianna climbed onto his lap.

# 8

EVERYTHING INSIDE HIM STILLED AS SHE SPREAD HER LEGS TO SIT astride him, her hair brushing the roof of the car. Time stopped. Chase held his breath and enjoyed the warmth of her thighs surrounding him. It had been so long that everything felt new to him.

She tapped the bottom of his glass. "Drink." She sipped from hers at the same time, then bent her head to his. "Kiss me with the bubbles."

Her lips sizzled against his, his tongue tingled with her sweet taste and the pop of champagne. He didn't touch her anywhere else, just thighs, the press of his hard cock along her center, and their mouths. She was so much more delicious than the fine champagne, with a sweetness all her own. She smelled of ozone and rain, wisteria and fresh grass, or maybe she just made him imagine all his favorite scents. He wanted her under him, on him; he wanted inside her. He wanted it all so badly he could do nothing more than kiss her as the fall of her hair teased his neck, his cheeks. She backed off and nipped his lip lightly, then licked along the seam.

"You like to play," he murmured.

"Don't you?" She smiled for him.

"I've forgotten how." It had been so damn long. Since long before—

"Stop," she said against his lips. "You can *think* when you're
alone in your bed. Or when you're driving to work. Or even in
some boring meeting." She rubbed her nose back and forth against
his, lowered her voice. "But not now."

Then she backed off, gulped the rest of her champagne. "Finish so we can put the glasses down and I can have my very wicked
way with you."

His heart stuttered, but he downed the champagne. The bubbles flooded his head with desire and need. He wanted anything
she'd give him.

"Define *wicked*," he said. Words were as seductive as touches.

She leaned once more over the backseat, getting rid of their
glasses. Her hair brushed his shoulder, her breast stroked his arm
as she settled back onto his lap.

Her eyes alight with mischief, she finger-walked from his abdomen to a button on his shirt. "Well, first, I'd undo this." She
flicked it open, then another and another, and laid her palm on his
chest.

"That's not particularly wicked." Yet it was fun. It raised his
pulse. Could she feel the beat beneath her fingers?

"Wicked is this," she murmured, pinching his nipple hard.

He gasped and surged against her, his cock suddenly as hard as
gunmetal. "Christ."

"Wicked?"

"Diabolical." He liked having his nipples pinched, the harder
the better, as if they had a direct line to his dick. "How'd you
know?"

She swept in to lick his ear and murmur, "Because I like my
nipples pinched hard. And if I like it, why shouldn't you?"

He molded his hands to her breasts, pushing her off slightly. Holding her gaze, he rolled both nipples between thumb and forefinger.

"Do it hard," she whispered, head falling back, lids drifting closed in anticipation.

He pinched, she peaked. Then she leaned into his touch and moaned for him. "I haven't had sex in two years." She rode his cock through his pants, undulating against him. "And this feels so good."

"I thought you—" He stopped. "I mean, don't you—" He didn't know how to finish without offending her.

She opened her eyes slowly. "You're my second date. And I didn't have sex with him, at least not in the traditional sense." She tipped her head. "Is it okay that I don't really know what I'm doing as a courtesan?"

Her second date? It was difficult to believe, yet he found it hard to doubt her sincerity. Maybe it was part of pretending she was his girlfriend. What the fuck, he didn't care. She was with him for now. He shoved her hand inside his shirt again. "You know exactly what you're doing."

She pinched and laughed delightedly when he put his head back on the seat and groaned, his body rising involuntarily, cock grinding between her thighs.

"Maybe I know a little bit, then," she whispered.

He laid both hands on her hips and held her tight against him, shifting slightly, rubbing until the heat of her pussy seeped through his slacks. "Tell me how you had sex with him in the nontraditional sense." He was curious, turned on, and slightly jealous, too, a heady combination.

She gathered the hem of her shirt and yanked it over her head. Her nipples peeked above the black lace of her bra. "Lick them first."

He loved that she threw her clothes aside with abandon and asked for what she wanted. Sliding his palms up the smooth skin of her back, he pulled her to him. "Tell me while I suck," he murmured the moment before taking her pebbled nipple in his mouth.

Her low moan vibrated in her chest. "It was a party, a big ballroom." She jerked as he bit lightly, then put her hand to his head, holding him close. "We went out to the terrace." She moaned. "Oh yes, don't stop that." He sucked harder, pinched her opposite peak. "I can't remember now," she laughed, cutting herself off mid-gasp.

He let her go long enough to ask, "What did he look like?" Not that he cared about other men, but he wanted an image.

"He was older, fifty-five maybe. Not too bad-looking." She cupped his cheeks in her palms, held his gaze. "But not like you. Nothing like you."

He liked knowing she found him more attractive. He popped the front clasp of her bra, and her breasts filled his hands. "They're beautiful," he said, with true reverence.

"Thank you." She shimmied out of the lacy garment and threw that, too, just as she'd tossed her shirt.

"I like that you're uninhibited." He liked that she'd lost her earlier nervousness.

She laughed, low, huskier this time. "I'm not usually. But you're different."

He let himself believe her. "Tell me what you did out on the terrace." Sliding his hands beneath the skirt, up her thighs, he stroked her ass.

She held his shoulders, captured his gaze. "I put my hand down his pants and rubbed his cock. No kiss. No petting. Just right to it where anyone could have seen us." Her hazel eyes deepened to the color of the ocean, and he knew that last part had turned her on the most. His cock throbbed in his pants.

"Did he come?"

"Oh yeah," she whispered, her lips curving in a seductive smile.

He couldn't resist pinching her bottom, then gliding along the elastic band of her panties to palm her damp pussy. She didn't balk or tell him he was moving too fast. Her skin was smooth, her belly slightly rounded, her pubic curls trimmed and soft to the touch. She shivered, and it flowed into him, until his body shuddered with need. "Did he touch you?"

She shook her head.

"Did you want him to?"

She shook her head again.

"Why not? Because it was your first date with a man?" He didn't stress the word, but they both knew it was a euphemism.

Her fingers flexed slightly on his shoulders. "Because I liked being in control of his orgasm."

Heat streaked through him. He stroked her curls, lightly, without delving deeper. "I want to control yours."

With her deep inhale, her breasts rose, begging him. He'd never been so entranced with a woman. It was the kinky act of paying for sex, the date being *only* about sex, the fact he hadn't even thought about sex in over a year. Suddenly he was consumed by it. Yet there was also a connection. He'd revealed a tiny hint of his turmoil. She'd given him a glimpse of her insecurities. It made what passed between them now so much hotter.

He wanted to give her this, an orgasm that required nothing in return.

HOLDING HER GAZE, HE HOOKED HIS FINGERS ALONG HER WAIST-band and tugged her skirt, catching her panties, too. She blinked, bit her lip, but said nothing. Lifting, she allowed him to slide the material along her thighs, then rolling to the side, she shoved everything down her legs. Settling once more, completely nude in his lap, her skin flushed a rosy pink.

Marianna shivered again, and it wasn't cold. Oh no, she was hot all over. And terrified. A man she'd never met before, fully clothed. Her, totally naked, legs spread and vulnerable. She was wet. She'd never wanted anything more than she wanted this, and part of the allure was being at his mercy. With Brock, she'd been the one in control; at least that's how she'd felt. With Chase, she had no control at all. And she loved it.

His hand hovered just over her mound, his green eyes seeming almost to glow like jewels. "May I touch you?"

"Yes." Her voice cracked. It was one thing to slide your hand down a man's pants, quite another to be totally exposed yourself. Yet she needed that orgasm badly. She wanted to give him her need, her desire, her control.

"Please touch me or I might go crazy."

Sliding his hand between her legs, he parted her folds, and stroked her with two fingers. She almost cried out, it felt so damn good. Her head brushed the roof as she tipped back and let her body roll with his caress. It was better than fucking, gentler, sweeter.

He stopped. She opened her eyes without realizing she'd closed them. He slowly drew his fingers to his nose, scented them, then sucked one into his mouth. Oh God. She almost came watching him.

"I needed to taste you."

She wanted to put her own hand on herself. Nothing had ever been so entirely about her, never had a man enjoyed her with such sensuality. Need made her dizzy. She didn't care that she was the naked one. She wanted to come, she needed it now.

"Touch me, please, or I'll do it myself." She hardly recognized her own voice.

"Then do it while I watch." His breath was sharp, harsh, his pupils dilated, and his cock bulged hard against his zipper.

"I was just joking about that. I want you to do it." Yet the idea made her even creamier.

"It'll be more wicked this way." He used her own word against her. "Do it," he whispered.

The cash had been the prime motivator. Brock's money had gotten her off in ways a physical orgasm couldn't. But with Chase, it was him, the moment, her need, and money be damned. She dipped between her legs, and his gaze followed. His nostrils flared, his cock flexed. His reaction drove her higher. She'd masturbated for a man, but it had been mutual and just another bit of foreplay. Not like this.

Her body shuddered and shimmied against her fingers. His grip biting into her hips, he pulled her closer. The back of her fingers rubbed his cock with every frenzied stroke.

Then she felt his touch on her, his hand cupping hers, his fingers sliding inside her as she caressed her clit. He stroked deeply, slow, gaining speed, then she was riding his hand, the pleasure inside, outside, everywhere. The climb was unbelievably fast, like a rocket shooting her into space. All she saw was stars behind her lids, then her body imploded from the very center, and she cried out.

His arms were around her as she trembled and jerked, then, for just a moment, she wasn't in a car, she was in his bed, safe, warm, sated, wanting to sleep, wanting to wake in the morning to make him coffee and breakfast. Like a girlfriend.

He laid her across the seat and came down on top of her.

She opened her eyes.

"I'm not sure what I want," he said, his eyes dark, and the sky beyond the window black with clouds.

"Do you want to fuck me?" The harsh word ached in her throat, reducing what she'd just experienced to . . . sex for money.

"No."

Was that good or bad? "Do you want me to blow you?"

He shook his head.

*Do you want me to come home and sleep with you?* She couldn't say that.

"I don't want to do you in the car."

Her heart beat hard and fast. "Okay."

"I don't want to do you tonight."

Her stomach turned over. "You don't have to do anything you don't want to do."

He shook his head, so imperceptibly she almost missed it. "Tomorrow night." He exhaled in a rush. "I want to see you again."

"Yes." She'd promised herself she'd have that orgasm. And Chase had made it spectacular.

Now, as with any drug, she needed more. She needed Chase's taste in her mouth, his orgasm, and her name on his lips when he came.

# 9

HER SCENT WAS ALL OVER HIS HANDS, HER TASTE ON HIS LIPS. HE could have had her. But when she came, crying out his name, Chase couldn't do her in the backseat of his SUV like she was a hooker he'd hired. The hours he was with her had transported him back to a time when every moment wasn't filled with guilt and should-haves.

It might not have been Marianna. Perhaps he'd been ready to let go, even if for a short time. Yet he couldn't take the chance. He needed more of her. He wanted the fantasy she created for him.

He'd helped her dress. She'd smiled sweetly, then talked non-stop on the drive back to her car. About the housing market and how she'd never been able to afford her own home. "Yeah, my dad, he's totally about net worth, so my not having a house . . ."

In the backseat, touching each other, insulated by the rain, they'd been in their own world. Now they'd come back to earth. Her anxiety exposed itself in the way she crossed and uncrossed her legs, how she clasped her hands, then a moment later laid them beside her on the seat, tucking them beneath her thighs. And kept talking.

"My sister, she's got a gorgeous house and the most well-behaved teenagers. I know that's an oxymoron, but . . ."

He didn't have to answer. She most likely didn't know how

much she'd revealed about herself. Or how appealing he found her, insecurities and all. It put them on the same level, he with his guilt, she with her sense of never being good enough. Her revelations also made him evaluate his relationship with his daughter. He hoped to God he'd never made Krista feel less-than.

Storing Marianna's number in his cell, he told her he'd call in the morning, then the moment she drove away, he started planning where he'd take her tomorrow night. He had never, in his entire life, planned a date with the energy he expended on this one.

He needed to get ahold of Harve and find out how to book her for an evening. He'd take her any way he could get her, even if it meant paying for her.

MARIANNA HAD AN OPEN HOUSE THE NEXT DAY. JANUARY WASN'T usually a good month for sales. People tended to put things on the market in the spring, when the weather was nicer. But just as the flowers were starting to bloom early, the unseasonably warm days recently had encouraged sellers. Despite yesterday's rain, the morning sun was now bright in a cloudless sky.

That's how she felt: bright, cheery. Despite having babbled like a dork the entire drive back to her car after their picnic. She'd had a momentary case of nerves. But he wanted another date. That changed everything.

It was Chase who brought the sunniness out in her, not the twenty-five crisp one-hundred-dollar bills in the envelope on the vanity. She hadn't even opened it until this morning. A little less than what Brock had given her, but more than what Jewel had called average. Marianna's financial crisis had been averted.

Yet she wouldn't give up being a courtesan. If she did, she wouldn't see Chase again. She liked him. Her heart skipped beats at a time when she thought of him. It was that special time when you meet a new and interesting man you can't seem to stop thinking about. Her delight defied explanation.

The cell rang in the bedroom. She'd been waiting for Chase's call since the crack of dawn. Okay, slight exaggeration—but close. She jogged to the bedside table and checked caller ID. Isabel. Her heart skipped.

"You impressed him," Isabel said after Marianna's hello.

Her heart rat-a-tatted. He said he'd call her; instead he'd called Isabel. She didn't know what to think. "I had a nice time."

Isabel's laugh tinkled musically. "He's requested another date tonight. Are you free?"

God, yes. She wouldn't care why he'd called Isabel first. "I'll check my calendar." She counted to three. "I'm free."

"He's asked for a car to pick you up at six thirty."

"Okay." Excitement rippled through her. "Did he say what kind of engagement he'd like me to dress for?"

"Elegant dinner, then the symphony."

Yes! A real date, not just a hotel room. She did a little happy dance around the bed, then stopped as if Isabel could see her being such an infatuated idiot.

"I also received a call from Brock Ransom. He's asked for you again. Are you interested?"

Brock who? Yeah, yeah, she knew, but after Chase . . . "I can only handle dating one man at a time."

"That's perfectly all right," Isabel said.

Then Marianna's mind started working overtime on what to wear. An elegant dinner. Dress up. Sexy high heels—she had a closet to choose from. Black stockings. That lacy red bra she'd bought a few months ago and never worn. Panties? Or no panties? Condoms, definitely. Should she have her hair done?

At four o'clock, she raced home from the open house, as if two and a half hours was an impossible amount of time in which to get ready. She washed, dried, fluffed, and mussed her hair, deciding it looked as good as if she'd been to the salon.

She chose a midnight blue velvet dress that matched her favorite Jimmy Choos. The neckline plunged, and the skirt was fun and flirty, reaching past mid-thigh. She forgot she was meeting a client and dressed for the man of her dreams, especially the thigh-high stockings with a sexy back seam.

She was ready for anything. She wanted everything.

Her life would have been perfect if her bell hadn't rung half an hour before she was expecting it to.

When she opened the door, Marianna's stomach dropped straight to her toes. Her father stood miles tall in the hall. All her life, he'd seemed miles tall, totally out of her reach. This evening was no different.

Yet she was old enough to hide her insecurities behind a big smile. "Dad. Wow. Come on in. To what do I owe this pleasure?" He was checking up on her, that much was obvious; otherwise he wouldn't have come without her mother.

"Well, don't you look lovely."

She suppressed a shudder. She wouldn't let this ruin her date with Chase. "I'm going to a cocktail party. Business. A client invited me." It just wasn't a real estate client.

She closed the door behind him as he raised his nose to sniff. "Coffee. Thank God. Your mother's coffee is terrible."

Marianna loved a cup while she was dressing, whether it was morning or night. "I'll pour you one." Her insides shouted, *Tell me what you want*. Still, she led him into the kitchen with a chipper smile on her face and made polite conversation about nothing, none of which she'd remember later.

"Your mother sent me," he said, seating himself at the bar that separated the living room from the kitchen nook.

"*Mom* sent you?" God, it was serious.

"She told me I was a putz for not giving you the money." He hitched a hip and pulled out his wallet, unfolded it.

She felt like Alice sucked down the rabbit hole. It was a nightmare. They'd argued, and he'd given in to keep the peace, which probably made him pissed as hell. At her, not her mom.

Poised with his fingers in his wallet, he asked her, "How much do you need?"

She wanted to throw up. Until the moment she remembered she didn't need his money. "Dad, I'm okay now." It shouldn't have felt so good, considering how she'd gotten the cash. "I sold a house last week, and my broker gave me an advance on the commission, so I'm all set." She spread her hands to encompass her outfit. "That's what the cocktails are about. To celebrate finding their dream home." The lies were just piling up. Soon, she'd bury herself under them.

Her father beamed and slapped his wallet down. "Sweetie, congratulations. The talk we had must have gotten you off your duff."

She barely suppressed the wince. "It sure did. Without you, Dad, I would never have gotten busy. You were so right. All it took was a little hard work." She was laying it on way too thick, making even herself nauseous. "I've got some open houses tomorrow as well. So it's all looking good."

He smiled that big, toothy smile usually reserved for her sister. "Honey, I'm so proud of you. I knew you could do it when you applied yourself."

Not. He'd never believed she could do anything. She'd been applying herself all along, harder than he'd ever given her credit for.

"If I hear of anyone needing an agent, I'll pass on your card. Give me a stack, will ya, sweetie?"

She fished her holder from her purse and gave him what was in it. "I appreciate it, Dad." She wondered if he'd even handed out the last set. He had a ton of business contacts, but she was pretty sure that up until this point, he'd been too embarrassed by her to give out her cards. Maybe he even thought she'd screw up a deal and make him look bad.

He rose, his coffee only half-finished. Mission accomplished. He'd gotten her in line—no need to stay. "Now I can tell your mother she didn't need to worry so much." He leaned in to kiss her cheek. "Keep up the good work." He stopped with his hand on the doorknob. "If you want me to invest any of the money for you, let me know."

Good God. He really was proud of her. He actually was. It was unbelievable, a state of relationship she'd never had with her father. He hadn't even asked to see the check she'd received. There was a catch, there had to be. Maybe he was going to call her broker and verify the sale.

"Just let me build up my cash reserves, Dad, then we'll talk about it." Of course, she wouldn't do it. She rather die. Giving him money to invest was along the lines of borrowing from him, like making a deal with the devil.

She never wanted him to feel he had a right to ask where the money came from.


DINNER WAS DELICIOUS, SEXY FUN, WITH MARIANNA GORGEOUS IN blue velvet. But she went over the moon when Chase bought her the symphony program.

She grabbed his arm, sank her fingers into his biceps. "Oh my God. It's Ashkenazy." As if she were speaking in reverent tones about a favorite movie hunk actor, her breathless, husky voice strummed his cock.

"It was last minute," he said, "so we didn't have much choice."

Her eyes sparkled as she pulled him out of the stream of

symphony-goers heading into the auditorium. "Do you see what he's playing?" She stabbed the program. A Rachmaninoff piano concerto and rhapsody was all Chase could make out before she went on. "These are my two most favorite piano pieces in the whole world and he's my most favorite pianist. I saw him when I was in my teens, but he played some horrible discordant Dvořák music I hated."

"I did good, then, huh?" He felt inordinately pleased.

She went up on her toes to kiss his cheek, and he could have sworn moisture clouded her eyes. "Thank you," she whispered.

He'd racked his brain for something he thought she'd like and decided the symphony was a good bet. When he purchased the tickets, he hadn't even asked who or what was playing. He hadn't cared. It was simply the elegant ambience he'd wanted. Yet someone up there was looking out for him.

He took her hand to lead her to a less crowded set of stairs. "I hope you approve of the seats, too."

Upstairs, down a hall, he handed the ticket to a docent in a burgundy jacket. The man pointed several doors down.

"You got us a private box." Awe dripped from her voice as he opened the door for her.

He attributed the fact that a box was still available to the economy. People were no longer willing to pay exorbitant prices. He, however, wanted the privacy.

Like an excited child, Marianna scampered down to the railing to look out. The slightly angled box was three tiers deep, designed for a party rather than a couple. A small curtained-off landing lay to the right where the wall blocked the stage view. The champagne Chase had ordered, chilling in a silver bucket, stood beyond the drapery. He popped the cork while Marianna was entranced by the sights. The dress was primarily formal—Chase himself had chosen a tux—but there were a few tweed jackets over jeans.

Marianna dashed back up the three steps. "He's not out there yet, but the rest of the musicians are tuning up."

Which explained the cacophony of voices, laughter, the clash of instruments, and Marianna's bright cheeks. He handed her a glass and clinked. "Cheers."

She sipped, closed her eyes, moaned. "Oh God, that's good."

She enjoyed everything with gusto—Ashkenazy, champagne, Rachmaninoff, teriyaki drumsticks with peaches, his touch, her orgasm. As he let his eyes rove over her, her sweet sounds caressing his ears, his cock twitched, begging for more.

She opened her eyes, smiled. "That's orgasmic."

Her terminology amused and delighted him. He had so much more in store for her tonight. "Let's sit. The performance won't start for another fifteen minutes."

She settled into the second seat on the top tier. Chase noted that they were damn near invisible from most angles, though their view of the stage was undeterred. Perfect.

Marianna, however, concentrated on him, gazing over the rim of her glass as she sipped.

"I want to hear more about being a real estate agent." He allowed a smile to rise. "We got sidetracked yesterday." He wanted to sidetrack her again tonight, but he was a patient man.

Over dinner, she'd steered the conversation to him, getting him to talk about his work. They'd even covered current events. Now he wanted to learn more about her.

She sighed, a sharp inhale, then a puff of air. "The market is not the best right now, you know. My father says I got into the business too late."

Her father. Chase was beginning to visualize the man as an ogre. "So you haven't always been in real estate."

"I started out as a librarian."

He laughed, couldn't help himself. "Marian the librarian."

She smiled with him. "A naughty librarian." She ran a finger down his sleeve. "There are a lot of naughty things I didn't get to do to you."

A librarian, a real estate agent, a courtesan. The sad state of the market was probably why she'd had to supplement her income. Chase figured that was his gain. "What things?" he asked.

She wet her lips with champagne. "I could give you a back rub."

A laugh burst from him. "All you want to do is rub my back?"

She leaned in, smiled up at him, a sultry, seductive cast to her gaze. "I could rub your chest, too, if you want."

"It's not my chest that's getting hard and needs your attention."

"Dirty man," she whispered. "I can't rub *that* here."

Hell, yes, she could. No one would see. "The lights will be going down soon." The box would be in relative darkness.

"We would miss the music." Yet her hazel eyes glittered, the color changing, reflecting bits of gold, as she turned her head slightly to gauge how visible they were.

He touched the small jewel case in his pocket. He'd thought about giving it to her at dinner, but was glad he'd waited until she'd learned who was playing tonight.

"For you." The ring box lay on the flat of his hand. "I decided this would be preferable to money." He hadn't wanted to hand her cash, and Harve said presents were always welcome.

Chase was silent for three beats. The instruments suddenly got louder, the murmur of voices higher pitched.


MARIANNA FELT A THROB AT HER TEMPLE. SHE'D BEEN HAVING A marvelous time. She planned to have her wicked way with this man, touch him, stroke him, taste him, but she'd forgotten she was being paid to do it. "You open it," she said.

Inside, light sparkled on gold filigree and jade. "I thought it was the same color as your eyes just before the storm hit yesterday."

A wave of warmth rushed through her body. He'd actually *thought* about what to get her. Matched it to her eyes, for God's sake. "It's beautiful." Antique, an oblong jade stone set in intricate curlicues of gold.

It was a gift, not payment. Something he'd give a girlfriend, not a courtesan. Cash would have been so much easier. Or even a trip to a mall jewelry store. But this had taken time, thought, energy. It was part of the fantasy. He pulled it free, and she fit it to her middle finger.

She held her hand against her sleeve for him to see. "It almost matches my dress." Amazingly, it picked up the midnight blue.

"It's like your eyes, changeable depending on the mood." He smiled.

God. He'd actually looked into her eyes yesterday. He'd found her perfect music on a fluke, her favorite pianist. Now a ring that matched her eyes.

Marianna could get used to this.

# 10

MARIANNA CLOSED HER EYES, SWAYING WITH THE NOTES AS IF THEY came from inside her. Chase was awed, entranced. She made him feel the music rather than merely hear it. The piano, with orchestral accompaniment, hit a crescendo at the end of the adagio, and she smiled as if she were in heaven, her lashes against her cheeks, a tear of delight at the corner of her eye.

He'd always enjoyed a night out at the symphony, but she made it an experience. Marianna was the beauty in the music.

The piano faded away, only the echo of its strings in the quiet symphony hall. No one spoke, no one even breathed. The pianist flexed his fingers, readied himself, his hands hovering over the keys as he raised his eyes to the maestro. Violin bows rose, poised, on the brink. Marianna took his hand into her lap, squeezed, and made his heart beat faster with her smile.

Then the concerto entered the allegro, with a livelier tempo that brought a light laugh to her lips. It was as if the music told a story she could hear in her head. Shards of light danced in the ring on her finger. He'd found it in a shop in Los Gatos this morning, a jeweler he used to go to regularly years ago. He'd had to have it for her.

She bounced and rocked in her seat, raised her hands and conducted, even hummed under her breath, all as if she were aware of nothing but the music. Marianna was the performance in his box. He knew she would bring all of that and more to her love-making. He couldn't have said how long the piece was, but he could have wished for it to go forever. Yet it ended, and the audience rose en masse for a standing ovation.

"That was beautiful, wasn't it?" Marianna whispered, traces of mist in her eyes.

"Yes." A complete understatement. She'd never grasp how magnificent watching her had been.

The stage emptied, the intermission lights went up, and the crowd in the auditorium below exited for drinks, appetizers, and conversation.

Chase barely made out the knock at the box's door. Ah, the next phase of the evening's entertainment.

"What?" she asked, one brow raised, a smile growing.

He shook a finger. "Don't turn around."

She wandered down to the rail as he let in the waiter. You could get anything you wanted, as long as you were willing to pay. Chase had made arrangements he hoped would dazzle her.

He considered that he might be trying too hard, then decided he didn't give a damn. He wanted fun. He wanted fantasy. He wanted to forget his guilt for a little while. It would be there to rain down on his head come tomorrow. For now, he wanted to create an experience neither of them would forget.

He tipped the waiter, sent him on his way, and opened the bottle himself. Having poured a glass, Chase whisked up a silver tray of treats and headed down the steps.

Gazing out over the party atmosphere of the symphony hall's intermission, Marianna didn't hear Chase, she scented him. Subtle aftershave, sexy male aroma. She let herself be mesmerized by the anticipation of his next surprise and turned from the sights below.

The chandelier lighting glittered in the dark strands of his hair. The drink he handed her was little more than a shot glass filled with a deep amber liqueur.

"Port," he said when she lifted it to sniff the bouquet.

"Aren't you having any?" She noted he hadn't poured one for himself.

"This is for you. In Victorian times"—he ran a finger down her arm, a sensation she felt in every nerve ending of her body— "it was believed that port overly stimulated women, so they were forbidden to drink it."

"Stimulated how?" She played along, her excitement rising before she even tasted.

He cocked one brow. "Orgasmically stimulated."

"Mmm," she murmured. God, he looked deliciously devilish. He'd made the night so perfect. The symphony, the music, now this seductive tease. "Does it work?"

"I don't know." He smiled, just a crook of his mouth. "I'm trying it out on you."

She sipped, surprised at the fruitiness of it. She'd always thought port was strong and heady like cognac, but this was sweet and smooth.

She tipped her head one way, then the other. "I'm not feeling it yet." Liar. She was damp from thinking about all the things he might have planned for her.

"Ah, then you must have the dark chocolate to go with it." He offered a silver salver on which the confection was broken into chunks.

"I love the dark stuff. Better than milk chocolate." She took a small piece.

"Let a tiny bite melt on your tongue, then sip the port."

She followed his instructions as he focused on her lips. She savored the sweet bite as it melted.

"Now the port," he murmured, caressing her with his gaze as if it were a physical touch.

With the port, the chocolate turned smoky, rich, delicious, and the alcohol seemed to sweep through her body, heating her inside and out. His expression was enough to melt the candy all by itself.

"That's to die for," she whispered. "What does it do to men?"

He raised his gaze to capture hers. "Port itself doesn't do a thing, but the act of watching a woman imbibe drives him to bury his cock inside her hard, fast, and deep."

She lost her breath. She lost her mind. He held out another tidbit of chocolate on the end of his finger. She bent to take it in her mouth, then sucked his finger. Backing off, she followed the morsel with the port. Oh yeah, it overstimulated women. No wonder those Victorian men had forbidden it, but God, what they, both sexes, had missed. If she'd been wearing panties—she'd removed them in the ladies' room at the restaurant because it felt so sexy—they'd have been drenched. As it was, she was so creamy she could have taken him without a moment of foreplay.

Then again, *this* was foreplay.

Shifting to stand behind her, he bracketed her with his arms as they watched the musicians begin filtering back onto the stage. "Is it working?"

She did nothing more than twitch her hips, rubbing his hard cock against her backside. "Maybe I need more."

The chocolate appeared in front of her, this time on his palm. She licked him clean, then sipped the liqueur and moaned for him, letting her head fall back against his shoulder. Brushing her hair aside, he kissed the side of her neck. He stroked with his tongue, sucked, then nipped her lightly.

An orgasm surged like fireworks blooming in a night sky. "Good Lord, port *does* work."

"So glad to hear it." His voice rumbled at her ear, adding to the moisture building inside her.

Across the auditorium, down in the seats, a man glanced up, did a double take. Focusing on him, she reached behind to wind an arm around Chase's neck. "People are watching. Perhaps you should drag me back out of sight so they can wonder what we're doing."

He chuckled, his breath puffing against her hair. "Dirty girl."

"Or maybe I should drag you." She pivoted in his arms, then trailed her fingers down his arm and grabbed his hand. "Bring the chocolate," she whispered, "I'll bring the glass." It would be empty before they were done. "How much longer before intermission ends?" She glanced back over her shoulder as she led him up the steps.

"Do you care?"

She smiled. That said it all. "I can hear the music from up there."

"But you can't see Ashkenazy."

"He can't see me either." She blew him a little kiss, then twirled lightly on her heel as they reached the small landing. She loved teasing him, playing with him. "Now, what was that about overstimulation?"

The silver tray clattered on the table as he laid it down, then he tunneled his fingers beneath her hair and pulled her hard against his chest.

He gave her lips a seductive swipe with his tongue. "You taste good. Port, chocolate, and you."

Her heart beat faster. She needed more. She dipped her tongue in the port, then she took him with an amazing mingling of flavors. His arm across her back crushed her to him, and the glass almost slipped from her fingers.

She pulled back. "Wait, wait, I have to put the port down." Or she'd spill it all over.

"I'll take it." He slugged back the last swallow, then set it on the table, beside the remains of the chocolate and champagne.

Beyond his shoulder, the main auditorium floor was hidden behind the railing, but she could see into the other boxes.

When he straightened, Chase shifted, following her gaze. "Shall we take our seats?"

Marianna didn't even have to think. "Hell, no." She grabbed his tux lapels to pull him behind the curtain.

"You're an animal," he murmured with a teasing lilt.

"Kiss me, Romeo."

He took her with little nips and licks, finally sweeping into her mouth for a deeper, longer, sweeter kiss. She wound her arms around his neck, reveling in the imprint of his body along hers. His chin was smooth, freshly shaved, the spice of his aftershave filling her head. He slapped one hand to the wall next to her ear, imprisoned her butt in his grip, and pressed his hard cock against her. God, she wanted to lift her skirt for him right then.

He was sex and sweetness and Prince Charming all wrapped into one. She was the courtesan, duty-bound to please her client, yet he'd made the night all about her.

Pushing at him, she tried to catch her breath. She needed to give him something in return, not for the ring, but for how well he treated her. Like a lady. "Let me taste you."

He was so still. A bell sounded, the five-minute warning for the end of intermission, yet not a muscle flexed or an expression flickered on his face.

Then, slowly, he let out a breath and brought her hand to the zip of his tuxedo pants.

The hall filled with the bustle of returning patrons, strings being prepared, yet above it all lay the sound of his zipper. He wrapped her hand around his freed cock. "Please suck me."

The momentousness of the request flared in his eyes. He

hadn't done this since his wife died. He'd never said as much, but she knew the truth of it.

He'd chosen Marianna to give him that first time. She felt humbled with the honor. And unbearably slick with her own need.

She went to her knees before him, still holding him in her hand, head back, gaze locked to his. Her tongue darted out for that first taste, licking just the head, the drop of come salty-sweet. She closed her eyes and breathed deeply, dragging in his scent to blend with his flavor. She glided her tongue down his shaft. A vein pulsed. He let out a sharp breath. The material of his pants caressed her cheek. Then the lights dimmed, and the music rose. She knew every note by heart, Rhapsody on a Theme of Paganini, and there was no song more perfect by which to take this man. She wrapped her lips around him, sucked him deeply, then slid down until his tip tickled her throat. Burying his fingers in her hair, he guided her, and she caressed him to the rise and fall of the music.

She would never hear the piece now without thinking of him, tasting him on her tongue, feeling the texture of his flesh, smelling the lush scent of his body.

Marianna sank her fingers into his thighs to steady herself. Chase rocked, feeding her his cock, retreating, taking again, possessing.

HIS PULSE THROBBED IN HIS EARS, HIS BLOOD HEATED EVERY CAPIL-lary. He'd forgotten how good this could be. Yet she made it better than any memory.

Because he was starved for a woman's sensual aroma. His heart had shriveled without a woman's touch. He'd been only half-alive until she took him into the warmth of her mouth.

His hand slipped away from her hair; he braced himself flat-palmed against the wall and made love between her lips. Her tongue swirled around him, captured him, seduced him. His legs shook with the effort it took not to come. It couldn't end yet. He needed more. A sudden crescendo of music was almost his undoing, until he opened his eyes and met hers. Blond hair spilled over her forehead, down her shoulders. Her cheeks bloomed with color, her lips like rubies, and his jade ring gleamed on the hand fisted around the base of his cock.

She owned him in that moment. He needed a piece of her in return.

Pulling free of her mouth, he brought her to her feet. "I want you."

She blinked as if she couldn't hear or understand. Cupping her face in his hands, he put his lips to hers and whispered, "Let me inside you." He heard the catch in his voice. "Please." He didn't care how needy it sounded.

"Yes."

The word puffed against his mouth and touched his heart. From his pocket, he retrieved a condom and rolled it on as she raised her dress.

The brazen act made his cock impossibly hard.

Her pussy was bare. She'd been naked all night. No wonder her scent had tantalized him. It damn near drove him insane now. As if his hand didn't even belong to him, he watched a finger snake out and bury itself in her wet center.

"I'm a very bad girl for not wearing panties."

He felt the drumbeat of music in his ears, an insistent throb. "No, you're very, very good." He lost himself in her eyes, swallowing hard. "God, I so want to fuck you."

"Then fuck me."

He couldn't see her irises, only her dilated pupils as he lifted her, pulling her legs to his waist. Entering her with a hard thrust, he pushed her against the wall, his cock hitting high and deep. It was so damn fucking good, he rested a moment with his forehead to hers, savoring the clench of her pussy as if he'd never had this before and could never have her again.

"Chase." Her voice was sweeter than the music.

"I need to catch my breath." He needed to write the moment into his gray matter never to be forgotten, the lace of her stockings beneath his fingers, the silky caress of her pussy, the decadent scent of chocolate, port, and his semen on her breath. In his right mind, he knew it was simply that he'd been without a woman's body for so long. In his animal brain, it was all about her.

She tightened her thighs, urging him deeper. "Take me, baby," she said on nothing more than a breath.

When he moved, she was heaven. God, how he'd missed this. As he plunged again, she shivered around him. He'd never had *this*, an insatiable need. He didn't want to come, because then it would be over. He didn't want to stop touching her, because then she could leave.

His body trembled, his legs ached, yet the scent of her enthralled him and the feel of her sent him over the edge. He didn't know whether the crescendo of music was in his head or if it had covered his shout of release. He lost his very essence inside her. When he came to his senses, they were on the carpet, wrapped in each other.

Chase thanked God that he'd finally learned how to pretend the last year had never happened.


RACHMANINOFF HAD NEVER SOUNDED SO GOOD. IT WAS LIKE HER own personal fairy tale. At midnight, Chase helped her inside the Cadillac he'd called for her, and she sped away into the night as if she were Cinderella. Thank God the car didn't turn into a pumpkin.

She held out the gorgeous ring he'd bought her. The thought he put into it made her weak-kneed all over again.

The evening had been so perfect. Like a real date. All right, with a real date, she wouldn't have dragged him into the dark and taken his cock in her mouth. Being a courtesan gave her a boldness she'd never felt before, and she was glad. She'd wanted to give that to Chase. She'd wanted that for herself.

Jewel claimed it was the money that made being a courtesan so sexy. But Chase was what made it sexy for her. It couldn't be as good with another man no matter how much money she got. Marianna wanted Chase whether he paid or not.

Oh God, she was in trouble. High-priced call girls weren't supposed to become attached to their clients.

# 11

"I HATE TO RAIN ON YOUR PARADE, MARIANNA, BUT ARE YOU SURE you want to put all your eggs in one basket?" Wow. Isabel had used two clichés in one sentence.

Marianna stirred cream into her coffee. It was a not-so-busy Monday afternoon, and she'd dashed over to the coffee bar across the street from the brokerage to give herself the opportunity to return Isabel's call.

"I know we've had several dates," she said, which would sound innocuous to anyone listening in, "but I think this is working well."

"As a courtesan, that's not good, Marianna. It's best if you establish a clientele, a *list*."

Marianna didn't want a list. She didn't want Brock Ransom. She wanted Chase. In the week and a half since the symphony, they'd had two more fabulous dates. Their third time together, he wowed her with an elegant French restaurant up in the Santa Cruz Mountains. On the way home, they'd had sex in the back of a stretch limousine. He'd given her a sapphire-and-diamond bracelet, which he said he'd purchased because it was the only piece he'd seen that was fine enough to fit her delicately boned wrist. Her heart beat faster simply remembering the look on his face as he'd fastened it. He'd taken her dancing on the fourth date. He was surprisingly good, far more skilled than she was, but they'd had so much fun despite her two left feet. He made love to her hidden in a little alcove off a back hall of the dance club and rewarded her with a sapphire-and-diamond necklace that matched the bracelet.

Exciting, sexy, tantalizing, he swept her away. It wasn't the jewelry. It wasn't all the sex and fun. They actually talked. She felt like she knew his daughter with all the things he'd said about her. He'd told her about his work, that he was a CEO for a big company up in the city. They discussed their political and social views. The only thing he didn't talk about was his wife. Marianna understood. But she was starting to need a little more. Like a bed and a whole night with him.

She sure didn't tell Isabel that. She hadn't told Jewel either. Jewel would totally freak out, so Marianna hadn't had the courage even to call her.

"When he's no longer interested"—thinking about it seemed to curdle the cream in her coffee—"I'll consider increasing my client list." She grabbed a lid for her cup.

"Marianna, I just think that four dates in a little over two weeks is escalating beyond where a courtesan should go."

"But this was his fantasy, a girlfriend experience. That's what I'm giving him." A couple moved up to the condiment bar. Marianna grabbed her coffee and shifted away, lowering her voice. "We both know it's *just* a fantasy."

Except that sometimes Marianna dreamed it was more.

"I'm only suggesting that you keep it on a casual basis."

Marianna wasn't like Jewel. She wasn't good at casual sexual relationships. She knew that for the moment she was living in a secret world she'd created for herself. In a little while, she'd have to worry about next month's bills, but for now, today, tomorrow, she didn't care. She'd enjoy Chase for as long as she could. "I promise to just have fun and not get too serious. Might I ask if he called?" She didn't want to sound desperate.

"He did. He's planned something for Thursday night." Isabel sighed. "I don't need to ask if you're interested."

Marianna actually counted the days before she'd see him. "Thursday would be great." *So* great. "Did he mention where we'd be going?"

"Only that you should dress very casually—jeans, sweatshirt, that kind of attire. Meet him outside the San Jose Fairmont at six. You can park in the hotel garage."

The Fairmont. A ritzy hotel. What she'd been waiting for. But he wanted her to wear jeans and sweatshirt? That was odd. "Should I bring overnight things, then, since it's a hotel?"

"He didn't say to do that."

Her stomach dropped. Okay, *not* what she was hoping for. But gee, it could be something better, and she wasn't about to let herself get down. "I can be there by six." She'd have enough time to get home, shower, put on fresh makeup. If she hurried.

"Be careful not to get overly involved, Marianna."

"I won't."

Too late—she already was.


MARIANNA'S EYES DANCED WITH LAUGHTER AS SHE PERCHED ON the edge of her seat. The crowd went ape as the lights dimmed, and the mammoth shark's head dropped slowly from the arena ceiling. It landed, creating a tunnel from the locker room to the ice, and fake smoke swirled across the rink. Marianna's knee brushed Chase's as she screamed just as loudly as everyone else when the first player shot out of the shark's mouth.

"I cannot believe you wanted a date to a hockey game," she

shouted in his ear to be heard over the shrieks and catcalls as the opposing Hurricanes hit the ice.

Chase knew she loved it. "There's nothing like a game at the Shark Tank." Chase used the noise as an excuse to nuzzle her hair. "I was a fan even when they played at the Cow Palace."

The opening lines of the national anthem began, and everyone stood. Flush up against his side, Marianna belted out the words, slightly off-key when she hit the high notes. His ears rang with all the shouting, screaming, and laughter mixed with the scratchy music over the loudspeakers.

The spectators sat as the last note faded away, then came the coin toss, the slice of sticks across the ice, and the puck started flying.

Marianna grabbed his hand and shouted a curse as an opposing player did . . . something. Chase didn't see. He only had eyes for her, her cheeks glowing pink with excitement.

He'd worn his Sharks jersey. It hadn't been out of the drawer in a couple of years. After meeting at the Fairmont, they'd walked the three-quarters of a mile to the arena. He'd had her park in the hotel garage because it was safe there and because he'd wanted her to be surprised with their destination. She had been. Despite her comment, he felt her delight in his belly.

The Sharks scored fast, the fans jumping to their feet and screeching. Marianna did, too, pulling him with her, throwing her arms around him and dancing in the foot space in front of their seats. He felt as if her body touched him everywhere—thighs, chest, cock, heart, mind. He drank her in, fingers clenching in her sweatshirt. Then she threw herself back in her seat, clapping, shouting. She'd be hoarse tomorrow.

He watched her eye a steaming plastic container of nachos as a guy in the next seat started munching. She licked her lips. An overpowering urge to kiss her, touch her, took him over. A hand beneath the fall of hair at her nape, he pulled her close. "You want some nachos?"

She clutched the front of his jersey. "God, yes."

He felt her words as if she were begging for his cock, and when he rose to push his way out to the aisle, he was damn glad his jersey covered the evidence.

He returned to find her heckling a couple of Hurricane fans seated in front of her. She laughed, stuck her tongue out, the two guys shook their fists.

The symphony had been good, so had dinner and dancing. But this was fucking fantastic. He'd wanted something different, something unique, to watch her laugh, see her have fun. She surpassed every expectation he had.

Grabbing a cheese-laden chip, she closed her eyes, savored the bite, then licked her lips clean. He hadn't realized how much he'd needed to be with a woman who could enjoy a great big bite of life the way she did. She turned everything into an experience.

"God, that was good," she shouted. He could barely hear her.

She dipped another chip in the tangy sauce and fed this one to him. Half the cheese ended up on his lips. Leaning in, she wiped him clean with her tongue. Then she nipped, and finally, she took his mouth in a short, hot kiss that sent his blood pumping like fire through his veins.

If there hadn't been ten thousand Sharks fans there, he'd have pulled her on top of him right where they sat.

With the next score, she almost dumped the nachos on the floor. Chase rescued them. She covered her mouth and smiled an apology.

Had she a clue what she did to him?

He'd started out forcing himself to pretend she was a date, pretend what they were doing was reality, pretend the bad times with Rosie had never happened. But as Marianna sipped on her beer, then licked the foam mustache from her upper lip, he knew *this* was reality. Her. The way she laughed, the way she screamed an obscenity along with the rest of the crowd when a Hurricane player committed an egregious foul, the way she kissed, the way she made love.

He didn't have to pretend anymore. The way he felt about her was real.

MARIANNA SHOOK HER TICKET AT CHASE AS THEY WALKED BACK TO the Fairmont. "We get pizza!" Not only had the Sharks won, but they'd scored four times, so the ticket stubs were each worth a free mini pizza.

"You want pizza after the nachos and the hot dogs and ice cream—"

She put a hand over his mouth. "Not tonight. I'm totally stuffed. Another time." Then she realized she'd presumed there'd be another date.

A *real* date. Like this one.

Marianna dropped her hand and made her boldest move yet. "I think I won't see anyone else from Courtesans while I'm seeing you. Is that okay? I haven't yet, anyway, but I'm thinking things are less complicated if I don't." She held her breath, waiting, frightened. What if he said it didn't matter one way or the other to him?

His eyes roved her face, touched her lips, then he finally met her gaze. And smiled. "That would be fine with me. Next time we'll do pizza and miniature golf."

Her heart beat so hard she couldn't hear over it. Or maybe that was because her ears were still ringing from the arena noise. Her throat hurt, too. She shouldn't have screamed so much. Or so loudly. Or so long. But God, she'd had fun. Hockey. The date. Him. Most *especially* Chase. Now this. He wanted to be exclusive with her.

As they left the stadium crowd behind, she slipped her arm through his and hugged close, trying not to show he'd just totally rocked her world.

"Cold?" he asked, looking down at her, the streetlights gleaming in his hair.

She shook her head. Being with him made her warm all over. "Thank you for taking me."

"I haven't been in ages. I needed someone to go with."

She sensed he was downplaying what a spectacular date he'd given her. It was better than the others for the simple fact that it was what normal people did. Not what a courtesan and her client would do.

"Why don't you take your daughter?"

"She doesn't like hockey. I used to take my wife."

The words fell into a sudden vacuum. His wife. His dead wife. Cars began to fill the street, queuing up to get on the freeway. A deep bass beat out of the open windows of a truck. The pavement swelled with noise.

Did he want her to ignore it? Did he want to talk about it?

"You must miss her very much," she offered, wondering if she should stop clinging to his arm. Yet the moment before had been so good.

She glanced at him as he stared straight ahead, chewing on the inside of his cheek as if he were considering his next words.

Marianna took a deep breath and made the assumption that he wanted to open up. "How did she die?" Cancer maybe. Or an accident. Which would be worse to endure, a long illness or a sudden loss?

"She killed herself."

His flat statement slammed into her chest, literally thrusting the breath from her lungs as if he'd punched her.

Chase didn't stop walking. Cesar Chavez Park lay ahead of them. He waited for her to ask him why he hadn't seen something was wrong, why he hadn't helped Rosie, hadn't stopped her before it was too late. All the questions he'd punished himself with for all these months. But he needed to tell her. He needed her to know who he was, the crimes he'd committed. Especially after she said she didn't want to date anyone but him. She blown him away with that one, but he couldn't have it without telling her the truth about Rosie.

"I'm so sorry." She hugged tight to his arm. "That must have been terrible for you and your daughter."

The night air chilled his bones, but her voice, her body pressed to his as they walked, these things warmed him. "Krista is still working through it."

Sliding her hand down his arm, she laced her fingers with his. "At least she still has you."

"Yeah, right, she still has me." He heard the despair seep into his voice.

"That's why you don't wear a wedding ring, isn't it?" she said, her tone rising slightly. "You didn't think you deserved to wear it anymore."

"Yes." He'd removed it because he'd broken his vows. He hadn't taken care of Rosie. It did something to his insides that Marianna understood. It was almost like a little bit of forgiveness.

She didn't say a word, just squeezed his hand.

They rounded the corner and the lights of the Fairmont blazed before them. It was almost time for her to go. He'd wanted this to be a date. He hadn't intended sex. But then he hadn't thought he'd tell her about Rosie either. Being with Marianna changed things for him.

He stopped, pulling on her hand to get her to stop, too. "I just thought I should tell you about my wife before I asked you to spend the night with me at the Fairmont."

Despite saying she wouldn't date anyone else, she was still a courtesan, he was still her client—of course she'd spend the night. But he hoped she understood this was different for him. He couldn't say it, couldn't explain it. He just wanted her to get it.

He was used to her in high heels, but in tennis shoes, she seemed so much more petite. After an evening of her clinging to him every time there was a score or a foul or an excuse, her perfume was all over him. She wore the jewelry he'd given her, his ring on her right hand. It wasn't payment for sexual favors; it was a gift. She wasn't a fantasy. She was real.

She touched his cheek, smiled. "I'd love to spend the night with you."

For tonight, she was his.

# 12

MARIANNA WISHED SHE'D WORN SOMETHING SEXIER THAN A sweatshirt, T-shirt, jeans, and tennies for their first time. All right, it wasn't their first time *doing* it, but the first time naked, in a bed, in private, where no one could interrupt. The first time after he'd told her about his wife.

His confession changed things. She wasn't sure how yet, but in the telling, he'd given her his trust. This was no longer casual sex-for-hire. This was *real*.

Chase unlocked the hotel room door, then stepped aside to let her in.

God, how he'd suffered. She needed to make this good for him. Special.

The room was cushy and elegant, a thick cream comforter on the big bed, expensive wood furniture, luxurious light blue carpeting her shoes seemed to sink into.

There was only one problem. "Brrr." Marianna shivered and wrapped her arms around herself. Housekeeping had left the air-conditioning on.

Chase quickly turned on the heat. "I can warm you up in the meantime."

Marianna literally flung herself at him. "God, I've been dying to get naked with you." She'd never been so forward or so naughty, but she knew if she didn't do something quick, she'd get nervous.

Chase laughed, lifted her, and swung her around to the center of the room, right by the bed. "Get naked for me, then."

"Like a striptease?"

"Or tearing off your clothes. I don't care how." He toed off his running shoes as he spoke.

Her heart beating a mile a minute, Marianna grabbed the hem of her sweatshirt, dragged it over her head, and tossed it aside. Her hair floated back down around her shoulders, and she hoped to God it looked sexy instead of messy.

"Your nipples are hard," Chase said, his gaze brilliantly green and focused.

"It's cold in here."

He stepped closer. Her blood heated. "Are you sure that's the only reason?" he asked.

The T-shirt was white, tight, and thin as tissue paper. The lace of her bra made patterns beneath the material. His sapphire-and-diamond necklace rested above the scooped neck. He was close enough for her to scent his sensual male aroma, as he toyed with one breast, then the other. Just when she thought he'd step away and order her to finish stripping, he pinched her nipple hard. Orgasm rushed to her clitoris; she hissed in a breath, and manacled his wrist, holding off the moment. Not yet. She wanted to build toward it. With him.

"Do it again," she whispered, her voice hoarse from all the shouting.

He trailed a hand up her side, flicked the peak of one breast, then, locking his eyes to hers, he rolled both nipples between thumb and forefinger. And pinched. Hard and long. A pleasure-pain raced through her, so strong she felt her knees go weak, and she clung to his wrists, her head falling back.

Finally, he soothed her with his palms cupped to her breasts.

She searched his eyes. "How did you know I liked that?"

"You told me the first day."

Marianna couldn't remember. It seemed so long ago, as if they'd come so far. She'd had little emotion about him that day, at least in the beginning. She was light-years beyond that now. And he'd remembered.

"You like your nipples pinched, too." The memory came back to her in a flood. Everything about that day swamped her, how he'd tasted, how he'd made her play with herself for him, then helped her.

She reached out. He grabbed her hand. "Do mine later. When I'm inside you." Reaching deep in his back pocket, he pulled out a wad of condoms and tossed them on the bed like a challenge. Or a promise. "Pinch me right before I come."

"I will." It felt oddly as if they were making vows. "But first I'm getting naked." Then she pulled up her shirt with a sinuous roll. He backed off to watch.

If it was still cold in the room, she didn't notice. Chase's gaze warmed her. She unbuckled her belt, popped the top button, slid down the zipper, then wriggled her jeans over her hips. Bending over, legs straight, she shoved everything off along with the shoes. Then she posed for him, hands on her hips at the high-cut waist of her thong. Thank God she'd at least worn sexy lingerie, because the way his eyes traced her curves melted her bones.

She crooked her finger. "Your turn."

He was faster than her, and he stripped down to nothing.

His beauty awed her, from his hair-dusted pecs to . . . "Wow. You're so big."

He laughed. "You have seen me before."

And taken him in her mouth, too. "It's a new perspective, getting the whole show." She circled her finger. "Turn around."

His ass was perfect as he gave her a one-eighty view. "That's a very squeezable tush."

He glanced over his shoulder, laughter lighting his eyes. "You're ogling me like I'm a sex object."

"This is not ogling, this is total appreciation." Before Chase, she'd never really thought about making sex fun, yet he brought the giddy banter out in her.

He grabbed her, tossed her onto the bed, amid all the pillows, then came down on top of her. "Show me how much you appreciate me instead of just looking."

Lord, he felt good, his skin against her flesh, cock pressed between her legs, his weight on her. It had been so long since she'd felt a man's bulk pinning her to the mattress. "How would you like me to *appreciate* you?" There were so many delicious ways.

His eyes darkened to the color of a rain-soaked forest. "Suck me."

She wound her arms around his neck and turned the tables on him. "You should lick me first. As I recall, you've been remiss on that account."

"God, you're right." He stopped; something flared in his eyes, then he cupped her cheek and held her still for his kiss.

She closed her eyes and let him consume her. A long, drugging meld of lips, his tongue sweeping in to claim her. He surrounded her, filled her.

"You have too many clothes on," he finally murmured.

It was just her bra and panties. "Take them off with your teeth."

He chuckled, crawling down her body. Mouth to her nipple, he tugged the lace aside, swiped her with his tongue. He bared the other nipple the same way. Then he lifted his head to gaze at her through his lashes. "I really need to use my fingers for the clasp."

She huffed and waved a hand imperiously. "All right. If you must."

Her breasts were bared in an instant, her nipples hard beads from the pinching he'd given them. Suckling one peak, he tweaked the other, then laid a trail of kisses down her belly. Her flesh quivered.

This was so much more than they'd done before. The furtive fucks were fun, but she'd craved this. All night. Anything he wanted to do to her. Everything she wanted to do to him.

Just as she'd instructed, he used his teeth to tug the thong over first one hip, then the other, his fingers caressing her thighs. She lifted slightly, allowing him to pull the minuscule garment down her butt. The crotch clung for a moment to her damp pussy, then he whisked the panty down her legs and off.

"Christ, you're gorgeous." His rapt attention all on her pussy, he tested her with one finger, sliding along the crease, then dipping in at the top to tease her clit.

Marianna stifled the moan. Until, his eyes on hers, he sucked the finger he'd touched her with. A shiver raced through her body.

"Lick me," she begged. She needed his tongue. She needed him.

He didn't move quickly. He made her wait, stroking a hand down her thigh, forcing her to part her legs. Dipping down, he blew on her pussy. Sensation exploded through her as if he'd sucked her clit into his mouth. Her hips twitched. He pinned her down. Then he gave her what she needed, his tongue swirling over her clit.

Closing her eyes, she shoved her hands through her hair and rose to meet his caress, showing him exactly where she needed him.

Pushing her legs apart, he seated his shoulders firmly between her thighs and spread her lips, exposing her. Licking, sucking, teasing, he turned her into a wild woman she'd never thought herself capable of being. He filled her as he sucked, a finger, two fingers, and hit a spot like no other.

Marianna cried out, rocked, squirmed, panted. Her skin flushed, her pussy wept.

Then her muscles clamped down on his fingers, and Chase drank in her shuddering orgasm, rode it with her, kissed her, licked her, sucked her, until she started to laugh and grabbed his head.

"God, please stop. I can't take any more." Tears trickled down her temples.

She shoved him off and curled into a ball, her voice half laugh, half cry.

Chase gathered her into his arms, her sweet taste on his lips, her soft skin caressing the length of his body, her scent in his soul.

"I don't think I've ever come like that," she muttered against his chest.

HE WAS ENOUGH OF A SUCKER TO FEEL HIS HEART SWELL. THEN SHE reached up, held his cheeks between her palms, and whispered, "You need to be inside me. Now."

God, yes. He'd never been completely flesh-to-flesh with her; some bit of clothing had always been in between somewhere. Condom packages were scattered all over the bed where he'd tossed them; he grabbed one.

She stilled his hand. "Wait. I changed my mind. I want to suck you first."

"Too late now. Suck me later." He backed off, tore the wrapper, rolled on the condom, then, his hand on his cock, he held her gaze. "Let me inside you first."

Her taste was ambrosia, but when she lay back on the bed and opened her arms and legs to him, she offered him heaven. Bracing himself on one hand, he rubbed the tip in her juice, then savored the sight of his cock vanishing inside her.

She was tight. Her pussy had milked his fingers, clamping down on him when she came. He'd brought her to orgasm before, but nothing like that, not with a scream or a tear. The sensation would be phenomenal on his cock. God, how he'd missed the feel of a woman.

God, how he needed the feel of *this* woman.

He rocked into her. She raised her legs to his hips, her feet clasped at the ankles, and dragged him in. Biting her lips, she moaned as his cock massaged that already sensitized spot inside. Her body trembled, and she tossed her head on the mattress, then stopped and met his gaze. Her eyes were the shade of his jade ring on her finger. Color bloomed in her cheeks. Then her body moved with his rhythm, took him deep, let him loose, called him back again, forced him home. He felt her orgasm rise, working his cock from the inside. The ache built in his balls. And just as she began to spasm around him, she claimed his nipples, pinched hard with excruciating perfection, rocketing him into space, into mindlessness, into her.


HIS RELEASE WAS SO MUCH MORE THAN PHYSICAL.

Chase had disposed of the condom, turned down the lights, then laid a jewelry box on the bedside table while Marianna was in the bathroom. When she returned, he hunkered down in the big bed with her curled against him, her arm draped across his chest.

The sapphire-and-diamond bracelet glittered on her wrist. He liked his jewelry on her. Like a stamp of ownership.

She wore every gift he gave her. Which meant she hadn't hocked anything for the money. What they had between them was above money.

At least he liked to tell himself that. How she felt was another matter. He hadn't asked.

"Mmm," she murmured against his skin, then kissed his chest and tipped her head back to look at him. "That was very good." Her eyes sparkled as brightly as the gems he gave her.

He stretched out an arm for the oblong box, then laid it on his belly. "For you."

She smiled. "You shouldn't have."

He wondered if the words were part of the fantasy she'd fabricated for him. "I saw this, and it reminded me of you."

"My eyes again?"

He laughed, feeling corny. "Open it, and I'll explain."

She sat up and flipped the lid, making a little *ooh* sound as she lifted the intricately braided gold links, then let them cascade into her palm. "It's so heavy."

"It's an antique gambler's chain."

"What's that?"

"Like the chain for a pocket watch, gamblers had chains for their wallets so they couldn't be easily stolen."

She fingered the gold embellishments. "But it's too beautiful to be just an ordinary chain for a wallet."

"The more elaborate, the richer it made a man appear."

"I see." She tipped her head. "But I don't have a watch or a wallet that would fit it."

"You can wear it as a necklace." He snapped the box closed, then sat up to slide the chain around her neck. He didn't care that she already wore the sapphires and diamonds. He wanted to drape her in jewels. "It's classy, elegant, and unique." He kissed her neck. "Like you."

She traced it with her finger. "Thank you."

There was so much more he wanted to say, yet the proper words to describe his emotions wouldn't come. Instead, he showed her how he felt. Wrapping a hand around her neck, he pulled her down, took her mouth, kissed her, and long into the night, he made love to her.

SHE'D LEFT HIM AT FIVE THIRTY IN THE MORNING TO GIVE HERSELF enough time to get ready for work. She'd wanted to stay in bed, wrapped in his arms, rather than face another day at the brokerage with no sales, no leads, no calls. Gosh, those thoughts were totally depressing after such a spectacular date the night before.

Which was why Marianna ignored her real life and thought about Chase for most of Friday. He'd made love to her. Honestly, there was no other euphemism for it. Whenever she touched the gambler's chain, she *knew* it. Elegant, classy, and unique. That's what he'd called her.

Those thoughts sustained her until five o'clock.

She stopped for groceries on the way home. Her cell phone chirped oddly just as she'd grabbed a cart and headed into the produce section. She fished the phone from her purse, but it chirped again. Inside her bag. God. It was *the* phone.

Only three people had that number—Isabel, Jewel . . . and Chase. She'd been dying to hear from him all day.

Marianna dove once more into her purse before the cell stopped ringing. "Hello."

"Marianna?"

Her head was dizzied by anticipation, desire, the giddiness of relief, and the fear that the soccer moms shopping right next to her might overhear something naughty.

"Hello, Chase." Her heart beat wildly.

"I'd like to ask you to dinner."

"That's nice." She tried not to let excitement bubble over in her voice as she moved her cart closer to the organics and out of the way. He was calling *her* for a date, not setting it up through Isabel. Finally. Triumph sizzled through her veins. "I'd love to." She covered one ear to hear him better.

"Don't you need to check your calendar?"

Damn, he'd busted her. She didn't care when, she'd be free. "What day were you thinking of?"

"I was hoping you'd be available tomorrow night."

They sounded so polite, as if they were making an appointment for her to show him a house. She glanced at the crowded produce section. Okay, polite was a good thing now. "That will work. I'll report it to the agency, if you'd like."

"No," he said. "I don't want to report it. I don't want sex. I just want dinner. With you."

Oh God. He'd wanted a whole night. Now he wanted a *real* date. "Okay."

"And . . ." He stopped, and cleared his throat as if he were having difficulty speaking, or needed a moment to sort out his words. "My daughter's coming for the weekend."

"Your daughter?" She was sure her voice squeaked.

He cleared his throat again. "I thought if she met you, she would see that I'm starting to get over . . . what happened."

He was a good man; he cared about his daughter. The girl was probably as traumatized as he was. "I'd love to meet her," she told him with every ounce of sincerity she had. "Who will you tell her I am?" She'd play by whatever rules he chose.

He gave the briefest of pauses. "My girlfriend."

She closed her eyes. *Breathe.* "That's sounds all right. What time would you like me to be there?"

"Six is good. You can compliment the apartment, too."

She laughed. "Is there something wrong with your apartment?"

He laughed, though there was an odd note in it. "She complains that the walls are kind of bare."

After he'd hung up, she closed the phone and held it to her chest. He wasn't just a fantasy of Prince Charming that she'd created. He had all the qualities she'd always looked for in a man; he was loyal, caring, a good father, thoughtful, smart, and he had the ability to play.

He wanted her to meet his daughter. It had to mean *something.*

DAMMIT, HE DIDN'T SAY IT THE WAY HE MEANT IT. THIS WASN'T about showing Krista he was getting better. It was about showing Marianna that she was more than a date Harve had set him up on. He wasn't asking a courtesan to meet his daughter. He was asking a woman who had become terribly important to him.

She'd been an escape from his pain and guilt, but now the escape had become reality. After the first time, he'd never paid, he'd given her jewelry. She hadn't seen another man, she'd seen only him. He didn't fuck her, he made love to her. She wasn't a courtesan in any real sense of the word.

He should have said all that.

Except he'd been afraid she'd tell him that she *was* a courtesan and that to her this *was* all a fantasy Harve had paid for.

# 13

"I WANTED YOU TO MEET HER, SWEETIE." CHASE NUDGED KRISTA with his hip as he pretended to be helping her in the kitchen. "Plus I needed someone to do the cooking."

"You really like this lady, I can tell."

Krista was right. Chase had laughed more in the last few weeks than in the previous two years. Marianna was good for him. By osmosis, she'd be good for his daughter. Krista hadn't glowed like this in ages. She used to be such a happy kid. As a baby, she was always smiling, cooing at strangers, laughing. After Rosie died, she'd beaten herself black and blue with guilt, too. He wasn't the only one.

"Besides"—Krista did one of her typical eye rolls—"anyone can make lasagna." She sprinkled parmesan on the bread. Lasagna and garlic toast might seem like simple fare, but Krista jazzed it up by combining unexpected spices for a distinctive taste. She'd harbored dreams of becoming a top chef. The practical side she'd inherited from Chase had won out, though, and she'd chosen graphic design as her college major.

"They say the way to a woman's heart is through her stomach," he said, "so I'm counting on you to make me look good.

Which is why I went to all the trouble of buying proper cookware for you to make it."

Krista grinned, and he was struck, as always, by how much he loved her, wanted the best for her.

"At least Marianna got you to invest in some kitchen stuff." She laid her head on his shoulder for the briefest of moments. "Love you, Dad," she whispered, then, ever the efficient hostess, she added, "We'll put the bread in a little bit after she arrives. That way we can relax for a few minutes without rushing her to the dinner table."

The doorbell rang, and Chase froze, suddenly nervous, like a sixteen-year-old who has to meet his date's father.

Krista pushed his shoulder. "I'm going to love her, and she's going to love me, Dad, so stop worrying."

How had he managed to raise such a beautiful, intuitive woman?

He opened the door, heart choking his throat. Marianna. Low-rider jeans and sweater top. And the gamblers' chain around her neck.

She grabbed his hand, pecked his cheek, then stepped around him. "You must be Krista. It's so nice to meet you."

His daughter gave him an up-down look. "So he told you my name and everything."

Unbelievably, a flush rose in his cheeks.

"He pretty much never stops talking about you."

*Little liar.* They hadn't talked about Krista for quite a lot of the time they'd spent together. But Krista beamed.

"God, something smells divine." Marianna closed her eyes, inhaled deeply, then sighed.

"Krista made lasagna for us."

"I haven't had lasagna in ages. Yum." She patted her stomach, then set her small purse on the table by the door he reserved for tossing his keys when he walked in. "I don't have wine or flowers or dessert, but I've got something else." She skipped out the front door.

He'd been so mesmerized, worried, excited, terrified, that he hadn't even closed it. She hefted a flat package she'd leaned against the outside wall. "Housewarming present."

His heart hammered hard enough for him to feel it against his ribs. He took the package, a framed picture of some sort, then slid his index finger along the edging to slice through the tape. Krista crumpled the brown paper he let fall to the carpet. He flipped the fourteen-by-eighteen picture in a blue frame from one palm to the other, right side up.

"I got it on Fisherman's Wharf."

A stylized, colored-pencil drawing, fine lines and slashes that when you held it away sharpened into a semblance of the Bay and Alcatraz. Unusual, it wasn't to scale, but as he examined, the details popped out—sailboats drifting, seagulls diving, a ferry, buildings, even sea lions on the wharf.

"Thank you. I've never had anything like it." The drawing was like her: the longer he looked, the more depth he discovered.

"You're welcome." She blushed prettily.

He glanced at Krista. Her intent gaze flitted from Marianna to him and back. Then she smiled, so freely, beautifully, easing something in his chest, a tight band of stress that had made breathing difficult. Marianna had somehow managed to do the perfect thing. He'd asked her to compliment the apartment. She'd done him one better. It struck him that Marianna had awakened him with a kiss, drawn him from a deep sleep. His life was starting anew.

CHASE CLEARED HIS THROAT. "WINE?" HE POINTED BACK TO THE kitchen.

"Make it a small one, please," Marianna said. "I have to drive later." She hoped she'd hadn't gone overboard with the present. Chase looked a little shell-shocked, so she couldn't properly gauge his reaction.

Krista saved any awkward moment. "Can you put the bread in, too, Dad?"

He smiled. "Sure, sweetie." God, she loved his smile.

"Thank you for giving him the picture," Krista said after Chase disappeared into the kitchen.

"It was my pleasure. You don't have to thank me."

"It's just that he—" She stopped, and looked up at Marianna as if she suddenly doubted she should reveal anything at all. Her eyes, a rich milk chocolate, mirrored her anxiety.

"It's okay," Marianna said. "I'm not going to hurt your dad."

"Good, because if you did, I'd have to break your legs." Krista gave a shaky laugh, trying to make light of the moment.

Marianna would never hurt him. How could she not fall for a man who had such capacity for love? It shone whenever he looked at Krista, talked about her. Knowing what had happened to his wife, Marianna realized that his daughter was probably the only person that had kept him from giving up.

Chase returned, they sat, and she sipped the deliciously sweet wine. "So your dad says you go to Cal Poly," she said to start off the small talk. "What are you majoring in?"

Marianna admired the girl's poise and lack of self-consciousness. Krista told funny stories from school, laughed at her dad when he made faces about her boyfriend, teased him. It all felt so normal. So wonderful. As if Chase had asked Marianna here not just to ease Krista's mind about him but so he could get his daughter's stamp of approval on the woman he was dating. His girlfriend.

The timer went off. "My lasagna's ready." Krista jumped up,

dashing to the kitchen. The scent of tomatoes and herbs wafted into the living room as she opened the oven door.

Marianna touched Chase's hand. "She's beautiful."

A gentle smile softened his face. "Thanks for treating her like a grownup."

"She is a grownup." She put two fingers to his lips when he opened his mouth. "No buts. She's a beautiful lady, and she's filling this apartment with the most wonderful aromas."

"The lasagna will be set in five minutes," Krista called.

Marianna grabbed his hand and pulled him off the sofa. "Quick, show me the balcony."

"The balcony?"

"Yes. You're so high up, and I want to see all the lights." And she wanted a moment to enjoy him, the touch of his hand, the scent of his aftershave, to immerse herself in the fantasy he'd given her tonight.

Chase laughed as he followed. "It's just the airport."

She clung to the railing. "Oh my God, it's gorgeous."

He gazed at her, not the view.

"Look," she said softly. "The pattern of lights is beautiful, then they just end in the blackness over the water." She pointed. "Surrounded by the San Mateo Bridge and all the lights shining in the East Bay. It's like a secret world out in the middle bordered by all those lights." That was how she felt being with him, as if they were in their own fantasy world. "It makes you need to discover what's hidden there." Feeling his body heat along her side, she turned her head to catch his breath at her ear. "Don't you see how beautiful it is?"

"I see," he whispered. "I'm starting to see a lot of things I missed before." Something in his voice made her shiver, then flush with warmth.

"Dad?"

Marianna startled at Krista's voice behind them.

"Will you bring in the salad and dressing? And Marianna, the bread's in a basket on the counter, if you wouldn't mind getting it." Krista toted a large casserole dish with a couple of dishtowels.

"No pot holders, I guess," Marianna said, closing the balcony door behind them.

Krista smiled. "I can't think of *everything*."

"I see another housewarming gift on the horizon."

"Ladies," Chase warned.

Krista pecked his cheek as they passed. "You can't help it if you're domestically challenged."

God, this really *was* her dream. Marianna basked in the camaraderie. It was something her family had never had. She wanted what Krista and Chase had with an intensity that made her dizzy. She was like the department store commercial with the woman on the outside whispering, "Open, open, open." For tonight, Chase had opened the door to let her in.

Then they were seated, plates filled, and Krista's cooking was to die for. "I've never tasted lasagna as good." She swirled the flavors on her tongue. Tomato-tart and cheesy, it was sweet, but not any old sweet, something more, something—

"Secret ingredient," Krista said, her smile little-girl delighted.

"Everything has a secret ingredient." Chase covered his daughter's hand. "She had dreams of being a chef like Emeril."

Krista snorted. "He's a TV chef. I wanna be like Patricia Yeo or John Ash."

Marianna hadn't heard of them, but she assumed Krista knew her own icons. "I thought you were a graphic design major."

"I am." Krista shrugged, her glossy hair falling over her shoulder as she dipped her head. "The other thing's not practical."

That sounded like something Marianna's father would say. Chase wouldn't. Right? She glanced at him. He was devouring his daughter's divine meal. Even the salad was a profusion of color, with dried cranberries, mandarins, almond slivers, and blue cheese crumbles.

"Just because something seems impractical at first glance doesn't mean you can't make it work if you have a plan." Marianna avoided Chase's eyes in case her comment pissed him off. Maybe he didn't want his daughter to be a chef.

The girl flipped her hair over her shoulder. "That's what Dad says."

The ball of tension in her belly eased. Chase wasn't shades of her dad. She was letting her relationship with her own father paint her view of everyone else's.

"See? Now there are two of us saying you should think about it, sweetheart." Chase forked a mouthful of lasagna, the gooey cheese and tomato staining his lips before he licked it away. He closed his eyes to fully appreciate the blend of flavors, and when he looked at Krista again, he murmured, "To die for," the very same thought Marianna had.

Krista blushed with pleasure.

"Think about doing what makes you happy, sweetheart, even if it seems like it might be hard. You're smart, and you can do whatever you put your mind to." He meant it. He wasn't lying.

Marianna marveled. Then again, maybe Chase thought chefs made a ton of money and they were all famous.

Krista clasped her hands. "I know, Dad, but . . . well . . . I have to think about it. I mean, having the career you want is fine, but if you're struggling to pay the bills . . ." She trailed off, picking up her fork to toy with the food on her plate.

"If it takes you a few years to get yourself going, I'm here to help you out, honey."

Her throat tight, Marianna watched them—Krista's sweet smile,

Chase's adoration, a curve to his lips, crinkles at his eyes, and his gaze a deep, rich green focused on Krista.

If her own father had encouraged her this way, would Marianna still be a librarian, a *happy* librarian? Which made her want to laugh hysterically, because instead she was the happy hooker, with delusions of being part of a family like this.

Then again, if she was very, very lucky, maybe it could be hers.


CHASE WALKED HER TO HER CAR. "THANK YOU."

Marianna didn't beep the remote. She couldn't bring herself to leave him yet. "I didn't do anything."

His subtle aftershave did funny things to her insides as he cupped her cheek. "Krista smiled a lot. And she loved that you complimented her dinner."

She wanted to wrap herself in his words, his praise. "She's a sweet girl."

Sliding his hand beneath her hair, he leaned his forehead against hers. A tremble passed through him, one she wouldn't have felt if he hadn't pressed so close. "I can't explain," he whispered, "how important tonight was."

Marianna made the move, touching her lips to his mouth, caressing him with her kiss. A fire built in her belly. Chase shuddered, engulfed her in his embrace, took over the kiss, his taste still sweet with dessert. It was a romantic kiss, more than sexual, a bonding, soul-deep, full-body, so perfect that moisture rose to her eyes.

He pulled back slightly, held her face in his hands. "I'll call you tomorrow when Krista leaves. After dinner sometime."

There was so much promise in his eyes, his touch, his words. Marianna wanted to give him everything she had.

\* \* \*

CHASE LAY WIDE AWAKE, HANDS STACKED BEHIND HIS HEAD. Krista's soft bed-prep noises—water running, door opening and closing as she padded to the kitchen for something—all had ceased long ago, yet he couldn't sleep.

The evening had been perfect. Krista thought Marianna was awesome, and they'd spent another hour talking after Marianna left. Real talk. For the last year, Rosie had been a specter hanging over them, something they couldn't talk about yet was always between them. Tonight, he hadn't felt Rosie. For the first time, he believed they could heal, move on. Krista agreed to consider cooking school. Whatever the expense, he'd swing it. He wanted her to be happy.

That's why Marianna's offhand comment about Krista's career options had meant so much. It gave him another foot in the door to get Krista thinking about going for what she really wanted.

There were so many special things about Marianna. Christ, she could even find beauty in runway lights. She had a joie de vivre he needed her to help him relearn. She made him young again. She offered him a way to start his life over.

He wanted her to give up being a courtesan. He wanted her to be his. He'd gone into free fall with that good-night kiss, wishing he could go home with her, make love to her, sleep in her arms.

Tomorrow night, after Krista left for school, he'd have a long talk with Marianna and ask for everything he wanted.

# 14

LAST NIGHT WAS SO PERFECT. ISABEL WOULDN'T APPROVE, OF course. Marianna had done the unthinkable and fallen for one of her clients. That only happened in fairy tales and movies like *Pretty Woman*.

She couldn't wait for Chase's call tonight.

Her cell rang in the afternoon as she was managing the first of two open houses. She prayed it was Chase calling her earlier than planned. Until she realized it was the wrong phone. She dug out her real phone, and her dad's number popped up. God, talk about killing a great buzz. What had she done wrong? Thank God the house was empty. She didn't want potential clients overhearing an argument.

"What's up, Dad?" She headed for the kitchen. She needed caffeine to deal with her father. She'd recommended the homeowners leave a pot for prospective buyers to enjoy, but also because the rich scent of coffee made a house seem like a home.

"Listen, honey, your mom's pitching a fit about having to go to a charity thing tonight. It's the third one I've dragged her to in a week. Want to come with me instead?"

Marianna held the phone away, checking the ID to make sure

that really was her dad's number. Yep, it was. "This is Marianna, Dad. Did you think you'd called Tina?"

"I know who I called, honey. Sorry it's last minute."

Tina was honey. If their mom couldn't make it, Tina stepped in when he needed a companion to one of his big events. Ah, that was it. Tina had turned him down.

"Well, if Tina can't make it—"

"I didn't ask Tina, I asked you."

He didn't ask Tina? Well, jeez, she wasn't going to look a gift horse in the mouth, to quote the old saying. He wanted *her*. "Sure, Dad, I'd love to. What time?"

"I'll send the car for you at six thirty, and you can pick me up on the way."

Six thirty. Chase was supposed to call after dinner, but she couldn't talk to him with her dad there. Dilemma, dilemma. Okay. She'd call him today, very brief, tell him about the change in plans, and suggest they talk tomorrow.

"Cool," she told her father. "I look forward to it."

"See you then, honey. Dress up with a really nice pair of the choo-choo shoes."

"Great." Shoes. They were his concession. Now she was supposedly making money, she could have her Jimmy Choos. She'd take what she could get. "Thanks for inviting me, Dad."

"My pleasure, sweetheart."

Sweetheart. A house sale, that's all it took. She should have started lying to her father years ago.


MARIANNA CHOSE A SLEEK BLACK EVENING DRESS, BEADED JACKET, a darling pair of mini-boots, and the gambler's chain Chase had given her. Elegant, stylish, and above all proper.

Chase hadn't answered. She'd left him a message instead.

"You look lovely, sweetheart." Her father complimented her as he climbed into the car.

"Thanks, Dad. You look wonderful, too." Distinguished and handsome in his black tux, no one would guess him to be sixty-two—late fifties at most. She couldn't resist telling him her news. "A couple at the open house today was very interested in the property. We're meeting tomorrow to go over an offer." It was no lie. She was damn lucky to have scored this couple. Most people were lookie-loos checking out their neighbors' decorating scheme and getting an idea of their own house value.

"Congratulations, honey." He kissed her forehead.

*Another* endearment. She was suffering from shock.

They chitchatted during the short drive to the opera house where the charity event was being held. It was like standing back and watching someone else. She was amazed her father chitchatted with *her*.

And once they arrived . . .

"I'd like you to meet my daughter, Marianna. She's a real estate agent on the Peninsula"—he beamed at her like a thousand-watt bulb—"and you can't find better advice in this market."

Good God, he was advertising for her. He seemed to know absolutely everyone. Patrons filled the opera house's front lobby. Most dressed in black and white, with a few women going wild in navy or green. Conversation echoed against the high ceilings, laughter, glad-handing. Half an hour in, Marianna was parched. Champagne. She snagged two glasses from a passing waiter, handed one to her father, and applied a death grip to her own.

"It is a down market with the whole credit crisis, but if you choose the right price . . ." She tried to sound intelligent. She wanted her father to be proud of her, but the stress made her head ache. She'd earned his respect, but she could easily lose it with one stupid remark.

"Oh, yes, the south of France is a must during the winter," she said, agreeing with . . . some woman. Marianna had never been to the south of France. And she couldn't remember the lady's name.

She sipped faster on her champagne, the bubbles fizzing in her head. When were they were serving dinner? She should have eaten something.

The woman left, a man replaced her. "You're a pretty little thing. Where's Asa been hiding you?" He was old—white hair, florid cheeks—and his tone was mildly suggestive.

"Just work, work, work," she said, quipping, "so I don't get out to many functions."

"You know what they say, all work and no play." He winked, and a tic started at the corner of his eye.

Yuk. He was hitting on her right in front of her father, though Dad was deep in discussion with a CFO about . . . reserves, or something obviously involving money.

Then, as if he felt her discomfort, her father exited his conversation and shot out an arm to draw her in. The white-haired man drifted off. Thank God.

"Having a good time, honey? Making lots of contacts?"

Okay, her mother had to have put him up to this, saying he wasn't doing enough to help her. Because it was all starting to feel surrealistic. "Yeah, sure, Dad. A ton."

"That's great. Now let's mingle."

She'd *been* mingling, but his gaze was already darting around the room looking for business associates he hadn't spoken to.

As he started to pull away, a heavy arm slipped around her shoulder. "Asa, you sly devil."

Her stomach plunged. She knew that voice. Oh God, she *knew* that man. Brock Ransom. Her first "date." Her blood seemed to shudder to a complete stop in her veins.

Good God, Brock was a friend of her father's. The color drained from her dad's face as if he'd had a premonition and knew something momentously bad was coming.

Marianna wanted to run. She wanted to hide. She wanted to shut the man up before he said another word. "I—"

Brock didn't wait for her to finish. "I'm sure this one's worth every penny." He chucked her under the chin. "So don't be stingy, Asa." Oblivious to the panic swirling around him, Brock beamed down at Marianna.

Then he slapped her father's back. "Don't do anything I wouldn't do, kids." With a wink, he trundled off as if he hadn't just brought her life crashing down around her.

All the oxygen was sucked out of the room. Spots danced before her eyes. The voices and laughter all around secluded them. Just her. Just her father. Maybe he didn't understand. There could still be hope. Brock had said so little. It might have meaning only to her guilty conscience. In their bubble of silence, she couldn't look at her father. Then he cleared his throat, and she couldn't *not* look at him.

Oh God. *Worth every penny. Don't be stingy.* Oh yes, he understood. Horror had bleached his skin white. His eyes were both a big round O of disbelief.

He took two steps back. As if being too close to her was repulsive. "I have to go," he muttered, minus his usual commanding tone.

Turning his back on her, he disappeared through the big brass front doors. Marianna couldn't move for a full five seconds. Then she dashed after him. Maybe she could explain, say something, anything.

Outside, a doorman put his fingers to his teeth, whistled, and a cab shot to the curb. Her father climbed in without looking back, and the cabbie darted into the traffic.

Exhaust seeped into her nostrils. A pounding started in her

head—the noise, the car horns, the roar of engines, a homeless man shouting.

Even if she could have caught up with her father, there was nothing to say. He would probably call Brock and ask for the full story. She could never explain it away.

In two minutes, *everything* had changed.

TUESDAY MORNING. TWO AND A HALF DAYS SINCE HE'D SEEN MARI-anna. Sixty hours since she'd walked out of his apartment.

Isabel was polite but adamant. "I'm sorry, Mr. Ramirez. I understand your desire, but under no circumstances can I give you Marianna's home number."

Goddammit. He wanted to wring the woman's neck over the phone, but it wasn't her fault. Marianna had cut him off.

Sunday afternoon, she'd left a voice mail saying she had to spend an evening with her father, and she'd talk to him in the morning. He'd called on Monday. She hadn't answered. He left a message in the afternoon and another that night. Then today, her phone no longer worked. What the fuck? Saturday night had been perfect. She'd liked Krista, and his daughter had liked her. He hadn't even gotten around to asking her to give up being a courtesan, so it couldn't be that. It didn't make a fucking bit of sense. Why would she do this? How could she drop him without a word after everything they'd shared? After he'd let her meet his daughter?

He wanted to bash heads.

With the Tuesday morning staff meeting coming up in half an hour, he'd closed his office door and given in to his obsession by calling the agency to try to track her down. Isabel, however, wasn't giving her up.

"It's nothing personal, Mr. Ramirez."

Hell yes, it was fucking personal. He needed to calm down. He needed to think.

"Thanks for your time." He sounded surly. He felt panicky. He didn't know Marianna's real name, her address, or her phone number.

She was simply gone, and he had no way of finding her.

SITTING BY THE FOUNTAIN ACROSS THE SQUARE FROM THE BRO-kerage, Marianna soaked up the Tuesday noontime sun. She'd been cold since Sunday night, her hands numb. She could not get warm no matter what she did, even when she'd resorted to lying in the bathtub, refilling it when the water cooled. The midday air was crisp, a slight breeze tossing leaves to and fro, then swirling them in little eddies. But the sun seeped deep into her bones. Hopefully it would kill the chill.

Like the leaves, people rushed this way and that, grabbing a bite to eat at the deli stand, nabbing a bit of shopping time during the lunch hour, nipping into the bookstore for a magazine. Her lunch? An apple cut into quarters. An apple a day keeps the doctor away. She couldn't stomach much more than that.

Her sale on Monday, after Sunday's open house, was unheard of. Everyone knew that couples making the rounds at open houses weren't ready to buy. The most you usually picked up from it was a new contact. If you were lucky, someone might ask you to show them houses in the area. But make an offer Monday morning, much less have it accepted that evening? It was nothing short of miraculous. Everyone in the office looked at her as if she'd suddenly been elevated to goddess status. She'd have real money, enough to make rent, pay bills, even save a little.

It didn't mean a damn thing. Her family had disowned her. None of them had called since *it* happened, that horrible thing.

She'd contacted Isabel to sever the tie, thrown her special phone down the garbage chute, and answered Jewel's messages to say she was okay. Isabel had apologized profusely. Brock Ransom's privileges would be revoked. Way too late for her. Marianna kept hoping she'd come up with a way to fix what had happened. She *had* to find a way.

Her family was bad, but the worst was Chase. She'd been living on lies and fantasies. She'd built up this dreamworld where he actually cared about her when the truth was she was just a hooker. He'd called, she hadn't called back. It was cowardice, but she couldn't face him. She couldn't have him tell her that's all it was, that she was just a panacea for his guilt and loneliness. Because it had been so much more to her. She'd actually believed her own fantasy.

God, she had gone so wrong thinking she could be a courtesan without repercussions. If only she could handle things the way Jewel did, without fuss, without emotion.

A cloud blew across the sun, and she shivered. Time to get back. She had so much to do. Her fantasy world might have crashed and burned, but her real life kept rolling right on over her. She had mortgage calls, insurance, inspections, a thousand things she needed to hear back on for the sale. Sure enough, her phone beeped as she approached her desk. Four messages. It hurt that not one of them would be from Chase.

She plugged in her earphone and got out her pad.

Her father's voice hit her right in the heart. "Marianna, I'd like to talk to you. Could you come over after work?"

He asked, he didn't demand. He didn't even sound angry, but he didn't sound normal either. In fact, a hint of worry threaded through his voice.

What did it mean?

Honestly, she couldn't take much more.

# 15

HER MOM OPENED THE DOOR. "DARLING, IF I'D KNOWN YOU WERE coming, I'd have waited on dinner."

Following her inside, Marianna searched her mother's face for a clue as to how much she knew about Sunday. She smiled the same as always. "Didn't Dad tell you he called me?"

Clucking her tongue, her mom shook her head. "That man. What am I going to do with him?"

Marianna would have sworn he hadn't told. Why not? "Well, I'll see what he wants, then maybe I can warm up a plate for myself." She kept her voice genial and the comment innocuous, though the thought of food right now made her ill.

Her mom waved imperiously down the hall. "He's in his office."

Marianna's high heels on the hardwood floor sounded like her death knell.

The office door slightly ajar, she found her father sitting behind his desk, chair turned slightly as he stared out the window. Hands clasped over his abdomen, he was so lost in thought, he didn't hear her. With only the desk lamp on, the light shining up on his face created deep craggy shadows and highlighted the bags beneath his eyes.

Her stomach tumbled. On Sunday, he'd appeared five years younger. Tonight, he looked his age. She'd done this to him.

The carriage clock ticked on the leather-top desk. Marianna couldn't stand the guilt. "Dad."

He startled, and when he saw her, something unreadable flashed across his features. "Marianna." He swallowed. "Would you please close the door?"

He was unnervingly polite. With the door shut, the wood-paneled room lay mostly in foreboding darkness. Marianna couldn't stand that any more than she could stand the guilt, and she switched on the standing lamp by his leather sofa.

"Please sit down." He pointed to the couch. She sat on the ottoman of his easy chair instead.

"Dad." The excuses and explanations wouldn't roll off her tongue despite how she'd practiced on the drive up.

"Please don't tell your mother."

God. She should be the one begging *him* not to tell. "I won't."

"I love your mother very much."

"I know." Actually, she didn't. He'd never been demonstrative. But then, her mom didn't seem to need it. "I won't do anything to intentionally hurt her," she said. With her father, Marianna's conduct had resulted in deep disappointment. She hated even to think how it would affect her mom.

Her father leaned forward, scrubbed his hands down his face, then rested both elbows on the desk. "I can't explain away what I've done. Maybe it was a midlife crisis." He laughed harshly. "But I'm a little old for that."

Okay. Right. He wouldn't tell her mom what Marianna had done because *he* was having a midlife crisis. In an alternate reality, maybe that made sense.

"I promise you I'm never going to do it again."

Marianna sat frozen on the ottoman. Her skin prickled. She

got a really bad feeling in the pit of her stomach that this was something she didn't *want* to understand. "So you promise not to do it again if I promise not to tell Mom," she said to clarify. Of course it wasn't clear at all.

He nodded his head, his face grave. "Yes."

"And 'it' would be what that man was referring to on Sunday."

His nostrils flared, and for the first time, his tone hardened into the voice of the man she was used to. "Don't make me give you all the dirty details of what I've done, as some sort of penance."

Her brain started to whirl like a washing machine on spin cycle. Her father thought Brock Ransom had been talking about *him*.

"I don't want any details," she said softly, trying to remember everything Brock had said that night. The exact words wouldn't come. What she did remember now was the blood draining from her father's face *before* Brock said anything to Marianna.

*Asa, you sly devil.*

Oh yes, she remembered that. Brock knew her father. And he knew Marianna as a courtesan. And he'd assumed . . .

She couldn't wrap her mind around the truth. It had never occurred to her. It was too much of a coincidence. And yet it fit exactly with what her father was saying.

Brock made the assumption not only because of Marianna, but because he knew her father was a client of Courtesans. *Her* guilty conscience said it was about her. *His* conscience was just as guilty. They'd both heard what they feared the most.

This big man, her father, the all-important man she'd striven her entire life to please, the father she always seemed to disappoint—this man had cheated on her mom. And he was afraid Marianna would tell.

A rush of anger welled up, choking her. He'd been cheating. He was a total asshole. He'd lorded it over them, not just herself, but her mom and Tina, too. Holier than thou, he'd told them all how he thought they should live, what they should do.

But he was a cheat.

She stood, her fists clenched. She wanted to shout at him. God, she even wanted to run right out to the kitchen and reveal his dirty little secret, because it was exactly what he deserved. Marianna wanted to pay him back for the way he'd treated her for as long as she could remember.

"Marianna, please." Fear trembled through his voice.

She realized that was what she'd seen on his face when she first arrived. Fear. He saw his comfortable life crumbling around him. Her mom would take him for everything he was worth.

"Please forgive me."

She didn't want to forgive, she didn't want to—

She closed her eyes, breathed deeply, the oxygen like a calming drug. She didn't want to judge. She didn't want to persecute. She didn't have the right, not unless she wanted her own secrets revealed. Her father was no worse than she was. The difference was she'd learned he was no better either.

She unclenched her fists, the blood flowing back into her fingers. "I've lived my whole life based on your expectations, Dad." She'd even dumped Chase because she couldn't measure up. "I jumped jobs so many times trying to make you happy."

Her father rolled his lips between his teeth and nodded. Listening to her, not citing dirty details, was his penance.

"I gave up a career I loved because I was trying to make you happy. But it only made *me* unhappy."

"I pushed you to help you."

"I know. You wanted to get me off my duff." She felt the anger storm up again and she tamped it down. "My duff was okay." All right, not totally okay, because she'd overspent a *lot*. She'd forced her dad to bail her out. Funnily enough, she could see both sides clearly now, his *and* hers.

"We've both made a lot of mistakes." She stopped, waiting for him to lift his gaze from the leather top of his desk. "But we're not going to make the same mistakes again. We're not going to talk about what happened on Sunday." She took one step closer. "We're going to start over."

He closed his eyes, rested a moment, then nodded. "I won't tell you how to live your life anymore."

"And I'm not going to expect you to bail me out of my own problems either."

The room echoed with a light knock on the door.

Her father grimaced, glanced from her to the door and back again.

She knew what he needed. "I will never talk about this with anyone because this is *your* problem. *You* fix what you did. *You* make it up to her." Then she opened the door.

Her mom's gaze flicked between them. "I heated up a plate for you, darling."

Marianna wasn't hungry. Food wouldn't satisfy. Chase was the only thing that would. Opening her eyes to her father's faults had suddenly opened her to everything. She needed Chase. It didn't matter how she'd met him; she had to tell him tonight that she wanted him in her life. If it was just a fantasy world she'd created, so be it, but for once, she was going to follow through instead of jumping ship at the first sign of bad weather.

SITTING ON THE BALCONY, A HOODED SWEATSHIRT ZIPPED AGAINST the cool night air, Chase nursed the last glass of wine from the bottle he'd bought for Saturday night.

After talking with Isabel, he'd gone from despair to anger when Harve confirmed he didn't know how to find Marianna either. Chase had shared something special with her. It wasn't merely a fuck. It wasn't just sex-for-hire. It wasn't even a fantasy. Yet she'd tossed him out along with her phone. He deserved an explanation.

On the drive home, he'd realized he'd given her no indication of how he felt. He'd asked her to help him with his daughter. He never mentioned what Marianna had done for *him*.

When he'd pulled into his parking spot in the underground garage of his apartment building, what she'd said in Sunday's message actually hit him. She was meeting her father. The ogre. With his bruised ego, Chase had been thinking that she'd thrown out her phone to get rid of him.

Maybe something entirely different had happened.

So here he was, sitting in the dark, considering his options. Of which he didn't have many. He could call Isabel again and ask her to give Marianna a message. He could go to Courtesans—Harve had the address—so that Isabel could personally see how important this was to him.

The only option he wouldn't take was letting it alone. He belonged with Marianna. He would do everything to find her. He *would* find her. And they would talk through what really went wrong. After a year of guilt and apathy, he was not going back to the way he'd been, living with a specter.

He propped his feet on the balcony rail as if the action were a punctuation mark.

"May I have a taste?"

He almost dropped the damn glass.

"I knocked and rang the bell," Marianna said, "then I was about to walk away when I decided to try the doorknob." She rescued the glass from his fingers, sipped the wine, then handed it back. "It's dangerous to leave your door unlocked." She spread her hands, shrugged. "Who knows what the cat might drag in?"

The dim light falling through the balcony door revealed the pulse beating fast at her throat. She wasn't feeling as flippant as she wanted him to think.

Chase didn't care. She was here, that's all that mattered. "I don't remember leaving the chain off the door."

She pulled a deck chair close and sat beside him. "Then maybe I was supposed to walk right in, cosmically speaking."

"Would you have returned another time if I wasn't here?" That *did* matter to him. A one-shot deal she'd done while she had the courage? Or something with more meaning?

"I would have kept coming back until you answered me."

He set the wine aside, thinking he should explain himself, disclose his inner feelings as he'd planned to on Sunday. He did none of those things. "Why?"

"Because I've given up being a courtesan, but I don't want to give up you."

Chase closed his eyes, savored the relief and joy deep inside. "That's what I was going to ask you to do. Give it all up." He let that settle between them. "I don't want to share you. You've come to mean a lot to me."

She rose, climbed onto his chair, straddled his lap. "I made a big mistake becoming a courtesan. But there was one really good thing to come out of it." She cupped his cheek, stroking the five o'clock shadow along his jaw. "You." Then she dipped down to take his mouth.

No kiss had ever tasted so sweet. She made him whole again.

Marianna pulled back. She wiped off her lipstick glistening on his lips. She'd been terrified he'd slam his door in her face. "I'm sorry I simply disappeared without telling you first. I couldn't think straight."

"We moved very fast. I can understand needing some time."

True, she'd been a goner almost from the beginning. "That was no excuse. I should have told you about . . ." It was still hard to say.

"Something happened with your father, didn't it?"

She closed her eyes. A deep breath cleansed her. She could tell him everything. He somehow guessed parts of it anyway.

He put his hand over her mouth. "I take that back, I don't want to know. You're real. You came back. That's all I care about now."

Maybe. Marianna owed him an explanation, about her father, about what went on Sunday night, that she couldn't call because she'd let her fear take over. Yes, she owed Chase, but she'd give him all the answers later, after making love, when she was snuggled in his arms, the moment perfect for divulging secrets. For now, she had something more elemental in mind. "Wanna hear my plan?"

"Woman, I always want to hear your plans." His eyes crinkled at the corners.

"We should have a piggy bank where we put . . . say"—she wagged her head thinking what was just right—"five hundred dollars."

He played along. "What will we use the five hundred for?"

She adored that he played the game. "We'll take turns paying for sexual favors." She rubbed noses with him. "Because I really did love the power trip. I think you'll love it, too."

Especially when she thought of all the things she could make him do when it was her turn to pay. "The naughtier the favor, the higher the price."

"Deal." He snugged her close against him, rocked lightly to let her feel how much of a *big* deal they had going right now. "I pay first. Tonight you have to do whatever I want." He gave her a lip-smackin' kiss. "And my idea is so downright nasty it'll be worth a helluva lot more than five hundred."

God, he was the best. He had such a delightfully dirty mind, too.

She'd gotten her Prince Charming fantasy after all.

# PAYBACK

# 1

DOMINIQUE LOWE HAD BEEN WITH TREVOR MCDOWELL EXACTLY one and a half hours, but she had him pegged. He didn't fork over five hundred dollars a plate for a benefit dinner because he was a philanthropist. He did it so people would *believe* he was. And to make sure they knew he had more than enough money to fund a worthy cause.

The worthy cause, however, was Trevor's own ego.

"She's got to be at least ten years older than he is." Trevor shook his head as if he were mystified instead of just snotty, "What the hell can he possibly see in her?"

Dominique wondered what any woman could possibly see in Trevor McDowell.

Festooned with valentine hearts and cupids dangling from the ceiling, the hotel ballroom was alive with laughter, chatter, and the clink of glassware. Hopefully Trevor's rude remarks couldn't be overheard by the couple fifteen paces away. Still, wearing stilettos that gave her two inches up on Trevor, Dominique turned her head slowly to gaze straight down her nose at him.

He interpreted the stare. "Her fifty years are way different than your forty-five, my sweet. Not even comparable." He looked her up and down. "Especially in that hot dress."

"Thank you, Trevor." Her shoulders bared, the red satin showed off Dominique's generous curves, fitting snug over her breasts, tummy, and behind, then cascading to the floor. Despite the compliment, he was fast losing points with her. It wasn't the woman's age that bothered Dominique. It was Trevor's need to nitpick a quarter of the ballroom's two hundred fifty occupants in the hour since they'd arrived. Dominique didn't tolerate rudeness well in her escorts.

"A woman at fifty," she said with a slight edge, "is coming into her own. Someone your age"—he was mere baby at thirty-five, and she gave him the same up-and-down perusal he'd given her—"would benefit from helping her to release her inhibitions."

She surveyed the ballroom, sipping her cosmopolitan. In celebration of Valentine's Day, the pink drink flowed from the mouths of Cupid-shaped fountains.

"*You're* coming into your own. But her . . . ?" Trevor shrugged, leaving his critique at that. "She's got to be paying him."

The "him" in this case was definitely delectable. Fortyish, six feet, he was trim and sexy in a black tux with a charcoal shirt. His dark brown hair was long enough for a woman to run her fingers through but short enough to be neat. Dominique had never been the long-hair type. She glanced at Trevor. His black hair brushed his shoulders. While probably all the rage with a teenybopper crowd, it didn't do much for her.

The handsome gentleman's date? She was matronly, true, with a thickening waistline, but when she smiled, she literally shone. Obviously a magnificent smile meant something to this man. That, in her estimation, raised him far above Trevor.

Trevor was too young or too self-absorbed—or both—to appreciate a smile. "Come on, Dominique, admit it. He's damn hot, and she's"—he shrugged and quirked an eyebrow—"not."

Odd. Men didn't generally call other men hot, but Trevor

wasn't gay, at least not as far as Dominique knew. After all, this was a sex date set up through Courtesans. If he impressed her, she'd allow him to have sex with her. If he wanted to impress her further, he would bestow upon her a gift of high value, be it cash or jewelry. She adored jewelry.

So far, though, he wasn't making a good impression. They hadn't mingled, instead standing by themselves as he muttered catty remarks like a teenage girl. She didn't have high hopes that she and Trevor would make it to the sex or gift stage.

Not for the first time that evening, the tall stranger's eyes flicked toward them. Either he was checking her out or he sensed he and his female friend were being watched. Evaluated. Dominique decided it was the latter, and she hating making people think they were the subject of gossip, especially since she'd been the victim of it herself. Enough to last a lifetime.

"Stop staring, Trevor. Didn't your mother teach you it's rude?" His mother hadn't taught him manners at all. He was your typical rich, disdainful playboy, totally uncaring of anyone else's feelings. In addition to that, at five-seven, he had a bad case of LMD, commonly known as Little Man's Disease, in which he tried to make up for his lack of height by being an ass. Why Isabel thought they'd be a good match, Dominique hadn't a clue. She liked her men handsome, fit, intelligent, humorous, and respectful. Trevor was the first two, but a malicious wit was neither smart nor funny. And forget about courteous.

Seating for dinner would begin shortly, and after there would be dancing. A string quartet was setting up in the corner for some light music during the meal. She'd give Trevor the length of dinner and dessert before she made her final decision. There was always the possibility he'd redeem himself. After all, just because she'd been dumped on by her ex-husband didn't mean all men were bad. She refused to color them all with the same bitter paintbrush.

She was not a man-hater, but since joining Courtesans, she did make sure her escorts knew whatever happened between them was only by her good grace.

And wouldn't it tweak her ex's nuts to know how much some men were willing to pay for what he'd thrown aside like trash?

"I'm going to powder my nose," she told Trevor. She needed a break. Dinner, dessert, coffee, then, if he was still uncivilized, she'd take a taxi home. Even as a courtesan, when she went on a date, sex was a gift she gave, not something a man could expect.

Trevor waggled his fingers at her.

Unlike the warm, stuffy ballroom, the mezzanine was cool, the scent of fresh rain rising from the open doors down on the lobby level. She loved the smell of rain and the *shush* of the car tires on the wet concrete. It always reminded her of playing in warm summer storms when she was a child back in Michigan.

She turned toward the restrooms.

And pulled up short, her pulse thrumming in her ears.

"Hello, Dominique."

It would have been so much easier if she could have said he'd gotten fat and bald since the breakup, but lounging against the wall, Edward was still as lean and handsome as he'd been that day a year ago when he'd told her he wanted a divorce. If possible, at fifty-one, he was even better-looking than when they'd exchanged vows sixteen years ago.

"Hello, Edward." She didn't care anymore, of course. Her heart had picked up speed at the unexpectedness of the meeting. For eight months, since she'd found Isabel and Courtesans and given up fighting the divorce, she'd been expecting to see him at every function she attended. In the beginning, there'd been a few sightings, but they hadn't talked. Dominique didn't know whether Edward had actually heard of Courtesans, and she certainly didn't want to know if he'd ever utilized their services, but she had run his particulars by Isabel to make sure there was never an accidental match. After the divorce became final, Edward seemed to disappear from the social circle they'd frequented together. Dominique had let down her guard.

"You're looking well." He did not look at her dress or her cleavage, just her eyes.

"Thank you, Edward. So are you." So polite, so careful. She didn't want to reveal a smidge of her inner anxiety, yet her breath seemed to come faster, harder, and a headache began to nudge at her temple. How to get away? Simply walk past him to the ladies' room? Easy enough. Her feet wouldn't move. Her high heels made her ankles ache.

Then the blonde turned the corner out of the restrooms. "Okay, sweetie, I'm done." She slipped her hand into Edward's, and he laced their fingers. Her gold wedding band and two-carat diamond engagement ring glittered.

Dominique wanted to die.

"Oh." The blonde's smile died, and her hand went to her belly. Her very pregnant belly.

"This is Dominique." Something flickered in Edward's eyes.

Dominique interpreted it as pity and hated him. She wanted to hate the blonde, too, a Barbie look-alike, but her Ken doll was old enough to be her father. "And this must be Francine." Dominique extended her hand smoothly, forcing the girl to shake. "I've heard all about you." The gossip had made the country club circuit. All those whispers behind her back that she'd heard nonetheless. Dominique knew Edward had remarried right on the heels of the divorce. She knew his young wife was pregnant. And that was all she could take knowing. She'd pretended it wasn't true and hadn't been back to the country club in months.

"It's so nice to meet you." Francine smiled, but in her eyes the flicker was very clearly fear. She rubbed her belly like a talisman.

Pretty, long blond hair, perfect blue eyes, thirty-two years old. And at least seven months pregnant.

Yes, Dominique had known, but actually faced with it, the impact was far greater than she'd expected.

Half the country club believed Edward was cheating long before he asked for the divorce. The other half claimed he wasn't. Dominique didn't know, and she'd tried so damn fucking hard not to care. She was desired by many men. She was special enough to command whatever price she asked. She didn't need a husband. She didn't need a baby. She was long over that desire, that want. She'd truly accepted life without children. So many other things had fulfilled her.

"You look lovely in that dress." It tore her apart to give Francine the compliment, but she managed to say it with a stone face. In fact, Francine did look lovely in her maternity wear, a simple yet elegant drape of sky blue with spaghetti straps and a bodice that molded to her breasts, then flared to encompass her child.

"Thank you so much." Francine looked down, then reached out to flare the skirt even further. "I was embarrassed coming out looking like such a cow, but Edward assured me I look fine."

"You don't look like a cow," Dominique offered. Partygoers flowed around them, to the restrooms, the lobby, mingling. Though aware of them, she couldn't actually hear them, as if she were trapped in a bubble with Edward and the pregnant wife.

"Of course you don't," Edward concurred, a fond, indulgent smile lifting his features.

Francine looked like a Madonna, so beautiful it hurt to look at her, her cheeks glowing with health; fresh, dewy, young, motherhood personified. Dominique's eyes ached. At Francine's age, she'd dreamed of motherhood. Her body wouldn't cooperate. She'd had the fibroids removed, and with them, the doctors took her uterus.

They'd talked adoption, but Edward said they were fine as they were. She thought he'd forgiven her the hysterectomy because they had each other. As she got older, she believed he saw past the wrinkles and the sagging flesh to the woman inside. She thought he loved her. Until a year ago when he announced he was filing for divorce. No discussion, no question.

He wanted young, he wanted fresh, he wanted a child. He had it all now.

"I'll leave you two, I have to pee badly." She giggled and didn't care how ridiculous she sounded. Edward would know he'd affected her, but she couldn't care about that either.

If she had to stand here one more second, she would die. Or worse, she'd burst into tears.

GABRIEL PRICE LOUNGED BY THE RAILING OVERLOOKING THE lobby. He sipped his Scotch neat, the froufrou drinks served in the ballroom too sweet for his taste. He'd left Brenda schmoozing with the other guests. She was a great chum, and he always gave in when she asked him to attend one of these things. Currently a city supervisor for one of the smaller Peninsula bedroom communities, she was launching a campaign for state assembly next year. Which was why she liked a man on her arm instead of her preferred gender. With a career in politics, she feared coming out of the closet. Gabriel believed it could actually be in her favor, working for gay rights, but she was old school and her private life was simply that, private.

Normally he found these events tedious, but tonight he'd hit the jackpot. He'd followed the lady in red to the lobby. She'd stopped to talk with a couple, the wife noticeably pregnant.

There was something there, the lovely slope of her shoulders tense, her back ramrod straight, her hands behind her back, fists clenched, then open. She'd laughed, a brittle sound, whereas in the ballroom, her laughter had carried a musical quality.

That's how he'd first noticed her, her laugh. He'd met her eyes several times across the room. She was interested. He was interested. Her lush curves in that stunningly red dress drew his gaze. Her red hair should have clashed with the dress, yet the gorgeous tones blended perfectly. She was with a man, but he was young, and the look she gave him spoke of boredom, morphing to downright disdain. Gabriel didn't think they were together, not in any meaningful definition of the word. The man was like a mouse to her tigress. She batted him down with an elegant paw.

When she left the ballroom, Gabriel drifted after her. While she spoke with the couple, he observed her. And he learned two things. This man meant something to her. He'd bet on either an ex-husband or an ex-lover. And the pregnant woman was a slap in the lady's face.

No. A slap was too mild. This was a harsh blow. Within minutes she extricated herself and entered the ladies' room.

The couple argued, not loudly, but soft, a shake of his head, a brief slash of her hand in the air. The man took the girl's hand, kissed her knuckles, and ran a finger down her cheek as if he were wiping away a tear. Then they made their way to the ballroom.

Oh yeah. Bad scene. Though he was sure he was the only one who noticed the exchange. There'd been no histrionics, no heated words. But the devastation left in its wake was evident just the same. Oddly, the hint of vulnerability he'd witnessed attracted him. It made the woman human. Real. It made him want to touch her, hold her, offer the comfort of his arms. In the business settings through which he navigated 90 percent of his time, women sported a bigger set of balls than most of the men. They had to or end up as hyena bait, torn limb for limb. Corporate environments weren't for sissies. Yet that very fact of life gave him a yearning for something softer.

Gabriel waited for the lady in red to return.

IN THE STALL, DOMINIQUE BLINKED UNTIL THE PAIN AT THE BACK of her eyes receded. She did not cry. She hadn't cried since the week after Edward announced his intention to divorce her. She would never cry for him again. It was just seeing that pregnant girl, and the reminder of how badly Dominique had wanted a child. But you grow up, you come to terms with your life, enjoy the things you have instead of forever mourning what you've lost. The same was true of Edward. She'd gotten over her need to punish him. In the beginning, she'd wanted to take him for everything they owned. Then she'd met Isabel through a mutual friend, learned about Courtesans, and found a better payback. On the arms of rich, handsome men who paid a fortune to have her.

She might not have seen much of Edward since the divorce was finalized, but she knew he'd heard all about her active social life at the country club. A different handsome, attentive man at every event.

Isabel and Courtesans had saved her. She'd proven she was hot, desirable, special, and not the vengeful bitch he once accused her of being. She was also stoic. Having finished business, she yanked the stall door open, washed her hands, and proceeded to powder her nose and repair her lipstick.

No one would see a single sign of her encounter with Edward and his beautiful, young, and very pregnant wife. She was so over that little burst of emotion.

Her game face back in place, Dominique strolled across the mezzanine, a seemingly unconscious sway to her hips. It came from feeling sexy. Before the divorce, she hadn't had a clue how to sashay. Since finding Courtesans, the delicious little wiggle had become as much a part of her as breathing. Sex permeated her life. She fantasized. She'd bought herself a vibrator. She adored shopping for lingerie.

She loved making a man wonder what lay beneath the dress.

Like the gorgeous man in the charcoal shirt and black tux, from the ballroom. Trevor was right. The man was definitely hot. Leaning against the railing as she passed, he watched her, his gaze like a gentle caress down her spine, a warm breath, a tingle of anticipation.

Too bad all she had to look forward to was Trevor McDowell.

# 2

DOMINIQUE HAD ONLY ONE SELF-IMPOSED RULE AS A COURTESAN:
You didn't dump one date for a better offer. At least, not unless
you'd already disposed of the first one. Besides, that exceptionally
attractive man was taken. Dominique considered it bad manners
to try to lure him away. You never purloined another woman's
date. But if she gave him to you? Then you had carte blanche to
do anything. Everything. And Dominique had.

But not tonight.

As soon as she reentered the ballroom, she spotted Trevor by
himself at the edge of the dining tables, watching the minglers
down their last cocktail before dinner. He didn't engage. He observed. And damn if she didn't catch him checking out another
man's butt. It was a nicely shaped ass, but . . . Dominique decided
to give him the benefit of the doubt. Maybe he wasn't so much
checking it out as wondering how his compared from a rear view
perspective. Trevor was so self-involved, Dominique wouldn't put
it past him.

Now, to Trevor or not to Trevor. Hmm. On the one hand, she
felt like some naughty, nasty sex tonight. On the other, she didn't
feel like doing it with Trevor. Her multispeed silicon penis with
dual twirl-and-vibrate mode would do a better job.

He didn't notice her until she was at his elbow. "I'm back," she murmured softly.

Trevor flinched, then pointed at the nearest female ass and said, "Doesn't she know that tight pink jersey across her butt makes it look like the back end of a donkey?" He glanced at Dominique.

"Trevor." She shushed him. The volume of his voice had climbed, and despite the chitchat, laughter, and music, they were close enough to the pink bottom to be overheard.

Trevor turned to her, his face flushed, a shaft of light from the chandelier making his eyes spark. "That dress shows every dimple and bulge in all that flab."

That's how men were. They tore you down behind your back. The woman in the jersey probably thought she looked gorgeous and flamboyant in that dress. Dominique imagined the middle-aged lady twirling in front of the mirror, viewing herself from all the possible angles except the one that mattered, blissfully unaware of all the dimples and bulges and flab. Until her husband walked in one day and dumped her for a younger, prettier model with no dimples or bulges and not even an ounce of flab.

In desperation, Dominique had gone on a crash diet the day after Edward made his announcement. She'd lost twenty pounds in a ridiculously short period of time. Edward hadn't come back. She lost another ten pounds. She would have kept going, except that she actually stopped one day and looked at herself in the mirror. She didn't look fit and gorgeous. She'd looked haggard and gaunt, her flesh sagging on her face.

She'd joined a gym, hired a nutritionist, and gained back all the weight with healthy eating and exercise. Real women have curves, and she now had them in abundance, along with being fit, toned, and amazing her doctor with fantastic HDLs and LDLs. She was better than she'd ever been.

And she deserved better than an ass like Trevor McDowell. Every woman, including the pink-jersey lady, deserved better than Trevor McDowell.

She stood to her full height in her four-inch stilettos and glared. "Trevor. I worry that you have this tremendous fixation on a woman's posterior." She leaned in. "You would be lucky if that gorgeous curvy woman decided to give you a blow job under the table. Except you'd be too self-absorbed to appreciate it."

He blinked rapidly. "It was just an observation. I've been trying to entertain you all evening."

"You're not entertaining. You are rude and demeaning to women. I'm going home. I'll get myself a cab."

He touched the pocket of his tux. "But we have a deal. For later. I've got the money right there."

"We do *not* have a deal. We never had a *deal*."

"But all this money." He widened his eyes, the brown catching her reflection.

"We have nothing in common, Trevor."

"Who cares about having anything in common?" He actually sounded mystified. "I chose you because I was told you were the highest priced."

She smiled. She *was* the highest priced courtesan, and proud of it. "That's your mistake. *I* do the choosing, not you."

"But"—he tapped his pocket once again—"I've got ten thousand dollars in here."

She almost laughed. What an idiot to be carrying that much cash. "Ten thousand is nothing. A sheik once gave me a diamond worth thirty thousand." Bitchy and self-aggrandizing, it still felt *so* good. "For you, even that's not enough."

"But—"

"You're catching flies, Trevor." She tapped his jaw with her fingers. "I don't sleep with men who have no manners."

She didn't just leave, she made an exit, stalking straight through the throng of partygoers, forcing them to part for her. It was marvelous.

Almost as good as the day she'd decided to be a courtesan and show Edward just how much men were willing to pay for her.

THE WOMAN KNEW HOW TO MAKE AN EXIT, THAT WAS FOR SURE. She sashayed from the crowded ballroom and every male eye followed the sway of her hips in that hot, slinky red dress.

Following the direction of his gaze, Brenda leaned close. "Go for it," she urged. "I've been looking for an excuse to ask Maureen to drive me home anyway."

"Naughty slut," he murmured.

"That makes two of us." She beamed a smile at him. Brenda and Maureen, a public defender for the city, had been doing the dance for weeks.

He glanced down at her. "I don't want to have to worry that you didn't make it home."

"Darling, I'll be fine." Her eyes sparkled with just how *fine* she planned to be. He hoped this thing with Maureen would help Brenda to accept herself, come out of the closet or, at the very least, find a little happiness.

He bent to kiss the tip of her nose.

"Now hurry"—she swatted him playfully on the behind—"before she changes into a pumpkin like Cinderella."

"It was the coach that changed into the pumpkin."

"Whatever."

Gabriel turned to follow his lady in red. He'd unashamedly eavesdropped on what he could make out of her conversation, enough to hear her remonstrate with her partner about a rude comment he'd made in far too loud a voice. She actually gave a damn about someone else's feelings. They'd spoken in hushed tones for a minute or two after that, then she'd walked out.

It didn't take a rocket scientist. The guy was an ass, and she'd left him. Since Brenda had her own plans, Gabriel wasn't about to miss the opportunity.

He exited the ballroom as the lady, having retrieved her wrap from the coat check, stepped onto the lobby escalator. He made a quick call to order his car around, then caught up with her outside the hotel, where she'd had a doorman signal a cab.

She stood back beneath the canopy, out of the rain and the bite of cool night air. Pulling her wrap tighter around her shoulders, she followed his progress across the lobby and through the revolving doors. A slight smile kicked up at the corners of her lips. As if she knew he was coming for her.

Once at her side, he spoke easily, no introduction. "I have a car and driver and would be more than happy to take you wherever you want to go."

"I don't know you. What if you're planning to kidnap me?"

He leaned in close, her scent rising to him, something sweet mingled with the elemental aroma of rain and aroused woman. "My name is Gabriel Price. I live in Atherton, I work in San Francisco. My driver wouldn't be a part of a kidnapping. And you can hold your cell phone on 911 just in case."

She laughed, that tinkling musical note that first captured his attention in the ballroom. "Maybe I should hold my stiletto shoe at the ready as well."

"Such torture won't be necessary."

She jutted one hip, putting a hand to it, her long nails crimson like her dress. "What about your lady friend?"

He liked that she asked, that she cared. "Brenda has her own plans for the rest of the evening, which don't include me."

"So you're just friends."

"Good friends, but that's all." They'd once considered a three-some together with a bisexual mutual friend, a woman. But in the end, they'd both decided that sex in any form had the potential to screw up even a really good friendship.

She gazed at him, deliberated, then finally waved her hand at the doorman to cancel her cab. Returning to him, she fished a cell phone from within the elegant but tiny evening bag. "I'll make a call first." She gazed up at him through her lashes. "One should never go anywhere without telling someone else."

"I agree."

Turning her back to him, she hit a speed dial, spoke softly, laughed briefly, then closed the phone again. "I'm Dominique," she said, holding out her hand.

He shook, and observed his car pulling up curbside. "A lovely name." A lovely voice, a low, sexy tone that vibrated on his insides. "My car is here."

He'd ordered a limousine because sometimes Brenda liked to bring friends, cocktails before, nightcaps afterward. She liked last-minute decisions in her social life.

The driver jumped out, holding the door for them both as Gabriel ushered Dominique into the plush interior.

Dominique realized this was a crazy idea. But she was a cour-tesan, and she liked to spice things up with a little risk. In the scheme of things, this one wasn't particularly dangerous, plus she'd checked in with Courtesans, leaving a message with the re-ceptionist that she'd had a change of plans. Tomorrow she'd call and give Isabel the full scoop on Trevor McDowell.

For now, she simply wanted to enjoy Gabriel Price's subtle spicy aroma in the luxurious car. Maybe she'd enjoy a lot more.

"You never even asked how far you'll have to drive me," she observed.

He leaned forward to pop a small door, revealing a snazzy bar with crystal glasses and decanters. "That's because I don't care." He turned his head slightly to gaze at her from dark eyes. "I'll take you as far as you want to go."

There was a wealth of meaning in that. Distance, yes, but far more. She wondered how far she needed to go tonight to clean out Trevor's nasty attitude and the vision of Edward's Madonna-like wife. "I live in Saratoga." If she let him take her all the way home, he'd know where she lived. She had an hour to think about it, since the San Francisco streets were packed and getting out of the city wouldn't be a quick jaunt.

"Atherton isn't all that far from Saratoga, so it's not particularly out of my way."

Except that her house was up in the hills, along winding roads. She was sure, though, that he wouldn't calculate the extra distance and regret his offer.

"What can I get you to drink?"

She slipped closer, ostensibly to look at what was available, yet more than that, she wanted his scent to fill her head, make her forget everything else. She wanted the heat of his body to shoot warmth through her.

Dominique had always loved the way men smelled. Earthy. Salty. The hint of sex in the air around them. Men seemed to live and breathe sex, perfuming the atmosphere with their thoughts. When they looked at you, sex was written in the way they caressed you with a glance. Some women thought it objectified them, and they found it offensive. For Dominique, it was the core of being a woman. Invoking that predatorial, elemental, caveman look.

"Brandy?" she asked before her thoughts ran away with her and she begged him to take her in the backseat of his limo.

He selected a decanter and one of the squat glasses. After preparing one for himself as well, he closed up the bar, leaned back, and tipped the crystal to hers.

"To meeting gazes across a crowded room." He sipped, watching her over the rim. The city lights reflected in the rain-soaked streets flashed over his face as their driver successfully made it through a green light.

"Is that a subtle question as to whether I was watching you tonight?"

"I might be flattering myself, but I wasn't questioning that at all. And I was watching you."

She wondered if she should tell him her reason for watching was Trevor and his cutting remarks. Then again, she would have noticed Gabriel even without that. "I'll admit I was watching. I like your name."

"Gabriel the angel?"

"No. Like Gabriel Byrne, the Irish actor. I think he's incredibly hot."

Gabriel laughed, the mirth reaching his eyes. "Well, that's a set-down."

"Not really." She'd always had secret yen for the actor. She sipped her drink. Despite the brandy's relative smoothness, it was liquid fire down her throat, setting her body alight. Or maybe that was caused by his brown eyes, the same dark amber of the drink, seeing through to her soul.

Leaning back against the seat, she crossed her legs, letting her foot swing. Nonchalant. At ease. Though she was anything but. "Tell me what you do for a living." Innocuous. Meaningless chit-chat. The question restored her equilibrium. For a moment there, she'd wanted nothing more than to touch him, taste him, take him.

She put the wild need down to a bad night.

"I invest in start-ups." He shifted and laid his arm along the back of her seat, close enough for her to feel his heat.

"What kind of start-ups?"

"Mostly telecommunications. In all its different forms."

She stroked the leather seat. "You must do well then."

"It's all in knowing the exact moment to enter. And the perfect moment to pull out."

She smiled, chuckled. "Is that a sexual innuendo?"

Light sparkled in his eyes as the car pulled to a stop again. The heavy window glass insulated them from the city noise outside. The quiet interior enveloped her in his warmth and spice even as the alcohol worked its magic on her limbs.

"It was definitely a sexual innuendo." He twirled a lock of her hair around his finger, then drew back, letting it fall as he studied the light streaming across it through the back window.

He had a way of looking at a woman, really seeing her, the tint of her hair, the color of her eyes, making every part of her special.

"Are you married?" It wasn't a question she usually asked. In her line of work, the question was irrelevant. She was well aware that many of her clients were married. It was in the nature of what she did. But he wasn't a client.

And she was hoping he could make her forget about the shock of seeing Edward's pregnant wife. At least for a little while.

# 3

"NEVER BEEN MARRIED. DEMANDING CAREER, WOULDN'T FOIST A workaholic type on a family, never met the right woman," Gabriel recited, as if he'd been asked too many times. The truth could have been all of the above, none, or something entirely different. "And you?" He picked up her left hand, running his thumb along her ring finger.

She suppressed the quiver his touch stirred. "Divorced."

He continued to stroke her finger, staring at it. "He was there tonight, wasn't he?"

Dominique was glad she hadn't been sipping the fiery brandy, or its burn might have consumed her. "Why do you ask?"

When he lifted his gaze to hers, she saw . . . something. He'd never been married, so it couldn't have been empathy. "The pregnant blonde" was all he said.

Her blood began to beat against the backs of her eyes. He'd been watching her way too closely. Heat rose to her cheeks. So much for forgetting. "That was nothing."

He dropped her hand to lightly trail a finger down her cheek, as if he were following the tracks of tears she hadn't cried.

Gabriel the angel. He'd seen it all. Including her pain.

Dominique turned abruptly and stared out onto the rainy city streets, people running to and fro in the rain, covering their heads, hunkering down beneath their umbrellas. The lights of the neon signs glittered on the wet concrete.

God, she needed, she wanted. Needed to *be* wanted. Yes, it was all tied up with Edward and his pretty Francine, the cutting remarks Trevor had made so blithely, hits on her age, her weight, her ass. Though the digs were about other women, they all led back to her own insecurities.

She'd spent months rebuilding herself, only to feel it all come crashing down in little more than an hour.

"Sorry. That was out of line. Not my business." His voice was pure sex. Deep yet soft. Over the phone, he'd have made her come at the count of ten.

Sex was power. Mindless relief from bad thoughts. From the moment she'd contemplated becoming a courtesan, it had never been about the sex itself but about the peripherals, feeling on top, in control, desired. One would think she'd done all sorts of wild things, too, but she'd kept everything vanilla. Nothing kinky. Just straight-up sex, in many ways like her marital sex. She winced. Everything came back to Edward. She needed to erase him. Wipe him out. Obliterate him. The man beside her was the perfect panacea, the beguiling stroke to her figurative bruises.

Dominique turned slowly. The limo broke free of the gridlock and finally hit the freeway ramp. Setting the edge of her glass to her lips, she downed the rest of the brandy. It burned away any remaining inhibition, freed her to the moment.

"I was never very good at small talk," she murmured, holding her empty glass out to him.

He took it. "You're doing fine." He followed her example and drained his brandy, then opened the liquor cabinet long enough to stow the glasses. He didn't offer her another.

"You didn't let me finish." She arched her feet, letting her shoes drop to the car floor, then curled her legs beneath her as she faced him.

"So sorry. Didn't mean to interrupt."

Dominique moved in on him. Gabriel didn't back off an inch. "What I was going to say was that I'm not good at small talk when I want something else entirely."

She was fast. Gabriel found that extremely hot. A woman who knew what she wanted and went for it.

"What else do you want?" Hell, *he* wanted everything. The smoked glass concealed them from the driver, but he wouldn't have cared if the man could see the whole thing. He got the impression she didn't give a damn either.

Rising slightly, she pulled her skirt high, then looked at him, a hint of mischief in her green eyes. "I'd like a kiss."

"I'm okay with that."

"In order to *really* kiss you, I have to get on your lap."

He'd been half-turned in the seat toward her. Now he backed off, sitting straight against the back. "Be my guest."

Bunching the dress at her waist, she climbed on top, legs enveloping him, her heat seeping through to his cock. "There, that's better," she whispered. Putting her hands to his shoulders, she snuggled closer.

Christ. His eyes drifted shut as he enjoyed the feel of her, her hips beneath his hands, the cool slide of material separating him from bare flesh. He didn't keep his lids closed for long. Her lush breasts were a feast for the eyes, begging for his lips, his tongue. And her flowery, sexy woman scent hardened his cock.

"By the way, I want to fuck you, too, Gabriel, but first I need that kiss."

She blew his mind. A woman who knew what she wanted, who asked politely, but took nonetheless. He didn't think he had a choice in the whole matter, and damn if that wasn't the biggest turn-on. He'd been intrigued and attracted by that early hint of vulnerability, but in the heat of sex, he liked the I-want-I-will-have approach just as much.

And take him she did, her lips tasting of brandy. She didn't devour like a she-creature from hell, but licked, sucked, and nipped, her tongue dipping inside for quick forays.

"Mmm, you taste good," she whispered against his mouth.

This time she went deep, for a bone-melting kiss that sent his blood sizzling through his veins, yet was all too brief. Then once again, her breathing a little faster, she murmured against his lips. "I have to tell you a secret, Gabriel."

In that moment, he'd have killed to know her every secret. "What?"

She rested her forehead against his, her eyes closed. "I'm not wearing any panties, and I need you to put your hand between my legs right this minute and make me come."

There was definitely a god looking out for him when he'd decided to take Brenda up on her invitation. He'd never have had this woman, never have known her, touched her, desired her. Even if it was only for this one night.

"How many times?" he asked.

She backed off, laughed. "I'll tell you when I've had enough."

Capturing her chin, he held her. "You'll never get enough," he murmured.

She blinked, her expression unreadable for the briefest moment. Then she recovered. "Maybe *you'll* never get enough."

He liked the challenge. "Let's see." He tunneled beneath the yards of fabric with both hands, grabbing her butt cheeks.

She gasped. "God, your hands are warm."

He laughed. "I thought you'd say they were cold."

"No." Closing her eyes, she hummed a sexy sound. "Warm."

Sliding his hands forward, he caressed her thighs, slipping up to the juncture, his fingertips brushing her curls.

She opened her lids again and gazed down at him with a sultry smile. "And you're getting warmer," she urged, as in the child's game of warm-warmer-hot.

He eased along the plump lips of her pussy, watching her pupils dilate. Her nostrils flared in anticipation of his touch on her clit. He held off, stroking on the outside. "Warmer still?"

"You could certainly step it up to hot."

That would be too easy, too fast. Lightly clamping her pussy lips closed between his fingers, he used her own flesh to caress her, rotating slowly. He felt the bite of her fingernails on his shoulders even through his tux, as she moved against him, trying to force him to a faster pace, a deeper penetration.

Then she huffed. "You're a tease, you know."

"I just want to make sure you get really wet."

"Trust me, I'm wet."

He relented only because he needed to feel how wet she was. "Christ." He slipped in all her moisture. God, he wanted to bury his face in her, inhale her scent, taste her.

"More, more," she chanted, her hips writhing against him, her eyes closed.

He didn't think it mattered whose hand she rode, but he wanted to make sure she didn't forget it was his. Wrapping one hand around her neck, he played her with the other, shoving two fingers deep in her and working her clit with his thumb. "Look at me."

She moaned, but didn't obey. He lightly pressed a pulse point at her throat. This time she gave him what he wanted, her eyes the deep green of a priceless emerald.

"Do you like this?" He pushed her.

"Yes." It was barely more than a hiss. "Make me come."

He snaked an arm around her hips, held her tight, and fucked her with nothing more than his fingers inside and his thumb on her clit. She panted, then tossed her head back and came with a long shudder and a throaty tigress growl. He didn't want her to come down before he got his cock in her, but he suddenly realized the lack of condoms. He hadn't come prepared to make love in the backseat. He hadn't been expecting sex at all tonight.

Yet he craved it more than anything in a long time. Hot, fast sex in a car with her. Then later, a long, slow seduction. And after that, who the fuck knew.

She finally collapsed hard against his chest, trapping his hand between their bodies.

"God, I so needed that," she muttered into his collar.

"Ready for another?" He'd give her as many as he could.

She shimmied against him, backing off just enough to ease her fingers down his abdomen, touching his wrist, his waistband, then settling her palm over the hard ridge of his cock. "I'm ready for this now." She murmured once more into his collar, her breath stirring the hair at his ear.

"I'm afraid I didn't bring the necessary protection."

She backed off, knocked him senseless with a luscious smile, and leaned over for her purse. "Have condom, will travel," she quipped and held up the package as if it were a prize out of a Cracker Jack box. "Always prepared, like a Boy Scout," she added.

"Ah, that was my problem. I wasn't a Boy Scout."

She fluttered her eyelashes. "Neither was I."

It amused him that she wasn't embarrassed to have condoms in her evening bag. Despite the sexual revolution, women's rights, and a new millennium, most ladies his age still weren't supposed to be out trolling, so to speak. That she'd attended a gala affair fully stocked both delighted and amazed him. As he would a jewel, he wanted to explore her many facets.

But first, he wanted to bury himself inside her.

Gabriel took the packet, tore it open, then held out the condom. "Will you do the honors or shall I?"

DOMINIQUE CONSIDERED WHETHER SHE WANTED TO PLAY OR JUMP right to the action. The orgasm had been so damn good, his fingers magic. But there was nothing like the feeling of a big cock deep inside, filling her. And he was big, overflowing her palm as she cupped him. She leaned forward, nipped his lobe, then whispered against his ear, "I want cock. Your cock. Now."

He shoved his fingers through her hair, taking her by the nape with his hand, and held her tight against him. "Woman, I don't think I've encountered anyone quite like you."

"I assume that's a good thing."

He gazed at her with those brandy-colored eyes. "Most women my age do not seem to like sex as much as you do."

She liked that the compliment was embedded in sex talk. "I do believe I'm probably older than you. Maybe that's why."

"I do believe it doesn't fucking matter." He pushed her skirt up her thighs, baring her and exposing the hard cock burgeoning in his pants. "Christ, you have a gorgeous pussy."

She liked a combination of neatly trimmed and clean-shaven, the lips of her pussy freshly smooth and sensitive. "It's very wet, too."

"I noticed." With his free hand, he slipped down her slit, dipping in her cream. Capturing her gaze, he raised his hand to his mouth, sliding the very tip of his finger along his lower lip, then he sucked it into his mouth and licked it clean. "I had to know how you tasted."

The sensuality of it set her pulse racing. She usually had to slow men down, guide them to take stock of her body, to use it fully the way a woman's body was meant to be used, with reverence and joy. Few men, though, were good at it. They gave capable orgasms, excited her blood, but she rarely got that something extra. It had never mattered. She gave herself what she needed anyway.

Gabriel Price was the absolute personification of *extra*. Her pussy tightened, moistened, her nipples peaked, ached, and a flush rode her body. All from the look on his face as he ran his finger along his lip, the heat in his gaze as he licked off the very essence of her.

He could make a woman come without even touching her.

"The condom," she whispered. "Put it on now. I want you inside me." With enough intensity that if he didn't hurry, she'd take him bareback. And Dominique *never* let a man ride bareback.

He shoved the condom into her hand, then unbuckled, unbuttoned, and unzipped, pulled his cock out, holding it in his fist. Squeezing.

"God," she murmured, in awe, in fear. "You'll never fit."

"Hell yes, I will, baby. I was meant to be inside you." The pitch of his voice mesmerized her, and she found herself wrapping her hand around the gorgeous monstrosity, testing the girth. Pre-come beaded on the tip. Just as he'd tasted her, Dominique gathered the drop on her finger and raised it to her lips, sucking it, rolling it on her tongue, savoring it.

"I love come," she said, but his was . . . extra. She closed her eyes so that nothing detracted from his scent, his taste.

He extracted the condom from her fingers.

"If you keep doing that"—she wasn't sure which "that" he meant: the way she relished him, talked to him, or stroked his cock—"I'm going to come before I ever get inside you."

He donned the condom with an expertise that even as a courtesan she hadn't quite mastered. A man always knew his own cock best.

"Hold your dress up," he directed, his hand gripping her thighs. "I want to watch every centimeter sliding inside."

Pushing her hips forward to meet that hot, succulent tool, she crumpled her dress against her belly with one hand while stretching behind with the other to brace herself on his knee. Legs spread, she gave him maximum view. He flipped on the overhead light, spotlighting the head of his cock at her entrance. Then he reeled her in with two hands on her butt.

"Oh God, yes." Once again, she closed her eyes to steep herself in the sensations. He was big, fitting her snugly. He flexed his hips a couple of times, teasing her.

It was enough to drive a woman mad.

He squeezed her ass. "Look at us," he urged. "Watch us."

She gazed at his flesh filling her up. He pulled her inexorably closer, feeding his cock to her, stealing her breath with the overwhelmingly sensual sight of man taking woman. Owning her flesh. Her clit was a red bud between her pussy lips. Even as she saw it, thought about it, he put his thumb to the nub and rubbed as he eased another inch deeper.

"I love fucking," she murmured. "I love sex. I love orgasms. I love cock."

It was the first time in a year that she could say she loved all those things over and above the power of taking a man, making him want, making him beg. It was the first time in a year she'd had sex without getting paid for it.

She pushed the excess material of her dress beneath her to hold it aside, then stretched both hands behind and clamped down on his knees for leverage.

"It's the hottest fucking sight, isn't it? My cock buried in your pretty pink pussy."

God yes. She'd never have thought she could love the sight so much, or be so utterly turned on by it. She leveraged herself to ride him, shifted her butt back and forth on his lap, pushing relentlessly with her hands.

"Told you I'd fit," he said, a gleam in his eye as he circled her clit.

"Oh, you fit all right." So well. He was high, deep, at the very entrance of her womb. She'd never been so full.

Not even with Edward.

*Oh God, please don't think of Edward now.*

"Fuck me, Dominique." Gabriel's voice brought her back to the moment.

She wanted to rise over him and pump hard, but somehow, the angle of his cock was stroking that special place deep inside, and she didn't want to move. She rode faster, her arms aching. Then she was repeating his words over and over. "Fuck me, fuck me." Though she'd never been a fuck-me girl.

He had turned her into one. And it was good. The orgasm shot in, a rush of heat, an implosion, then an explosion.

And Dominique screamed.

# 4

THE ORGASM HAD DAMN NEAR GIVEN HIM A STROKE, IT WAS SO powerful. For long moments afterward, he'd been unable to move, to speak, to do anything more than reel her in flush to his body.

Her skin was hot to the touch, her cheek against his face. She lay like a rag doll in his arms. With the strength of her climax, it was no wonder. What was surprising was how damn good she felt against him, how good it was to remain seated fully inside her. While he enjoyed sex, he didn't tend to tarry long after the act. He glanced up, saw they were almost to Palo Alto, and realized he'd been holding her for ten minutes.

He must have shifted slightly, disturbed her. She raised her head, pushing the red locks out of her face.

"Wow." She smiled.

"Double wow." He smiled, but all the while he wondered what came next. If he wanted her to come home with him, they'd have to double back.

She sat straight, stretched, her hair brushing the roof of the car. "My arms and thighs will be deliciously sore tomorrow."

"Hopefully it was worth it."

"Definitely." She smiled again, yet something flickered in her gaze. Her mind was working the issues. How to get off him. How to dispose of the condom without getting messy. How to ditch him without hurting his feelings.

He always made sure his dates realized there was no sleeping over, so he didn't have to deal with any fuss. It was almost amusing to be on the receiving end.

Yet he didn't want to let her go.

"Come home with me."

"No." She slid back on his lap, his cock falling free, then she dexterously pulled her leg over him and plopped back onto her half of the seat. "But thank you for the offer."

He disposed of the condom, zipped, buckled, straightened.

Why, of all women, did he want her in his house? Though she was older than him, she was beautiful and completely comfortable in her skin, devoid of inhibition, at least as far as he could tell. She laughed easily, yet she didn't tolerate bad behavior. She fucked like a goddess. Still, he had met a few other women like her, comfortable with who they were. So why *her*?

Then he saw it, that wary glimmer as she dropped her gaze searching for her purse, a hint of the vulnerability that had initially attracted him. She was more than the façade. He was interested enough to want to find out what was behind it. He wanted her secrets, to learn what made her tick. Women who needed to be coddled and cared for hadn't appealed to him since college. Yet she was an exciting mixture of assuredness and vulnerability. Not a needy cream puff, but not an ice queen with brass balls either.

She found the lighted mirror in the console in front of her, fixed her lipstick and the smudge of mascara under her eyes, fluffed her hair, then set about righting her dress. Finally, she slipped on her shoes, putting away her lipstick with a snap of her purse. And looked at him.

"Good as new." This time the caution shading her eyes was

gone. Just as she'd mentally fixed herself up in the ladies' room after seeing her ex-husband, she'd done so in front of that tiny mirror. Transforming herself from the woman who'd begged him to fuck her into a date done for the night.

The driver took the turnoff for Highway 85 down to Saratoga. Like a portent, they'd reached the halfway point between his house and hers.

All right, so she wasn't coming home with him. He chose the next best option. "I'd like to get together again."

She opened her mouth, then just as quickly shut it on whatever she'd been about to reveal. Clicking the clasp of her purse once more, she pulled out a card. He wondered idly how a woman managed to fit so much into such a tiny pocketbook and figured it was somehow a statement on the whole nature of male-female relations: women knew how to pack a wealth of meaning into one tiny act.

She handed him the card. "Call this number. Ask for Isabel. Tell her you'd like a date with Dominique." She waved a hand at the window in front of her. "Now, please ask your driver to take the next exit and drop me at the hotel on the corner."

The demand was so unexpected, he did exactly what she said, pushing the intercom button. Sure enough, there was a Wyndham on the corner.

She opened the door and, with one hand on the latch, leaned across to peck his cheek. "Thanks. That was hot. See ya."

Then she was out and striding to the lobby doors, disappearing inside.

"Sir, where to?" The tinny voice came through the intercom.

He didn't know. She'd taken him completely off guard. She'd surprised him. Hell, he actually liked being surprised. "Home," he finally said.

He turned the card she'd given him to the light. *Courtesans*.

And a San Francisco number in a cursive font. A courtesan. Wasn't that a high-class prostitute in days of old?

Reaching in his pocket for his cell phone, he punched in the number.

"Courtesans." A male voice, surprisingly.

"I'd like to speak to Isabel."

"Just one moment."

After a second or two, he heard the click of a transfer.

"Hello, this is Isabel. How may I help you?" She had a sultry, smoky voice that reminded him of Dominique's yet didn't strike quite the same chord in him.

"I'd like to make a date with Dominique."

"Have you seen her before?"

"She just left me."

There was a beat of silence. "Well, Mr. McDowell, I assume you had complete satisfaction if you're calling so quickly."

"This isn't Mr. McDowell."

The silence was longer this time. "And you are?"

"Gabriel."

"Gabriel, this sounds like a situation I need to discuss with Dominique. May I return your call in a few minutes?"

"By all means." He disconnected, assuming the woman had caller ID. He hadn't blocked his number.

Mr. McDowell, the short guy Dominique had walked out on, had been an arranged date. A john. A mark. Whatever. And she was an escort. A call girl. A courtesan.

The woman was a prostitute. And she'd just given him a freebie. He wasn't averse to paying for a woman. He was just averse to paying for one he was already in lust with before he'd known there was a price to pay. Yet she'd hooked him like a slow, dumb fish who saw only the bait and snapped for it. He had to go back for more.

He just had to figure out how to do it on his terms.

* * *

DOMINIQUE STARED AT HERSELF IN THE LADIES' ROOM MIRROR. Miraculously, she'd managed to fix her makeup in the car, getting even the lip liner right on. Surprising when her hands had been quaking with orgasmic aftershocks.

Good God, she couldn't believe she'd done it—fucked him, then Lord, given him a Courtesans card. There'd been that split second where she wanted to see him again. Wanted to date him. Man, woman, no gifts, no remuneration, just . . . a date.

But she didn't date like *that*. She wanted sheiks with thirty-thousand-dollar diamonds and men like Trevor with ten thousand cash in their pockets. Cash for *her*.

Besides, she didn't want to have to worry later on down the road how she'd tell Gabriel that men paid to have her. That she liked men paying to have her. Loved it.

So here she was hiding in the restroom of the Wyndham in case he decided to come looking for her. It reminded her too much of how she'd licked her wounds in the ladies' room after encountering Edward.

Her phone rang. It scared her so badly, she jumped. Thank God the stalls were empty and no one had witnessed her antics. For a second she thought it was him; he'd already called and Isabel had given him her special number. She dug in her purse, yanked out her cell. Isabel. She didn't know whether she was relieved or disappointed.

She answered just before the call went to voice mail.

"Darling." Isabel always called her "darling." "I just got the strangest call."

Good Lord, he'd phoned already, but she chose another interpretation. "So Trevor's already complained to you."

"Haven't heard a peep from him, darling, but someone named Gabriel called, and really, inquiring minds want to know."

"Trevor was an ass. I found Gabriel instead."

"You 'found' him?"

"I—" She stopped, unsure how to explain, then decided the truth wasn't the worst thing she'd ever done. "He picked me up. I did call and leave a message with your reception, just in case. I liked Gabriel enough to have sex with him without receiving payment." "Like" didn't fit. She'd done him out of desperation after being trounced by Edward's pregnant bride.

Why she didn't reveal that part of it, Dominique wasn't quite sure. After all, it was Isabel who'd shown her that Edward wasn't worth the pain and misery. Isabel had helped her move on—in a most unconventional manner, true, but Dominique had moved past the divorce. At least she thought she had until tonight. And presto, there was the answer. She didn't want Isabel knowing she'd taken a big step backward.

"If he wants to have sex again, he can go through normal channels," she finished. He was hot. She'd see him. But the next time, the necessary rules had to be between them.

"Does he understand what the normal channels are?"

"No. I didn't fully explain. I thought I'd leave that up to you. You're so much more diplomatic about it than I am."

Isabel laughed. That was one of the things Dominique liked about her. Laughter came easily to Isabel, taking offense did not. They'd met at a cocktail party given by one of Dominique's friends, one who hadn't gossiped about her at the country club. There'd been a spark with Isabel—nothing sexual, just a general "I'd like to know this person better" sense. They'd met for a friendly lunch, and Dominique ended up pouring out her sob story. After a few such lunches, Isabel had offered her an alternative to spiraling down into bitterness and misery.

Isabel was her lifesaver and her guardian angel.

"So," Isabel said, "you want me to give Gabriel the basic spiel about escort allowances and gifts being nice but not expected, yadda yadda."

"He's a big boy. I'm sure he'll get the full gist of it from that." Most clients did, because they only got the Courtesans number through a recommendation. No one at Courtesans talked money, because that would constitute prostitution. But there were so many ways to get the point across, and Dominique had earned the reputation of being very expensive. She chose only men willing to make it worth her while. Yes, there'd been a few times she'd gotten stiffed, so to speak. But those men were no longer allowed access to Courtesans.

"May I ask you a question, Dominique?"

"Of course." Something tingled up her spine. Isabel was sometimes too astute.

"Why don't you do him without the gifts if you like him?"

At least Isabel hadn't brought Edward into it. Dominique didn't mind giving a straight answer. "I'm a courtesan, Isabel. I can't go back to a normal life with a normal relationship. I like the power too much. And a man is never going to accept what I do for a living. You know it as well as I do." She snapped her purse closed as if that solidified her decision on the matter. "He pays like everyone else does."

"You're right. It doesn't work any other way." Isabel had her own story, though Dominique only knew there was once a man. And now there was not.

"Give him the spiel, see what he says." Dominique wanted him enough to hope he didn't balk, but if he did, she wanted her freedom and power more.

"Fine. What's your schedule if he wants to make a date?"

"I can make adjustments to accommodate him."

Silence. She could hear the tick-tick of Isabel's mind working. Dominique didn't usually do the accommodating. But Gabriel was good at what he did. He paid attention to her body's needs. And she liked it. Big deal. "Just give him this number. I'll make my own arrangements.

"Will do," Isabel finally answered.

"I'm turning the phone off, though, so just tell him to leave me a message." It sounded so nonchalant, as if she didn't care one way or the other. She wanted Gabriel to wait for just a little while. Or maybe she was afraid she'd beg him to come back. "Oh, and I'm going to block Trevor's number. I don't know what you saw in him that you thought I'd like."

"Trevor has special needs, and you're so good at figuring out what a man doesn't even know he wants and giving it to him."

"Thanks for the compliment. But I didn't have the patience with him."

"I'm sorry for the mistake." Though Isabel didn't make many of them.

The restroom door opened and a couple of ladies entered, laughing. One of them, a little tipsy, stumbled and her friend caught her. "Not to worry," Dominique said, "but I've got to go now." She didn't want to have to think about how to say things in code because there was an audience.

"I'll call you when I've got something. Sleep tight."

She closed the phone. The girls went into the large handicapped stall together, as if they needed help. Being that drunk, maybe they did.

Dominique intended to get a room here at the Wyndham. Calling a cab now was too much hassle. She just wanted this dress off. She checked in and twenty minutes later burrowed beneath the bed's big down comforter. Her last thought before sleep claimed her was how much she wished she'd taken Gabriel's cock in her mouth before she'd fucked him.

That was the question. Could a girl have her cake and eat it, too? Or cock, as the case may be. Could she have Gabriel and still retain her power?

MMM, YUM. SHE'D BEEN HAVING A LOVELY DREAM WHICH SOMEhow now eluded her. Dominique snuggled among the comfy warm bedding. The morning sun streamed through the curtains she'd forgotten to close. The rain must have ended sometime in the night. She snaked a hand out from the coverlet and grabbed her phone to turn it on. Just like that. First thing. Had to check if he'd called.

Maybe this wasn't such a good idea. She looked forward to her dates, but not *a* date with a particular man. She only dated men she enjoyed, so they were all pretty much equal. But here she was dialing in to find out if Gabriel had left a voice mail.

The first message. She didn't like how marvelous it made her feel. She wasn't a woman who got excited about a man's call.

"Have coffee with me and we'll talk." Then he rolled off a number. Oh, they'd talk all right. She'd lay out her terms and he could take them or leave them. She listened again so she could write down his number. His voice was like whipped cream and chocolate. It made her warm and gooey like a teenage girl.

The second message was from Isabel. Trevor begged her forgiveness. He was contrite. He didn't know what came over him. Dominique rolled her eyes. The man just didn't like that he couldn't have her at any price. It offended his self-worth.

She punched in Gabriel's number instead. It rang four times then went to voice mail. She left him a message. "Meet me at Stevens Creek Park off Highway 280 at Foothill. Noon. Bring your hiking boots."

# 5

WITH LAST NIGHT'S RAIN, THE SIX-MILE LOOP WOULD BE MUDDY, but Dominique never missed her speed walk. She preferred a walk over the gym, especially on a day like this, when the rain had washed the smog out of the sky and the sun was blindingly bright. A speed walk was also getting one up on Gabriel Price. She wondered if he'd be able to keep pace with her.

She'd made it home in a taxi, showered, put her face on, suited up, and was halfway through her stretches in the park's lot by the time Gabriel arrived.

She'd expected an expensive luxury vehicle, but he drove an ordinary SUV. When he climbed out, she realized her mistake in suggesting a workout. While hot and sexy in a tuxedo, he was devastating in runner's pants and a long-sleeved black T-shirt, every muscle defined, including the delicious package between his legs. Something about hiking boots versus dress shoes got her pulse throbbing, too.

He leaned into a stretch beside her. "You look edible."

It was unnerving how her blood suddenly raced through her veins. The man had the ability to rob her of her very next breath. She ratcheted back and pretended his words didn't mean a thing. "Thank you."

She allowed him three hundred sixty seconds of stretch in different positions, admiring his taut calves, the tight thighs, and the curve of his ass as he stretched out his hamstring.

Then she was off, her arms pumping. She could walk like this for hours, a fast clip that ate up a mile in twelve minutes.

He didn't ask her to slow down, but the path was barely wide enough for the two of them, so he settled a half pace behind her. "I called your friend Isabel."

"She told me," she threw over her shoulder.

"She explained how this works."

"Good."

They started the incline. It wasn't tough, but it did quicken her pulse—though having him so close on her ass could have caused that.

"I think you should explain it, too." His breathing didn't change an iota, dammit.

"It's quite simple. I'm an expensive woman with expensive tastes." She looked back to catch his eye, but his sunglasses reflected the sky. "Last night you had your one and only on-the-house session."

She waited for him to sputter or tell her to take a flying leap into the reservoir. She hadn't intended to be so blunt or to come off sounding rude. Then again, it was good to learn right up front how liberal he was. True, he'd taken her in the backseat of a limousine, but he might very well get his back up when asked to pay for the privilege. She wanted that out in the open now. She was used to men knowing the rules from the start. Doing it the other way round, screwing him first, felt like she'd given him the advantage. She wanted it back.

"How much do you charge?"

She knew it wasn't entrapment, at least not of the law enforcement kind, but she still wouldn't let him pin her down. "I don't charge. You simply show your appreciation."

"And the more appreciation the better?"

She glanced back once more to gauge his reaction. Without tripping, though, she couldn't observe long enough. The walk wasn't working to her advantage. She badly wanted to stop and ferret out every nuance playing across his features. Instead, she continued to climb so *her* nuances weren't visible. "That's exactly it. A woman likes to be appreciated."

"And desired." His voice gave nothing away. Dammit.

"Naturally."

"And the level of a man's appreciation is based on the amount of his . . . gift." He gave the barest pause, but it was there.

It drove her mad. What did it mean? Dominique couldn't stand wondering, worrying anymore. She turned and walked up the hill backward. "Good for the thighs and the glutes," she explained, hoping he wouldn't see the through the lie. "You're picking up the idea clearly."

The sun was bright, they both wore shades. Now she could see his face but not his eyes. "I understand completely," he agreed, a totally noncommittal reply.

"I don't normally have sex on the first date," she went on, trying to draw him out. Really, what did the man think of the fact that she was a courtesan? All right, dammit, a call girl.

"That wasn't really a date, now, was it. I didn't call the number, we didn't prearrange. In fact, you were with another *date*." He bit down on the word.

She felt the burn of the backward walk in her thighs. "Yes."

"Why did you get rid of him?"

"He made several insulting comments about the people at the party. I didn't appreciate his disrespectful attitude."

"Admirable." Was that a hint of a sneer in his voice?

What was it about him? Why did she care what he thought? He was devastatingly handsome, he gave great sex. His demand that she watch his cock taking her was sexy, hot. Last night wasn't just everyday sex. She liked his sensuality. But even more, he'd expunged her emotions about Edward and the baby, made her forget for a bit. The problem was that very fact put him above other men. It made her need him more, like a panacea to her self-esteem. The only way to have him and maintain her control was to make him pay.

"So we're set on the rules," she said, "and the proper appreciation—"

"Look—"

She tripped on a root and went down on her ass hard.

"—out," he finished.

The puddle soaked through her walking tights and mud squished through her fingers where she'd tried to save herself from the fall.

He hunkered down in front of her and pulled off his sunglasses. "Are you all right?"

She snorted. Then spluttered. Then a laugh burst out. "I can't believe I just did that."

"I tried to warn you."

She'd thought he was about to tell her he'd changed his mind because she was too much damn work. "Yes, you did try, but I was too busy spouting off." She'd deserved it. She'd been acting the total bitch.

"You even splashed mud on your cheek." He pointed out a spot. She swiped at it.

He touched her hand, and then, a sparkle in his eyes, he drew his finger down the length of her nose. "And look at that, it's on your nose, too."

"You put it there," she squeaked in feigned outrage. Raising her muddy hand, she slashed a finger down his nose, then across both cheeks. "Oops, I accidentally got you all dirty, too." He looked like a war-painted Indian.

"So you did. Maybe we need to get a little bit more on you." He shot a hand around her neck, grabbed her nape and yanked her forward, taking her mouth in a kiss before she could even react.

Hard, then softening, his lips across hers, taking her by surprise with the sweetness of it. She opened her mouth to him, bracing her hands behind her. He tasted so good she didn't give a damn about the mud between her fingers. He filled her senses, took her over. She could drift in this nirvana with him forever.

It was like pain when he pulled away, short, sharp, up under her ribs like a knife blade. He was close enough to scent, far enough that she didn't have to look at him cross-eyed. On the heels of that kiss, his dark amber gaze disarmed her.

"Why?" she murmured.

"Why did I kiss you?"

It had all started in the ballroom. "Why did you follow me last night?"

He didn't even deny it. "I saw you, I wanted you."

"That simple?"

"There was nothing simple about it. Sex is simple. This was more."

"So you saw me across a crowded room like in some fairy tale, yadda yadda." She tried to make light of it.

"I wanted you badly. I made sure I had you."

It was the lust-at-first-sight fantasy. You meet a guy in an elevator and boom, your heart starts pounding, your knees go weak, and if there was a power failure, you'd be doing it with him up against the door panel in two seconds flat. If she'd been twenty years younger, she'd have used the word *love*. Love at first sight. Yet lust could be so much more powerful. Like a drug. She relished his words, the slight puff of his breath coming faster than when he'd walked behind her. Because he'd kissed her, touched her. He was just what she needed after Edward.

And so much more dangerous because of that.

His eyes darkened to melted chocolate. "Did you feel the same?"

It was obvious she had. Why bother dancing around it now? "Yes." Not the first moment she saw him, but he'd grown on her quickly. Less than an hour after she'd met him, she'd hiked her skirt, straddled his lap, and begged him to make her come. That wasn't her usual style. In being a courtesan, sex wasn't her ultimate goal.

"I'll fuck you anytime you want," he whispered.

She felt his voice as if he'd put his hand between her legs. She'd take him here, now, and you couldn't get more down and dirty than a mud puddle. But she'd been Edward's doormat for fifteen years, and now she couldn't give in without a fight. "And I'll fuck you anytime you want to pay," she countered.

He settled, hunkered down before her, one foot balanced, his forearm resting on his raised knee. You'd think he'd show some reaction, even something so small as a twitch of his nostrils or slightly dilated pupils. The man showed nothing.

Then he leaned down and tied her shoelace. "It seems we skipped the first date where you don't actually fuck. Why don't we go back there and get to know each other?"

It was a slam. A rejection. Wasn't it? Yet he'd called Isabel, left Dominique herself a message, and pushed another meeting. He had to want *something* from her. Just as she wanted it on her terms, perhaps so did he.

Wouldn't it be fun to see who won?

\* \* \*

SHE HAD GREAT CALVES IN HER THREE-QUARTER-LENGTH TIGHTS. Great calves, a great ass, and she was walking the pants off him. Figuratively speaking. Gabriel had an interesting time keeping up with the woman, literally and figuratively. Not that he'd let her know it was even the slightest exertion. His breathing remained even, and he hadn't broken a sweat yet. But she tested his limits in so many ways.

"It's only another mile," she said ahead of him.

He'd never paid for sex, but if the right moment arose, he had no compunction or moral against it. But he'd had her without the money, and now he was loath to reduce what happened between them to a transaction. He wanted Dominique to give herself freely the way she had in the limo. He'd kissed her in the mud to prove they weren't all business. She'd have let him do her right there on the path, he knew it.

He wanted her on the edge, willing to give in, wanting him as badly as he wanted her. Screw the gift, screw the monetary "appreciation."

In truth, he hadn't been completely hooked when he'd followed her out of the hotel lobby. Interested, yes, but not hooked. Then she'd done him in the car. Watching his cock slide deep inside her, *that* was the hook. He wanted more of her. He just didn't want it to be a mere business deal.

"I'm thinking Palm Springs," he mused.

The slightest hitch marred her firm step. "For a date?"

"Yes. I thought we'd fly down on Saturday, maybe take the tram up to the top of the mountain, have dinner, spend the night at one of the resorts, and come back on Sunday."

She tossed the answer over her shoulder without even looking at him. "That's a weekend, not a date."

"It's a date if we have separate rooms."

"It's more than twenty-four hours. What if we get sick of each other?"

"Haven't you ever gone on a weekend trip for one of your regular dates?" He assumed men would pay for something like that, the pleasure of a good-looking woman's company for more than a night. And some hot sex as well.

She stopped, half turning, a hand on her hip and one foot balanced higher on the path. "Actually, I haven't." Her lips curved. "It could be fun."

He liked the idea of being first in something with her. "Next weekend."

"That sounds fine."

"Don't you have to look at your schedule or check in with Isabel?"

"Most men aren't like you. My dates are usually more last-minute."

"I'll make the reservations then."

And he would plan her seduction. At some point during the weekend, she'd be begging him to do her in every position imaginable.

# 6

IT WOULDN'T TAKE GABRIEL TWENTY-FOUR HOURS TO BREAK DOWN
and beg her to stuff his money in her purse so he could have her.
How long? After dinner? When they settled into their hotel rooms?
On the plane?

God, she was such a conniving bitch. And she loved it, because
she would make it worth every penny Gabriel paid.

"Truly, Dominique, I was beastly, and I need you to forgive
me. Please." On the other end of the cell phone, Trevor didn't exactly whine, but close.

*Concentrate.* Since her early afternoon walk with Gabriel, he
was the only thing on her mind. She'd been sitting on the sun-
porch with her tea in her hand thinking about him, which was
delicious and frightening all at the same time. Maybe that was the
reason she'd agreed to talk to Trevor when Isabel called this afternoon, again claiming he was contrite; consumed by Gabriel, she
hadn't been listening properly. Now she was stuck on the phone
with Trevor. If she didn't concentrate, she might agree to something she didn't want or need.

"I appreciate the apology, Trevor. Let's forget the whole episode."

"But I'd like to see you again."

"Thank you, but no." One should always be polite.

"Please. I realize the price will go up, but I'm willing to pay whatever it takes."

Some men couldn't take no for an answer, and they didn't know how to handle rejection. As soon as she told him she wouldn't take his money, Trevor had to have her. She wasn't even sure he wanted *her*. She was in many ways like the women he trashed— older, with abundant curves. She liked herself exactly the way she was; in fact, she'd worked out for months to get this body.

"Trevor, I—"

He cut her off before she could say no yet again. "I'll do anything you want. You name it."

What's up with that? His desperation was almost . . . sad. But he'd already shown his true nature. Besides, she had her date with Gabriel. They'd be flying out Saturday morning. He was so much more a man than Trevor McDowell ever could be. She didn't need another—

Good God. The thought brought her up short. Some courtesans went exclusive. They had one man, put themselves at his beck and call. She would never do that. She had her favorites, of course, but she never used the word *need*.

"Trevor, I'm thinking." Friday night with Trevor would put her weekend date with Gabriel in perspective. It was *just* a date. Gabriel was *just* a man. And he would pay like any other.

"Please, Dominique, tell me how to make it up to you."

Again, Trevor gave off the scent of desperation, even over the phone. She had a thought. A brilliant thought. Actually, it was Machiavellian. She'd gotten that odd vibe when Trevor commented on the men. What if . . . "There is something I've always wanted to experience but haven't found the right man for."

"Yes, yes, tell me more." He jumped on her suggestion like an eager little puppy.

He'd either hang up in outrage—with which she'd be fine—or he'd agree because he had a secret hankering he couldn't admit to. Unless he was forced. "I've always wanted to watch two men together," she purred.

Silence. She sat in the sunroom of her hilltop Saratoga home—the one Edward agreed to give her in the divorce because she'd been ever so reasonable about everything else—and let the afternoon sun warm her. Curled up on the rattan sofa cushions wearing a pair of comfy velour sweats, she sipped her green tea, a slice of lemon giving it that needed kick. Trevor wasn't gone. Even with her earpiece in, she detected his breathing.

"Earth to Trevor," she singsonged, as if she hadn't just suggested the most outrageous thing.

"I don't know what to say."

Hmm. He hadn't said no. "That's what I want, Trevor."

"But—"

"It's all right to say no. I'll understand perfectly if it offends your sensibilities. Why don't we make it a little easier on you? Instead of full-on sex with a man"—she paused long enough for him to get the image in his mind—"how about we just go for jerking off?" She stopped, thinking, imagining. "You stroke his cock, then he strokes yours. Then you two have a nice mutual orgasm."

The more she thought about it, the more she saw this as Trevor's chance of a lifetime. If he was so inclined, he got approval and acceptance without having to admit it was something he'd wanted, perhaps even dreamed about. If she'd misread his strange comments, all he had to do was say no.

"We'll do it Friday." Because then she'd be planning her date with Trevor instead of mooning over a weekend with Gabriel.

His silence was shorter. "Who would we do this with?"

Oh my. Oh Lord. He was going to say yes. "Isabel will find

someone appropriate." Someone like Gabriel. She couldn't help the comparison. But it was only about appearance; she didn't want to see *Gabriel* with Trevor. "I'm leaning toward fortyish, good-looking, fit."

"I'm nervous." His voice actually trembled, as if he were driving over a very bumpy road.

"You can say no at any time. Even once we meet him. Even once you take your clothes off."

"I have to take my clothes off?" His tone rose.

Dominique sighed. "Yes. You both have to be naked. This is not some quickie in the backseat of an old car."

His breath sounded like a hum over the cell phone line, one long *ahhhh* of sound.

Was she trying to teach him a lesson, fulfill a fantasy, or just being a plain old bitch? She opened her mouth to tell him to forget it, that she realized she'd gone overboard.

He spoke first. "All right. But I'm a newbie at this."

She took air in two gulps. He'd agreed. She'd committed herself. "I won't push you to do more than you want," she said, reassuring him as if he were a virgin. Maybe she needed reassurance, too.

"And make sure he's not some ugly old dude."

She ignored the age slam. "You should know I would never do that to us, Trevor." *Us.* Making it about them, not just him. "I'll call you with the time and place, darling. Toodles."

She hung up, then held the phone to her chest a long moment. She'd never been so adventurous. She'd never even thought about two men. But now, the slightest tingle shimmied through her body. It could be good. She'd *make* it good. Because she didn't want anyone—not even her own conscience—coming back later saying she'd only done it as payback, taking out her anger with Edward on Trevor McDowell.

And she didn't want to contemplate that she'd made the date in the first place because she needed to get Gabriel Price out of her mind.

ISABEL BOUGHT INTO HER PLANS FOR TREVOR. "I TRUST YOUR judgment" was what she'd said, but Dominique feared her own personal feelings were out of control. She'd jumped into this date with Trevor because she didn't like how much she anticipated seeing Gabriel. Then she'd come up with a truly Machiavellian solution. Certainly her emotions played a huge role in the men with whom she chose to have sex. Why else would she have this need to be the highest paid, the most sought after—all to prove Edward had made the worst mistake of his life. She'd never before been quite so manipulative, though. Yet when she told Isabel what she wanted for Trevor, her friend didn't offer so much as a word of caution. In fact, Isabel found the perfect partner almost right away.

So here she was, Friday night, meeting Isabel's choice in the bar of a downtown San Jose luxury hotel, near the arena. Ten minutes to go before Trevor was scheduled to call with the room number. She half expected him to back out, but Trevor would view it as losing, and he'd already lost once when she walked out on him at last week's benefit.

The soft strains of musical standards masked the quiet conversations around her. The bar was refined, the drinks costly, the orchid in the center of the table real and well cared for. Flickering candles augmented the low lighting.

Dominique sipped her expensive chardonnay and set her glass back on the table as Simon Foster slid into the booth beside her.

"You must be Dominique."

She'd arranged with the hostess to send Simon her way when he arrived. "And you're everything I expected."

The man was incredibly hot. She liked older men, not because she was older but because they were seasoned, a few lines, a knowing glint. Simon Foster had it all. With George Clooney looks, his silver hair was shot through with the remains of dark brown. Eyes the gray of a fox, he perused her up and down the way she did him. She looked good in a long-sleeved teal T-shirt dress. It wasn't fancy, but the material hugged her curves and made her feel sexy. Beneath it she wore a bra and minuscule panties. She liked the glimmer of appreciation in his gaze. He dressed up exceedingly well in a navy suit and white shirt. He'd dress down to nakedness just as beautifully, she was sure. She judged him to be close to fifty, but he'd taken good care of his years. At six feet, he was bulked up from working out, like an ex–football player who hadn't allowed himself to go to seed. His hands were big, his shoulders wide. He would dominate Trevor, but she figured that was good for the boy.

She could enjoy watching the two of them from a purely artistic perspective.

"Isabel told you what we were looking for?" Dominique trusted Isabel implicitly, but still, she needed to confirm that he understood the story.

"Experimentation appeals to me. I've never done this, but the idea of a woman watching takes the nervous edge off the experience." Then he smiled, the creases at his eyes testifying to the fact that he smiled a lot. She didn't, however, believe he'd ever be nervous about anything. He had that strong jaw and solid strength to his shoulders that said he'd never be unsure of anything he did. Like Gabriel.

Drat the man for being on the edge of her thoughts even now.

"I'm an exhibitionist," Simon was saying, "and the idea of such a gorgeous woman watching me"—he shrugged expressively—

"I've had some of my most powerful orgasms in ages just thinking about it."

"It doesn't bother you that I want to watch you with a man?" He was surprisingly masculine, considering what he'd volunteered for.

Again he shrugged, following it up with a half smile. "Sex is sex. The hottest part of it is fulfilling a woman's fantasy, giving her what she wants." He tipped his head. "I'll want you to masturbate for us."

Though his words, his desires, dampened her panties, she had no intention of exposing herself to him. This was about Trevor, not her. But she was glad Isabel had found a man who wasn't afraid of his own sexuality. "Masturbation isn't part of the scenario."

He leaned in. "You're going to feel so fucking hot you'll have to do it for us."

His knowing words and heated tone jerked her back to that night in Gabriel's limousine and how badly she'd needed his cock. If he'd demanded that she masturbate for him first, she'd have lifted her skirt in a second. It was her emotions, it was him, but it was also the naughtiness of opening herself to a stranger. Just as part of the allure of being a courtesan was getting money for sex. It was taboo and therefore so damn hot. The thought gave her an insight into Simon Foster. "Is that what appeals to you about my request?" she asked as if he could follow her thought processes. "I mean, the forbidden nature of two heterosexual men having *those* kinds of fantasies?"

His lips curved, then the smile rose to his eyes. "I didn't think a woman would understand. It's the idea of doing something you're not supposed to do, like fucking a woman on the dance floor in a crush of people, or fingering her to an orgasm under the tablecloth in a fancy restaurant." He blinked slowly. "Or stroking another man's cock and making him come because a woman asked you to do it."

She shuddered deliciously with the vision of Gabriel touching her the way Simon had described. She enjoyed sex, but she'd remained vanilla about it. Isabel sent her men that suited her in that way. Some people, however, needed kinkier, riskier things to excite them. She wondered about the things Gabriel would need to excite him. He was a sensual man. He wouldn't be satisfied with nothing more than a wham-bam-thank-you-ma'am in the backseat.

Dammit, why did she keep letting him intrude when she was conducting business here? The whole point of this exercise with Trevor had been to exorcise thoughts of Gabriel, and here she was allowing him in over and over again. The frightening thought occurred—and not for the first time—that what was happening between her and Gabriel had nothing to do with business.

Her cell rang before she could work herself into a tizzy about what Gabriel would or wouldn't want and whether she would win or lose.

"Excuse me a moment, that should be our boy." Then she paid attention to the phone. "Trevor."

"Room fourteen-oh-one." His voice rose slightly on the last number.

"Good boy, Trevor. We'll be right up."

Hanging up, she sidled out of the booth, then held out her hand to her partner in crime.

She'd worry about besting Gabriel when she saw him tomorrow.

FOR A MAN WHO'D NEVER GIVEN IT A HELL OF A LOT OF THOUGHT before, Gabriel had to admit he'd planned the date perfectly.

Women liked romance, and he'd give her all she could handle. By the time he got her back to their suite, she would beg him to climb into her bed.

He had to laugh at himself. There was an equal chance he'd give her the envelope of cash he'd stuffed in his computer case. Just the fact he'd withdrawn the money this afternoon was telling.

He wanted Dominique, and he meant to have her on his terms. But just in case . . .

Standing in front of the picture window of his Atherton home, Gabriel downed the last of his brandy before retiring. The moon was bright, reflecting in the pool he rarely used. It was there for business entertaining.

He had to acknowledge what rumbled in his belly. Dominique slept with other men. A lot of other men. She had a date tonight. When he'd suggested an early flight down to Palm Springs, she'd made him push out the time. She needed her beauty rest, she claimed. In his opinion, she had all the beauty he could handle. He also guessed the real reason she'd wanted a later flight. She'd be fucking a client tonight. Doing what she'd done with Gabriel. And probably a hell of a lot more. Sucking him, letting him fuck her from behind, any way he wanted, every way he wanted. Because he was paying for it.

And Gabriel was jealous as hell.

# 7

TREVOR LEFT THE DOOR UNLATCHED, AND HE LOUNGED NAKED ON the bed as they entered. Propped against the headboard, he was the picture of relaxed except for the quake of his hand as he set his wine on the bedside table.

"Trevor, this is Simon."

Simon simply gave him what Dominique had come to think of as his signature smile. Trevor lifted his chin in acknowledgment. But his gaze dropped to the front of Simon's slacks, and his cock hardened.

His LMD—little man's disease—didn't include his cock. Trevor was actually quite impressive. And growing.

Okay, what to do now? Dominique had thought she'd have them undress each other, but Trevor had wrested that idea from her. Instead, she tossed her purse on the desk, kicked off her shoes, and crawled across the bed to the head, next to Trevor.

Pulling her dress to her knees, she curled her legs beneath her and sat back against the headboard. "I think Simon should give us a show, don't you?" Just like the other afternoon on the phone, she made it about them, her and Trevor together.

"So I'm the evening's entertainment," Simon drawled, tugging off his suit jacket and tossing it across a chair back.

"Of course you are." She winked. "And you love it. You said you were an exhibitionist. Give us a really good show."

Trevor was uncharacteristically silent, as least compared to his behavior at the benefit on Saturday. He watched avidly. Hungry was the only way to describe his gaze, as if he were drinking in Simon's every physical detail.

She had to admit there was a lot to drink in. Simon whipped off his tie and unbuttoned his shirt to reveal a hairless muscled chest and whipcord abs. The man definitely worked out hard. He tossed the shirt. It landed across Trevor's thighs. Trevor's cock flexed, and his fingers twitched as if he wanted to grab himself, caress, stroke, jerk as he watched. But he didn't move.

Simon's silver-fox eyes weren't on Trevor. Instead, they devoured her, which unnerved her. As if the expectations were all about her instead of the two men.

"More," she said, flapping her hand at him, smiling, throwing him off the scent of her nerves.

Bending to untie his shoes, he afforded them both a nice view of his well-formed ass. "Now, that's a tight end, don't you think, Trevor?" she murmured.

He grunted. She glanced down to see he'd moved Simon's shirt to cover his crotch. His cock tented the material.

Footwear disposed of, Simon rose to his full height of six feet. That could be another reason Trevor was already on the bed naked; Simon wouldn't see how short he was. She pinched Trevor's nipple, hard. Some men hated it, some it drove insane. Trevor hissed in a breath, then moaned.

"Hey," Simon called, "quit playing without me."

"Then hurry up and show us your big tool."

He laughed, large teeth, wide smile, a bit like the big bad wolf ready to gobble up Trevor and her in one bite.

As handsome as he was, he made her think of Gabriel for the

very fact that he *wasn't* Gabriel. If he were, she'd have been undoing his slacks and taking out his delicious cock.

This was getting ridiculous. What was it about Gabriel that made her do all this comparing? The harder she tried *not* to think about him, the more she did exactly that.

Simon slid out his belt, popped the button on his slacks, and slipped down his zipper, revealing bronzed flesh. He'd gone commando. Then he shoved his pants over his hips, down his legs, and kicked them aside. This man was no shy, retiring mouse.

Trevor's eyes widened. Beneath the cover of Simon's dress shirt, his dick flexed.

Simon stroked his cock proudly, bringing it to life. "Nice, isn't it?" he murmured. Again, his gaze pierced her. And all she could think was *wow*. He was big, thick, his balls shaved smooth. Excitement rippled through her, heading to her clit.

"You want to suck it, don't you." It wasn't a question.

Beside her, Trevor moaned. Then, as if he couldn't help himself, he shoved the shirt aside and took his cock in his fist, pumping lightly to Simon's rhythm.

The two men actually made her salivate. Trevor's small, lean, compact body versus Simon's large, muscular, toned bulk. She imagined Simon's big hand wrapped around Trevor's cock and experienced an intense rush of moisture she hadn't anticipated.

Good God, her panties were soaked. She'd teased Trevor with the idea that watching him would make her hot, but she hadn't expected the sensations to take her over this way.

"You want my hand on that cock." Simon seduced them both.

"Yes," she whispered.

"Please," Trevor said on an exhale, the word almost unrecognizable.

Simon retrieved a small bottle from his jacket pocket. Flipping the top open, he stalked them, forcing their gazes to follow his bobbing cock as he rounded the bed.

"On your back," he commanded, and Trevor slid down to lie flat. Dominique almost did the same.

Holding the bottle high, he squeezed, the lubricant spilling over Trevor's groin.

"What do you want?" Simon held Dominique with the power of his gaze.

"Stroke him. But don't let him come yet."

Trevor groaned at her words, closed his eyes, and threw his arm across his face. She yanked it down.

"Don't you dare," she whispered. "I want you to watch. I want you to know it's a man making you feel good." The play of agonizing pleasure across his face made her hot. God, she wanted Gabriel's cock right now. She wanted to ride him while she watched Simon's hand wrap, finger by finger, around Trevor's throbbing cock.

Trevor arched into the tight grip as Simon started to pump him. Faster, twisting his hand at the base. Then he squeezed Trevor's balls with his other hand, worked them as he worked his cock. Trevor groaned, tossed his head, closed his eyes, and arched back into the pillow. She didn't correct him, didn't tell him to watch. He *knew* a man had his cock. A woman couldn't perfect that rhythm, that stroke. It took a man to know a man.

How could one man's hand wrapped around another's cock look so intensely masculine? The sight stole her breath.

"Do yourself now," Simon ordered her.

"No." Watching burned her up, but she kept imagining Gabriel across the room. If he'd been watching her from the chair, she'd have spread her legs in two seconds flat. And come just as quickly.

God, she needed to concentrate on Trevor's pleasure. Leaning close, she whispered in his ear, "Tell me how good it feels."

He gasped, his mouth opening and closing like a fish. "God, fucking incredible."

She grabbed his chin, pulled his face to hers, forced him to meet her eyes. "You've never had anything better."

"No." He pulled away, blinking, staring down the length of his body to that manly hand stroking him relentlessly. "Oh God, it's so good." He gulped air, moaned, tossed his head on the pillow again. Drops of pre-come leaked from the slit of his cock.

"Stop," she said. "Don't let him come." She wanted, needed to see Trevor take Simon's meaty cock first. She wanted to see in his eyes the weighty feel of a penis in his hand. She needed to know she'd done the right thing forcing this on him. She wanted him to want it badly. "Let Trevor stroke you now."

"A greedy little bitch, aren't you?" Simon's words should have pissed her off, but she *was* greedy, a fact she'd never known before. Until Gabriel. And now this. Simon kept on smiling. But he loosened his grip, then rose to his feet. And for the first time, he concentrated on Trevor. "Stroke me."

Trevor rolled over, sat up, and spread his thighs. Simon stood between them. Dominique slid down to her stomach, improving the view of Trevor's cock jutting between his legs as Simon's penis bobbed close to his face.

"Use some lube, Trevor," she directed, then she raised her gaze to Simon. "And I want you to make Simon come."

The man gave her that same damnable smile. "You think I won't let him, don't you?" he challenged.

Why did he phrase everything as a question, yet not a question? As if he knew her thoughts. Why did he make it all about her?

"Oh, I have no doubt you will," she murmured. Instead of the male hand on his cock detracting from his masculinity, his attitude only enhanced it. This man would do anything. He had no limits.

She had too many, her goal being to bring a man to his knees, to pay the highest price for her. Nothing else meant anything. For one moment she'd let herself go with Gabriel, but then she'd wrested back her control by forcing this on Trevor.

If he wasn't enjoying it so much, she would have felt ashamed of herself.

Yet she couldn't turn her eyes away.

Trevor poured lube into the palm of his hand, then smeared it all over Simon's cock. Simon let his head roll back on his neck and muttered, "Stroke it, do it now."

Trevor took to jerking a cock like a duck takes to water, to use an old cliché. For the first time, he gave voice to what roiled inside him. "You like that," he murmured. "You like my hands all over you. It makes you feel fucking nasty and hot."

Simon shoved a hand through Trevor's hair, grabbed hold and pulled his head back. "Fuck yes."

The crass talk pooled moisture between her legs. The unyielding caress of Trevor's hand on that big, thick cock heated her skin.

"He's so fucking hard. Look how hard I make him." Trevor displayed the cock proudly, holding it out for her.

"Make him come, Trevor." She wanted to give him the glory of it. And she needed it for herself.

Trevor stroked faster, talked dirtier. Until Simon's hips pumped in a matching rhythm. She poured more lube over the engorged tip, the slip-slide sound of Trevor's fist filling the room.

"You love how he feels, don't you, Trevor?"

"Christ yes," he muttered without looking up, his gaze only for the cock in his hand.

Simon broke free, pushed Trevor to his back on the mattress, shoved both hands beneath his armpits, and hauled him higher across the bed. Then he straddled Trevor's hips.

He took both cocks in his big fist, squeezed them together,

forcing pre-come to the surface. Her mouth watered. She hadn't taken Gabriel's cock in her mouth. She'd been so stupid not to. She wanted it badly, the sweet-salty taste of his come on her tongue, more than just the drop she'd licked from her fingers.

"Lube," Simon demanded from her.

God. The sight mesmerized her even as she managed to drizzle lubricant over them, watched it dribble down to his hand.

Dominique had never seen anything like it, that big hand taking command of both cocks, stroking, caressing, sealing them together from tip to shaft to balls. It was beautiful. It was powerful. It was pure sex without inhibition. And she wanted more.

She wanted the freedom they had, the freedom *she'd* given them. Complete and total approval and acceptance.

Trevor shouted first, his cock pulsing in Simon's grip. A spurt of come shot across his stomach. And without a sound, Simon started to come with him, their streams of come merging, becoming one.

She couldn't breathe, it made her so hot. She couldn't move, it made her so desperate. It should have appalled her, and yet it was so damn sexual, so uninhibited, so perfect.

She wanted that uninhibited perfection for herself. With Gabriel. Inside her, all over, everywhere. His nipples, his cock, every part of him. On her, in her, taking her in any way possible or imaginable.

She just didn't know how to ask for it without giving him the power.

DOMINIQUE SANK DOWN IN THE BACKSEAT OF THE CAB. SHE HADN'T driven, so she'd have the option of enjoying a glass or two of wine if she chose. The effects of the alcohol had long since worn off, but her mind still buzzed with a potent sensory intoxication. She couldn't have handled her car.

Wrapping her coat around her, she snuggled into the seat, closed her eyes. Her body still pulsed as if Gabriel had his hand between her legs. One would have thought Simon Foster's big hand would fill her imagination. But no, everything was still Gabriel. It was just *more*. Dirty, nasty, unbelievably delicious sex.

Simon had wanted to have sex with her while Trevor watched. Trevor had been in such a shell-shocked orgasmic aftermath that he'd barely been able to speak, let alone say what he wanted.

God help her, she'd needed something badly. She just didn't want it with Simon. The phantom feel of cock inside her belonged to Gabriel.

Dominique shuddered. She'd never wanted it like that with Edward. She'd loved Edward, but she'd never been all that into sex with him. They could go months without . . . and even then, everything was so vanilla. Was that part of the reason Edward left? He wanted a child, he wanted a wife who hadn't lost her libido, he wanted someone young. Maybe he also wanted a taste of something wild. Perhaps denying him that was her biggest mistake. In her defense, he'd never asked for anything outrageous or different.

And now she wanted wild. Badly. She was so consumed by her roiling emotions and needs, she'd almost walked out of the hotel room without her reward. Trevor had paid her in diamonds and emeralds. He'd been listening when she told him about the sheik's gift.

Yet all she could think of was Gabriel's come, almost as if she could taste it on her tongue.

She fished her cell phone from her purse and punched in his number. The call went directly to voice mail. He'd turned off his phone. Dammit. She fumed for a moment. Okay. It was a good thing. If he'd answered, she'd have begged for his address and had the cabdriver drop her off at his house. She listened to Gabriel's voice, imagining how he would have tantalized her with words as they'd watched Trevor tonight.

God. Why couldn't she stop? She closed her phone without leaving a message.

Thoughts tumbled around in her head. This wasn't about Gabriel. She was reacting to a very hot scene. Though she'd imagined him there with her, taking her from behind as she watched— well, that didn't mean anything. It was an extreme reaction to an extreme date. She hadn't done anything that outrageous before.

But she wanted it again. She was a vanilla courtesan. What she needed was adventure like she'd had tonight. Hot, exciting, thrilling adventure. She wasn't Mrs. Edward Lowe anymore. She was the new and improved Dominique.

Her clients weren't going to know what hit them.

And Gabriel? She would so completely seduce him, he wouldn't be able to get to his wallet fast enough.

# 8

THE AIRLINE ATTENDANT SERVED THEM CHAMPAGNE AT TEN o'clock in the morning. Dominique had hers laced with orange juice. Gabriel wasn't a champagne man, but he realized it was romantic.

She was different this morning. He couldn't put his finger on it, but she reminded him of a big cat excessively pleased with the kill she'd just made.

"Thank you for arranging a later flight."

"It was my pleasure. Anything to accommodate a lady."

She smiled, sipped her mimosa. First class was full, but the seats were large, comfortable, and the engines of the plane masked their conversation from eavesdroppers. The attendant brought a bowl of warmed cashews, setting it on the console between them. Dominique had kicked off her sandals and curled her legs beneath her. Turning her torso toward him and leaning in, she increased the intimacy of their seats and consumed a nut one tiny bite at a time. She licked the salt from her fingers, then followed it with a mimosa chaser. She fascinated him, her looks on a par with Grace Kelly's ageless beauty as she grew older.

"I trust you had a good evening." He shouldn't have asked, but he was a glutton for punishment.

Her smile grew, rose to her eyes with the glimmer of a secret. "It was marvelous, thank you."

"What did you do?" He could have rolled his eyes at his own idiocy, but he felt compelled, like a witness to a bloody crash.

She drew a daintily painted fingernail along the back of his hand. "I shouldn't say anything. It will terrify you."

"I assure you, if it doesn't involve a lot of violence, I'll muddle through."

Her flowery scent drifted around him, as intoxicating as champagne bubbles. "I was with two men," she whispered against his ear, then backed off to observe him.

He raised one brow. "A threesome?" Christ. His cock jumped, wanting to be a part of it.

"Not a threesome." Her lips rose in a half smile, and again that faraway secretive light shone in her eyes. "I watched." Then she looked at him. "Still say you aren't terrified?"

Holy shit. His cock turned to rock in his jeans. The idea of two men together did nothing for him, but that she would go so far did a hell of a lot. He hadn't thought of her as kinky. Then again, she was a courtesan, so why was he surprised? "And you enjoyed it?"

With a deep breath, her chest expanded beneath the tight, low-cut sequined top she wore with her black pants. A sexy, satisfied sigh slipped from her lips. "It ranked right up there with you and the limo."

"Amazing." At least he was close to the top of her list.

"Incredible." She batted her eyelashes. "I never thought something like that would turn me on."

"But it did," he murmured. Then he drew back, looked down at her. "But you're not expecting me . . ."

She trailed a finger down the arm of his long-sleeved shirt, letting it slide all the way to his thigh. "Don't worry. We're not going to have sex this weekend, remember?"

Yet her sexy scent teased him, made his balls fill with need and his cock ache. "I remember."

"I suppose it's equivalent to men liking to watch lesbian videos," she went on, leaning close again, her breasts brushing his arm, a beaded nipple tantalizing him.

"I've never really gotten into porn, at least not since I was in my teens."

She laughed softly, deeper than one of her full laughs, and he felt it inside like the subtle stroke of her fingers on his thigh. "Now you just get the real thing."

He shook his head. "More because I don't have time to search out something only to find it's total crap."

"I've never watched porn, I've only heard about it."

He chuckled low, matching her tone. "Yeah, right."

"No, it's true." She frowned a second. "I don't know even know why."

"It offended your sensibilities, I'm sure."

"It never occurred to me." She tipped her head and looked deep inside herself for a long second. "My husband never asked."

The deep look carried a measure of pain with it. "And now you've watched two men . . ." He let the words trail off. "I'm not sure I can bear to hear." But he wanted the tale, for the sake of hearing her tell it, reliving it. "It excited you."

She laid her temple against the seat back and gazed at him. "It was extraordinary. Like they knew exactly how to excite each other, the way to hold each other, manipulate for the greatest pleasure." She demonstrated with a twist of her wrist, then speared him with her gaze. "Is that how you jack off?"

Christ. There was a mixture of innocence and mischief in her eyes, wonder laced with a knowing. He pushed her hand down. "Someone might see that." Not that he cared. He liked the playfulness, the tease.

"But is that how you do it?" She stared him down.

He reached up and pressed the attendant button, never taking his eyes off Dominique. When the woman arrived, he asked for a blanket. "My lady friend is cold."

Reaching above, she handed down two, and smiled at his thank-you.

"What are you planning?" Dominique whispered.

Gabriel spread the blankets over her lap and his, finishing with the rasp of his zipper beneath the material. "Give me your hand."

Dominique glanced around, her blood pumping faster. "We cannot do that here." Especially with him directing the action. *She* was supposed to surprise and shock *him*. But God, she was warm and wet. This is what she craved after last night—risky business.

He grabbed her hand and pulled it beneath the blanket. "Oh yes, we can," he said, low and enticing.

His cock was already hard, his flesh heated, a tiny drop of moisture tracing her palm as he wrapped her fingers around him. "I'll show you how I do it," he murmured.

"I can't see." She didn't want to miss one lovely sight.

"You can feel."

Was this sex? Dominique didn't care. She let him guide her, following his movements, losing herself in the silky feel of his flesh. He pulled one hand out and yanked their blankets high on their chests, then abruptly ceased any movement.

"For breakfast, we have—"

He cut the stewardess off, directing his question to Dominique. "Are you hungry, sweetheart?"

Hell yes, she was hungry, but not for any food they offered in first class. "No, honey, I'm fine. And weren't you taking me to lunch when we get to Palm Springs?"

He drew his finger down her nose, and squeezed her hand around his cock until she felt the beat of his pulse through it.

"Whatever my lady wants, she gets." Then he raised his gaze to the attendant. "We'll pass, thanks."

"You are a bad man," Dominique murmured when they were alone again, or at least as alone as they could be on a plane. She glanced to her left. On the opposite aisle, an elderly gentleman snored, and next to him, his wife had her nose buried in a book.

Gabriel nuzzled her ear. "No one's watching."

She realized he wouldn't care if someone was. "This is sex," she whispered back.

"It's a demonstration." He moved her hand, twisting at the base the way Simon had, then back up, closing her fingers around the crown. Precome coated her thumb, forefinger, and palm.

"Like this," he said, pulling her down again, her pinkie finger hitting the open zipper of his black jeans.

"I can do that." She needed to do it, badly.

"I know you can." He tipped his head down, getting her to meet his gaze through her lashes. "You just have to be shown."

Her breath caught in her throat, trapped there by an overwhelming need to have this man. Here. Now. Make the mile-high club, as she'd heard it called.

"There's more." He seduced with a whisper, sliding her back up to the ridge beneath the crown. With only their thumbs and forefingers, they stroked right there, a fast, tight pump just below the ridge.

"Yeah." He groaned low, barely more than a rumble in his throat. "Just like that." Their hands bobbed beneath the blanket, then he tightened his grip, holding her still, encompassing the head. He shuddered, but didn't come.

"That was close. Almost went off." He smiled, capturing her eyes. "Can't come though. That would be considered sex."

Her skin flushed with heat, air almost painful in her throat, and her panties wet with need, she didn't give a damn about whether it was sex or not. She wanted it. And dammit, that's exactly what *he* wanted. Her capitulation.

No way. She was supposed to be teasing him to the point of begging, not the other way around. She would make him crazy.

Withdrawing her hand from beneath the blanket, she raised her damp fingers to her nose. First, her eyes closed, she scented his come, salty like sea air. Her mouth watered. Raising her lids, she mesmerized him with her gaze and her fingers on her lips. Then she let his taste take her under. Sliding one finger all the way in, she sucked and licked it clean as if it were his cock. God, the man was ambrosia. She'd never found the taste of come so sweet. It was Gabriel. It was the moment. It was the way his eyes darkened and his nostrils flared. She was getting to him.

She licked the rest from her palm, then closed her eyes with a hum of appreciation as if she'd eaten . . . bread pudding with brandy sauce at Vatovola's.

"You're going to pay for that," he murmured.

She opened her eyes, smiling with a self-satisfied grin she knew would make him nuts. "I like come," she said. She'd never have said that before. Yes, she'd sucked men's cocks and she'd swallowed, but she'd never . . . savored any of it the way she did his. Why not admit it? "But I *love* your come."

"Wench," he muttered, followed by the rasp of his zipper.

"Slut," she purred, "and proud of it."

Then he grabbed her hand and sucked her finger just as she'd done. "You will dine on my come one of these nights."

Yes. She would. She might even do it without payment.

HE'D BOOKED AT A SUMPTUOUS RESORT WITH A SUITE FACING THE golf course. In Palm Springs, everything was on a golf course. He gave her the large bedroom with the Jacuzzi tub and took the smaller room. The beds, however, were of equal size. She could do him in either. She could even do him in the tub. The living room and full kitchen lay between them like an ocean.

They met in the middle.

"Would you like a swim?" she asked. They'd passed a massive pool complex on the way in.

"How about a little shopping instead?"

"Shopping?" What man liked to shop?

"I'd like to buy you a special outfit for tonight."

An outfit didn't constitute payment. Okay, maybe if it was designer quality.

"It's just a gift," he said, "not a *gift*."

All right, not payment. "I brought a short strapless cocktail dress."

"Will you allow me the pleasure of picking for you?"

He waited. She couldn't read his expression.

"I've never dressed a woman before. I'd like to try."

Edward had never chosen her clothing. Most of the time, he barely seemed to notice. She couldn't have anticipated the thrill Gabriel's desire would give her, a rush of pleasure straight to her chest. "That would be very nice."

He took her to El Paseo Drive in Palm Desert, which was considered the Rodeo Drive of the Palm Springs area. Good Lord, the man had actually researched on the Internet. The store names sported all the major designers and some she didn't even recognize. The weather was exceedingly warm even for February, in the low eighties. She'd changed into sandals and a short sundress that left her shoulders bare.

He directed everything, choosing outfits for her to model, from sexy cocktail dresses to long evening gowns.

"Let's find something with a little more cleavage showing," he told a salesgirl in one exclusive little boutique, then waved her away to do his bidding. The threat of exposure sent a thrill through Dominique, straight to her pussy.

"We need something tighter," he instructed an older female clerk at the fifth store they entered, then winked at Dominique. Her heart fluttered in her chest.

He had her parade before him, circling his fingers for her to turn, giving him a three-sixty view.

In a corner jewelry store, he fastened diamonds at her throat, sapphires at her wrist, and silver around her ankle. His light touches made her tremble. In the end, he chose the anklet.

Of course, nothing had price tags, and he didn't let her see the bill. "This isn't payment for sex," he said as he carried the packages to her room in the suite.

"Certainly not." Yet the gifts delighted her.

"I simply wanted to dress you in beautiful things."

The sentiment made her stomach fluttery.

He flipped his wrist to glance at his watch. "I've got reservations in two hours." He glanced up, a smile lurking in his eyes. "Enough time to get ready?"

"Barely," she said dryly, "but I'll make it."

She ran a bath in the huge tub and soaked with the fragrant salts provided. Dreamily she imagined him with her, what she'd do to him, what she'd have him do to her. She lay back, a hand between her legs in an idle stroke. She didn't want to come, just heighten the desire. Then, finally, she took care of all the necessary womanly activities. Everything was in the prep.

The short black velvet dress he'd chosen caressed her bare skin as she slipped it over her head. The cut was low, with a squared neckline revealing her breasts almost to her nipples. The sleeves were long, thank God, keeping her warm. The dress was smooth over her abdomen, then the skirt flared, reaching to her knees, and he'd given her black thigh-highs and a lacy thong to wear beneath. Balancing one foot on the edge of the tub, she fastened the silver anklet. Instead of jewels, he'd opted for tiny bells. "So I can hear you coming," he'd whispered in her ear.

The double entendre heated her through.

He'd finished her off with high-heeled strappy sandals. Standing before the mirror, twisting from side to side, she glowed with how perfect the outfit was. Red hair, green eyes, and all black.

He was already in the living room and looking luscious in a black tux and charcoal shirt.

"Do you ever wear anything besides black?" she asked.

"Black is easy: I always match." Then he raised one brow devilishly. "And I match you perfectly."

He didn't say she looked gorgeous, but his eyes followed the length of the dress all the way to the fuck-me high heels and back up, sweeping her breasts and nipples, then rising to her face. "I was remiss in not getting you a necklace." Then he held out a matching velvet cape. "You're going to need this."

That look of his made her tremble as she wrapped herself in the luxury. "Where are we going?"

He shook a finger. "It's a surprise."

God, she wanted his surprise. Badly.

She wanted so badly, she was in danger of paying him to give her what she craved.

# 9

HALF AN HOUR LATER, THEY PULLED INTO THE LOT AT THE BASE of one of the area's largest mountains. Rising like a behemoth, it blended into the night sky behind a low-slung building.

"They're open after dark?" She'd been to Palm Springs before, but never taken the tram to the top.

"They're open to us," he said, climbing out and coming around to her door.

The night air bit into her cheeks as she stepped out. She pulled the velvet cape close. The building was empty, with few lights gleaming. Gabriel rapped on the glass door. An elderly man unlocked and let them in, then led them to the tram.

She gazed at Gabriel in awe. "You rented this just for *us?*"

"You challenged me. Our date had to be spectacular."

No man—not Edward, not a client—had ever done anything like this for her. What was Gabriel trying to prove? All he had to do was pay her what she was worth and she'd sleep with him.

The tram car itself had a heater, yet once they were in and the door closed, Gabriel moved close behind her and wrapped her in his arms. Framed in the building's window, the elderly gentleman tapped a few controls, and the car pulled away, rotating slowly as they rose above the valley floor.

"It rotates three hundred sixty degrees," Gabriel said at her ear. "You won't see as much at night, except the lights."

The lights of Palm Springs and the surrounding towns looked like a thick carpet of bright stars. Far out they ended and gave way to another rise of mountains silhouetted in the distance. Dark against darker, then above, the twinkle of real stars.

"It's gorgeous," she whispered as the tram car turned slowly, revealing more lights, more city, more mountain.

"Yes." He leaned over her shoulder, his cheek close to hers as he nuzzled her hair. "You smell like grapefruit."

She laughed. "I found grapefruit bath salts by the tub."

He tightened his arm beneath her breasts, easing her ever closer against the bulge of his cock at the small of her back.

He licked the nape of her neck. "It tastes good, too."

She felt so warm, so mesmerized by the slow turn of the car, his heat surrounding her, his scent, something subtly spicy with a hint of musk. And the soft kiss of his lips against her neck.

"I bet you taste like this everywhere." He caressed her belly, then made a brief foray between her legs.

She thought her knees would collapse. They might have if she hadn't been leaning against him. God, she needed sex, she needed him. Her body moistened, readying her. Her mouth watered, anticipating the salty deliciousness of his cock.

"You're trying to seduce me," she murmured as the car turned slowly away from the light, into the darkness of the mountain.

"Is it working?"

She laughed softly. God yes. "I once heard someone say that oral sex wasn't sex." She turned in his arms, setting her hands on his shoulders. "It might have been an ex-president."

"Then it definitely must be true." He leaned back far enough for her to see the sparkle of stars in his eyes. "Does that mean it's okay for me to bury my face in your hot pussy?"

His dirty talk excited her, the thrill of it pebbling her nipples. "It means that as long as I don't swallow, I can suck."

Against her, his cock surged. She rubbed him with her abdomen. He clamped his hand on her butt and rocked harder. "I'm okay if you don't swallow."

"Okay" wasn't good enough. She waited for him to beg.

"But you want to swallow all of me, don't you?" More sparkle in his eyes.

The car revolved, the lights now appearing behind him, and his gaze became a dark pool of desire.

"I can take it or leave it," she lied. She wanted his taste on her lips, her tongue, sliding down her throat, filling her. "But only if I don't ruin my lipstick."

He took her mouth in a hard kiss, licking, sucking, going deep, backing off, taking her again. Until she couldn't think, couldn't breathe, couldn't stop wanting.

The car jerked to a stop as they docked at the top.

If the ride had lasted five more minutes, they would have arrived with her down on her knees, his cock in her mouth, and she damn well wouldn't have cared who saw.

The man was too potent.

The bells on her anklet jingled as Gabriel guided her from the tram, past a young man who'd been handling the controls. Gabriel smiled and handed the boy a bill just as he had the older guy manning the control box at the bottom.

"Up the stairs, sir," the kid said. "The observation deck is pretty much freezing right now, but you can see virtually the same view from the restaurant."

The lights were low, perhaps only a quarter of the normal number lit, as Gabriel ushered her to the top of the stairs and pushed through a set of glass doors to the outside.

The wind blasted them, the cold bite of mountain air tearing through her velvet. Gabriel pulled her to the railing, then co-cooned her with his body heat as he had on the tram. "Isn't it the most magnificent sight you've ever seen?"

The wind roared so loudly, he had to yell, and yet it was beautiful, the lights across the valley floor, then the darkness of the mountains opposite. The puniness of man's creations against the vast awesomeness of nature. She felt small against it, yet special in Gabriel's embrace. His touch transformed the sight from simply beautiful to absolutely spectacular.

Tears stung her eyes from the brutal cold whipping past them. Yet for this moment, there was nowhere else she wanted to be, wrapped in Gabriel's strength and warmth, safe.

Then he pulled her back inside. The howl of the wind still rung in her ears. Gabriel traced a finger beneath her eyes, gathering the moisture. "You had to feel it, you had to see it."

She had to feel *him*, see *him*. The view was immense, but Gabriel was here and now, bigger and better. "I have to fix my lipstick," she said because she was afraid anything else might reveal the feelings that had swamped her out on the observation deck.

He took her hand. "Your lipstick is perfect."

She knew it wasn't, but she let him guide her along the hall, a row of floor lights leading the way, moonlight falling through the windows. Up another flight of steps, they entered the restaurant, where again, the lights were low, candles on the tables bathing everything with an intimate glow.

An unobtrusive piano instrumental filled the room from hidden speakers. Gabriel led her to a table at the bank of windows overlooking the city lights and pulled out a seat for her. Taking her cloak, he laid it across a chair back behind them. Then he sat beside her, facing the glorious view without the wind biting through their clothing. Champagne chilled in a bucket. French bread and salad had already been laid out, a silver dish brimming with dressing. She didn't see the waitstaff but they were obviously there somewhere.

With only the candle sending flickers of light across the table, their reflections in the window didn't obscure the vista beyond the glass. "You thought of everything."

He smiled. "Best date ever?"

"Fishing for compliments?"

"Just wanting to know if you're ready to beg."

She couldn't help the laugh escaping. "I'll never beg." Never say never. "I didn't say you had to give me the best date. I just said you had to show me the proper appreciation."

Tilting the glass, he poured her champagne without foaming it over. "Appreciation isn't about money or gifts. It's treating you the way you deserve to be treated."

Edward had money; she hadn't lacked for comfort. Yet every present he gave her was ordered by his secretary, every vacation she arranged herself. And on a beach in Hawaii, he was on the phone conducting business. Even during sex, she felt as if he were thinking about what stock he'd purchase as soon as the market opened. Maybe that's why she'd been so vanilla.

She hadn't once seen Gabriel's phone since the taxi had picked him up at his home this morning for the ride to the airport.

He tapped his champagne to her flute. "Drink." Sipping, he watched her over the rim of his glass.

She was afraid to ask why he thought *she* was worth being treated this way.

"I was the best man at a friend's wedding right out of college."

She spooned a creamy dressing on her salad as he talked.

"His fiancée wanted a massive engagement ring that cost fifteen thousand dollars."

"Fifteen isn't much." She raised her hand in question, and he indicated for her to drizzle dressing over his salad, too.

"It's a helluva lot if you're fresh out of college, starting your first job, and you haven't got a trust fund to live on."

"Did *you* have a trust fund?" The salad was a mixture of bitter greens, sweet mandarins, and Italian spices.

"No." Flat tone, steady gaze. She'd already pegged him for a self-made man. "Back then, fifteen thousand was a down payment on a modest starter home in the East Bay, but she believed the cost of the ring showed how much he appreciated what he was getting in a wife."

Dominique didn't miss his emphasis on *appreciated*. "Did he buy her the house later?"

"Yeah." He speared his salad, but didn't raise the fork. "Then she divorced him because he wasn't making enough money, and took the house, the car, and the kids."

She tipped her head to eye him. "And the moral of the story is that a greedy woman ends up screwing you over?"

He laughed from deep in his belly. "The moral is that money doesn't buy happiness."

She smiled with him. "You're trying to weasel out of paying."

His gaze turned serious, and he put a finger to her chin to hold her. "Maybe you're worth more than trinkets and cash. Maybe I'd like to find out how much more."

She trembled beneath his touch. She'd had more than enough men in the past few months, received a veritable fortune by some standards, yet somehow, she still hadn't proven to herself that she deserved more than being divorced for a younger woman.

Gabriel gave her more worth than mere money.

Behind them, the subtle sounds of pots and china underscored the gentle instrumental through the speakers. Instead of answering him, Dominique tasted a mandarin spiked with the Italian dressing.

It was the bastard husband that had done this to her. Gabriel would have liked to beat the man senseless. On the one hand, she was gorgeous and confident. But beneath that lay the need to be shown. A tangible demonstration.

Still, he wanted to taste her and take her without the transaction between them. He wanted Dominique as a woman, not an object he had to buy. The dress, cape, and lingerie, even the jewelry—they weren't payment. He'd simply picked out what she would be wearing when he buried himself deep inside her. He'd remove the panties, but the rest would remain.

"Are you done with your salads, sir?"

Gabriel hadn't heard the waiter approach, nor had he realized their plates were almost empty. Too much damn thinking instead of doing. In the tram car, he'd almost had her on her knees with her luscious lips around his cock. He wasn't taking proper advantage of his opportunities.

"I'm finished," Dominique said, leaning back slightly so the waiter could whisk away the plate.

He was barely beyond his teens, blond, tanned, and lusty, his eyes drinking in Dominique's cleavage. She didn't glance up or she would have seen. She was a beautiful woman who attracted men young and old. She didn't need paying clients to keep proving it to her.

Alone with her once again, Gabriel ran a finger along the edge of her bodice, skimming her breasts, easing close to her nipples. She grabbed his hand and shot a look behind them, to the dark recesses of the restaurant and the door through which their server had disappeared. "What are you doing?"

He removed her grip, then deliberately pushed the material lower to reveal a touch of nipple, the beads already peaked. "He was looking. I made it easier for him."

She tugged the dress higher. "He's just a boy."

"I liked watching him try to sneak a peek."

She huffed, but candlelight sparkled in her eyes. "That's naughty."

This time when he ran a finger over her nipple and pushed the bodice down, she didn't stop him. Her cheeks colored. He could almost hear the beat of her heart. "There, perfect."

"Now why would you want to let that boy see my breasts?"

"He's not a boy, and I want you to see that he's looking." Then, holding her gaze, he raised the skirt, revealing the lace tops of her stockings.

The creak of the kitchen's swing door alerted them.

He saw her swallow, heard the intake of breath and the slow exhale. Closing his eyes, he drank in her scent, grapefruit and hot, creamy woman.

"Lobster for you, sir." The waiter slid the plate in front of him, then rounded the backs of their chairs. Holding Dominique's dinner, he took the time to rearrange her utensils. Slowly. Getting them just right though his gaze wasn't on the table at all. "And crab legs for the lady."

Dominique smiled up at him. "Thank you so much."

"My pleasure, ma'am. If you need anything, don't hesitate to ask." His glance fell to her lap, then he backed away, and turned on his heel.

Gabriel put his hand between her legs. "You're wet."

Her skin flushed pink, yet she pushed him away. "Behave."

Little liar. She wanted his touch badly. "I was going to reprimand him for serving me first, but I realized it was by design." One elbow on the table, he raised her tiny crab fork. "Would you like me to rearrange the cutlery for you?"

With a barely there smile curving her lips, she pretended to ignore him. Tucking into her crab legs, she daintily pulled the meat from the already cracked shell, but the little fork left half of it behind.

"Eat with your fingers," he said.

She tipped her head, looked at him through her lashes, and continued digging with the fork.

He pulled apart his lobster, tore off a piece of the tail, dipped it in butter, then held it out to her. "Try it."

When she reached for it, he pulled back. "From my fingers."

A drop of butter landed on her lips as she took the white lobster between her teeth. He didn't let go, so she licked his fingers, the butter, the lobster, him. If it had been his cock, he'd have blown sky high. As it was, he pulsed in his tux pants.

Her green eyes darkened to a deep emerald, glittering in the candlelight. A gust of wind buffeted the window. Overhead, the music hit a faster beat.

"Feed me," he murmured. He'd almost said *Fuck me*.

"How did you know I liked crab better than lobster?" She pulled out a hunk with her fingers, dipped it.

"I didn't. I thought we'd share."

She offered the succulent morsel to him. He took it, going for *her* succulent morsel at the same time. Licking her fingers, he slid his hand up her leg to the lace edge of the thong, then slipped beneath.

Sitting back, she parted her legs slightly to give him better access. The ankle bells tinkled as if signaling her arousal. "Is the crab good?" she asked, pretending his hand wasn't between her legs.

"Excellent." Her pussy was warm, wet, delicious.

She gasped when he hit just the right spot. "Would you like another piece?"

"Oh yeah." He almost groaned, wanting her badly.

Instead of crab, she fed him lobster from his own plate. As she drew the butter and meat along his lips, she raised her hips, arching into his touch, her breath ragged, the ankle bells going off again.

He finished the juicy bit of lobster meat. "Do you want more?" he asked.

"Yes." She turned her head, gazed at him with a deep, sensual caress. "More."

He slid deeper into her pussy, running his thumb over her clit at the same time. With his free hand, he grabbed a hunk of crab meat already drenched in butter and put it to her mouth. "Open."

She tugged her skirt high, exposing the strip of curls arrowing down to her pussy, his hand against her pink flesh. Accepting the crab from his fingertips, she closed her eyes, licked her lips.

He wanted to taste her, bury his tongue against her clit, and make her scream.

"I think this might be sex," she whispered.

"Nah. It's eating." He shot her a big grin, but God, he wanted to feast on her.

# 10

"SEMANTICS," DOMINIQUE SAID ON A GASP AS GABRIEL HIT A PAR-
ticularly sensitive spot inside. This time, instead of going for a bite
of lobster, she went for his cock, stroking him through his pants.

Gabriel closed his eyes, gritted his teeth.

It was like that first night. In such a short time, Gabriel had
made her crazy. Except that they'd been teasing each other all day,
building to this moment.

"If it's not sex, then I want your cock in my mouth." She
didn't care that the young waiter could swing through the door
without warning. The thought sent a jolt to her clitoris. Almost as
if she were preening for an audience, she stretched, ran her fingers
through her hair, then down over her breasts.

Oh yeah, the waiter could watch. Gabriel made her want to
push her limits, do things she'd never done.

His eyes sparked brighter than the candle flame on the table,
but his hand never let up on the delicious play between her legs.
"As long as you don't make me come while you're sucking," he
said, "it's not sex and everyone wins."

She was skirting around her own rules. No sex on the first date,
no sex without money. So now they simply changed the definition
of sex. If it worked for a president, it certainly worked for her.

She pushed him back in his chair, his hand falling away. She was on the edge, her body humming, and holding off would make the pleasure that much greater. Anticipation was 50 percent of the turn-on.

Then he licked his fingers clean, tasting her, closing his eyes to savor her, the sight spiking her desire.

She rose far enough to tap the chair out of the way, her anklet chiming. "Push away from the table," she instructed.

Positioning his chair, he yanked her to her knees between his legs. Right where she wanted to be. His cock bulged in his pants, stretching the seams almost beyond their limits.

She'd dreamed of this in the deepest part of the night. A light perfume of male arousal rose off him, musky, salty, a taste and a scent all rolled into one.

She was a courtesan, she was trained, yet she fumbled with his buckle and zipper. He didn't tell her to slow down, but put his hand over hers and helped. Together they pulled his cock free.

"God." She was awed all over again. "You're beautiful."

He chuckled, then pressed a kiss to her forehead. "No one's ever called my cock beautiful before."

She smiled as a bead of pre-come pearled on the tip. Biting her lip, she dragged in his sensual scent, let it fill her up. Then she bent to swipe away the droplet with her tongue. Tilting her head back, her eyes on his, she relished the sweet taste. His eyes darkened, glowed. She didn't want to rush. She wanted to savor him.

"Take me," he whispered, his need seducing her.

Wrapping her hand around his cock, she slid down over the crown, sucking hard just there, then soothing with a lick, her tongue along the little slit. He put his hand on the back of her head and rocked into her.

She reached beneath him, on the outside of his slacks, and cupped his balls, squeezed. His whole body tensed.

"Christ," he groaned, and she glanced up. Lines of strain and desire etched his face, and he watched with an avid light. "More. Please."

She'd never done this right for Edward. She'd never made him look at her that way. Gabriel was a gift. His need fueled her own. His arousal deepened hers. She lifted her hand from him and slid all the way down, as far as she could. He was so much, so big. His tip caressed the back of her throat. She sucked hard on the retreat, grazed him lightly with her teeth all the way back up to the ridge of his crown.

His hand on the back of her head guided her down again; a hand on her cheek set her pace. But then she backed off again to feast on the droplets of come at the tip.

"Easy," he murmured. "Or I'll come."

He was beautiful, he was delicious. She wanted all his come, she needed everything. She raised her eyes, his cock still fully between her lips, then slid slowly off, feeling him pop free. He still rested between her lips, and she drowned in his musky scent, his hot gaze, the flare of his nostrils.

"Then come for me," Dominique invited, a wicked smile on her lips. "I'm pretty sure it's not sex unless there's penetration."

SHE WAS SO GORGEOUS DOWN ON HER KNEES BETWEEN HIS LEGS, the glimmer of his come on her lips, his cock so close yet so far. He didn't want to come in her mouth. He wanted inside her.

And Gabriel gave in.

"You want me to beg, I'll beg." He held her chin tight, forced her to look at him. "I'm begging to fuck you."

For the longest moment of his life, she simply returned his gaze, then her eyes touched his cheeks, his mouth, and finally, God, after fucking forever, she said, "I'm begging you to do it."

That was all it took. Gabriel pulled her up, rising with her, grabbed her hips, his fingers slipping on the sleek velvet. Spinning her to face the chair, he planted her hands firmly on the back.

Then he raised the dress. The globes of her ass were creamy buttermilk, her skin smooth as glass.

Something flickered to his left. A face, shadows, at the window in the kitchen door. "They're watching," he told her.

She glanced at him over her shoulder, light beaming in her eyes, a glow to her skin. "I know."

Pushing the dress higher, he angled her for the perfect view, better than anything beyond the huge picture windows. He stroked down to her center and the drenched crotch of her thong. "You love that the boy's watching, don't you"—it wasn't a question—"that he's called them all to watch." The cook, the washer, the waiter, the candlestick maker, even the kid that let them in. "Tell me how hot it makes you."

She moaned, focusing on the swing door. "It's unbearable." She slipped her hand inside her panties, her fingers moving beneath the material. "I'm so wet." She tipped her head back over her shoulder, gave him the most sultry of looks. "I need to put on the best show."

He fell into her gaze, into the playfulness and the heat of her. "Lose the panties."

Even as she started to wriggle out of the lacy thong, setting the ankle bells to jangling, he caught his fingers in the edge, gliding his hands over her delectable rump. He kissed her ass as together they shoved the thong down her legs.

"Do I look forty-five?"

She'd never said her age, but he'd guessed. It wasn't so much looking her age, with the negative connotations, as much as walking, talking, and owning the self-confidence a younger woman couldn't hope to achieve. Yet everyone had vulnerabilities. Dominique needed reassurance. He wanted to give it to her. Her need ratcheted his desire up a notch, pulsed through his cock. "You're the best damn fucking forty-five I've ever seen."

She sighed with a throaty purr, obviously pleased. "Then you better fuck me before I get a minute older."

"My pleasure." He donned a condom quickly, then stroked his dick along the crease of her ass to her moist opening. Sliding forward in all her succulent, fragrant juice, he coated himself in her natural lube, nudged her clit until she moaned.

It was a show, all right. The best. Her hip secured in one hand, he guided his cock to her sweet pussy and buried just the head inside her. Flexing his hips, he pulsated right there, short little bursts.

"Oh God." She widened her stance, gave him better access, then slipped one hand between her legs to caress her clit.

It was slow, languorous fucking, the angle of their stance giving their audience a clear shot of cock taking her. The kitchen lights were out now, to improve the view, the window in the door a dark hole. And he felt them just on the other side.

Sliding an inch deeper, he pumped short and fast, loving the gasp that fell from her lips. "Is it good?" He wanted her words, her sweet voice.

"It's so good, Gabriel." Her fast breath threaded through her voice. "Fuck me harder, fuck me deeper. Please, Gabriel." She ended on a sob of need and desire.

She was a lady. She was a whore. He wanted both. "Beg me," he whispered.

She bounced against him, driving him home, high and deep. "Please, please, please, please. I need it, Gabriel. Fuck me good. Fuck me hard." She gasped as he gave it to her. "I think this is sex," she muttered, ending with a low moan.

"It sure as fuck is." She made his balls ache, so full they'd burst any second. "You only want it to be me, don't you."

"Yes, Gabriel, only you. Only your cock." She cried out, her pussy contracting, milking him, her orgasm dragging him under.

He came, hard, gut-wrenching, knowing he'd never survive another man taking her this way.

Dominique was his now. And he was hers.


*MINE, MINE.*

Gabriel's words echoed as she lay against his chest, his heart beating beneath her ear. When they'd arrived back at the resort, he'd taken her to his bed, fucked her delirious again, then fallen asleep with his arm anchoring her securely to him.

They'd never made it to dessert. Gabriel had gathered her up, laid her cloak around her shoulders, and whispered that he needed to get her home. Home, the hotel. The young man operating the tram had been flushed, sweaty, unable to meet her eye, fixated on her chest. His wide-eyed look had loosed a rush of moisture in her.

On the way down, she'd taken Gabriel's hand between her legs and ridden his fingers to another shuddering climax, her arms and the cape wrapped around his shoulders.

She couldn't get enough of him. The idea set her trembling against his sleeping body.

The dark surrounding them, the hum of the air conditioner, his sweaty sexy male scent tantalizing her nostrils—she wanted more, she wanted it all. She'd never bargained for this.

After the glow of new love had worn off her marriage, Edward had stopped the compliments and the late-night talks snuggled in bed. But she'd become dependent on those things, and struggled to get them back, thinking of a million ways that never worked. The hysterectomy had been the end. She'd been too stupid to see it, and Edward had been too lazy to do anything about it.

Until he hit fifty and dumped her. Maybe it was his need for a child. Maybe it was his desire for a young wife with whom he could relive his youth. Whatever the reason, it was *his* midlife crisis and hadn't had a thing to do with her. Nothing she did would have changed the outcome. She recognized it so clearly now. Perhaps her feelings for Gabriel had ripped the blindfold from her eyes.

She loved how Gabriel made her feel, the brush of his hand on her skin, how he'd dressed her for his pleasure, the way he fucked her for their audience. He didn't care that she was middle-aged. He'd raised her out of the despair she felt if she thought too long about Edward, Francine, the baby.

When she was with Gabriel, Edward ceased to exist. No other man had done that. Not the sheik with his thirty-thousand-dollar gift. Not Trevor with ten thousand dollars or diamonds and emeralds. No amount of money, no present, made her forget. It only gave her power when she imagined showing Edward her worth to other men.

Gabriel made her powerful without the symbol.

But she was new and different to him. Just as she'd been new and different for Edward in the beginning. She couldn't depend on Gabriel to go on making her feel that way. And when he was gone, she'd feel lower than she had since the day Edward dumped her. As low as the evening she'd faced Francine's pregnant belly and borne witness to the woman's motherly glow.

As Gabriel's breathing evened out and his body relaxed, still she didn't sleep. She was thinking. Thinking was never a good thing. You discovered truths you didn't want to see. Just as she could have done nothing to make Edward stay, when Gabriel got tired, she had no arsenal of foolproof feminine wiles to keep him.

She could wait for the newness to wear off. Or she could end this before she got to the point where she couldn't live without him. When she'd met Isabel, she swore she'd never be emotionally dependent on a man again, yet here she was close to falling into that trap.

Dominique slipped from beneath his arm. Gabriel didn't stir. Sex had zonked him out. Good sex. Fantastic sex. Out-of-this-world sex. No, it wasn't just sex. It was something more.

She was in so much trouble. She'd survived Edward, but she couldn't do it again.

It was three in the morning, but the front desk was manned. If you're willing to pay, you can get anything. Within twenty minutes, she was behind the wheel of a rental car heading out to the freeway. The desk clerk had been kind enough to print out directions navigating her through LA. She'd be home by noon, before Gabriel even stepped on the plane.

"SONUVABITCH," HE MUTTERED, DOMINIQUE'S NOTE IN HIS HAND, dawn still an hour away, the inky blackness of night broken only by the stars hovering over the golf course.

At least she'd left him a freaking note so he wouldn't think she'd been abducted by aliens or kidnapped by a serial killer. Not that the note said much besides thanks for a great time, wanted to get home early, have a nice life.

What the fuck? He didn't know where she lived; he had only the number for Isabel and Courtesans.

He called as soon as the sun came up. It was Sunday; no one answered. The voice-mail voice sounded like a sweet young thing, and he left a message.

When he got off the plane in San Francisco, he had a reply.

"This is Isabel of Courtesans. I'm sorry to inform you that Dominique's number has been changed with no forwarding. If you'd like to inquire further, please feel free to call again."

*Feel free to call again and get the same fucking answer.*

Goddammit. He wasn't a man who liked to overanalyze his actions, but last night had been fucking perfect. He'd *made* it perfect for her.

So why had she left in the middle of the night?

# 11

ANOTHER WEEKEND, ANOTHER PARTY. DOMINIQUE WAS BORED OUT of her skull. The laughter was too high pitched in the hotel ballroom, too much perfume drifted in the air, and the crush of bodies stifled her. For the first month, she'd been afraid she'd run into Gabriel at one of these events. But she hadn't. Nor had she stumbled across Edward or his luscious Francine. She would have preferred that over facing Gabriel.

If she saw him, she might bleed.

It had been two months since Palm Springs, but she'd recognized her mistake after only a week. It was too late to get out unscathed. Her need for him had already taken root, and like a bulb lying dormant through the winter, she'd woken one morning and found her feelings had blossomed with the warmer weather.

She'd been on several dates, but not one single man had passed muster. There was always something wrong.

"Darling, I've got your champagne cocktail." Timothy Alten III handed her the fresh bubbly.

He was British, and she didn't like the way he called her darling. She appreciated that he was tall—the same height as Gabriel—but she didn't like that he was so skinny. She wanted muscles and strength. Like Gabriel. She admired the gray shots in his dark hair—it reminded her of Gabriel—but the strands were stuck to his head with too much gel. She couldn't run her fingers through his hair—like she'd done with Gabriel—without the *ick* factor.

Other than that, Timothy Alten III was fine.

But . . . "This music is giving me an enormous headache, darling." She couldn't resist the slight emphasis on the word. "I'm going to the powder room for a bit."

Her inner voice screamed, *Get me out of here!*

"I'll be right here when you get back." Timothy smiled.

He was sweet, pleasant, polite, and rich. The problem was her. She was Total Numero Uno Bitch.

She put her fingers to her temples, massaging as she passed through the double ballroom doors. This had to stop. She shouldn't treat her clients this way. She couldn't keep comparing them to Gabriel. None of them stacked up.

"Dominique?"

She snapped her head up, two bodies suddenly looming in front of her. In the teeming lobby, she'd almost run headlong right into them. Then she stared. "Trevor?"

He smiled. It wasn't malicious, it was . . . nice. She almost didn't recognize him with that smile. "I can't believe you forgot me so quickly," he said. "I could never forget you."

Oh God. That night. The night before that night with Gabriel. See how everything reminded her of Gabriel? Pathetic.

But, God, her eyes burned with how much she missed him.

"You look good, Trevor." And he did. He was dressed as nattily as before, but he'd grown a goatee, and there was something about that smile of his.

It was completely genuine.

"I want you to meet Raymond."

She glanced at Raymond, held out her hand. "It's so nice to meet you, Raymond."

Raymond stood a head taller than Trevor, and the lack of lines on his smooth face said he was perhaps five years younger. His tailored suit accentuated a lean, hard body. His black hair was artfully mussed, and his lips curved in a sly, sexy Brad Pitt smile.

Raymond didn't let go of her hand. Instead he engulfed it both of his. "Trevor's told me all about you, so I'm glad to finally get to meet the icon."

She glanced at Trevor. He beamed through his goatee. What was going on? "I didn't know I'd become anyone's icon." Maybe it was the fact that she was darn near old enough to be this boy's mother.

Then Raymond smiled at Trevor, and electricity arced between them. They didn't touch, but Trevor's gaze, the way it flitted over Raymond's face, lighting on his eyes, then his lips . . .

Good God. They were a *couple*.

"You made me see what I was missing," Trevor said.

"I didn't do anything."

"You helped me accept the part of myself I'd been denying."

Her breath wouldn't seem to work its way out of her lungs.

Raymond pressed her hand. "And I'm the one who benefited. We never would have found each other."

"I didn't do that." She felt small, mean. Trevor had done it on his own after she'd tried to force him. *He'd* faced himself. *He'd* accepted himself. It had nothing to do with *her*. She'd been Lucrezia Borgia. True, she'd fed him a fantasy she believed he'd entertained, but so many of the reasons she'd done it had been about her own needs, not Trevor's.

Trevor linked pinkies with her, turning the three of them into a triangle. "You're so modest. That's what courtesans do; they fulfill your greatest fantasy and change your life." He kissed her cheek.

"Sweetheart, it was worth every dollar," he whispered against her ear. "I should have paid more." He grabbed Raymond, laced fingers with him, then held up their clasped hands. "See? I'm not afraid. I want everyone to know how happy I am."

Dominique swallowed, her eyes blurring with moisture.

"Don't cry, honey," Raymond said. "This is a good thing."

She sniffled, willed the tears away. They weren't for these two; they were for her own idiocy. "It's just that I'm so happy for you both." And she was dying inside.

Trevor had had the courage to jump for what he wanted. To change. To accept. He'd been afraid, but he'd conquered.

While she'd run away in the dark of the night, a coward.

"I'm so glad what we did wasn't a mistake." Not like *her* mistake, where what she needed was standing right in front of her and she'd been too afraid to grab it. All the power-mongering she'd been getting off on since Edward left had not rejuvenated her. The tenderness Gabriel showed had accomplished that. Yet she'd walked away from him and forever doomed herself to punishing men for what Edward had done. Forever punishing *herself*. Gabriel was right: money and revenge didn't buy happiness.

Trevor shook his head slowly. "It was the best mistake I ever made."

Raymond squeezed her hand again. "But don't let us keep you. You were on your way somewhere."

She was on her way to hide in the ladies' room. She'd done a lot of hiding in ladies' rooms. And a lot of running.

On impulse, she kissed first Raymond's cheek, then Trevor's. "Thank you."

"What for?" Trevor asked, eyebrow raised.

"For opening my eyes the way I opened yours."

"Sure, sugar."

She left them wearing the cutest bewildered expressions.

If Trevor McDowell could set himself free from his fears, then she could do no less.

IT WAS ALMOST ELEVEN AS DOMINIQUE PULLED HER CAR INTO Gabriel's circular drive. Light fell through the curtained front windows of the long bungalow, and two Chinese-style lanterns illuminated the stone stoop. He was home. Her heart stuttered, then raced.

She'd driven her own car up to the city tonight because she didn't want to wait on a driver. Even before she left home, she'd been subconsciously planning her escape from Timothy Alten. All the way down here from the city, she'd rehearsed what she would say to Gabriel, yet now the glib words flew out of her head. A rush of nervousness cooled her blood all the way to her fingers and toes.

*You can do this. You want to do this. You need to do this.* She had to move past being a divorcee, and she wanted to step forward with Gabriel. But then she wondered if he'd even been asking for that. He'd only ever said he wanted sex without paying.

If she sat in his driveway much longer with the engine running, he'd hear and wonder what the hell was going on. Shutting off the car, she grabbed her purse and climbed out. Her high heels tapped the concrete all the way to his door. She pulled in a breath and held it as she pushed the bell, a simple *ding-dong* inside.

Waiting, waiting, she was aware of her quickened heartbeat and a low buzz of nervousness in her arms and hands.

Footsteps, the doorknob turned, and she wanted to run as badly as she wanted to throw herself at him.

The entry lamp backlighted him, disguising his eyes, yet he was beautiful in his usual black, casual tonight in jeans and a button-down shirt.

One second, two seconds, three. She found her voice. "I wanted to apologize for running out on you in Palm Springs."

He kept one hand on the door as if afraid she might try to leap past him and he'd never get rid of her. "It was the first time a woman has rented a car and driven five hundred miles to get away from me." His voice was as expressionless as his face, yet with that sexy, sensual note that struck a chord deep inside.

"It wasn't like that." But of course it was exactly like that.

Like Spock, he raised one brow in question.

"I was running away from myself."

"That's illuminating." An edge had crept into his tone.

"I didn't mean that to sound trite." But it had. Dammit, when she'd worked this out in the car, she'd been so eloquent.

He waited for her to go on. God, this was hard. "I thoroughly enjoyed everything we did together," she said.

Silence. He was determined to make it difficult for her. But she had been the pissy one throughout, always pushing for her way, her terms, her everything. So why not say that? "I was a total bitch. You treated me like a princess, and I gave you crap the entire time."

One corner of his mouth rose. "I wouldn't say it was the *entire* time."

Her heart lifted in response. "You're being generous. I've been a bitch since my husband left me, and I've relished taking it out on all the men I dated. But you especially."

"And what earned me that honor?"

His features seemed to swim before her eyes. "Because you were so damn hot and you made me feel all the things I hadn't felt in a long time, but you wouldn't pay me. I needed that."

"Money turns it into a business deal." His voice remained level, his facial muscles even. Yet she sensed there was more in that statement than she grasped.

What was she supposed to say? Again, honesty was the best policy, as her mother used to say. "Money has become how I measure myself."

He raised a finger, shot it at her. "That's the problem. I don't have that much money."

But the Atherton house, the Palm Springs trip, renting a mountaintop for her—he had more than enough money.

He noted her widened eyes and interpreted correctly. "None of what I did was enough, was it." He didn't question, he knew. "Hence my point that I don't have enough. I'm not sure anyone does."

She stared at her sexy black pumps. "You're right," she whispered. She'd been trying to buy back the self-esteem she'd let Edward's defection rob her of. "I don't know what you were offering me, but I want to—"

"Gabriel, what's going on?"

The sight of the blonde stepping into the entry hall ripped the rest of the words out of Dominique's mouth. He wasn't alone.

Gabriel raised a hand. "It's nothing, Carla."

Dominique was nothing? While the blonde was gorgeous. And younger. Thirty-five perhaps. God had graced her with a lithe, model-thin body, big baby blues, and blond curls, in perfect contrast with Gabriel's darker looks.

Dominique felt light-headed, as if she'd stood up too quickly. "Sorry, I didn't mean to disturb you." She backed down one step.

Her fears had ruined everything, stolen the beautiful opportunity. Wrong. Nothing had been stolen. She'd thrown it away. "I won't bother you again."

She'd learned her lesson the hard way. Fear of getting hurt didn't protect you, it just screwed your chance at happiness.

\* \* \*

"ARE YOU DOMINIQUE?" CARLA ASKED.

Dominique stopped, one foot on the first step. Gripping the door so hard his knuckles hurt, Gabriel didn't move. "Yes, this is Dominique."

Why was she here? What did she want? Simply to apologize, to explain? Fuck, he needed more from her.

Carla rolled her eyes. "I should have listened to Brenda."

So his good friend had been talking. He'd met Carla a week ago at one of Brenda's parties. He'd liked her. Trying to pretend to himself he wasn't already hooked on another woman's line, he'd asked her out.

It was clear to him within half an hour that he'd made a mistake. His cock didn't feel the slightest urge.

Her heels clicked on the tile floor. "Don't go," she said to Dominique. Then Carla ran a hand along his arm to capture his hand. "You're a sweet man"—he'd never been called sweet before—"but I think your mind is elsewhere." Her purse already on her shoulder, she pulled out her keys.

"I'm sorry it showed." He wasn't normally an asshole.

"It didn't. It's just—" She stopped, shrugged eloquently, then wrinkled her nose. "A woman knows."

Then he'd been a double asshole.

She kissed his cheek, smiled at Dominique as she passed, and headed out to her car at the far end of the circular drive.

"I didn't see her car. I wouldn't have—"

"*Does* a woman know?" he interrupted her.

She tipped her head, her silky red hair brushing the shoulder of her elegant midnight blue evening gown. "Know what?"

"When a man is interested."

"I . . ." She stopped. "Yes."

"Come here."

Her bare leg peeked through the slit in the dress as she returned to the porch and stood in front of him.

"So what do you know about me?" he asked.

"You're interested," she whispered, her green eyes soft.

"Hell yes, I am. Isabel wouldn't give me your number. I wanted to reach through the phone and strangle it out of her."

"It was a shitty way to leave things."

He'd gone over what he could have done differently, but he'd found no satisfactory answers. "What did I do to make you afraid I'd hurt you?"

Moisture flickered in her eyes, then she blinked and it was gone. "You did everything right, Gabriel. I haven't been myself for months. The divorce, Edward's new wife, the new baby—" Her pain rippled through her eyes. "I'd like the chance to show you I'm not the greedy, power-hungry bitch I've been acting like."

He laughed, the first genuine laugh in two months. "You are not a power-hungry bitch. Single-minded, yes, but not a bitch." He touched her cheek with his fingertips, her skin soft, smooth, her scent sweet and fruity, like the grapefruit bath salts she'd used in Palm Springs. "I saw you with your husband that first night, and I knew you'd been hurt. I didn't expect anything to be easy." He drew a thumb lightly across her lower lip. "But I didn't expect you to disappear in the middle of the night without giving me the chance to convince you I was worth the risk."

She blinked again, the slightest tremble at her mouth. "Will you give me that chance now? Can we start over?"

"First date, no sex?" He shook his head, a wry smile finding its way to his lips. "I'm pretty damn sure I can't go that far back. But I also can't give you the money you want." He stroked her cheek, then dropped his hand. "Money diminishes what we could have together."

"I don't want you to pay. I don't want any appreciative gifts." She raised her chin almost defiantly and met his gaze. "I had specific reasons for becoming a courtesan, and they were primarily because of my husband. But you showed me that money doesn't buy happiness." Then she smiled and everything about her changed. She was suddenly the woman he'd taken shopping, the lady who'd teased him mercilessly on the plane. "How's that for a perfect cliché?"

He took her hand, pulled her in. "I've missed you. I would have paid Isabel anything she wanted to tell me where you lived, but she couldn't be bought."

"I've been an idiot." She came into his arms, leaned her body against his, and tipped her head back. "But I've officially taken my head out of my . . ." She trailed off, smiled. "And I called Isabel tonight to tell her I'm leaving Courtesans."

"You don't have to do that for me." But he couldn't help the reflexive tightening of his arms across her back. The thought of having her all to himself simmered through his blood.

"But if I'm not doing that, you're going to have to work extra hard to satisfy me."

"In any way you want."

She arched a brow and gave him a naughty half smile. "Anything?"

"Anything. You're worth it."

Both brows went up this time, and he knew he was in trouble. "Remember what Trevor did for me?" she asked, that wicked half smile turning his heart over.

"I remember."

"Well . . ."

"No."

"But you said anything." She pouted. His cock surged.

"Let's think of something else."

"Like what? Remember, you have to top renting a mountain restaurant and making love to me in front of the staff."

*Making love* instead of *fucking*. He liked her word use. Skimming a hand down the front of her dress, he delved lightly between her legs. "Mile-high club."

She squirmed against him, her musky feminine scent of arousal rising. "Sex on a plane?"

"Yeah." Anywhere, as long as he got to taste her.

"We already did that," she huffed, then curled her foot around his calf.

"I didn't come, so it wasn't sex."

She snorted, then gave in. "All right. Think of something else anyway. Something really exciting and naughty."

His hand at the base of her spine, he hitched her closer. "How about a threesome?"

"Only if it's a man. Everything should be about me." The playfulness in her gaze gave way to something different, tenderness. Then she went up on her toes to wrap her arms about his neck, hugging him tight, her face buried against his throat. "I'm the one who should be paying you for how you make me feel."

He breathed in her sweet, citrus scent, letting it fill him to the brim. "I'm very expensive."

"And worth every penny," she whispered.

# TRIPLE
# PLAY

# 1

"I FEEL LIKE I'VE BEEN EATING TOO MUCH VANILLA ICE CREAM."
Noelle St. James toyed with the rim of her double nonfat caramel
latte. The barista art in the foam, a maple leaf, was starting to
disintegrate. She hated to destroy it completely by drinking. "I
need something exotic." She tipped her head, her long hair falling
across her shoulder. "Like Pistachio Crème. Or Blue Moon. I don't
know"—she rolled her eyes—"something *new*."

"How about a bukkake?" Isabel sipped her tea. According to
her philosophy, tea should be served in bone china cups and made
only with boiling water. She'd found a San Francisco café willing
to cater to her needs.

"What's a bukkake?" With her maple leaf finally melting away,
Noelle tested the delicious brew. Yum.

It was ten in the morning, and despite the cool of an early
March day, the sidewalk tables were packed, hot air blowing from
vents beneath the striped awning. The street teemed with passers-
by. Isabel lowered her voice so she couldn't be heard by the college students to the right or the two middle-aged businessmen to
the left. "You get five or six hot guys to stand over you while
you're naked. They jack off and come on you."

Noelle almost spit out her latte. "I can't believe you just

suggested that." Noelle was joking, of course. Over the years, she'd come to consider Isabel a friend. They could say anything to each other. Which was one of the reasons Noelle had asked for this little face-to-face. She'd need Isabel's help in redirecting her energies.

Isabel made a face. An elegant blonde, she still had the slack-jawed "duh" look down pat. "You're a courtesan. What's wrong with something outrageous? You said you wanted exotic."

Noelle had become a courtesan about two months after her last divorce, when a male friend suggested she'd make a perfect companion. A client of Courtesans, he'd made the introductions. In the ensuing two years, Noelle had done a lot of things, some she'd loved, some she'd decided once was enough. But this was a new one. "There's no personal connection if you've just got them masturbating on you."

"Think about this. It's five men hot for your naked body."

"True." Noelle knew she was still attractive even at forty. With long silky black hair, dark almond-shaped eyes, a slender build, and standing five-nine in her bare feet, she'd been called striking. Part of the courtesan thrill was being desired by men. She needed validation as much as the next girl.

Isabel fluttered her lashes and set her elbows on the table to lean close enough for Noelle's ears only. "And five times the guys is five times the tip."

Noelle had to laugh at that. Isabel was always about the bottom line. That's why she was the brains behind Courtesans. "You're right about that. But it's more than the money. I need . . . something." Noelle just couldn't define, even for herself, what that was. "Something new, something *else*. I feel like . . ."

"I know. It's too much vanilla ice cream when you're craving pistachio."

"It's not boredom," Noelle tried to explain. "It's excitement."

She frowned, then immediately caught herself. She preferred re-laxation over Botox to banish the wrinkles from her forehead. "That's not the right word either." Closing her eyes, she visualized what she was searching for. "It's that giddiness when you're with someone new and hot and delicious. How you look forward to seeing him with a fervor that takes you over, makes you breath-less even when you just think about him." She craved it. She knew she was desired, she had great orgasms, but the kick was missing. The thrill of getting paid for sex was no longer enough.

"Noelle." Her eyes popped open at Isabel's sharp tone. "You're a courtesan." She set her teacup down with a *clink* of china. "It's not good to get your emotions involved."

"Our emotions are always involved. But I'm talking about the illusion, Isabel. I know it's not real. I like to *think* myself into it. I like to pretend. I just haven't been with anyone I *want* to pretend with."

"It's dangerous to want these things. You think you can handle it, but you'll only get hurt in the end."

Noelle understood just how dangerous giving in to her needs could be. She'd been married three times. She *knew* how badly it could end. But she was an infatuation junkie. She loved living dangerously. She thrived on those first few weeks of a new rela-tionship. She freely admitted it was her greatest flaw. So she'd de-cided after the last divorce that marriage wasn't for her. As a courtesan, she wouldn't hurt anyone, not ever again.

"Why don't we just go a little kinkier than your usual fare?" Isabel suggested. "That should give you excitement."

"Kinky's great, but I want something personal, intimate." Where meeting a man's eyes carried her away with that giddy, trembling sensation.

"I've been searching out just the right match for a new client I've got."

"What are his details?" Noelle squirmed in her seat.

"He's a wicked one, I'll say that much for him."

If Isabel thought he was naughty, he liked way more than your normal level of kink. Noelle didn't hold it against him. "What's he look like?"

"Hot."

Noelle snorted softly. "That says a lot." Sometimes what Isabel thought was hot didn't match Noelle's idea.

"He's a Viking. Six-four, two hundred pounds, blond, and blue-eyed."

She loved a man who wouldn't be intimidated by the five-inch heels on her gladiator boots. "What's his name, Thor?"

Isabel laughed. "Dax Deacon. Forty-five. I know you don't mind the older guys."

Older men were hot. Two of her husbands had been ten years older than she was. Her first, her high school sweetheart, was a year younger. They were married right out of college, but it lasted only a year. There was something to be said for the yearning of a long-distance relationship, especially when you were lusty twenty-year-olds.

"So what are his kinky desires?" Noelle was intrigued. She liked his stats. She wanted his fantasies.

Isabel glanced to the right. Their college groupies had stopped talking and conspicuously concentrated on their mochas. Eaves-droppers. Turning slightly to put her back to them, she lowered her voice. "He likes to watch. He'll want you to do things for him with other people."

Noelle shivered. She was the ultimate exhibitionist. She loved to be watched, to be told what to do. It made her performance spectacular. She didn't fool herself into thinking she was a good person. She wasn't. She'd hurt people in her past, badly. She lived with the guilt and strove never to cause that kind of pain again.

She kept the vow by doing what she excelled at, giving men their wildest fantasy, their greatest desire. "More than one person?"

"He did mention threesomes and foursomes. Perhaps a party."

Group sex. She'd tried those things, but again, the connection was missing in a mass of bodies. With two or three partners, though, especially with a man watching, that could definitely work. "He doesn't want to participate?"

"Sometimes, but he'll choose his timing for jumping in. He's more the organizational type, getting off on setting up scenarios designed to drive a woman insane."

Noelle fought the urge to bite her lip in her excitement. Beneath her warm sweater, her nipples pebbled. A man directing her pleasure, planning, watching, perhaps joining in, but still making everything about her. She'd fantasized about having a husband give her to another man for one night.

None of them ever had. She'd never had the courage to ask. But with each of them, she'd imagined him sitting in the corner, observing everything, then taking her hard and fast after the door closed behind their visitor. Oh, the thought of him getting so excited as he watched her that he had to have her the moment they were alone.

Her panties were warm and wet with her fantasies.

She raised one eyebrow and smiled. "I could get into that."

"He might be perfect for you, darling," Isabel murmured like a wicked devil on Noelle's shoulder. "If everything clicks, he wants to make it an ongoing relationship. That might give you the connection you're looking for."

She did have repeat clients, but they lacked the indefinable *something*. Lacing her fingers and leaning her forearms on the table, she bent closer. "Maybe he could be the answer."

"It's worth a shot."

"I'm excited just thinking about it."

Isabel winked. "That's half the battle, isn't it? Thinking ourselves into arousal before we even meet him."

"Except"—Noelle laughed—"when you build it up in your mind then find he's a total dud." She'd been known to do that, too.

Her smile sultry, Isabel settled back and crossed her legs. "I assure you, he's no dud in the looks department."

"Then it's a date."

Anticipation could often be way more than half the battle, plus a great big bite of the fun. But you also risked a bigger bite of disappointment. That had been her problem over the past six months. The anticipation had been the best part.

If Dax Deacon lived up to Isabel's description, though? Well then, he might be Pistachio Crème and Blue Moon on a sugar cone with sprinkles on top.

WITH HER USUAL APLOMB AND ATTENTION TO DETAIL, ISABEL arranged everything for the following Friday evening. She catered to Noelle's need for surprise and excitement. The Lincoln Town Car arrived at her San Francisco flat at seven. She lived near the marina, and the driver took her across town to Market. Noelle loved the city—the lights, the sounds, the rush, always busy, always moving. It made her feel alive.

At the downtown high-rise hotel, the driver—midthirties, sharply dressed in his pressed black suit, white shirt, and black tie—held the car door for her, offering his hand as she climbed out. His eyes dropped to her thigh revealed by the long slit of her elegant calf-length dress. Emerald green. She favored vibrant colors. She liked the slight flare of his nostrils, the compliment in his brief glance down her leg. The night air would have cooled her if it weren't for the heat of his gaze. She liked big Latino men. All right, she liked all men, for the most part, if they dressed well. The one thing she couldn't abide was sloppiness.

Noelle smiled her gratitude and palmed him a tip. His hand was hot, big, a tight grip that lasted a moment longer than necessary. Then he handed her a card. "Please call fifteen minutes before you're ready for me."

She had such a dirty mind, imagining a double entendre in his businesslike words. "I will."

He handed her off to the doorman, who directed her to the express elevator for the restaurant on the top floor of the hotel. She stepped inside and expected to see walls. Instead, the elevators were all glass, looking out over the lobby. Alone in the car, she hung close to the windows. As she was whisked skyward, the lobby, with its fountain and fern garden in the center, fell away, growing smaller until the people were like ants.

She remembered times in her life when she'd felt like the ant, scurrying everywhere, worrying. Those feelings had ended with Isabel and Courtesans. Until recently, when a strange longing for something indefinable had struck her once more. A damn good thing she'd sworn off marriage or she'd be in danger of hurting someone all over again.

The elevator dinged and slid to a smooth stop, the doors opening onto a marble entry. The maître d', a short man with a goatee and a fast walk, led her into the restaurant, which was famous for its three-hundred-sixty-degree view of San Francisco and the Bay as it circled atop the hotel. Noelle always felt a moment of disorientation as she passed from the entryway to the rotating floor.

"Your gentleman friend has reserved one of our private balconies for you." The goateed man swept his hand in front, bidding her to enter. Approximately one-third of the restaurant's circumference was given over to balconies open to the sky.

Noelle stepped into a jungle. Ferns and exotic flowers bloomed from pots on the concrete floor, climbing the walls, an explosion of color and scent. On one side, two crystal glasses and a bucket with champagne already icing adorned the center of an elegantly laid, glass-top table. Dax Deacon adorned the rattan sofa on the opposite side of the intimate balcony.

Meeting his brilliant blue eyes, Noelle felt a moment of dizziness much as she'd had stepping onto the revolving floor.

He was all Isabel had said and more. With gentlemanly aplomb, he rose to his feet. His height stole her breath, his tailored black tux fitting him like he'd been born to wear it.

Behind her the maître d' closed the frosted sliding-glass door, leaving her alone with Dax. She was oddly nervous. "I thought it would be cold, but it's toasty warm out here."

"Heaters." He raised a hand to indicate two standing electric torches. "And a windbreak."

"It's a perfect design." Outside the wind howled, yet the clear canopy above diminished the wind but not the sparkle of stars, and the heaters pushed back the cold. Damn, she felt totally inane talking about the architecture.

He was just so . . . hot. With short blond hair, he made her think of Peter Graves in the old *Mission: Impossible* TV show—strong features, square jaw. And his hands . . . big hands, long fingers. She hadn't felt tongue-tied with a man in ages. After all, she was a courtesan.

Then she recognized it—the breathlessness, the quickened pace of her heart, the butterflies in her stomach. Infatuation. Lust. It was his looks. It was the things Isabel said he wanted. It was her own fantasies seducing her.

# 2

WHO CARED WHAT CAUSED IT? NOELLE REVELED IN THE EXCITE-
ment. God, it had been so long. She closed her eyes to savor the
moment, the man, the spice of his barely there aftershave blending
with the perfume of exotic blooms.

"May I pour you champagne?"

His deep voice set off little charges along her nerve endings.
This was what she'd been looking for. True, her own fantasies had
fueled the fire burning in her, but wasn't that always the way? The
mind was the real sex organ.

She opened her eyes. "I'd love some." Oh, he was delicious.

At the table, he popped the cork without shooting it over the
balcony. She wanted to giggle at the thought of it landing at
someone's feet thirty-six stories below. He poured expertly, creating a minimum of foam, and handed her a flute.

"Cheers," he said, clinking glasses. "Shall we sit?" He extended
a hand toward the sofa, its bright cushions mirroring the jungle
theme. "I left instructions for our dinner to arrive in half an hour.
So we can chat and enjoy our drinks first."

"That's so accommodating of you." He was a planner. He'd
arrived early, made sure the setup was ready and to his liking.

She hoped his attention to her pleasure was as exacting.

"I chose filet mignon for you. Isabel said you weren't a vegetarian."

"I'm not. I adore a good steak. Thank you for checking." Some women would go crazy with his presumption, ordering for her. She viewed it as an appealing attention to detail.

"You're welcome."

They were, however, becoming annoyingly polite without really saying anything at all. She kicked off her high-heeled pumps and tucked her feet beneath her, the slit of her dress baring her leg to mid-thigh. "I must say your sexual requests have me very intrigued."

He smiled, one corner of his mouth higher than the other, giving him a slightly naughty quality. "You don't beat around the bush, do you?"

She could have laughed at the image, but decided not to get crass. "What's the point? We both know why we're here." Meeting a stranger simply for the purpose of sex excited her. It always had. And such a magnificent specimen? Even better. But would he turn out to be the *something* she'd been looking for?

He gave a little chuckle. "Since you're here, I assume you didn't find any of my desires too reprehensible."

"Of course not. Every person has a right to his or her own fantasies." She shrugged. "They may not always mesh with mine, but you certainly have a right."

"Did ours mesh?"

She inhaled, aware of his eyes falling to the swell of her breasts, and let a naughty smile grow on her lips. "I like to be watched," she whispered, leaning ever so slightly closer for emphasis.

"I love to watch," he whispered back in kind.

"Then we mesh perfectly." She let his looks, his voice, her desires, and the intimate surroundings weave a spell around her. "Tell me everything you love." Sharing fantasies was her foreplay.

He laid his arm along the back of the sofa, resting the cool and sweating stem of his glass next to her elbow. His knee brushed her shin, sparking like static electricity. "I've got this fantasy of the perfect relationship with a woman who allows me to be a party to all her sexual adventures." The blue of his eyes seemed to deepen as he spoke.

"That sounds interesting." So exciting, her heart fluttered in her chest. "But maybe you should be more specific." She sipped her champagne, feigning calm, but inside her blood pumped fast and hard through her veins. A rush of warmth shot to her center. If she touched herself, she'd be wet, her panties damp.

He seduced her with his fantasies. "Sometimes I'd want only to watch, sometimes I'd want to be an active participant. But I always want to be involved, this perfect woman telling me what she's doing, sharing every taste, suck, and swallow."

His wording made it theoretical; she brought it back to them. "But what if my client doesn't wish to be watched?"

"I'd want you to call me, during the act if you can, or right after."

"Then what?" She shuddered to think of all the possibilities. Phone sex was such a turn-on.

He leaned close. As if he were taking in her perfume, his nostrils flared, his eyes turned to sparkling sapphire, and she knew he'd scented her arousal. His reaction seduced her as well. Everything about Dax Deacon seduced her.

"I'd want you to describe every dirty, naughty, nasty detail to me," he said. He glanced down her body. Her nipples tightened beneath the silk.

She wanted him to touch her. He stroked her only with his gaze. For the moment, it was enough.

"Will you jerk off while I talk to you?"

He tipped his head—"Maybe"—then tilted the other way. "Or maybe I'll want you to meet me so I can taste his come on you."

Her breath simply stopped. "Taste it?"

"On your fingers, your lips, your tongue." He blinked slowly. "Sip it from your pussy."

A flush of heat raced from her nipples to her toes. "That's hot," she murmured, trying to keep her tone light, when the thought of what he wanted consumed her.

"You will never have sex without telling me first."

"I have to ask your permission?" It was the first thing she'd heard that she didn't like.

"No. You're a courtesan. You'll do whoever you contract to do. But you'll tell me ahead of time. We'll decide if your client can handle me watching, perhaps being active in the date." He was on a roll now, listing all his requirements. Oh yes, the man was a planner, and he'd thought of everything. "Sometimes I'll arrange dates for you," he went on. "Perhaps a couple. Perhaps two men. I might make myself a fourth."

A finger to her chin, he tipped her to meet his eyes. She hadn't realized she'd been staring at his groin, imagining his cock hard and thick beneath his tux pants.

"Is there anything you won't do?" The husky timbre of his voice captured her.

"I'm not into other women. I don't like to be tied down. And I abhor pain."

"Would you suck a man's cock with another woman?"

"I could do that." She had done it. They'd touched tongues. She'd just never had the desire for sex with another woman. It wouldn't freak her out, but she didn't want him to show up with a woman and expect to watch her perform oral sex.

"If there's anything I ask that you find yourself uncomfortable with, you can tell me."

"And you can tell me to do anything you'd like." She gave him a sassy grin. "As long as I have veto power."

"Agreed."

Her mind whirled as if she'd drunk the whole bottle of champagne. He was too good to be true. "How long would our relationship last?"

He held her with a steady gaze. "Until one of us tires of it."

She wondered how long it would take her to get bored, to need something different again. She was notoriously bad about requiring a new level of excitement. "We agree to have no hurt feelings on either side if one of us wants to opt out?"

He nodded. "No hurt feelings."

She had the notion that he was so controlled, he didn't have feelings close enough to the surface for them to get hurt. It was the most attractive thing of all. "So are you a Dom?"

He caressed her with that naughty half smile. "No. I just enjoy acting out some of the nasty scenarios running around in here"— he tapped his temple—"and finding a . . ." He paused, as if searching for an inoffensive word. "A courtesan," he finally said, "means not having to worry about the negative aspects of most relationships."

"Let's face it, you can't ask your girlfriend to let you watch her do another couple."

He laughed, a deep chord strumming her body, not too loud, but with real mirth and no derision. "It takes a special woman to allow a man to give her to another."

"You're not giving me to anyone. I'm simply letting you into my world." She didn't want him to get the idea he owned her. This was a business deal. Exciting, thrilling, but still a deal in which they were equal partners. As soon as the giddiness evaporated, she needed the freedom to get out without causing any fuss or pain.

He bestowed a quick bend of his head. "I stand corrected. What I meant was in a relationship such as I'm suggesting, we do away with the jealousy that can potentially ruin everything."

Jealousy. It was the bane of her existence. It was why she couldn't be married. "I think we have a deal, then."

He set his champagne on a small table and glanced at the frosted sliding door. Raising his hand slowly, he gave her plenty of time to say something—*no, hell no, yes, please*—then he circled her nipple with the tip of his finger.

She lost herself in his gaze. Her breath quickened, her pulse fluttered. She wanted to close her eyes and lean into the pleasure, but the power of him kept her lids from drifting down.

Slowly, so she saw it coming, anticipated it, felt her panties dampen with it: he pulled her nipple between his fingers and thumb. Then he pinched. Gently. Harder. Tighter. Until a tingle of pain arced straight to her clitoris. She gasped.

"Tell me," Dax whispered, "is that too much pain?"

Noelle cupped his hand, held him to her. "No."

"Does it feel good?"

She leaned into him. "Yes."

DAX TOOK POSSESSION OF BOTH NIPPLES. HE DIDN'T WANT TO HURT her, only give her exquisite pleasure. She moaned, lowered her lids, and tipped her head back, inviting him to plunder her lips.

"It makes me want to come." She shifted on the sofa, wriggling her bottom, then opened her eyes.

They were black as night, as dark as her hair. Dax could barely see where her irises ended and her pupils began. She was a gorgeous, perfect creature, more than he'd hoped for, better than Isabel had claimed.

She wasn't just a hooker who fucked for money. She was a courtesan who had sex because she loved it. The money was incidental.

She was exactly what he'd been looking for.

With a hand to his chest, she pushed him back. "I want to hold off the orgasm for a little while."

"You can come now *and* later." Unlike men, who needed a little recharge, he'd found that one orgasm made a woman want the second one more desperately.

She cocked her head, her silky mane falling across her shoulder. "But no one's watching."

"The waiter could walk in at any time." The possibility provided enough kick for this first brief adventure.

"Ah, so you like the risk of discovery, too." Her dark eyes sparkled in the intimate lighting.

"Everything's good." He picked up his champagne. "But you're right. I'm rushing." He smiled. "You have the ability to make me get carried away."

She'd never relinquished her champagne, and she held the glass out to him. "May I have more?"

He'd give her a hell of a lot more. Just not right here and now. First he wanted to learn more about her. "How long have you been a courtesan?" he asked, refilling her flute from the bottle chilling on the table.

"Two years."

He handed her the champagne and sat beside her once again. "Why do you do it?"

Mindful of her glass, she crossed her arms beneath her breasts. He recognized it for the defensive posture it was. Even some of her clients probably looked down on her. It was fine for a man to pay for it, but it was the woman who got vilified for accepting payment.

He sought to assure her. "I'm not judging, just curious."

She relaxed, the tension in her shoulders releasing. "I'm very sexual. I always have been. I'm not good in relationships because of that. And I've never been happier." She flashed a smile. "They do say you should do what you love." She leaned in. "And I love sex. I love men. I love how they smell." She closed her eyes and drew in a deep breath of him. "I love how their skin feels." Raising a hand, she caressed his cheek, slid her fingers down his face, stroked the side of his neck, then pulled away again. "I love how they taste." Her eyes fell from his mouth to his lap, and he knew the taste she loved.

The tux jacket covered his cock. He'd been hard almost from the moment she'd sauntered through the door, dressed in emerald and smelling like fresh summer fruit. "Careful," he murmured, "or I'll beg you to taste me right now."

"Did I mention I love to tease?"

"No, but I'm figuring it out."

A shadow passed over the frosted-glass door, followed by a discreet knock.

"Our dinner has arrived."

He rose, opened the door, and their waiter wheeled in the cart. In brief minutes, he'd transferred the champagne bucket, set the table, and whisked the warming covers off their plates.

"God, that smells scrumptious." She rose, leaving her shoes tipped on their sides, and crossed barefoot to the table. Eyes closed, she drew in the scents of meat and béarnaise, then licked her lips.

She was a carnal creature, employing all her senses to get the most from her experience.

With the waiter gone, Dax pulled out her chair and seated her. She flapped her napkin and laid it over her lap. "God." She smiled around the first bite of steak, her lids lowered, her eyes rolling up slightly as she savored.

Christ, she was going to be a fantastic fuck.

# 3

"SO TELL ME WHEN YOU FIRST REALIZED YOU WERE SO KINKY."

Dax put a hand to his chest in mock offense. "Kinky? Me?"

Noelle shook her fork at him. "Yes, you. Tell me when."

It was one thing to say you liked kink as an adult. It was another to admit you'd probably always been that way, like you needed a psychiatrist. "My older sister had a friend. They had sleepovers."

"Naughty boy." Her eyes gleamed. "You watched the friend. How old were you?"

"I was fourteen."

She leaned forward, affording him a clear view of her gorgeous, sensitive nipples. "I bet she knew. She probably made sure she undressed in places where you could see."

Several times. "She had a penchant for undressing with the door open if my sister wasn't around."

Noelle laughed. "See? She wanted you to watch. And you've loved watching ever since." She cut off another slice of steak and smothered it with béarnaise, then moaned as she chewed.

Christ. He could get off just watching her eat. "There's more."

"Ooh," she purred, and whether it was her sound or his own memory, his cock hardened. "Tell me," she urged.

"My sister had a slumber party on Halloween. The girls watched horror flicks down in the basement. *Friday the Thirteenth Part One Million* or something like it. I sat at the top of the stairs because she wouldn't let me come down and join." He'd taken pleasure in all the pretty girls, their brightly colored pajamas, their laughter and shrieks doing odd things to his insides. "The girl, my favorite one, excused herself to use the restroom, and as she passed me on the stairs, she whispered 'pervert.'"

"Even then you were." Noelle smiled without censure, as if she understood exactly what he'd been feeling.

"Even then," he agreed.

"And you followed her."

He snorted. "Of course I did." He was sure she'd wanted him to. "I gave her a five-minute head start."

Noelle nibbled her bottom lip, dinner forgotten. He could swear a pulse beat double-time at her throat. "And?"

He discovered he loved teasing her as much as he enjoyed the memory. "She was already on the bed in my sister's room, her pajamas and panties around her ankles, her legs parted and her fingers doing a magic dance."

Her eyes glittered with the reflected glow of the heaters. "Oh my, that was bold."

"It was one of the hottest things I've ever seen in my life. Her pussy was pink and glistening." His mouth had watered, his heart pounding in his chest. "And the sounds she made"—he closed his eyes remembering—"soft little moans in the sweetest voice. She thrashed around on that bed, and I could smell her juice on the air, this citrusy, musky perfume, like she'd smoothed lotion between her thighs." He lost himself in the sensual memory, smelled her all over again, but then Noelle's scent was so closely related.

"You wanted to jack off, didn't you?" she whispered, bewitching him. "But you didn't because you were afraid you'd miss something miraculous."

"Yes." It had been exactly like that. "Then she came. I knew it was something special even if I didn't know exactly what it was. And after, she raised herself on one elbow and licked her fingers." He would have killed to lick them for her.

"And that's when she saw you?"

"I don't know. She didn't look at me, didn't acknowledge me. She just pulled up her panties and pajamas, and I went back to sit on the stairs before she came back down."

"And she still didn't say anything?"

"No. But she trailed her finger along my cheek as she passed. And I could smell her." He'd never forgotten the sensual aroma of feminine arousal. He'd fallen in love with the sight of a woman pleasuring herself, the scents she gave off, the sounds she made. He'd sought to re-create that moment ever since, yet somehow it had eluded him.

Until he'd decided to pay to produce it.

He shook off the introspection. He wanted to know about Noelle. "What about you? When did you first know you were kinky? A friend of your older brother?"

"I'm an only child."

"Ah, then who was it?"

Her cheeks flushed a deeper red. "I babysat his two kids. He was a single father."

"An older man."

She trembled as if the memory were tangible. "I love older men. I was sixteen and I loved him with all my heart. I used to dream about him at night, how he'd ask me to marry him and be mother to his children. It was all so romantic. He was twenty-six." She rolled her eyes. "I thought that was sooo mature."

"Unrequited love?"

"Shh," she said, covering her lips with a finger, "you're interrupting my story. One night I fell asleep on the couch because he had this really late business meeting."

"Right. A business meeting."

She glared. It made him hot.

"He was down on one knee by the side of the sofa when he woke me up. I felt like Sleeping Beauty. I was so mesmerized, I kissed him." She bit her lip, gaze unfocused, suddenly deep in the long-ago moment. "He kissed me back. It was so beautiful. He kept kissing me. I put his hand on my breast. And he squeezed. I laid his hand on my leg and moved it up under my skirt. It was one of those pleated schoolgirl types. I thought he'd get scared, stop. But I wasn't scared at all. I wanted to know what it was like to have a man touch me there."

Drinking in every word, Dax wanted to reach beneath the table and stroke his cock.

"I parted my thighs and set his fingers on my pussy. He kissed me as I made him rub me through my panties. They were an ugly old cotton pair, and I remember how much I wished I'd worn something pretty. Then I pulled the cotton crotch aside and helped him touch me. He was breathing hard, and any minute I knew he was going to run away. So I kept my hand on his, caressing myself with his fingers. It was the most beautiful thing I ever felt. I was so wet and so turned on, and then he put a finger inside me." She hugged herself, eyes squeezed shut. "Oh, it was the most wonderful sensation. I could feel this heat building, wanting to get out. Then finally it burst. I think I screamed, then I started to cry because it was so good." She opened her eyes and gazed at him as if she'd been aware of him listening the whole time. "My crying scared the crap out of him. He thought he'd molested me, but really, I'd molested him."

Dax had a hard time putting a coherent sentence together. She was a teenage boy's wet dream come true.

She shrugged eloquently, with a hint of remembered joy and a touch of sadness. "He never called me to babysit again. They moved away a few months after that. I never made a pass at an older man again." She smiled mischievously. "Well, not until I wasn't jail bait anymore. Besides, I fell in love with a boy in my junior class. I married him."

"How many times have you been married?" Isabel had mentioned divorces, plural.

"Three." Though most of the food was gone now, she picked up her utensils and concentrated on her meal. As if waiting for his censure. "I wasn't good at marriage," she said. "I was a bad wife. I'm better at being a courtesan."

Across the small table, he cupped her cheek. "It's good when a woman finds her calling." It was the finest compliment. Her faults as a wife didn't concern him. She was an extraordinarily lusty woman. It didn't surprise him she'd needed more than a husband could possibly give. "What did you do before becoming a courtesan?"

She laughed. It suited her much more than the negative introspection. "I was an accountant."

Interesting. The lady was no slouch. He'd been prepared for her to tell him she was a socialite who got huge sums out of her divorce settlements. It wouldn't have mattered, but he liked that she was a career woman. In more ways than one. He shook his head, smiling. "I always thought accountants were boring."

"Oh, you'd be surprised." She winked. "I've got some tales." She pushed her plate away. "What about you? Married?"

Though he hadn't polished off everything, he set his fork aside. She was the only meal he was interested in. "I never got married. I realized my tastes were beyond what most women could handle in marriage."

She nodded, her eyes turning a misty midnight. "I wish I'd learned that earlier. But"—she brightened—"I'm on the right track now. So what do you do for a living?"

"Executive." He was CEO of a San Francisco–based Fortune 500 company.

"Ooh. Executives are hot."

He felt the sizzle in the word *hot* all the way to his balls. She had a way of looking at a man with those dark eyes, a sultry lowering of her lashes, a smile so barely there it was too damn sexy for words.

Tonight's date had been about checking her out, deciding if they had common ground, if their fantasies played into each other or against. He hadn't expected sex; he'd only wanted to make a decision. But she had him. He imagined watching her undress for him, suck a man for him, get herself off while he sat close enough to drag in her aroused scent.

He wanted it now.

"Are you wearing panties?"

She nodded her head slowly, a knowing sparkle in her eyes.

"Give them to me."

Her hands beneath her skirt, she wriggled, then tossed him emerald panties that matched the dress. Pressing them to his nose for a brief second, he inhaled her hot female scent, then laid them by his water glass.

"Spread your legs." He held her with his gaze.

Her nipples tight buds beneath the material, she put a bare foot to his knee, shifted, and pulled the dress to her waist. He shoved her plate aside to see through the glass tabletop.

Indistinct, like looking through old-fashioned glass, he could still see she was as dark there as the hair on her head. A trim line arrowed down to the cleft between her legs.

"Touch yourself," he whispered, then allowed himself to be mesmerized by the slide of her fingers down to her pussy.

Her lips parted, and her lids drooped halfway.

"How wet are you?"

"Very wet." She removed her hand, held out her fingers. "See?" Moisture glistened on her fingertips. "Taste it."

He couldn't resist. Sliding her finger in his mouth, he found her sweet, spicy, all woman, and very wet. "Thank you," he whispered. "Pull your dress down before the waiter comes back."

"Do you care if he sees?" she challenged.

"It's hotter if he just spies your panties on the table." He liked the subtlety of it.

A pulse rippled at her throat, the idea turning her on as much as it did him.

He began to plan the things he'd make her do for him tonight. And for many nights to come.

# 4

NOELLE'S BODY BURNED FROM THE INSIDE OUT. DAX DIDN'T CARE she was a three-time loser. She'd stopped short of telling him the full extent of her crimes against her husbands—she hated to think about it, much less say it aloud—but he was a big CEO; he had to have figured out she'd cheated, yet still he wanted her.

They'd left her panties on the table and skipped dessert. Heat suffused her as she imagined the waiter finding them when he cleared the remains of their meal.

Dax was so perfect. She'd never told anyone about her baby-sitting crush, or what she'd made Mr. Howell do to her. Not even any of her husbands. Secretly, she'd been afraid they'd call her a nymphomaniac. A slut. A pervert. Or accuse her of trying to trap the poor man like the evil teenager in *Poison Ivy*. Noelle admitted she was bad from a very young age.

At fourteen, Dax had watched his sister's friend masturbate. He was an equal pervert. It gave Noelle validation. Or expiation. Acceptance. She wasn't sure which, maybe all three.

She settled next to him into the backseat of the Lincoln. Since she'd given her driver fifteen minutes' notice, when she and Dax exited the hotel, the Town Car sat at the curb.

"Where to, ma'am?"

The handsome Latino addressed her rather than Dax, as if he were hers to command. The thought evoked an awesome tingle of power. Still, she deferred, glancing to Dax. She wasn't sure if he wanted to hit a club for dancing, fuck her senseless, or get rid of her on her doorstep. Though the fact he'd rushed her off the balcony before dessert arrived had to mean *something*. Noelle wasn't ready for the night to end.

"A drive along the coast." It wasn't quite a question, but he waited for her nod of agreement, then added to their driver, "Take the quiet streets to get there."

Noelle glanced from Dax to the Latino and relished the contrast. Dark looks versus sexy blond. She'd rarely been with a blond man, for no particular reason other than the fact that there were more dark-haired people than blond or red, the recessive gene thing. "May I touch your hair?"

Dax shot her one of his naughty smiles. "I don't think a woman's ever asked to touch my hair. Be my guest."

The driver's eyes on her in the rearview mirror were a physical caress as she leaned into Dax's space. Combing through his straight hair, she closed her eyes to absorb the textures with her fingers. "It's soft." Smooth, fine. Like silk.

The car turned, traversing a more residential street, leaving the heavier traffic behind.

Noelle sat back, her fingers tingling. As in a chess game, the next move was Dax's. He glanced at the rearview mirror on the inside windshield, then the man's profile, and finally at Noelle.

"Suck my cock."

The words fell into the quiet vacuum of the car, not loud, yet unmistakable even in the front seat. His gaze brushed her nipples, bringing them to hard beads against her dress. Her body clenched. Without her panties, her thighs dampened with evidence of her need.

A pair of brown eyes, unblinking, met hers in the mirror.

Everything she did, the handsome Latino would see.

Noelle's clients were dignified in public despite how nasty they might get behind closed doors. She'd had sex at clubs, she'd been watched, she'd loved it. But what she'd done hadn't been out of place for the venue. No one had asked her for this.

A big dark hand reached up to adjust the mirror, tilting it down, aiming it as Dax shifted to the middle of the seat and took her chin. "You want it." Again, the statement lacked the question mark, but it was nevertheless a question. Or permission to say no.

She wanted this now as badly as she'd wanted Mr. Howell to touch her at sixteen. She fumbled unzipping Dax, her fingers clumsy in her excitement.

"Easy," Dax murmured, stroking her hair. "There's no rush, baby."

With a deep breath, she willed herself to calm, and finally freed him. "God." The word simply fell out in awe. Long, thick—all that hard flesh was almost too much for her hand. "You're beautiful."

He chuckled. She tipped her head to look up at him. "I mean that."

"I know." His eyes darkened to a stormy ocean blue. "Now suck me."

The console flipped down between the two front seats, improving the spectacle in the mirror. She angled herself to give their driver the maximum view of all Dax's lovely flesh disappearing into her mouth. She sucked on the crown, sipping a drop of pre-come. Deliciously salty, agonizingly sweet. She murmured her pleasure, and Dax shuddered against her. Holding him at the base, she caressed him with mouth and tongue until her lips met her fist, and she could take no more. She grazed her teeth along him, worried the ridge beneath the head, then sucked hard on the plum of his cock. His hips surged, blood rushing, turning him diamond hard in her grip.

"Christ." Breath hissed through his teeth. He pulled the hair back from her face, making sure every inch of her lips around his cock was visible.

She took him deep, began a fast slip-slide, then slowed for another hard suck of his crown. A gentle groan drifted to her from the front seat. She met the driver's dark greedy eyes in the mirror. She wanted to come, with the big man's gaze on her and Dax's cock in her mouth.

"Fuck me," Dax demanded.

God yes.

He pulled her up, yanked on her dress, and she didn't care if it tore. She wanted him to rip it in his excitement. He guided her over his lap, her back to his chest, his hips to her ass. She'd lost her shoes on the floor of the car.

"Condom," she managed, shoving her evening bag into Dax's hand. She never traveled light.

Streetlights along the road flashed over the hood of the car as it glided through the near-empty neighborhood, then headed downhill toward the vast blackness of the ocean.

Sliding forward, balancing herself with hands on both front seats, she felt Dax's fingers work the condom on. Her driver—yes, *hers*—the padded shoulder of his jacket lay only an inch from her fingertips. She stretched, touched, dug her nails in deep enough for him to feel through the material.

He grunted.

She almost came.

Holding the hem of her dress out of the way, revealing her pussy to the hungry gaze in the mirror, Dax lifted her hips. He pulled her back, breaching her with the head of his cock. She moaned, closed her eyes, held still to relish the feel of him, just there, right there, pulsing. Then she snapped her lids open because she couldn't miss a moment. Clutching the seat in front of her, fingertips still connected to her big, beautiful driver, she pushed back and took Dax's every magnificent inch deep inside.

"Oh yes." She spoke for all of them. Then she rode him hard, his grip guiding, her breasts bouncing, her nipples breaking free of the dress's scooped neckline. One hand still in contact with the beefy shoulder, she pinched her nipple hard. A lightning strike zinged to her clitoris. Inside, Dax touched a spot high and deep, forcing a cry from her lips.

Ahead lay the ocean and a red light. God, she was plainly visible fucking a man in the backseat. While the street wasn't crowded, neither was it completely empty. If they had to stop for that light, anyone could see them. The risk made her hotter, slippery, wild.

"Touch yourself," Dax demanded. Maybe he didn't see the light. Probably he didn't care.

The Latino didn't slow, as if he wasn't even aware of the intersection. They were going to die, fly straight into the ocean. Yet she rode the edge of orgasm, incapable of stopping until Dax's cock reached all the way to her throat.

At the last moment, the light flashed to green, and they careened around the corner with a high-pitched squeal. She held on tight, her knuckles white against the driver's black jacket until the car straightened. He reached out to raise the mirror, focusing it on her face.

"Touch yourself." Dax's harsh voice rasped at her ear. "Your left hand."

So much, too much, overload, yet she wanted everything he asked for. She had to do it or die. Her pussy was coated with her own cream, the nub of her clitoris so sensitive it almost hurt to touch. A raw pleasure-pain swept through her.

"Let him scent you on your fingers."

The thought made her dizzy. The way Dax must have felt watching that nubile girl take her clothes off, revealing herself, performing for him. Noelle raised her hand once again to the seat in front of her. Dax held her hips still, took control of her body, pistoned deep. And Noelle stretched for the hot young man to smell the perfume of her come. She was close enough to hear his breath, hard puffs through his nostrils. Then he grabbed her fingers in one big hand, his gaze capturing hers in the mirror as he pulled them to his mouth, sucking her juice from her skin.

Dax's cock inside her, this big sexy man sucking on her, it was more than she could take, more than she'd ever had. Then Dax whispered, "Come. Come now."

And she was lost.

She burst into flames, screamed, and let her body drag her under, either to heaven or to hell.

HOLY HELL. SHE LAY IN ORGASMIC EXHAUSTION ACROSS HIS LAP, her hair obscuring her face, her breathing in the easy rhythm of sleep. Or she'd passed out. She'd come so hard, Dax didn't dismiss the idea.

Disposing of the condom, smoothing her dress, pulling her close—nothing had disturbed her.

"Where to, sir?"

"I think it's time to take us home, Manuel."

"Your home or hers, sir?

He answered without a moment's hesitation. "Mine."

Manuel made a slow, careful U-turn, unlike the left he'd made while Dax had been buried hilt deep in her.

He'd planned to have her suck him in the back of the car, visible to Manuel in the front seat. The rest of it? She'd inspired him. He'd watched her watching Manuel—in the mirror, mesmerized by her moans, her sounds, her dilated pupils—and the familiar ache rose in him. He'd wanted to test her limits, see how far she'd let him take her the first time. When she'd touched Manuel's shoulder, he was a goner. He'd fucked her deep and come hard as Manuel licked her come from her fingers.

It was beyond voyeurism. Yet it only whet his appetite for more of her. God, the things he wanted her to do for him.

He stroked her shoulder. She didn't stir. "Thank you, Manuel, I appreciate your participation. I trust we didn't make you uncomfortable."

A passing car lit Manuel's face, and his smile. "It was my pleasure to help out, sir."

When he had need of a driver, he always chose Manuel. And it just so happened that Manuel also drove for Courtesans. Coincidence? He preferred to think of it as providence.

She turned then, as if she'd heard his thought. Providence. Divine intervention. She opened her lovely eyes, pushed her hair back from her face, and gazed at him through long lashes.

"That was incredible," she whispered, her voice almost reverent in the quiet glide of the car along the street.

He nodded, oddly overcome, with no words better than hers.

She pushed herself up, twisted slightly to look out the side window. "Where are we?"

"On our way home."

She blinked. It was enough of a question.

"My home."

She didn't argue, didn't ask if Manuel was coming in to fuck her, too, or if Dax would take her alone this time. She simply laid her head down upon his lap and wound one arm around his waist. "Wake me when we get there."

\* \* \*

SHE SHOULD HAVE CARED WHERE HE WAS TAKING HER AND WHAT he planned for her once they got there. She should have called Isabel or someone at Courtesans to let them know where she'd be. Instead she simply snuggled into the warmth of his body, his salty male scent teasing her, the gentle glide of his fingers over her skin lulling her.

The car rocked into the turns, then finally slowed to a stop. She heard them talking but was too sated to listen.

This was better than Pistachio Crème and Blue Moon all rolled into one. First the rooftop dinner, the sexy talk, sharing secrets, then the hardness of his cock inside her and the heat of Manuel's gaze, his tongue caressing her fingers.

The car door opened, and she felt herself lifted against Dax's firm chest, her shoes dangling from one hand. She wasn't petite and couldn't fathom how he carried her so easily. Cold air caressed her, the salt of the ocean tickled her nose, the crash of waves was like music.

He lived on the edge of cliff overlooking the ocean outside the Golden Gate. With the beep of a remote he unlocked his front door. The aroma of expensive leather permeated the house. A wall of windows stretched across the back, only blackness beyond.

Upstairs in the bedroom, he let her feet slide to the floor. Holding her against him, pulling her arms around his neck to steady her, he reached behind to unzip her dress. He backed off, allowing the silk to pool at her feet, then lifted her out of it.

"Get into bed, sleepyhead."

She wasn't sleepy, she was dazed, and she adored the way he pampered her. No one had ever carried her before.

She was wet for a slow, lazy fuck in his big bed.

When he raised the covers, she slid between cotton sheets. The soft pad of his feet headed across the carpet, a light went on, water ran, sounds, the rustle of clothing.

Then his warm body heated her back. "Spread your legs," he murmured, his breath minty with toothpaste.

What delicious thing did he have planned now? She parted her thighs. Draping her leg over his, he pressed a heated washcloth against her pussy. Oh God. He was cleaning her, soothing the flesh he'd ridden.

"God, that feels good."

"You worked hard. You deserve it."

She tipped her head back to look at him. He was an inky spot in the dark. "I was very naughty for you."

"Yes, you were. It was too fucking hot for words."

She laughed from deep in her belly, satisfied. He leaned back and tossed the washcloth. It landed with a wet *thwap*, then he surrounded her.

"Go to sleep, baby." His voice was like a lullaby. She was sure he'd wake her in the night and take her. Again and again. She fell asleep dreaming about his tongue on her.

She woke twice to the darkness and his even breathing. He never moved, never let her go.

In her chest, something grew. In her sweetest fantasies, she'd dreamed of this, a hot, naughty episode, one special man watching, even participating, then afterward, his heat all over her.

She'd never been able to ask it of her husbands, not any of them. She hadn't stopped wanting the men she'd married; she'd just needed excitement. It had become an obsession. Each time. Ruining everything. She'd hated herself for cheating.

But what if she'd had this? A man whose excitement peaked when other men wanted her. His voyeuristic needs fueling her desires.

She fell asleep once more to dream of Dax watching her go down on another man.

In the morning, he was gone, the bed and the house empty. Her stomach trembled. He'd left her cash and a note.

"When's your next Courtesan date?"

*Thank you, God.* For a moment, she'd thought he was giving her the brush-off. For the first time in a long time, she couldn't bear not to see a man again. This man.

She held the note to her chest. Her heart swelled. Infatuation. Lust at first sight. It was exactly what she'd been waiting for.

# 5

"TELL ME ABOUT HIM," DAX CAJOLED HER.

Almost two weeks later, Thursday night, ten p.m. Dax lay naked on the bed, lights off, Bluetooth in his ear, cock in his hand, Noelle's voice making him hard.

"He's close to six feet, a hundred and ninety pounds, nice, thick medium brown hair, brown eyes, about my age, a very nice smile and—" She paused; Dax could hear the rumble of a male voice, then she laughed, the music of it making his dick twitch. "And he told me to tell you he's incredibly hot."

"Do *you* think he's hot?"

"Mmm." The purr thrummed along his cock.

"Have you ever done him before?"

"No, he's new. From—" She paused again. "Fargo, North Dakota. Can you believe that? Just like the movie. It's snowing back there."

"Tell him to get naked, but I want you to keep your clothes on."

She snapped her fingers right near the mouthpiece. "Off. Now."

She'd gone on three dates since he'd seen her, and after each one, she'd called him, described in detail the things she'd done, turning him inside out with her erotic words and sexy voice. Then on Tuesday, she'd informed him she'd arranged a date for Thursday night with a guy willing to play their game, allowing Dax to listen in. The man probably found it hot as hell. She was going in hands free and plugged in, ready to do anything.

It was too fucking hot. Dax had always wanted this. He'd once had a woman friend who called him after she'd fucked another guy, but he'd never had every facet illustrated for him, punctuated by the emotion she felt and the sounds she made.

He'd never had a woman like Noelle. She was addictive. The night she'd lain in his arms had been heaven. He'd never slept so well, hated to leave her in the morning, and he wouldn't have except for an early golf date with a major supplier. If he'd known the effect she would have, literally enthralling him, he'd have canceled the game despite the fact that a lot of business was conducted over golf.

"Oh my God, Dax, he's huge." Awe dripped from her voice.

Male laughter drifted to him. He closed his eyes and lightly stroked his dick. Not too much yet; he wanted his tension to rise as theirs did, as if he were in the room.

"Describe it to me."

She made little noises, and a deep voice reached across the distance. "That's it, baby, take a real good look." She'd obviously moved closer.

"I'm down on my knees, Dax. He's longer than my hand, and when I wrap my fingers around him, they don't overlap."

He pictured her stroking, felt her touch on his cock, his balls tightening. A groan rumbled across the phone.

"He likes that," she said. "He's hard already."

"Fuck, sweetheart." The male voice was tinny with the slight distance to Noelle's earphone. "Listening to you tell your boyfriend all about it makes me fucking crazy."

It made Dax nuts, too. He pumped faster, twisting his wrist, stroking from base to tip until a bead of pre-come oozed from his slit. He palmed his crown and coated his dick.

"Pour some lube on him," Dax demanded. "I want him real slippery for you." He wanted to hear it.

"Yes, sir," she murmured, laughter threaded through her voice.

"Holy shit," the guy muttered, groaning again. "This is fucking kinky, sweetheart, and I love it."

Dax liked the term of endearment rather than a curse. Noelle deserved respect. She was more exceptional than her client could ever grasp. He visualized it all behind his closed lids, as if he were there with the light musk of semen permeating the air. Grabbing the lube, he drizzled a small amount over his cock. She was stroking *his* dick, crooning to *him*.

"Tell me how you like his cock," he whispered to her.

Her breath came faster, light puffs in the mouthpiece. "He's so smooth. His balls are shaved, and they feel so good in my hand. When I squeeze like this, he makes all these sexy sounds."

Dax heard them, a low growl, a rumble in the throat, soft words in a deep voice, *shit*, *fuck*, *baby*.

"Reach up and pinch his nipples."

A harsh gasp, a sharp exhale, then a hiss. "Bitch."

In this case, it *was* a term of endearment.

"He likes that a lot. He just flopped flat on the bed, with his feet on the floor while I work him."

Dax imitated the position and pinched his own nipple. She was so perfect. He should have thought of paying a woman to do this years ago. Then again, he wouldn't have found Noelle. Right time, right woman. Providence.

"Tell me how it makes you feel," he urged. He needed her emotions as much as anything.

"Powerful. He's putty in my hands, his flesh is all mine. I can make him do anything."

The cock's owner grunted, refuting her, then in almost the same moment, he cursed, groaned. She *did* own him.

"I love cock, Dax, the way it feels, all that smooth flesh marred only by the veins along it, how hard it feels yet how utterly soft against my palm, how it pulses, the way it changes color, almost purple right there"—pause, a shocked male gasp; she must have done something extraordinary—"his crown all covered in his own come. My mouth waters . . ." Her voice finally trailed off.

His head was going to explode.

"Suck him," he whispered, the devil in her ear.

The warm, wet sound of it filled his mind. Her lips were on him, the way they'd been in the car, pulling, sucking, teasing, biting.

"Give him the phone."

She moaned, a hollow sound, her mouth full. "Uh-uh."

"Yes. I want him to tell me."

She suckled, slurped; it drove him wild, but he needed more. "I want him to describe how it feels. I want you to know how much he loves it, baby. Do it now."

She let out a low moan, swallowed, then the sexy sounds ceased. "Yes, Dax." The breathy quality of her voice, need lacing her words, tied him in knots. The phone crackled and rustled, her fingers fumbling over the mouthpiece.

"Man, you two are fucking nuts," the guy said once he had her earphone in. "I fucking love it. Christ, if I had a woman like her, I wouldn't need to pay."

He didn't say his name; Dax didn't ask. But he totally agreed with the sentiment. With a woman like Noelle, a man would never need anyone else. Ever.

"Tell her to suck you."

"He says get busy sucking me, baby." The guy emphasized the line with a dirty laugh.

"How does she feel?" Dax needed to know.

"Fucking good. Really hard on the tip until I feel like my fucking head will blow."

Dax shared the sensation. He didn't know what this was called, whether it was voyeurism or something completely new and undefined. Whatever it was, her lips sucked him just as she sucked this nameless, faceless stranger. His eyes closed, the touch on his cock was hers, not his own, the ache in his balls was destined for her mouth.

"More." He could barely manage the word.

"Oh fuck. She's taken me so damn deep down her throat." The groan was gut-deep. He panted, swore, and beneath it all, Dax detected her moans and sighs.

"Christ, I wanna fuck her. Christ, she's so fucking good. How can she do that to a man? How can she take my dick so far? God, my nuts are full. It almost fucking hurts." He cried out. "Oh fuck, oh shit, she pinched my fucking nipple."

Dax felt the white-hot streak of pain himself, and his cock became impossibly hard in his fist. "Come in her mouth."

On the other end, in the heaven between her lips, the guy choked, sobbed, begged. "Oh man, her lips, her mouth, her teeth, all those little bites. It's like she can't get enough of me, like she's devouring me." Then he shouted.

Dax exploded. He emptied himself and gave it all to her. He shot high into the night, became one with a man he didn't know, and together they fucked Noelle's mouth.

He'd never come harder, better, longer. It was more than double the pleasure. It was life-altering. She wasn't even there, and he knew he'd finally found that precious something he'd searched so long for. A woman who was so sexual, so open, so uninhibited, so in love with sex itself she would never stop surprising him. She was undoubtedly the perfect match for his appetite, a woman he couldn't tire of, a lady who wouldn't eventually look upon him with disgust.

He willed her to call him when she was done. He needed one more thing from her tonight. Just one thing, and he would be utterly replete.

CHUCK, HER CLIENT, INSISTED ON GOING DOWN ON HER, GIVING her an orgasm, making sure she was satisfied. As if it were his duty, when her pleasure was really not a prerequisite.

Noelle could have done without the orgasm. She'd wanted to snatch the Bluetooth out of Chuck's ear. Dax was gone when she finally regained possession. Damn.

She left the hotel giddy, as if she'd downed three glasses of bubbly. Champagne always made her light-headed, but this time it was Dax's voice dizzying her on the other end of the phone. He was her alcohol. This was the fourth date she'd gone on since she'd met him, and it had come to the point where calling him before, during, or after was more important than the date or the client. His voice was the adrenaline shot, the drug in her veins. She needed that breathless, heart-racing, pulse-pounding kick that only he gave her. But tonight, it had been above and beyond anything she'd ever experienced.

Was she really that good? Sure she knew how to make men come. But listening to Charles Winstead IV, king of a North Dakotan manure empire, extolling her cocksucking virtues over the phone . . . it had done something to her. Set her free. Pushed her to never-before-reached heights. She wanted Dax to know what she was capable of, as if she were sucking him right through the phone. Swallowing him. His unique, sexy, spicy scent had filled her head. Chuck was merely a conduit.

In the back of the cab, she rattled off the address, dizzy with anticipation. Excitement thrummed in the pit of her stomach. Like being sixteen years old, waiting for a phone call asking her to babysit, her hand in the air right over the receiver so her mom couldn't get to it before she did. Ah, then the sweet caress of his voice and the fear: Would he look at her differently tonight, see her as a woman, touch her?

What if Dax didn't answer the door? What if he answered, then closed it in her face? What if he dragged her in and fucked the hell out of her? God, she just wanted to see him. Honest, she'd be satisfied with that.

His voice on the phone—he couldn't know what that had done to her. Even now, she was wet and close to the edge. So close that she sighed and parted her legs, catching the cabby's eyes in the mirror.

Maybe she could tease Dax with a story of how she'd masturbated in the backseat on the way over. Then he wouldn't throw her out.

This was lust and infatuation. Part of the high was the uncertainty, the giddiness, the ups, the downs, and everything in between. Her fingers itched to punch his number into her cell. But what if he told her not to come over? God, she loved this manic feeling. She was alive with it, every nerve sensitized, stretched, on edge. You couldn't get this from sex alone. No, you had to have the emotion, too.

The cab pulled to a stop at the gate. His home was a freaking seaside estate, but the driveway gate was just for show. She'd discovered that morning a couple of weeks ago that the wooden gate beside the brick column wasn't locked.

Climbing out, she gave the cabby a bill and a smile. "Could you wait please?" It would be embarrassing if Dax turned her away and she was stuck.

He was standing in the open doorway as she climbed his steps, silhouetted against the wall of windows over the ocean. Not a single light burned. She couldn't see his eyes, yet intensity sizzled off him.

She reached him. Snagging her with one hand at her nape, his fingers curled into her hair. She had to rise up on her toes to touch her lips to his mouth.

That first kiss was electric. His lips taking hers, his tongue invading and conquering, stealing her thoughts, her soul. He smelled so good, she wanted to melt into him, and he tasted all minty and sweet. Hard muscles melded to hers, as if she were becoming a part of him. And she was completely taken.

He let her go. She licked his taste from her lips.

"You taste like him."

Her heart stuttered. "I'm sorry."

"It's too damn hot for words." His eyes, deep, dark pools of blue, glittered in what little light they grabbed from the moon. "I needed that."

"Needed what?" As much as she'd wanted the sight, touch, and scent of him, she had to have the words, too.

"You. Here. Tonight. After you'd done him. That kiss."

She wanted to go in, push him to the floor, take him, fuck him. Instead, she backed away. "Thank you," she whispered. He'd given her everything. Anything more, in this time and place, would be too much. She wanted to savor each separate moment rather than immerse herself in sensory overload. She'd have it all next time.

"Good night."

He didn't ask her to stay. He understood her emotions precisely at that moment, as if the same need to relish, the same intensity rocked his world, too.

She backed down the steps one at a time, her fingers to her lips. "Call Isabel when you're ready."

"I'm ready."

It was a tease. She loved it. She turned, gathered her coat around her, and ran back to the cab as if it were her Cinderella pumpkin and he was the prince who would be driven to find her by her shoe.

His gaze tracked her the whole way.

God, he was perfect.


SHE WAS SO DAMN PERFECT. HE'D BEEN CALLED A PERVERT FOR RE-ceiving his pleasure by watching women he cared for make love to other men. He'd been told he needed a psychiatrist, but for him seeing and hearing was as exciting as doing. Especially since he'd had Noelle. He could *feel* what her client experienced, a tactile journey. Most men would call him a crazy SOB for failing to drag her inside and fuck her, for achieving orgasm with his own hand earlier in the evening while some stranger drove him nuts with how well she sucked cock.

Yet he couldn't have asked for anything more ideal than what she'd given him.

Drinking in the sights and sounds of a woman's pleasure—it couldn't be appreciated in the same way if you were part of the action. You overlooked the subtle nuances. You lost your concentration. You'd miss the kick of validation knowing another man could borrow but not own what you had.

Of course he had his moments of doubt that she belonged to

him. Until she stood on his doorstep. He'd tasted it in her kiss. She wanted to be shared as much as he wanted to share her. He imagined endless scenarios. Some he'd finish by taking her, others he'd simply enjoy the glisten of pleasure on her body. A woman's orgasm was a sight to behold.

Next he needed to be there to watch her come.

# 6

"DID DAX CALL FOR A DATE YET?" IT HAD BEEN ALMOST A WEEK. THE suspense made her bitchy and cranky.

Instead of answering, Isabel just gave her a look.

"What?" Noelle knew she shouldn't have asked. She never asked about clients. If they called, fine; if they didn't, whatever. She wasn't unfeeling, she had just never invested enough in one particular man. Which was probably her whole problem now with the boredom. No emotional investment, no emotional payback, but no one got hurt either. That had worked for a while.

The pool was warm. Noelle loved water exercises. They eased the work her joints had to do, yet added resistance to every movement. Oddly, she loved the smell of chlorine, too. Fresh. Unlike the sweaty bodies in the gym. Not that she disliked a hardworking male scent; she just didn't like to get sweaty herself. At least not while working out. After forty-five minutes of water-resistance exercises, she'd finish her regimen with laps in the big pool to get the aerobic workout.

"Do not look at me like that." She pursed her lips as Isabel continued to stare pointedly without a word. "I know what you're going to say."

"You don't." Isabel wore her blond hair piled in a neat knot on her head. Noelle marveled that not a strand fell out of place, even while exercising. Isabel was always together.

"You were going to say I'm getting too involved." Laying her arms along the pool edge, Noelle began a set of thigh repetitions.

"I wasn't thinking that at all," Isabel said, glancing past Noelle to an elderly woman climbing from the water.

The lady had walked the length of the pool, bobbing back and forth, for half an hour at a fast clip. That was a hell of a lot of resistance, and she'd gotten her aerobics at the same time. Noelle herself wanted to be able to keep up the pace at eighty. She still wanted to have sex, too, sagging flesh and all. She turned back to Isabel. "All right, what were you going to say then?"

"I'm jealous, actually."

That had her giving Isabel a second look. "You said putting too much emotion into a client was dangerous." And maybe Isabel was right. Dax consumed Noelle's thoughts. She went to sleep thinking about him, woke up dreaming about him. If he walked away now, she didn't know how she'd handle it.

"Sometimes a girl needs a little danger to keep her on her toes," Isabel said.

Noelle keyed into Isabel's almost wistful tone, wondering if something was going on with her. "Everything okay?"

"Just great," Isabel said, her smile a tad brittle.

Isabel was a listener, not a talker. Noelle could count on one hand the number of times Isabel had needed advice. If she wanted it, she'd ask when she was ready. Noelle let it go. "So did Dax call?"

"Yes." Isabel winked. "He had some special requirements."

Oh, thank God. Despite the warm water, Noelle shivered deliciously. Dax had called her every night. He'd gotten off listening to her get off. But he hadn't mentioned another date. Noelle couldn't ask. That ruined the anticipation. But waiting had been killing her. Which was probably how Dax wanted her to be, right on the edge. "What kind of requirements?"

"He gave strict instructions not to tell you anything."

Noelle forgot her count as she glided her left thigh through the water, so she switched to the right. "But you're not going to obey him, are you?"

Isabel's eyebrows shot up. "I don't *obey* men anywhere else, but a client request is inviolate." Then she smiled, a wicked angel smile. "Besides, it would spoil the surprise."

Ooh. Her legs weakened with a rush of heat straight to her sex. "I like surprises." She sounded like a child, but the tension coiling inside was all woman.

"He told me to set the date, time, and place, and when the details are worked out, he'll forward instructions through me on what you're to wear."

Noelle bit her lip. Anticipation. Seduction. A thrill circled in her belly. "That's kind of hot." Totally hot.

Isabel nodded slowly, and lowered her voice to a mere whisper. "That's why I'm jealous."

MIDAFTERNOON TWO DAYS LATER, DAX COURIERED A GOLD-embossed envelope to her apartment. The envelope was attached to a box wrapped in deep red. She could barely contain herself once the delivery man was gone.

Inside she found a fur coat. Fox. She didn't like the thought of killing animals, but the fur was sumptuous as she wrapped the knee-length coat around her shoulders. She was a sensual animal, and she couldn't resist running her hands through the thick pelt, savoring the softness, the warmth. She'd wear it once, just this once, then send it back.

Her hands trembled as she tore at the envelope and the note-paper caressed her fingertips.

"Wear the coat and nothing else. Meet me on the corner of Powell and Geary at seven o'clock." Union Square, with a myriad of hotels. Her insides creamed. Her legs weakened, and she fought the need to crumple to her knees right there in the entry hall. What did he plan? To fuck in her a restaurant, a doorway, on the elevator in Macy's, the Rotunda at Neiman Marcus? Or maybe he'd parade her down the street, approach the first man they saw, and order her to suck him off in a dark alleyway. Her body trembled with equal parts terror, excitement, and desire.

She'd agreed to do whatever he told her to. She just didn't know how far he'd go. Of course she always had veto power if things got too intense, yet the intensity was what excited her. Catch-22.

FIVE HOURS LATER, NOELLE HUGGED THE FOX FUR COAT TIGHT against the cold of the March night.

Dax saw her from afar, and his heart stopped beating. Her silky black hair cascaded over the silvery white fur. Tall and graceful, her bare legs were impossibly long and luscious in her fuck-me stilettos. Heads turned, gazes trailed after her. One woman bopped her husband on the arm for looking too long. Yet it wasn't her beauty that captured Dax. It was that she was his, that she waited on the corner as if it were a precipice she was ready to dive off. For him. The power brought him to life with a rush of exhilaration like none he'd ever experienced.

How far could he push her? What kinky things could he get her to do for him?

She turned then, saw him, and a smile curved her lips. Half-angel, half-vixen, sultry, sexy, yet elegant in the coat. His heart started its beat again, faster, louder. She'd do anything he asked. If he wanted her to suck one cock, she'd beg for two. If he told her to touch herself, she'd turn on a toy designed for dual entry. Her naughty mind would always outdo his. He could not have dreamed up a more spectacular woman.

Or maybe it was so much wishful thinking after years of disappointment. He'd always found the fall was harder when you truly believed your dream had come true. Only to find it hadn't.

He ambled to her, his gaze flicking over her, up, down, touching her eyes. Then he strolled past. The click of her spiked heels followed him on the sidewalk. He crossed Geary and headed up the street. A cable car clattered down the hill, and the noise was damn near deafening—car engines, horns, laughter, voices, a street person screaming at himself—yet beneath it all her shoes tapped close behind on the concrete. He turned into one of the older hotels, a doorman dressed as a beefeater holding the door for him. Mouthwatering scents drifted up from the restaurant—garlic, the zest of tomato sauce, something sweet he couldn't identify.

"Welcome, pretty lady," the man said in a low rumble.

She laughed, thanked him. Dax turned to catch a glimpse of bare skin where she held the lapels of the coat loosely. With that flash of thigh and deep slash of cleavage, the guy had to know she was naked beneath.

Dax's cock pulsed. His balls tightened. One step ahead of him, that's what she was, and he adored it.

As a couple with two children approached from the other direction, she wrapped the fox jacket around her. And hit Dax with a smile hot enough to knock him off his feet. On the other side of Reception, he headed up a wide set of carpeted stairs and turned right at the second level. Lengthening his stride, he hoped to lose her for a moment, force her to wonder and skip to keep up. Around another corner, he tugged an ornate door handle, slipped inside, and let the door close slowly behind him. Then he let out his breath. The setup was flawless.

The lighting was low and intimate, the table was laid, the chairs occupied.

And she was the feast.

NOELLE LEANED BACK AGAINST THE DOOR, FINGERS CLUTCHED IN the soft fur. She couldn't get enough air, spots danced before her eyes. Not a word, just a hungry look flaming in his blue eyes, and she'd had to follow Dax up the street. He made her crazy.

But the sight in that room liquefied her.

It was a small ballroom meant for intimate parties. Wall-to-wall mirrors reflected intricate moldings along the ceiling, a chandelier dangled in the center, its crystal glittering like dewdrops, and lush carpeting swirled with pinks, reds, and purples. In the middle, one table that would easily seat ten was set with damask tablecloth, silver cutlery, Waterford glasses, gold-trimmed china.

And two chairs.

Dax stood between the two, a wineglass in his hand. He held it out to her.

Noelle couldn't take her eyes off the two men seated there. Isabel had chosen them, she knew, because Isabel had two years of practice giving Noelle what she wanted. They were older. God, she loved older men. They made her slick and hot and needy. Especially with Dax watching, reading every thought, interpreting each emotion flitting across her face.

The first was completely bald. She loved a shiny pate where she could leave a kiss of lipstick on the crown. Wire-rimmed glasses, a ruddy masculine face, big hands, and a massive, sculpted chest. He was *The X Files'* Assistant Director Skinner personified. She'd always had a thing for Skinner.

But then she'd always had a thing for Burt Lancaster in some of his earthier classic roles, too, like rolling around on a Hawaiian beach in *From Here to Eternity*. Oh yeah, the second guy was perfect, a dark, dirty blond, not as light as Dax's hair, but his eyes just as blue. His biceps bulged beneath his work shirt as if he spent his days tossing fifty-pound bags of cement.

Dax snapped his fingers. The sound jolted through her. She should have hated it—no man snapped his fingers at her—but goose bumps pebbled her bare legs with anticipation, nerves and excitement doing figure eights in her stomach.

She sauntered to him languorously, her hips swaying, her thighs playing peekaboo through the coat. She didn't look at Burt or Skinner, holding Dax's ice blue gaze. He was stone cold. Until she saw him swallow. He was as high as she was.

This was going to be amazing.

# 7

AS SHE STOOD IN FRONT OF DAX, HIS SEXY MALE MUSK SWIRLED around her, and beneath the black suit pants, Noelle imagined his cock pulsed. He held the glass of fruity sweet wine to her lips as she took a long swallow and licked away the last drops.

"What are we going to do?" she whispered.

He didn't say a word. Her tension ratcheted higher. Close up, she could see the blazing heat in Burt's blue eyes, the strip-her-naked, heavy-lidded stroke of Skinner's gaze. And she wanted it all, everything Dax had in store.

Even while it terrified her. Just how far would she have to go to please him? Fear was part of the high.

She didn't have time to think. Grabbing her at the waist, he forced a squeak out of her. Then he dumped her on her butt on the table. In the only empty place setting. The one he'd been meaning just for her.

"Wha-at?" She stuttered, caught herself. "What are you doing?"

He closed in on her, his mouth almost taking hers, his gaze a blur. "I want to watch."

"Watch what?" Her lungs felt light and fluttery, unable to process a full breath.

He spread the lapels of the coat and cupped her breasts. His cold hands chilled her, thrilled her, like ice straight on her clit. "I want to watch them make you come."

He pinched her nipple. She moaned, little stars floating before her eyes.

"Spread your legs," he demanded. Then he touched her between the thighs. "Look how wet you are, naughty girl." He glanced left, then right. "Which one do you want first?"

Staring into his sky blue eyes, she wanted both. She wanted him, them, everything.

He read her need. "You have to choose."

It was like selecting from a smorgasbord of expensive caviar, crab, and lobster. Snared by Dax's gaze, she pointed. "Him." Skinner.

Dax stepped back, and Skinner pulled his chair between her legs. He nipped her thigh lightly. Heat rushed to her clitoris.

"Look at me," Dax ordered. "Keep looking at me."

Falling back on her elbows, she couldn't have torn her gaze from Dax even as Skinner's mouth descended in her peripheral vision. Burt pushed glassware out of her way. Skinner's tongue, Burt holding her thighs apart, Dax's too-hot stare—she was suddenly there, right *there*, so close she could cry out. When Skinner licked her clit, she bit her lip until she tasted blood. His mouth devoured her while Burt played, stroking close to her pussy, easing away, then coming down beneath Skinner's jaw to test her wetness. Her juice dripped onto his fingers. Oh God, oh God. Lasered by Dax's gaze, her skin flushed rosy, heat rising to her cheeks, as if he took her, fucked her, owned her with nothing more than a look. Her pussy simply imploded, sensation rocketing through each individual nerve, sparking in her clit, her womb, the tips of her fingers, dragging her under, then shooting her into the glittering teardrops of the chandelier.

Noelle screamed, and Dax covered her mouth with his, tasting her orgasm, riding the crest with her, sharing her breath as he drank in every ounce of pleasure she felt.

When it was over, he pulled back, held her chin between his fingers. "You didn't keep looking at me. We'll have to try that again." Consumed by her pleasure, he'd taken her lips and missed the orgasm play across her features. He wanted that, needed it. Damn, he wouldn't miss it again by indulging in her taste.

"Switch places," he whispered, his gaze holding hers as he snapped his fingers at his cohorts. Then he whisked the fox coat from her arms, leaving her completely naked. She was too far gone to care. He kissed her, held her, and didn't let her go until the musical chairs between her thighs ended.

The blond put his mouth to her, and she arched off the table, moaning, a tear of pleasure slipping down her temple as she thrashed on the fine linen tablecloth. Her brow furrowed, she squeezed her eyes shut, pushed her fingers through the man's short hair, and held him tight to her pussy. Her hips rolled, and she curled one leg around his shoulder.

"Dax, oh God, Dax."

He loved that in the midst of another man eating her pussy, *his* name was on her lips.

"Fuck her with your fingers," he ordered the bald guy.

And the man got right in there along with Blondie, spreading her legs, stroking her thigh, and slipping beneath the tongue lapping at her to push two blunt fingers inside her. He glanced at Dax, a devilish smile creasing his lips. "She's so damn wet. And she tastes so good." He pulled out, licked his fingers, then slid back in.

Dax leaned close to her ear. "How does it feel, baby?"

She groaned, opened her eyes, met his. "It's too much."

"It's never too much."

She jerked as one of them hit a sensitive spot. "Dax." It seemed to be all she could manage, then she slid her arm around his neck. "Kiss me."

"I can't watch you if I kiss you."

And Christ, he had to watch.

Her gaze grew unfocused. She groaned, bit her lip, closed her eyes again, tossed her head. Another teardrop trickled down her temple and into her hair. Dax slid his hand over her soft skin, flicked the tip of one breast. She was so damn sensitized, she arched and cried out. He gazed down the length of her, a blond head bobbing between her legs and the top of a bald pate visible as they concentrated on her pleasure.

He pinched her nipple. She arched her neck and moaned, panted. Then she rolled up, hunching, her eyes tightly closed as she chanted his name, a guttural, damn near unintelligible sound. But it was *his* name, and when she came the second time, harder than the first, he savored every tear, every cry, every quake of her body. There had never been a more beautiful sight.

During the aftershocks, he gathered her in his arms, and when she quieted, he whispered in her ear, "We're not done yet, baby."


NOELLE COULD BARELY MOVE HER LIMBS. BURT AND SKINNER HAD licked and sucked her until one orgasm melted into the next. One of them held her head—or maybe that was Dax—and fed his cock to her mouth. She couldn't be sure in the end who did what. It was all a blur of mindless pleasure punctuated by Dax, stroking, talking, touching, kissing, loving her as she orgasmed. She'd never been closer to another human being. How that was possible, she didn't know, didn't care. It just was.

Dax now cradled her in the backseat of the car he'd ordered to take them across town, his fingers toying with her hair. God, she was tired. And so utterly satisfied.

Except for one thing. "You didn't come," she murmured into his tux jacket, not sure he'd even make out her words.

"I enjoyed watching you too much to interrupt."

"It turned you on?" Wrapped in his arms, she felt the evidence against her belly, yet she needed him to tell her.

"It was the most perfectly decadent scene of debauchery I've ever witnessed." His laugh rumbled against her ear.

"Really?

"Truly. It was too fucking fantastic for words." He tucked a lock of hair away from her face. "I'll never forget how beautiful you were with a cock in your mouth and a bald head between your legs."

God. He knew exactly what to say. But she needed more. Pushing upright, she let her gaze travel over his handsome features. He had the ability to steal the very breath from her lips, just as he had the first time she saw him. She rubbed noses with him. "I could lick and suck you now."

Manuel was driving again. She was sure he wouldn't mind.

"You're exhausted."

Her jaw ached, her body throbbed, and if she closed her eyes for too long, she'd be asleep. But she needed this. She needed him to want it. Batting her eyelashes, she said, "I don't mind at all."

He stroked her hair. She must look an absolute fright, yet he touched her with such tenderness. "The anticipation will be so much greater for the next time if I hold off." He smiled for her. "I'll be half-mad with lust by then."

She didn't want *half* later. She needed him completely insane now. "You might get a case of blue balls," she quipped.

Something didn't feel right. Didn't he want her? After the things she'd done and had done to her, how could a man wait? She knew the guilty signs, the debilitating symptoms when a person needed more than what he or she was getting. She'd hated feeling that way, hated the things she'd resorted to in her quest for what she needed, hated the person she became.

Was Dax already feeling that need for more, different, new?

He cupped her face in his hand without laughing at her silly joke. With the streetlights flashing over his face, she couldn't read his expression. Yet he must have read something in hers. Taking her hand, he caressed his cock with her palm. "Then you better suck me, baby," he whispered.

She fumbled getting his zipper down. He helped her. In her hand, his cock was huge, pulsing, a tiny drop of pre-come beading on the tip. She swiped it clean with her tongue.

"Yum," she murmured. "This is so much better than waiting."

He moaned the affirmation she needed.

Then she took him deep. His groan rumbled in his chest. With a hand to the back of her head, he urged her to devour every inch. Then she tucked her hand beneath his thigh, and licked and sucked, fast and hard. She forgot about Manuel, the twinge in her jaw, and the tenderness between her thighs. There was only this, the silk of his cock, the sweetness of his pre-come, the throb as she brought him close, closer, closest. Until he spurted in her mouth. She swallowed it all, every drop of his essence, and needed more. So much more.

When it was done, he zipped up and snuggled her deeper into his embrace. "Thanks, baby, that was great."

Just "great"?

She didn't want to think. He hadn't asked her to suck him. She'd offered. He'd refused because she was so exhausted. Sweet. But he hadn't taken her in the ballroom either. Beyond kissing her and pinching her nipples, Dax hadn't touched her since that first night. Now her blow job was only "great."

Maybe he didn't want her anymore.

AS THE CAR WENDED THE LAST FEW BLOCKS TO HER FLAT, NOELLE slept peacefully in his lap while Dax stroked her hair as if she were a child. The woman was insatiable. After the workout in the ballroom, he hadn't expected her to do him, too, despite the ache in his balls. Yet she couldn't get enough. He wondered if in the end he could actually keep up with her or if she'd tire of him long before he had his fill.

That was the thing. He was starting to believe he'd never get his fill. She was his teenage fantasy come true, with so much more added on top. He'd have said he had a limitless imagination, but Noelle was like no other woman he'd ever known. Her need for fantasy and kinkiness surpassed even his.

He knew what he was. His desires were enough to freak out most ordinary women. So he'd never allowed himself much emotion in his relationships. With this one, since he was paying, he'd thought to invest even less emotion. Yet he was in danger of giving her far more than any price they'd bargained for.

When she left, she'd take a piece of him with her.

Manuel took a corner, and Noelle stirred against Dax. A soft purr in her throat, she nuzzled his cock, then settled as the car hit a steady rhythm once again. Her sensual woman scent drifted up to him, the scent he'd become addicted to at the tender age of fourteen.

Goddammit, what the hell was he thinking? He wasn't one of her pathetic, cuckolded husbands. He knew what he wanted. He knew what *she* wanted. Fantasy, excitement, naughty, dirty things in secret, hot places. He was a man, a CEO. When things took a wrong turn, he righted them, steered the ship onto a true course.

He would give her the excitement she craved, always upping the stakes, always surprising her, never the same thing twice.

And she would *never* want to leave him.

NOELLE SAT IN HER FLAT'S BAY WINDOW OVERLOOKING THE MA-rina. It was a sunny, windy day and sailboats dotted the harbor and bay. On the marina lawn, a dog walker struggled with six leashes, finally getting her charges untangled.

The phone clutched to her chest, Noelle waited impatiently for Dax to set up their next date. In the week since the ballroom event, he'd called once for phone sex, only once, and that had been the very next night. Then nothing. He'd said he was planning a special date, and he wanted to heighten his anticipation by starving himself for the sound of her voice. It sounded so sweet, so seductive, so exciting. Until a couple of days turned into a week. For a woman who personified instant gratification, that was six days too many.

There just *had* to be another date. She didn't know what she'd do if she didn't see him again. He was better than any flavor of ice cream. He was buttercream frosting on red velvet cake or choco-late decadence with real whipped cream. He was everything she'd dreamed of and thought she'd never have.

He'd said she was fantastic, but he might have been lying. No, he'd said *it* was fantastic. The date. Burt and Skinner. God, did he say *it* or *she*? Damn, damn, damn, she couldn't remember.

Isabel had been right. Getting your emotions involved was dangerous. Noelle hadn't been on a courtesan date in a week. She hadn't thought about another man since she met Dax. She'd dreamed only of how to please him, what she could do to make him hot. To make him hers. From the moment she stepped onto that rooftop balcony, her clients had been merely reasons to call him, talk to him, incite him to orgasm. She'd wanted the excitement, the infatuation, the giddy I'll-die-if-I-don't-talk-to-him-right-now feeling.

Now she was trapped into needing it all to be real.

The phone rang, and she jumped, almost jostling herself out of the window seat. Then she jabbed the flash button without even checking caller ID. "Hello?"

"Noelle?"

Isabel. Thank you, thank you. She wanted to blurt out, *Did he call yet?*, but she managed to maintain a little decorum. "I hope you're having a good day, Isabel."

Isabel snorted. "You don't care about my day. You just want to know if he made a date."

"Who?" She sounded singularly innocent.

Isabel gave a tinkling laugh. "He called."

Noelle closed her eyes and held in a sob of gratitude. "Did he want to schedule something? I'll have to check my calendar."

"We both know your calendar is completely free. You can't pay your mortgage with a free calendar, you know."

Noelle didn't have a mortgage. Being a courtesan had been good for her. She'd paid extra against principal every month, and six weeks ago, the title had become hers. "Okay, I give in. My calendar is too free. Does he want to fill it?"

"Tomorrow night."

She exhaled in a long sigh. "I can do tomorrow night. Anything special?"

"He's chosen a couple."

Her heart froze to a standstill. "A man and a woman?"

Isabel laughed again, although it might have been closer to another snort. "Yes, a man and woman. He wants a foursome."

She'd have to share him. She'd have to watch him fuck another woman. He hadn't even made love to her after the first night, and now he wanted another woman. It wasn't fair. It wasn't— She shut herself down. "When, where, how should I dress, et cetera, et cetera?"

"Are you all right?"

Damn. Isabel was far too intuitive. That worked for making her matches, but it sucked when Noelle was trying to hide something. "I'm fine."

"You sound funny."

"I had too much fresh air, and it's made me all stuffy."

Isabel let the silence hang for five counts. "Nine o'clock. The date will be at a residence. He'll arrive at your place by seven, though. He has something special for you to wear."

That lifted her. For a very brief moment before she dashed herself down again. God, she was manic. "Did you choose the couple?" It would be so much worse if Dax had picked the woman himself, someone special he already had in mind.

"Yes, I did the match."

She wrapped her arm around her knees. At least there was that; he'd had Isabel do the selection. "Okay. Then it's a go. Gotta run now. Bye." She hung up before Isabel could say *I told you so*.

He wanted another woman. Noelle wasn't enough. She was nothing but a courtesan, a plaything. He probably wanted to dress her for the other man, not himself. And really, he'd never said he wanted *her*. *He'd* said he wanted a kinky relationship. *She'd* thought she meant something to him. The way he'd held her that night, soothed her body with a warm cloth, taken care of her.

Yet he'd been gone in the morning. She'd allowed herself to fall for an illusion.

Noelle set her chin on her knees and stared out the window. Comeuppance. Retribution. A reckoning. For the first time she understood how each of her husbands had felt when he discovered he wasn't enough for her.

For the crimes she'd committed against the men she supposedly loved, she deserved this.

# 8

NOELLE HAD GIVEN HERSELF A PEP TALK. FOR TWENTY-FOUR HOURS. She still didn't believe it. The gist was that, first, asking him not to do another woman in front of her would reveal all the illusions she'd dreamed up about their relationship and lay bare her insecurities, so no way, bad idea. Second, it would sound as if she had a proprietary interest in him. Which she did, but again, bad idea letting him know. And third, if he wasn't jealous of her naughty desires, she couldn't be jealous of his. It was two-faced. Or to twist one of her mother's clichés, what was good for the goose was good for the gander. Only it wasn't. Another man making her come was totally separate from how she felt about Dax. It was just sex, physical, nothing more. Her husbands hadn't understood that. Now here she was with the shoe on the other foot (God, she *hated* thinking in her mother's clichés), raging about it.

But that was the God's honest truth. If she did another man, it had nothing to do with her emotions about Dax. In fact, it was over the top for her if he was there to watch. When he did another woman, however, it meant he didn't want Noelle.

By the time the doorbell chimed, she'd freshly showered, applied her makeup, and dried and brushed her hair to silky perfection, yet beneath her satin Chinese robe, she was naked, ready for him to dress her up.

The butterflies had flown from her stomach up into her throat, choking her.

Dax was mind-altering in his usual black tux and crisp white shirt. Except the night she'd kissed him on his doorstep, she'd never seen him wear anything else. And when he'd crawled into his bed with her? She'd missed her one and only opportunity to view his fully naked magnificence.

Oh wait, she'd have another chance tonight. When he took off his clothes to fuck another woman. Bam. Direct hit.

"Hi." Her voice squeaked, hitting an out-of-tune high note. She needed to get her jealousy under control.

"Hi, yourself." His gaze caressed her from head to toe and everything in between, setting her body on a low light. His voice dipped to a husky note. "You look beautiful."

She wanted to take his words for the compliment they were, but it seemed there was a "but" in there somewhere. "Thank you."

She hated how polite they sounded, like strangers, as if he'd never been buried deep in her mouth or her pussy. "Is that for me?"

He'd wrapped the box under his arm in red paper. Or someone had. "I want you to wear this tonight."

"What is it?"

He pulled back when she reached for it. "First things first, you get to try it on when we've gotten you all ready."

"I'm ready. Shower. Makeup. Hair." She fanned the shiny tresses over her shoulder. Didn't she look perfect? Dammit, she needed to stop with the self-doubt.

"Let me in and I'll show all the ways we need to get you ready."

She'd kept him waiting on the landing without even realizing it. "How are we going to get me ready?" she asked, seduction seeping into her tone. She wanted to ignore the silly, maudlin thoughts and play the game. She'd told Isabel she needed excitement, not melodrama.

He stepped over the threshold. "Nice place."

"It's small, but it's all mine." A one-bedroom, it had the original pink and gray tile in the kitchen and bathroom, hardwood floors, big bay windows in both dining and living room, an ornate fireplace, and her own tiny one-car garage she used for storage.

"It looks like you."

She tipped her head in question.

"The blue suede lounging chair."

It wasn't actually suede, which would have been a nightmare to clean. But she loved that chair, like the old-fashioned loungers an elegant lady of the manor would drape herself over. "I like to snuggle up with a good book in front of the fire." She preferred a naughty erotic romance over watching TV. "So are you going to dress me?" She pointed at the package.

"I'm going to prepare you. Take me to your bathroom."

This was interesting. She felt her spirits lift as she led the way down the short hall.

"Wow," he said, "that's amazing." The tub was a huge porcelain in which she could fully stretch out her legs. Pink and gray tiles marched up the wall. Her cushy towels matched, and a full-length cheval mirror stood in the corner.

Dax was still staring at the tub. "You could fit two in that thing."

"Yes. I probably could. But I never have." Damn, she didn't mean to offer that.

She didn't bring clients home. He was the first to even ask. She hadn't thought a thing of it. It was just . . . natural.

He laid the box on the countertop, then pointed to the tub's rim. "Sit."

She perched demurely on the edge.

"Open your robe."

Ooh. This was *really* interesting. She untied the sash and parted the lapels all the way down, letting the satin fall away from her thighs. She got a delicious little catch in her breath as his eyes glided over every inch of her skin.

"Lean back, brace yourself on one hand, and put your other foot along the edge."

It was as if he were choreographing a musical or posing her for a photograph.

"Touch yourself and tell me if you're wet." The tenor of his voice mesmerized her. She didn't have to touch to know she was wet.

But she did, slicking her fingers through her folds. "Very wet," she whispered.

"Good." He reached to the inner pocket of his jacket, then stopped, looking at her. "Close your eyes."

From behind her lids, the sounds he made were exquisite torture. Something chinked on the sink, and he ran the water long enough to turn it hot. The pipes were old, it took a minute, and she could feel each second ticking away in her chest.

The snap and pop of hands being soaped up filled the room, the delicate scent of her lavender bar tingling her nose. He was close enough to exude an enticing male musk, the air currents shifting around him, touching her.

He covered her mound, caressed her curls, soaped them. Good God, he was washing her. A finger slipped along her pussy, and she hissed between her teeth.

"Don't open your eyes," he warned, then shifted away for a

moment, returning the next. "Spread your legs wider." He helped her with a hand on her thigh.

"What are you doing?"

A razor rasped over her delicate skin. Her eyes shot open, and she stared at his darker hand against her pussy. He shaved carefully along one fold. "Don't move," he whispered.

She held her breath. Her body wanted to shudder. The cool glide of the razor, the warm touch of his hand, the sudden wash of air along her denuded flesh. She trimmed, but never shaved completely.

"Wider," he urged.

She leaned back on the tub, opened her legs fully, exposed herself. He bent to his task, shaving, reaching to the sink to dip the razor in hot water, then back.

No man had ever ministered to her this way, the erotic tilt of his head bent between her thighs, the cool razor leaving delicious prickles in its wake. Her body heated on the inside, melted for him, slicked deep in her channel. Her hips moved with the rhythm of his shaving, and she barely kept a moan in check. Then he pressed a warmed washcloth to her folds.

And speared her with his gaze.

"Why are you doing this?" she asked low, tantalized.

"Because I've never seen or felt a woman's bare pussy. And I wanted it tonight."

Then, like a magician revealing magic, he whisked the cloth away. "Now you're all pretty and pink."

She was bare, smooth. Her clit, a burgeoning nub, peeked out. Moisture glistened.

"Touch yourself," he murmured, taking one hand and guiding her there. "Christ, that's a beautiful pussy."

She laughed, but choked it off. His hand, her hand, her pink flesh, the feel of all that smooth skin. She traced the folds. "It's so soft." Reverence dripped from her voice. He'd made her so gorgeous down there and accomplished it with such heart-wrenching tenderness. Just like the first night in his bed.

Her eyes ached with unshed tears.

He followed her movements, touching where she touched. It was better than having two men. She tingled, then shivered.

"He's going to lick this." His lips at her ear, Dax seduced her. "He's going to fuck this sweet, smooth, bare, kissable pussy." He skated over her clit, and she jerked. "I'm going to watch him bury his cock in all that beautiful pink flesh."

Her lips parted, her skin flushed.

He forced her finger down on her clit, rubbed with her. She shuddered.

"I want to see his cock drenched in your juice."

She was so smooth, so wet, so warm. She'd never known how soft and delicate she was down there, every touch, every flick of his fingernail magnified by the bareness of her freshly shaved, sensitized skin. He'd once again given her something new she hadn't known she'd craved.

"Oh God, Dax, I'm going to come." She whimpered. Sensation shimmied up her torso.

"Then come." He licked her ear, blew on the wet spot.

Surrounded by feminine pink and gray tile, his heat, and her bare flesh against porcelain, Noelle screamed out her orgasm.

DAMN, SHE WAS BEAUTIFUL, HER SKIN FLUSHED A ROSY PINK, HER dark hair sliding over her shoulders, her pussy bare and gorgeous. Plump lips beckoned his tongue, her clit full and needy.

He'd surprised her, and he loved that he'd given her the unexpected. Tonight he would excite her with a cock, big, thick, filling her to the very brim. He was glad now that he hadn't let either of the men fuck her in the ballroom. He wanted to give her this instead. He wanted to lean back, hold her between his legs, flush to his body, as they both watched that massive tool enter her freshly shaved pussy. The sensations would drive her mad. And when she was close to the peak, he would rise and feed her his cock.

It was a fantasy come true. For both of them.

# 9

DAX REACHED ACROSS THE CONSOLE OF HIS PLUSH LUXURY CAR and fingered the silky dress he'd bought her. "Christ, you're gorgeous in red. You should always dress in vibrant colors."

Noelle always did. Hadn't he noticed? "Thank you."

God, she was manic. The orgasm in the bathroom had been fatal, too, too good, too overwhelming. She'd never be able to lie in the tub without remembering him, smelling him, wanting him.

She just wanted tonight to be over. The drive was interminable. The couple lived in Pacific Heights, the palace next to Danielle Steel's mansion. All right, she didn't *know* that, she was just . . . jealous as hell and feeling bitchy. She hadn't even discussed her price with Dax. For him, she didn't have a price. She'd give herself away for free. If only he didn't do the woman. But Dax had been sending her gifts after every phone call. He'd even given her an envelope after Burt and Assistant Director Skinner. He obviously still thought of this as business.

That was the problem. She should have returned the gifts and the money, a subtle statement without making a *real* statement.

"Are you all right?"

Why was he driving? Why hadn't they gotten Manuel this time? Maybe that was good, then he couldn't send her home by herself.

Unless the couple had a chauffeur, which was highly likely because they were so rich. They were in his class, his kind of people. She was just a whore. "I'm fine."

*Please make it stop.* She needed a psychiatrist and some really good drugs.

He was quiet then, negotiating the streets. She hadn't meant to snap. "I'm sorry. I'm just nervous."

"We don't have to do this. We can work up to it in baby steps."

"You had two men do me, Dax. What's the difference if it's a couple?" Because one was a woman who was supposed to do him.

"I don't expect you to touch her or let her touch you. I know you said you weren't into that."

God, she'd rather do the woman herself than have Dax touch her. She was probably beautiful and naturally thin without having to work out every day. And young.

She was such a bitch. Selfish. This was why she hated herself. She was all about me-me-me. She'd ruined her marriages because of it. She was ruining everything with Dax. Whether she was the one who needed something different or the person she was with had the itch, she screwed it all up. She wasn't good at monogamy, but now she had to face that she was also a selfish, jealous bitch as well. "I'm sorry. I'll be fine. And if you want me to do her, I'll do her."

He stopped at a massive iron gate supported by pillars topped with lions' heads. "I don't need you to do her." Pulling up to a pedestal with an electronic pad on it, he keyed in a series of numbers. "Whatever you want is fine."

"Fine?" God, she was even getting picky about his word choice now.

The gate slid open, and he continued up the drive. The grounds were magnificent, a topiary surrounding the house, oak and cypress masking the street below. You'd never know you were almost smack-dab in the middle of the city.

Dax glanced at her. "It's a perfectly *fine* word."

It struck her how like a married couple they sounded, the fights in the car before you get to the in-laws' house, because his mother thinks you're a slut who isn't good enough for her son, or because you always bring store-bought instead of something homemade, which shows you really don't care enough to put out the effort. But really, even though neither of you are saying it, the real reason for the fight is because he doesn't like to go down on you, which you love, and he doesn't even care if you have an orgasm.

Tears pricked her eyes. She had destroyed every marriage, torn apart every relationship. Courtesans had been her lifeline and she was damaging that, too.

She climbed out of the car before he could see the ridiculous moisture welling along her lids. *Please don't touch her. Don't want her more than me. Don't think she's better.*

That's what her life had been about. Always seeking a man who thought she was the prettiest, the sexiest, the most desirable. She'd lied to Isabel. She'd lied to herself. She hadn't been looking for something new and exciting. She'd been looking for a man to make her feel special again.

Men paid her. She was never more special than the next woman they could buy.

"Noelle." He grabbed her arm as she started up the wide stone steps.

She wanted to be watched and shared, but she couldn't stand doing the watching and the sharing. She was a self-centered bitch, and she didn't care. She'd die if she had to watch him. "You should just do them by yourself." She headed across the flagstone porch for the lighted doorbell.

"I want to watch you. I don't give a damn about doing them."

Right. That's why he'd fucked her once and once only. "You don't have to lie. I'm a courtesan. I'm all about anticipating someone else's pleasure. And I know you want to do her, so that's *fine*." With extreme effort, she tried to say it without sounding whiny. "I'll just have them call me a cab before the fun starts."

He pushed her up against the wall before she could tap the bell. "What's up with you? I thought we were doing great. Hot as fucking hell."

*Don't say it. Please, don't say it. Don't make him have to spell it out for you.*

"I just don't feel like watching you fuck her, that's all." Okay, that was *definitely* whiny. She couldn't stop herself. "What's wrong with that? You shouldn't have made me come in the bathroom. Now my heart's not in it." Her heart. God. Her heart was *so* in it. It ached that he didn't want her. During the drive, it had shriveled to the size of a dried pea. She had no proprietary claim on him. And even if she had, she'd long since lost the right to ask a man to keep himself only for her.

He held her shoulders to the wall, his big hot body flush against the length of hers, his blue eyes hot with anger. "Do you have some sort of split personality or something, because this is fucking weird, Noelle."

It had been building in her for days, almost two weeks. Even longer, perhaps from the moment she'd woken up alone in his bed, only a note on the table. But Dax, the poor man, didn't have a clue.

"Some other time," she whispered. "I'm not in the mood."

"*I'm* in the mood." He shifted his hips, rubbed his cock over her. He was hard. That didn't mean it was for her. "So tell me what the fuck is going on," he insisted.

He deserved to have what he wanted: the other woman. She

just hated admitting how badly she'd wanted him to choose her. "She'll take care of you."

He shook her slightly. "I don't want her to take care of me. I want *you*."

She was willing to take her punishment, letting Dax do the woman, but honestly, was part of her penance admitting aloud how selfish she was?

DAX TRAILED DOWN TO HER ASS, THEN HER THIGH, LIFTING HER leg to his hip and holding her there, open for him. "You loved me shaving you. Don't tell me that orgasm wasn't the best, and you know you want more."

Seeing her in that dress, bare beneath, her pussy shaved smooth, Dax was close to crazy himself. All he could think of was plowing his cock deep inside her, and it had been all he could do not to take her with her eyes closed in her girlie pink bathroom. He'd be in hell tonight because he hadn't taken her at least once before the foursome got started. So, other than his cock, what the fuck was up?

"It was good," she said, staring at his chest.

"Dammit, that orgasm was better than fucking good." Parting the slit of the dress, he unerringly slipped between her pussy lips. "And you're fucking wet. So don't tell me you've changed your mind." They stood to the left of the door on a wide front stoop of decorative flagstone. The door could open at any moment. And he had his hand up her skirt. Then again, they were there to fuck, so what difference did it make? He fingered her, deep inside, then glided back out to rub her clit. A low, sexy moan fell from her lips, and her eyelids fluttered shut.

"Tell me you want me to fuck you." No way would he let her deny it.

She pushed higher on her heels, tightened her thigh around him, pulling closer, rocking against his hand. Then she opened her eyes. "Tell me you want to fuck me."

"Hell yes."

Her dark eyes got impossibly darker. "No. I mean *really*. Tell me. You haven't done me since that first night."

Goddammit. In building his own anticipation and desires, he'd neglected the most important thing, making sure she knew that no matter what they did or who they did it with, it was only hot because he did these things with *her*. Hell, he hadn't even thought much about the other woman. For him, the wife was incidental to the scenario. He'd asked Isabel to find a woman who was keen to watch her husband fuck a courtesan because that might make it even hotter for Noelle.

He eased back, pulled her hand between their bodies and pressed her palm to his achingly hard cock. "I want to watch him fuck you, then I want to fuck you."

Like a hypnotist, she held him prisoner with just her gaze. "Do it now."

If he hesitated, he was dead. Dax couldn't think long enough to hesitate. He unzipped, and she pulled him through the fly of his tux.

"I've always wanted to fuck on someone's front porch," he whispered, lifting her. She trapped him with her thighs at his waist and her arms around his neck.

"Your girlfriend's parents," she said, playing into his fantasies. "They could open the door and catch you at any moment." Her red lipstick beckoned.

He couldn't resist, taking her lips as he eased the head of his cock past her opening. Her freshly shaved pussy was soft, smooth, and incredibly erotic. His tongue in her mouth, he flexed his hips, teasing her with just the tip.

She groaned into his mouth, then pulled back. "I've always wanted to do it in a hotel hallway. Just outside the room."

"Naughty bitch." He surged forward, burying himself deep. And God, nothing had ever felt this good. She was liquid warmth over every inch of his cock.

"Or in an elevator that looks out over the lobby."

Like the one she'd ridden in to meet him that first night. He should have done her on the way down. "Next time," he murmured, retreating until she pulled him back with a flex of her calves at his back.

"Anywhere," she said, her head back against the wall, eyes closed, lips glistening.

"Everywhere," he agreed.

Then he showed her just how badly he wanted to fuck her, how he'd *always* need to fuck her.

SHE COULDN'T LET GO. HER ARMS SIMPLY WOULDN'T RELEASE HIM. It wasn't her cataclysmic orgasm, or being fucked on a doorstep, or the risk of discovery. It was how he still trembled against her, his face buried in her hair. Her eyes ached with the effort to hold back her tears. He'd taken her so sweetly; the warmth of his come was still inside, lusciously slick between her thighs. How could he be that good to her after she'd been such a bitch?

"I forgot the condom," he said, still holding her flush against the wall though he had zipped up.

She'd broken the courtesan cardinal rule. In her need to have him, she'd actually forgotten the cardinal rule. It had never happened before. And she didn't care. This was Dax. He was everything. "I'm clean. I get tested regularly."

Backing off, he tipped her chin. "I'm more worried about what you think of me."

"I—" See? There he was worrying about *her* again, above himself.

She closed her eyes, vaguely wondering why these people hadn't figured out they were on the doorstep. Hadn't they heard the car? And maybe thinking about them was an excuse not to face the truth about herself, not to make *him* face it.

Hard as it was for her, she met Dax's gaze. "I think only the best things about you." He'd done nothing bad to her. He'd treated her with respect, provided her with unparalleled pleasure, never judged her. In return, she'd let her insecurities, guilt, and fears punish him.

"I want you. I don't know how else to prove that."

Noelle put her hand to his cheek, her eyes drinking in every detail. "I have lied and cheated most of my life."

"You might have made some mistakes in your marriages—"

She covered his mouth with her fingers. "It's not like I can tell you every story and confess every crime right now." She pointed to the front door beside them. "But I will tell you. All of it. You need to know exactly who I am."

"I know everything I need to."

"Then maybe I'm the one who needs to tell you." She dipped her head, rested her forehead against his throat. She'd never been good at confessing. She'd always run when things got tough, found another man to satisfy her; then, in her guilt, she'd rushed headlong into Isabel and Courtesans. She'd never tried to change, never been honest enough to help any of her husbands see what she needed. If she didn't change now, she never would. And she'd lose another man. Perhaps the most perfect man who'd ever walked into her life.

"Dax, I know this sounds really two-faced, but I'd rather die than watch you make love to another woman. I'm selfish and vain, and I don't want you to walk away from me, but I can't reconcile myself to watching. I don't want you to want her more than you want me." Her lips trembled. She felt like a child. "I can do everything you want me to, anything, but I can't watch you do that."

He tipped her chin, forcing her to look at him. "So you're jealous of her, but the fact that I'm fine with another man or a bunch of men having you doesn't bother you?"

She shook her head. "No. Because you always end up making it about me. I don't know how you do that." She sighed. "That's wrong. I know exactly how you do it. You kiss me and you dress me and you shave me and prepare me for them. You make me into a present, and that's the hottest, most exciting thing I've ever known."

The blue of his eyes deepened to sapphire as his gaze roved her face. "But I take it all away if I want another woman."

He'd described it precisely. "Yes," she whispered. But did he *understand*?

"I don't need another woman."

"How can you *not* need it? How can you let me put that kind of demand on you?" She didn't completely understand her own need for it; it simply was.

"Because it doesn't compromise me or what I wanted out of this relationship." She opened her mouth, but he didn't stop long enough for her to say anything. "In the beginning I just wanted a woman to do this with me for fun. I didn't expect it to last very long. But now I want *you* to do it with me. It isn't any good if it's another woman. I get what I need with *you*."

"But I'm self-absorbed, and I—"

With a finger to her lips, he shut her up. "Listen to me," he said. "I love to watch you. I love to find new and exciting ways to give you pleasure. I've never had a woman who would allow me that. It's more important to me than fucking some woman Isabel found for us. I'd rather watch the two of you share her husband's cock. I don't care about any other woman as long as you let me be a part of every sexual adventure you have, whether you plan them or I plan them. Whether I'm there with you or you call me before, during, or afterward. If you're a freak, then I'm just as bad, because that's what I've been looking for since I was fourteen years old. We match seamlessly."

She couldn't do much more than stare at him. Words escaped her. She clutched his shoulders, squeezed, then ran her hands up and down his arms, the smooth material of the tux as sensuous as bare skin. Because it was him.

"You want to be mine, Noelle? Share everything? Every date you have as a courtesan?" His face descended with each sentence until his lips were almost on hers. "Share my bed? My fantasies? My nights? My days?"

She had never trusted a man to do that for her. She'd never trusted a man enough to tell him the truth about her feelings. Dax was different. For him, she wanted to be different, too. "I'd be a total freak if I said no."

"Then don't say no."

"I do, Dax." It felt like a vow. "I want to be completely yours."

"Good. Because we've got a date." He pulled back without actually kissing her. She found she could wait. Because he always had a surprise, he always upped the ante, he always provided exactly what she needed.

"And you look like you've just been fucked." He smoothed the lipstick beneath her mouth. "Properly fucked." With her hand still in his, he rang the doorbell.

She had thought she didn't know how to love, that she was incapable, unworthy. He made her see things so differently. With him, everything was different. "Dax," she said, her heart swelling in her chest, "I think I love you."

The corner of his luscious mouth lifted. "I know I love you. You're my dream come true, baby." He grazed her knuckles with a sweet kiss. "Now let me give you more pleasure than you've ever imagined."

She knew he always would.

# ABOUT THE AUTHOR

**Jasmine Haynes** has been penning stories for as long as she's been able to write. With a bachelor degree in accounting from Cal Poly San Luis Obispo, she has worked in the high-tech Silicon Valley for the past twenty years and hasn't met a boring accountant yet! Well, maybe a few. She and her husband live with Star, their mighty moose-hunting dog (if she weren't afraid of her own shadow), plus numerous wild cats (who have discovered that food out of a bowl is easier than slaying gophers and birds, though it would be great if they got rid of the gophers—but no such luck). Jasmine's pastimes, when not writing her heart out, are speed-walking through the Redwoods, hanging out with writer friends in coffee shops, and watching classic movies. Jasmine also writes as Jennifer Skully and JB Skully. She loves to hear from readers. Please e-mail her at skully@skullybuzz.com or visit her website www.skullybuzz.com and blog at www.jasminehaynes.blogspot.com.